VOLATILE BONDS

Prospero's War: Book 4

JAYE WE

"The meeting of two personalities is like the contact of two chemical substances: if there is any reaction, both are transformed."
–Carl Jung

"He that lieth down with dogs shall rise up with fleas."
–Benjamin Franklin

CHAPTER ONE

S

ome say fire and water are the two most destructive forces in nature. But, if I had a vote, I'd insist on a third option.

Magic.

A potion can destroy a man's flesh in a burst of violence or ruin his spirit by slowly consuming his humanity. Like fire and water, there are positive, even healing energies to be found in the arcane arts, but any fool who believes himself to be magic's master will soon find himself in a world of pain.

Case in point? The idiot who'd exploded his own potion lab in Copper Heights. The home went boom at three in the morning. The explosion had combined flames and magic, and fire crews had added water, the third element of the destructive trinity. By the time we arrived on the scene at ten a.m., the entire area felt like a pressure cooker and looked like hell on earth.

My partner, Special Agent Drew Morales, parked the SUV and leaned forward to take in the scene through the windshield. The explosion had vomited poison-green smoke into the sky, and the stubborn cloud resisted the force of Lake Erie's blustery winds. The air smelled scorched and ruined, and it shimmered with the ghost of spent magic.

The actual explosion site was a couple of blocks farther up the road. Normally we would have pulled closer to the scene, but dozens of vehicles representing several emergency response agencies already clogged our path.

"Is it safe to go in there?" Morales asked.

"Define *safe*," I said.

He shot me a heated look that had more to do with the lack of caffeine in his system than actual fear. I handed him one of the travel mugs I'd brought when we left my house that morning.

"Drink up, Grumpy," I said. "And I'm sure the fire burned off the worst of the precursor chemicals."

He pointed the coffee mug accusingly at the green cloud. "But what about the residual magic?"

I could have explained how being Adepts meant we weren't affected by magic in the same way Mundanes were. But the truth was, Morales had rejected being an Adept when he was young, so he didn't have the same power to avoid secondhand magic exposure I did. Instead, I focused my explanations on the practical reasons we'd be safe.

"When the fire's source is arcane, fire crews mix salt in with the water to dampen any lingering magic." I pulled down the collar of my shirt to show the edge of my ballistics vest, which was embedded with salt slabs. "Besides, between our vests and the protective amulets Mez gave us, it would take way more powerful magic than this to bring us down."

Mez was our task force wizard. In addition to providing the team with arcane defense tools, he also handled processing crime scenes. His potion-powered sports car was parked across the street, which meant he was waiting for us.

"All right," Morales said, "I can feel the caffeine kicking in. Let's go see a man about an explosion."

I jumped out of the SUV with uncharacteristic eagerness. Any time Detective Pat Duffy called us to a scene, it led to lots of pains in my ass. But I'd never been called to an arson scene before, so I was looking forward to seeing what was what.

Usually, when clandestine potion labs exploded, the wizards responsible were such small fish that the Magic Enforcement Agency task force I worked for didn't bother with them. The fact we'd been summoned that morning meant the lab probably supplied one of the major covens that ran dirty magic in the streets of Babylon, Ohio. If we were lucky, the evidence would be useful in our ongoing efforts to bring the coven leaders up on federal charges. But, when it came to magic, only fools trusted luck.

"Medical examiner's here." Morales nodded to the white van as we made our way toward the scene.

"Hopefully, they've identified the crispy critter by now."

When Duffy had called that morning, he'd mentioned they found a body in the rubble, but it had been too badly burned for finger-printing.

"You ever work a lab explosion before?" I asked.

He shook his head. "Back when I was undercover in L.A., the MEA had a special task force that investigated clandestine labs. They handled all the explosion cases. I had a buddy who worked for them. He had some stories that made my work undercover seem like a visit to a preschool. How about you?"

"I never worked one for BPD. But when I was a rookie, I was involved with the bust of a floating potion lab that exploded and set the Steel River on fire."

"I bet that impressed your superiors."

"Let's just say I made a name for myself early," I said. "Also, when I was little, my cousin Rico set up a lab in one of those old conversion van like the one Mr. T had on the A-Team. Anyway, he did something wrong with a new potion one day. I guess when the potion blew, it clung to him like napalm. He ran screaming down the road, trailing blue fire behind him. His clothes and skin melted as he ran."

"Jesus," Morales said. "What happened to him?"

"Uncle Abe shot him in the head. He said it was to put him out of his misery, but we all knew Abe was just afraid Rico would snitch if the cops got ahold of him."

Abe had been the leader of the Votary Coven until he'd been arrested for racketeering and thrown into Crowley Penitentiary for Arcane Criminals. Luckily, I'd left the coven a few years before he went down.

"I'm not a fan of your uncle," he said, "but it probably was the most humane thing he could have done, regardless."

I didn't respond because I didn't like to give my uncle any credit, especially if he deserved it. Instead, I waved to Mez, who was conferring with Val Frederickson, the lead CSI wizard on the scene.

We headed toward the pair, dodging fire hoses and cops scrambling around the burnt husk of the old house. Across the road, neighbors and rubberneckers gathered behind police barricades to gawk at the charred ruins.

"Did y'all bring the marshmallows?" Mez called. That morning, his dreadlocks were pulled back and woven with jade amulets and copper bells. He normally wore dark jeans with embroidered waistcoats, but in deference to the mess at the scene, he'd thrown coveralls over his clothes. Despite the outfit and the setting, he still somehow managed to look elegant.

Val rolled her eyes. The pair were both talented wizards, but they were total opposites. He was tall with Japanese features, and she was short with WASP-y blond hair. But together they made up a sort of yin and yang of magic.

"Good morning," she said. "I hope you don't like those clothes."

She wore blue scrubs, her typical uniform when working a messy scene. Her comment referred to the intense scent of smoke and the fact that there was no way we'd be able to enter the soggy, ashy mess of that house without destroying everything we were wearing.

"Luckily I decided to forego the ball gown today." I wasn't too

4

worried about the worn jeans and gray V-neck that made up my warm-weather work uniform, and my boots had slogged through way worse stuff than wet ashes. "Any new information on the vic?"

"They found a wallet on the scene, but until Franklin does his stuff, we won't be able to verify the deceased is the guy in the wallet."

"What's the name?" Morales asked.

"Basil Valentine."

Everyone looked at me for a reaction. As the only member of our task force who'd grown up in the Cauldron, they relied on me to fill in blanks when it came to major players. "He's related to Aphrodite. A nephew, I think."

Aphrodite Johnson was the Hierophant of the Mystical Coven of the Sacred Orgasm. As a sacred alchemical hermaphrodite, Aphrodite was both a he and a she, and both sides were vindictive as hell.

"If the John Doe is Basil," Morales said, "whoever killed him is gonna have themselves a real bad day once Aphrodite gets ahold of them."

"That's assuming Basil is the victim and not the one who set fire to the lab," Val added.

"Either way, I'm pretty sure someone's going to be visiting the Hierophant today," Morales said. "And I'm really hoping it's Detective Duffy and not us."

"No shit." To Val, I said, "It safe to go inside yet?"

She nodded. "Arson investigator is inside with Duffy. They said you should go in when you got here."

Morales and I left them and headed inside.

Homes in that area of Babylon had been built in the 1920s to house steelworkers and their families. The bungalows had deep porches where people used to gather on warm nights to chat with neighbors. But once the steel industry died, neighborhoods like this one had gone on life support. The ones not being used as hex dens or cook houses sat abandoned, just like the dreams of all those workers who lost their jobs.

Two darkened window frames resembled bruised eyes, and the doorway gaped in a silent scream. We went up the brick stairs and picked our way through the rubble to walk inside. A potion fire doesn't behave like a normal fire. Depending on the types of chemicals and magic used, the reactions can be extremely varied. In this case, the explosion turned everything made from natural materials deep blue. All of the synthetic materials, from plastic to polyester, melted on the spot.

From the outside, the structure had still been recognizable as having once been a house, but on the inside, it looked like something out of a nightmare. Anything not destroyed by fire or transformed by magic had been ruined by the water used to douse the flames. As we entered, our boots sank into a slurry of dark-blue water and black ash.

The walls between what would have been the living room and the kitchen were gone. In the other room, Duffy spoke to a man with a head as bald and black as an eight ball.

"Took you long enough," Duffy said by way of greeting. He had a receding hairline but the fit frame of a man who refused to surrender to the gravity of middle age.

"They got every road leading in here blocked off," Morales said.

The man I didn't know responded, "Had to evacuate earlier on account of all the chemicals." He stepped forward and held out a hand. "Ralph Perry, arson investigator, BFD."

Morales introduced himself and the fact we were with the MEA task force. "And this is Detective Prospero, Kate."

He wasn't a wizard, so I shook with my right hand. If he'd been an Adept, aka a "Leftie," I would have used my dominant left hand instead. "You had a chance to determine whether the blaze was caused by a cook gone bad?"

"Someone sure wanted us to think it was." Perry's lips twitched with the beginnings of a smile. "But it's pretty clear to me based on the fire pattern that the perpetrator used the Bunsen burners to set fire to the chemicals."

"How is that different from a normal potion-lab explosion?" Morales asked.

"Most explosions in alchemy labs happen when a wizard doesn't know what he's doing and mixes two chemicals that don't play well together. That can create a nasty fireball like we had here, but that sort of explosion doesn't leave much behind." He waved us to follow him further into the house. "Our boy had his lab set up in the master bath."

"Why not the kitchen?" Morales asked.

"It's too exposed," I said, answering automatically. "Bathroom labs are easier to hide from nosey neighbors and defend if someone breaks in to steal the stash."

Perry shot me a look.

"Prospero used to be a cook for the Votary Coven," Duffy supplied in a shitty tone.

"She's right, though," Perry said.

I decided I liked him a lot.

Down the hallway, we went to the second doorway on the left. Or what used to be a doorway. Dr. Thomas Franklin kneeled on the broken tiles that used to be the floor.

"Franky," I called.

"Prospero, you slumming today?"

"Oh, you know, I like to be where all the action's at."

He snorted and rose from the crouch until he towered over the cramped room. His white lab coat contrasted starkly against his dark skin. "Shiiiiit, I thought you were here to see me."

Duffy cleared his throat. "Can you update them on the vic?"

The ME moved to the side so we could get a better view of the body. The skin blackened with patches of pink and red showing through, and the clothes had melted like shrink wrap to the trunk and limbs. The smell was beyond description. Hot bile rose in the back of my throat.

"Damned shame when a perfectly good white boy gets fried like a Thanksgiving turkey."

"How do you know he was white?" Morales asked.

"The DL they found was a Caucasian male named Basil Valentine," Duffy said.

"Of course, that could have just as easily have fallen out of the perp's pocket," I said.

Franklin nodded. "Agreed. I've got my assistant calling in the dental records, so we're not confirmed on identity—or the race—yet. However, I have been able to identify cause of death."

Morales held out his hands. "Gee, could it have been fire?"

Franklin pursed his lips. "No, smartass, he was dead before the explosion." He knelt again and used a gloved finger to tilt the head. A wet *crunch* filled the small space.

That sound, combined with the nauseating scent of charred flesh, meant I wasn't too far from needing to excuse myself for some fresh air.

"He's got a bullet hole here." He pointed to a dark hole about the size of a fingertip next to the vic's left eye.

"Why blow up the place if he was already dead?" I asked.

Perry answered. "Because criminals are dumb. Or maybe they were sending a message. Or they just liked to watch things burn. We won't know the answer until y'all find who did this."

When he said that, he was staring at Morales and me, not Duffy, who was the lead homicide detective for the BPD. "Um. Duffy?" I said. "You forget to explain to Perry that you're the lead on this case?"

Duffy cleared his throat. "Can we talk?" He held out a hand, indicating we should precede him farther down the hall. Morales and I exchanged a look but marched back into the kitchen.

Once we were out of that cramped hallway, I sucked in a lungful of cleanish air. The windows there had been blown out, so a slight breeze reached me. It still smelled like smoke, but at least it didn't have the nauseating ozone and barbecue scent that permeated the bathroom.

Once Duffy came out, we rounded on him with identical bullish expressions.

"All right, here's the thing," he began. "I'm sure you've heard that murders are up for the last few weeks."

I didn't nod, and neither did Morales. Any indication we sympathized with his plight would only encourage him.

"Well, Captain's been riding my ass about closure rates. It's not our fault. Bodies have been stacking up since Easter. My detectives are working overtime just to process the scenes."

"What's that got to do with us?" Morales said.

He waved a hand back toward the hallway. "You saw it yourself. That's a potion lab, which means the guy who got whacked is probably a wizard for one of the covens."

"The main word in that sentence was *whacked*, as in homicide. We work arcane crimes that violate federal statutes."

"How many of those you closed lately?" he challenged. "Last I heard, your bosses in Detroit weren't too happy with how few major coven leaders you brought to justice lately."

He wasn't wrong. Less than a week earlier, our boss, Assistant Special Agent in Charge Miranda Gardener, had read our team the riot act about our lack of big busts.

"Pretty sure the suits in Detroit wouldn't consider solving the murder of a low-level wizard a win," Morales shot back.

Duffy smiled a smile I'd come to dread. It's the expression people get when they know they have you cornered. "That's where you're wrong."

He stepped toward the refrigerator. It was one of those vintage jobs with rounded corners, like people had in the '50s. The fire had left its exterior darkened so it resembled a sarcophagus.

"How would your bosses feel if you showed them this?" he said.

The heavy door required a couple of hard yanks to open. But once it did, his smile grew even bigger. Frowning, I stepped forward and used my flashlight to illuminate the dark interior. Inside, neat bricks of plastic-wrapped cash filled the top two shelves.

Morales whistled.

"You ain't seen nothing yet." Duffy pulled open the freezer. Water splashed to the floor from the melted ice. But nestled in the center of the space were several gallon zip-top bags of potions.

"Holy shit."

"Bet Gardner would love to see MEA get credit for a seizure like this," Duffy said.

The thing was? She totally would. Not that we'd admit that to him. The instant he thought he had the upper hand, he'd screw us over.

"Why in the hell would anyone leave this behind?" I asked.

"Lots of reasons," Duffy said. "Maybe they were in a hurry or they thought the fire would destroy it."

"Or maybe they didn't care about the potions at all because the murder was personal," I said.

Duffy shrugged, looking unconcerned.

"What's your angle on this?" Morales asked the same question I'd been thinking.

"I told you, stats."

I crossed my arms. "Sounds to me like what's really happening is Mayor Volos is putting the vise on Chief Adams, who's rolling that shit downhill to Captain Eldritch, who's passing it on to you. No way Volos is promoting Adams to Commissioner without a decrease in crime stats."

Duffy sighed. "Something like that."

"Which begs the question," I said, "did Eldritch put you up to this?"

"Doesn't really matter, does it? Because whether he did or not, if I tell him the MEA's balking at assisting us, he'll go right up the chain to Volos."

Which meant we'd probably get the case whether we wanted it or not. The MEA's continued presence in Babylon depended on a good political relationship with the mayor and the BPD.

"But it doesn't have to be like that," Duffy said. "No reason it can't be a favor I owe you."

Considering that the last time I'd spoken to Duffy, he basically accused our task force of being dirty, this was an interesting development. Either he had a secret he wasn't telling or his ass was really in a sling with Eldritch.

"We'll have to take this up with Gardner," Morales hedged. He wasn't lying, but technically, as the number two on the task force, he had the authority to accept or decline the case. Most likely he was buying us some time to work through the possible angles. "In the meantime, I'll leave Mez to help with the evidence collection. If we do take it, he'll need to be in on it anyway."

"And if you don't?"

"Then you'll owe us a favor."

Duffy snorted. "I'll expect your call by end of day or I'll bring in the FBI."

It was an empty threat. The FBI had stopped getting their hands dirty with arcane crime about a decade earlier. They mostly took cases with ties to domestic terrorism or Mundane organized crime. It was less messy than chasing covens and got more media coverage, to boot. America did love its mobster myths, after all. Far sexier and easier to believe than the truth—that the real threat to our cities was America's addiction to magic's easy fixes.

"You'll hear from us when you hear from us." Morales flicked a parting wave in Duffy's direction and we made our way back outside.

"Talk to Mez," Morales said. "I'm going to call Gardner." He walked toward where we parked, away from the eager ears of the cops on the scene.

I found Mez near an idling fire truck. The loud engine created enough white noise that no one could hear us.

"Duffy wants us to take the case," I said.

"You told him no?"

"Of course."

"Think that's gonna stick once you talk to the boss lady?"

I sighed. "Probably not."

"What do you need from me?"

"There are some party favors in the freezer that need analyzing. Let me know once you've identified the type of potions we're dealing with so I can start linking them back to the covens."

"I can do some basic field tests, but I usually need to bring samples back to the lab to verify the chemical makeup."

"Just see what you can do. I'm hoping I can talk Morales and Gardner into punting this one."

"Why?"

"Because it reeks of a shitstorm."

"Don't they all?" He laughed. "Did you see the body?" Off my nod, he whistled. "I don't know who that cat pissed off, but they sure wanted to send one hell of a message."

"I have a bad feeling we won't like the meaning of the message or to whom it was intended."

He shot me a weird look. "Nice grammar, Emily Dickinson."

I laughed. "One of the benefits of having to help a sixteen-year-old pass his English class."

"Speaking of," he said, "is Danny liking the new school?"

"It's fine. He says public school is way easier than Meadowlake had been. Now that he's settled, he's asking when he can start up lessons with you again."

Danny was my younger brother. In addition to being his annoying older sister, I also had been his legal guardian since our mother died ten years earlier. The lessons I mentioned were in clean magic, which was Mez's specialty. I would have taught him magic myself, but I only knew how to cook dirty.

"Tell him I'm ready when he is." He nodded over my shoulder. "Your boyfriend's back."

I elbowed him in the ribs. "He's not my boyfriend."

"Uh-huh. What do you call your little situation, then?"

I thought for a second before answering. "Partners with benefits."

"You two are a trip." He snorted. "Although I never thanked you."

"For what?"

"I won a hundred bucks from the office pool. Shadi thought you'd keep stringing Morales along and he'd eventually just get sick of your shit." He winked. "But I knew you'd come around."

I ignored the flare of temper. After all, I had resisted the attraction for a while. Still, I didn't love the idea of my sex life being the subject of a team-wide betting pool. But in our line of business, showing discomfort put a target on your back. "Seeing how I did all the work, I feel like I should have gotten a piece of that payday."

He smirked. "I'll buy you a beer next time we're near a bar."

I grinned. "Deal."

By that time, Morales reached us. "Gardner wants us to come to the office." We must have looked guilty, because he paused and gave us suspicious glares. "What are you two talking about?"

"Oh, you know, wizard stuff." I waved a hand. "Call me if you run into any snags here," I told Mez. "We'll let you know once you can take custody of the evidence."

He saluted me and sauntered off to rejoin Val.

"Ready?" I asked Morales.

"What do you think about all this?" he asked as he walked toward the SUV.

I squinted at the green clouds. "I don't know. I got a bad feeling."

"You just need to eat. You're always sort of nihilistic before you've had breakfast." He bumped me with his shoulder and shot me a roguish grin.

"I mean it," I said. "Something's off here. Why is Duffy so eager to give us this case?"

"Maybe because he doesn't think he's got the chops to solve it. He had to bring in the real heroes to get the job done."

I rolled my eyes. "Or maybe he's setting us up. I'm telling you—this one's gonna be messy. I can feel it."

"Admit it, Cupcake, you'd be bored if things were too neat and safe."

The words were delivered casually, but they felt heavy on my ears. Instead of analyzing that reaction, I elbowed him. "Seeing how you're so keen to be someone's hero, you can buy breakfast."

CHAPTER TWO

W e were back at the office by noon. Morales parked his
SUV in the scrub-brush parking lot next to the train
tracks. The old brick building that served as the task
force headquarters used to be a boxing gym owned by a man named
Rooster. The gym was on the second floor over a bodega that sold
cold sodas, cheap snacks, and nudie magazines. We passed the
entrance to the shop and went through a glass door that still bore the
Rooster's Gym logo.

My favorite part about coming back to the office was when the
stink of old vinyl mats and the ozone scent of magic hit me. After
working there for several months, I'd come to associate that perfume
with coming home.

As we climbed the staircase, the sounds of a busy office filtered
down toward us. Now that we had some new blood on the team, the
old gym was always pretty busy.

At the top of the steps, I spotted Shadi Pruitt on the phone at her
desk. Her combat boots were perched on the edge of her desk while
she talked. The other two members of her team were in the center of
the ancient boxing ring. They faced off over a table that had been set

up in the center with a bulletin board nearby that held pictures and other information pertaining to their sting.

"How's it going, boys?" I called. They were too involved in whatever their debate was to answer, but Dixon waved halfheartedly in my direction.

Deputy Dixon and Detective McGinty were our team's version of the Odd Couple. McGinty was a BPD gumshoe who only had a couple of years left before he started collecting his pension. His mustache was more salt than pepper, and he had a ruddy Irish complexion and blue eyes that looked sad even when he smiled. He had the soft body of a cop who'd spent a good part of his time sitting in a city-issued car, but he'd been on the job so long that there wasn't much he hadn't seen or done. He wasn't an Adept, but he brought tons of experience to the team.

On the other hand, Deputy Aaron Dixon had the trim physique of a runner. I hadn't seen him eat one carb in the month he'd been on the team. He'd only recently earned his sheriff's deputy badge after spending his early years working as a guard in the county prison. Gardner had pursued him for the team because he was an Adept— albeit one who rarely practiced the Arcane arts. But I suspected it was his rookie eagerness to please that made him so appealing to Gardner. Plus, he had a knack for technology that made him useful for surveillance and research. He might have been green, but he wasn't naïve. He'd grown up in the affluent Highland Hills suburb, where all the upper-middle class Lefties lived, but considering how few Black families lived there, I couldn't imagine he had an easy time.

Shadi hung up the phone and pulled her boots off the desk. "What did Duffy want?"

"Clandestine lab explosion," Morales said. "Someone offed the wiz before they blew the place up."

Shadi only stood as high as Morales's shoulder, but what she lacked in inches she made up for in badassitude. Her black hair was pulled back into a no-nonsense bun, and her face was free of makeup

—not that she needed it with her clear brown skin and high cheekbones. Besides running her own team, she also was a surveillance expert and was pretty damned handy with assault rifles. "He dumping it off on you?"

"He's sure trying." He shrugged. "Gotta talk to the boss lady before we know for sure. How's your case going?"

She pursed her lips and shot an annoyed look at the men in the ring. "Good, except those two knuckleheads can't agree on a damned thing."

I grinned. "Have you tried couple's counseling?"

She made a disgusted sound and raised her voice to be heard. "I'm about to give both those motherfuckers a time-out."

The two in the ring grumbled something but went right back to their bickering.

"Good luck with that," Morales said.

My phone buzzed at my hip. I checked the screen. The number was from the medical examiner's office. "It's Franklin," I said to Morales.

Just then, Special Agent in Charge Miranda Gardner opened the door to her office. "Morales, Prospero."

It wasn't a greeting—it was a command. She might wear the sensible pantsuits and heels of a public servant, but only a fool would miss the authority radiating from her or the raptor's eyes that missed nothing.

"Coming, sir," Morales said.

I nodded to indicate that I'd join them in a minute and lifted the phone back to my ear. "Talk to me, Franklin."

"Thought you might want to know we got the dental records. The vic was Basil Valentine."

"Interesting."

"He ain't been to the dentist in a couple of decades, but the records match."

"Did you call Duffy?"

"He told me to call you."

"Naturally. Thanks for letting me know."

After I hung up, I turned to Shadi. "You hear anything on your rounds about an O boy named Basil Valentine? Last I hear, he was pimping for Aphrodite."

"Doesn't ring a bell. Why?"

I crossed my arms and leaned against her desk. "That's the name of the vic from the explosion."

"I'll ask my CIs. See if anything comes up."

"Cool, thanks."

She nodded and marched off to play referee for Dixon and McGinty. I stowed my bag at my desk and went to join the conversation in Gardner's office.

My knuckle barely tapped the door before Gardner's voice barked out, "Come in."

Inside the cramped room, the tiny window let in cold, milky light. Behind the desk, Gardner sat in front of a stack of case files that were organized with military precision. She wore a brown suit that matched her hair, with a cream-colored blouse underneath that matched her complexion. She wore no jewelry.

Up until a few months earlier, she'd worn a tigereye cabochon ring on the middle finger of her left hand. Tigereye was the stone of truth and logic, and the middle finger was the Saturn finger, which represented responsibility and security. But after a run-in with a sadistic Brazilian shaman in the spring, the ring had been lost and the finger upon which it had sat was now permanently crooked and its knuckle swollen.

"Sorry, sir," I said, taking my seat. "That was the ME. He confirmed the identity of the victim as Basil Valentine." I said this more for Morales's benefit than Gardner's, but she nodded as if he'd already filled her in.

"What's your read on this?" Gardner asked.

I sucked in a breath and blew it out, buying time to gather my thoughts. Things were always tricky when it came to working with the BPD. I was still technically on their payroll, so I had to balance that with the fact I spent every day with the task force. "It seems weird. I don't buy Duffy's eagerness to hand it over. Last time, he acted like we'd pissed on him when we asked to take a case."

Morales spoke up. "He'd do it if word was coming down from the mayor's office."

"Explain." She tossed her pen on the desk and leaned back as if she'd just dared me to impress her.

"According to Duffy, the increase in murder stats got the brass nervous," he said. "Duffy said he needed to get this case off his books to up his percentages. Our guess was that Eldritch is trying to increase the closure rate to impress Mayor Volos."

"That's bothering me, too," I said. "What's with all the murders over the last few weeks? Ever since Puck got put in jail for Charm and the Brazilian's murders things have been hot."

Puck used to be one of the up-and-comers in the Votary ranks. He'd gone down six weeks earlier for the murder of one of the leaders of that coven, an old-school wiz named Charm. He'd also been charged with murdering two *A Morte* coven hit men who'd actually been murdered by our mayor. The fact Puck was still alive in jail probably meant *A Morte* wasn't buying him as the killer. But that was a pretty touchy subject in the office, since we'd all technically been accessories to that crime, and the idea of *A Morte* finding out about Volos's or our involvement would be serious bad news.

"Are you thinking that once Puck was off the streets, the Votary rank and file started jockeying for positions?" Gardner said.

I nodded. "Most of the murder reports I've seen have been happening in Votary territory. But the issue at hand is whether Basil Valentine's murder can lead us up the chain of command, and I don't think it can. Last I heard, he was a low-level pimp for Aphrodite."

"But you said yourself that the lab looked like a Votary cook," Morales said.

The Votary coven used magic that was the closest to traditional alchemy. It also happened to be the coven I'd grown up inside, so I knew it best. Unlike the Votaries, the O's practiced sex magic and the Sangs practiced blood magic. Neither of those traditions usually used complex alchemical lab setups to cook their potions.

"Is that true?" Gardner asked.

"Yes, sir," I admitted reluctantly, "but even if he was working with the Votaries, most of the deaths so far have been simple drive-bys involving potion-filled projectiles being shot from pellet guns. All the bodies are from low-level corner wizes. None of the big players have been involved."

"Yet," she said, crossing her arms. "I have to admit I'm curious about the connection. Plus, I'd sure love to send my boss a framed image of money and potions from a big bust."

I opened my mouth to argue, but she held up a hand.

"But," she said, "I agree that Duffy could be a problem. I didn't like how he was sniffing around after the Brazilian incident."

"So, you'll call Eldritch and turn him down?" I asked.

Captain Eldritch was my boss at the BPD. Ever since I'd started work on the MEA team, our relationship had become...complicated. Luckily, since Gardner was the leader of the task force, she got the pleasure of dealing with him on cases like this.

She smiled. "No. We're taking the case."

My stomach dipped. "Sir—"

"Your concerns have been noted, Prospero. But the potential bene-fits outweigh the problems here. If you can connect this murder with the rash of drive-bys perpetrated by the Votaries, we're looking at a huge case here. I want money and potions on the table at a press conference ASAP. Plus I'm looking forward to having Eldritch owe us for a change."

Morales held up a hand. "What happens if we don't find a connection between the murder and the Votaries?"

"Then keep looking." Gardner's smile faded. "I'm gonna be real grumpy if I have to hand all that money and those potions back to the BPD. Understood?"

Morales and I exchanged a quick glance. "Understood," he said.

She watched us for a moment. Just when I thought she was about to change the subject or issue another veiled threat, she nodded. "Dismissed."

She didn't have to ask us twice. We were back outside before she'd even picked up her pen again.

"Morales," Shadi called from the boxing ring. "You got a fax."

While he retrieved the message, I went grab my backpack.

"From Duffy," Morales said, waving the fax as he joined me at my desk. "Valentine's rap sheet."

"He's not wasting any time," I muttered.

Morales scanned it. "Damn. Someone's been busy. He'd been collared for everything from driving under the influence of arcane substances to assault with a magical weapon to pimping and pandering."

He pointed to a note near the bottom of the sheet. A list of known associates included the name Aphrodite Johnson. "I say we start here."

I sighed and threw my backpack over my shoulder. "Might as well."

"Where you two headed?" Shadi called from the ring.

She, McGinty, and Dixon were going over surveillance photos from a stakeout they'd recently done of a suspected stash house. Shadi's leadership on these small-buy operations had netted some good information and a few low-level wizes willing to turn on higher-ups. That's how we'd managed to justify needing the new headcount with Eldritch—the BPD loved that we were getting some of the rabble off the streets. But now it was up to Morales and me to bring in the big fish so we could keep the MEA brass happy, too.

"We gotta go see a sacred hermaphrodite about a murder," I called. "Y'all behave yourselves."

* * *

On our way to Aphrodite's temple, I got a phone call from my best friend, Penelope Griffin.

"Working hard?" she said by way of greeting.

"Oh, you know. Another day, another shit show. No biggie. What are you up to?"

Morales looked over and I mouthed that it was Pen. He shook his head.

A deep sigh carried through the earpiece. "I'm watching a terrible reality show about people who agree to be locked up in a house with strangers for a chance to win unlimited supplies of vanity potions."

"You have got to stop watching that crap."

Another sigh. "I know."

I shifted in my seat in an effort to control my rising irritation. "Why don't you get out of the house today?"

"Maybe."

"I guess this means you haven't had any bites on that last batch of resumes?"

"Not one, Kate. I don't get it."

"Something'll turn up. You just got to keep your chin up."

Morales cast me a side-eye. I ignored him. Even though I got frustrated with the constant calls, I felt guilty about my irritation. Pen had quit her job as a counselor at the private school Danny used to attend six weeks earlier—on the same day I'd pulled him out of the school. The reasons for both exits were complicated, but we were a big part of the reason she'd left. On top of the stress of not hearing back from anyone, she was nearing the end of her savings.

"Tell you what," I said, "Why don't you come over tonight? I'll order pizza and we can have a girls' night in."

"Actually, that sounds amazing." She already sounded perkier. "What can I bring?"

"Just yourself. I have some beer."

"Will anyone else be there?" she asked in a deceptively casual tone.

"Baba's got her book club at the senior center, but Danny might be. Why?"

"Oh, nothing. I just want to be sure your special friend won't be there so I can get the scoop."

"Pen."

"Kate." She dragged the word out in a false whine. Even though she was teasing me, it was good to hear some of her old humor creeping back in.

"Behave yourself," I said in a mock cop's tone.

"Ditto, girl." She laughed. "I'll see you around seven."

After we hung up, Morales said, "How's Eeyore today?"

"Be nice. She's struggling right now." I swatted his arm. "I invited her over so she'd leave the house. It should be nice, actually. We haven't hung out in a while."

"There's going to be a lot of giggling, isn't there?"

I scowled. "We're grown-ass women. We do not giggle."

He raised an eyebrow but said nothing.

"You got any plans tonight?"

"I was gonna meet a buddy. Grab a couple beers. Play some pool. No giggling, though."

"You, uh, want to come over after?"

He arched a brow. "Like a booty call?"

I met his gaze. "Pretty much."

His voice lowered to a husky tone. "Yes, ma'am."

"Good."

One of the things I loved about our arrangement was that we'd been able to keep things casual. Since we spent so much time together on the job, it would have been easy to slip into some sort of premature commitment situation. But thus far, we'd been able to keep private private and business business. When we wanted to sleep together, we did. When we had other plans, we didn't. No expectations, no jealousy, no complications. Exactly how I wanted it.

He parked on the road about a block away from Aphrodite's temple. "How are we going to play this?"

I shrugged. "Considering the fact s/he is only out of jail because s/he agreed to be an informant, I'd say we take the direct approach."

Several months earlier, Aphrodite Johnson had been arrested in connection with the murder of the city's mayor. S/he'd been absolved of the murder, but due to some shenanigans during the case s/he'd been charged with obstruction and some other felonies. A deal had been cut to get out of jail time, but the price was having to snitch on the other covens.

"Well, let's see which gender we're dealing with today." Morales turned off the car and got out. I joined him on the curb and we walked together toward the office building.

With a name like the Temple of Cosmic Love, one might expect the building to be covered in neon hearts. Instead, it was a standard-issue brick office building that looked like it housed an insurance agency instead of a brothel disguised as a house of worship.

Inside the lobby, we found Aphrodite's main security guard manning the front desk.

"How's it going, Gregor?"

He had a face that looked like a fist with a broken knuckle for a nose, and was about as friendly as a sack of hornets. "What do you want?"

"We're here to see the Hierophant." That was Aphrodite's official title as head of the Sacred Coven of the Mystical Orgasm.

"You're gonna have to make an appointment," he said. "They are extremely busy today."

"*They* are?" Morales said.

"The Hierophant decided that since they are getting married, they will be called *they* from now on."

I frowned at him. "Morales, I think someone replaced Gregor with the Sphinx."

"I'm not following that riddle either," he said. "Who is Aphrodite marrying?" he asked Gregor.

"Theirself."

"Hold on," I said. "Aphrodite is marrying…Aphrodite?"

He looked at us like we were a few bullets shy of a loaded gun.

"Okay," Morales dragged the word out. "What's up with the *they* and *their* stuff?"

Gregor rolled his eyes. "As the Hierophant's gender is fluid, they prefer to not ascribe to society's forced gender labels any longer."

I pressed my lips together and thought about it. "He's got a point," I said to Morales. "Besides, all that s/he stuff was pretty confusing."

"Not to mention insulting." Gregor scowled, as if he was tired of people not showing his boss the respect they deserved. "Once the marriage rites are complete, their two sides will be in perfect union so the binary gendered pronouns won't apply anymore."

"When's the wedding?" Morales asked.

"Next week."

I had about a million more questions about what exactly marrying oneself involved for a sacred hermaphrodite, but we were on the clock and solving the murder trumped wedding gossip on the list of priorities.

"Great," Morales said. "We'll send some 'theirs and theirs' towels. Now, can we speak to them?"

"Regarding?" Gregor said in an infuriatingly calm manner.

"Regarding their nephew, Basil Valentine," I said sweetly.

The red phone at Gregor's elbow rang. He held up a finger, indicating we should wait as he answered it. Morales looked at me like I was crazy. I shrugged. Aphrodite might be a pain in the ass most of the time, but I couldn't help liking them. If nothing else, they were never boring.

"You can have five minutes."

He clicked a button on his control panel. A split second later a door to the right of the desk opened. Through it I could see the court-yard where Aphrodite kept her poison garden.

"They're in their meditation room."

Morales and I shared a frown at that gem. Meditation? Aphrodite?

Gregor ignored our silent communication and continued. "Go through the courtyard to the door on the far end. Can't miss it."

"Thanks for your help," Morales said in a tone that implied anything but gratitude.

"Do not upset them," Gregor warned. "They need peace and calm as they prepare for the sacred marriage rites."

I forced a smile. "Wouldn't dream of it."

* * *

The courtyard beyond the doors looked like the kind of place you might find housing a sultan's harem. Low couches and lounges created the perfect spot to strike a pose under the sun's beams. In the center of the space, a lush garden unfurled and offered up bright flowers that glistened like jewels in the midday sun. Only, anyone who touched those particular jewels would find themselves quickly dead. Aphrodite was famous for their poison garden, which served as a warning to her enemies. Rumor had it several unfortunate souls had been the unwitting victims of the Hierophant's vengeance, but Aphrodite was good at covering their tracks and had the bonus of having religious protection for the coven's rites.

We skirted the garden, careful not to breathe too deeply or brush any of the dangerous petals. Just beyond, a pair of glass doors led into a foyer of sorts. The floors were bamboo and the walls were painted a soothing sage green. A pair of carved wooden doors guarded the entrance to what Gregor had called the meditation room.

"You remember this from before?" I asked Morales.

He shook his head. "Must be a new phase they're going through."

"Marriage changes a person," I quipped.

Before he could respond, the double doors opened. The scent of incense wafted out of the darkened room. I couldn't see beyond the doorway because it was filled with a real son of a bitch.

"Harry," I said. "What are you doing here?"

"Hieronymus," he growled. "And it's none of your fucking business, Prospero."

In addition to being a dick, Harry was also the head of the Sanguinarian coven. His daddy, Ramses Bane, used to run the coven out of some abandoned subway tunnels that ran under Babylon like a rat's maze. But after Daddy got pinched for trying to murder me and my ex-boyfriend/future mayor of Babylon, John Volos, Harry had moved the coven to a junkyard. Still, he looked like a guy who lived in a tunnel, with his pale skin, white hair, and pink-rimmed eyes. The only part of him that wasn't pale was the black ankh tattooed on the center of his forehead.

"I see you're still as charming as ever," Morales said. "How's the limp?"

A few months prior, we'd interrupted a fight between Harry and a Brazilian wizard who could shapeshift into a panther. By the time we got there, Harry was half-dead. But did he ever thank us?

"Go fuck yourself," he said, and brushed past us on his way to the door.

I called after him, "You keep that up and we're not going to vote you for Miss Congeniality."

Once Harry was gone, Morales shrugged. "You'd think as much as that guy has gotten his ass kicked, he'd learn some humility."

I made a *tsk*ing sound. "Some people never learn."

Morales opened the doors Harry had just exited and held out a hand for me to precede him. Gregor had called it a "meditation room," but it looked more like a cross between a bordello and a Buddhist temple. Screens painted with graphic sex scenes covered the walls. Candles flickered from metal stands that created an aisle down the center. At the front of the room, a raised platform held a golden statue of some sort of many-armed deity with both breasts and a phallus. And in the center of it all, Aphrodite Johnson sat crisscross applesauce on a meditation mat.

I stilled in shock at the first sight of them. The last time I'd seen the Hierophant, they'd been wearing half of a slinky black dress and half of a dark business suit. The left side of the body had been made up with glamorous makeup and luscious brown locks, and the right had featured artful stubble and a hip masculine haircut.

Now, their head had been shaved altogether. Neither side of the face had any makeup or stubble. Instead of wearing two outfits sewn together, they wore a saffron-colored tunic and loose-fitting pants. The right side still had masculine bone structure compared to the left's softer feminine features. But the stark distinction between the Hierophant's feminine and masculine dualities wasn't as noticeable.

They didn't open their eyes when we walked in. "You're interrupting my meditation." Their voice was more neutral than it had been in the past when they chose between their female or male sides.

"Sorry," I said, "but we have some news you need to hear."

The eyes opened slowly. "Basil is dead."

I couldn't get over how calm they sounded. The Aphrodite I was used to was vindictive as hell and loved to play with their prey like a cat. I couldn't help wondering if this display was just another of the Hierophant's elaborate games. After all, a person didn't just go from keeping a revenge garden to practicing meditation overnight.

"I'm afraid so."

They closed their eyes and whispered something I couldn't hear, but it seemed like a prayer. Finally, the eyes opened again. "I can't say I'm surprised. That boy kept rough company."

Morales cleared his throat, obviously as surprised as I was about their calm response. The noise sounded unnaturally loud in the sanctuary. "When was the last time you spoke with Mr. Valentine?"

They unfolded their legs and stood. Instead of joining us immediately, they bowed three times to the statue before leaving the dais. Their movements were slow and graceful on bare feet that whispered across the reed mats that covered the floor. "Several weeks ago. He asked me for some money, but I refused. I'm afraid he didn't like my answer."

Given the stack of cash we'd found in Basil's lab, it appeared he'd managed to find a more lucrative con to line his pockets.

Aphrodite held out their hands. "Please, let's continue our conversation elsewhere. My temple is not the place for such talk."

We followed them out of the room. Morales shot me a confused look, and I shrugged, as confused as he was.

They led us out into the courtyard to a low grouping of couches. Once we were all settled, they said, "You're wondering if I had him killed."

"Did you?" Morales shot back.

A smile spread across their lips. "Of course not. Didn't Gregor tell you? I am ascending."

"He said you were getting married," I said.

"Yes, the sacred marriage is an ascension to enlightenment. My preparation requires ritualistic cleansing of both body and mind. That means I can't partake in any activities that harm another living being."

"That's going to make running your business sort of hard, isn't it?" I asked.

"I am in the business of healing troubled souls through sacred sexual acts," they said primly. "However, there are certain...aspects of my operation that I can no longer oversee. My cousin Fontina Douglas will be taking those over. She arrives in a couple of days from Atlanta."

I sucked on my teeth for a minute and watched Aphrodite. This whole enlightened act stunk worse than sulfur. "What's your angle here?" I demanded.

"Enlightenment is not an angle, Katherine."

"I'm just saying it seems sort of sudden. Especially since your cousin was murdered last night."

"I wouldn't expect you of all people to understand spiritual matters."

The insult rolled off my back, but Morales sighed, clearly reaching the end of his patience. "Before you ascend, it'd be great if you could give us a list of Basil's known enemies."

"You should talk to his new girlfriend about that." The Hierophant's eyes sparked with some of that old cunning, but they recovered quickly. "Or at least, I assume he was still dating her."

"What's her name?" Morales asked.

"Some terrible name I can never remember. She's a Votary." An elegant hand rose to wave dismissively. "Trashy but ambitious, you know?"

"I'm familiar with the type," he said. "You got a description?"

"Never met her personally," they said, all coy. Interesting, really, since very little happened in the Cauldron without their knowledge. "Just heard they were together through the grapevine. I'm afraid I've been so focused on my spiritual lessons that I'm out of the loop."

"We'll look into it," Morales said noncommittally. Despite Aphrodite's claims to be leaving the game, it was never smart to believe anything a coven leader said. "In the meantime, if you hear anything about Basil, let us know."

"Of course." The agreement came too easily to be sincere. "Now, if you'll excuse me, I must resume my meditation."

"While you're at it, meditate on what will happen if we find out you're planning on going after Basil's killer yourself."

"Kate, dear, you really should give meditation a try. It might help with your trust issues."

I narrowed my eyes. I really hated this new Aphrodite. When they'd been proudly catty, they were way more likeable. "Trust, sure. Tell you what. You try that enlightenment crap on someone who wasn't raised by the biggest bullshitter in the Cauldron."

They laughed. "Fine, you want the truth? You don't have a prayer of finding Basil's killer."

"So, you know who killed him." A statement, not a question.

"I have a hunch, is all." They paused. "Listen, I like you both, so I'll shoot straight here. Basil was my blood, but karma's a bitch. He made his choices."

"You do understand that you have an agreement with the AUSA Grey's office, right?" Morales said. "If you refuse to cooperate as an informant, you're going to jail."

All pretense of mindfulness dropped as a mean laugh escaped their mouth. "Then lock me up. Just wait until after my wedding."

Something about the bravado seemed too forced. "You don't seem too concerned about the fact someone murdered your own blood. Doesn't that bother you?"

They didn't flinch. "Damned straight. Lots of things bother me, though. Like how there used to be rules in this town, order. Honor among thieves and shit. But these young wizes?" They shook their shaved head. "No honor at all."

"Which young wizes?" I demanded.

The courtyard door opened and Gregor marched in. He took one look at Aphrodite's stiff posture and stepped between the Hierophant and us. "Time to go," he said. "Now."

"We'll come back with warrants if we need to," Morales said. "Or you can tell us what you know and save everyone a lot of trouble."

"Help us bring Basil's murderer to justice," I added.

Aphrodite's eyes filled with the deadly determination that had helped them rise to the head of the coven. "Justice," they spat. "There's no justice in this town. There's only power and money."

"Why are you giving up?" I demanded.

"Because this game is rigged, sweetheart. You want my advice? Cut your losses now."

Before we could shoot back any questions, Gregor hustled the Hierophant off to the sanctuary room. He closed the door and stationed himself in front of it. He didn't speak, but his expression made it clear that our invitation had been revoked.

CHAPTER THREE

A fter leaving the Temple of Cosmic Love, we decided to knock off early. Until we got labs back from Mez, we didn't have a lot to go on, anyway. Besides, I was pretty sure I'd be putting in plenty of overtime soon enough.

The meeting with Aphrodite was further proof that the case was going to be a pain in the ass. On top of my instincts that Duffy was setting us up, I was now also grappling with a growing sense of dread. Aphrodite's dire words about karma had the stink of trouble all over them. Morales didn't seem to share my concerns and, before he dropped me off back at my Jeep, suggested we start early the next morning tracking down Basil's girlfriend.

As I walked into the kitchen that evening, I left those troubles outside. I rarely made it home before dark, so it was nice to get there with a couple of hours to spare before Pen arrived for our girls' night.

I stashed my backpack by the door in case a call came in the middle of the night and I had to grab and go. A few minutes later, Danny wandered in while I rifled through the mail.

When he saw me he paused and shook his head. "What's wrong?"

I frowned at him. "Nothing—why?"

"You never come home early unless something bad is happening."

I put the letters on the counter and joined him at the table. "We sort of hit a dead end, so we called it a day. Pen's coming over tonight. I'm ordering pizza."

"Sweet," he said. "I'll eat in my room. Chemistry test tomorrow."

Normally I would have found his willingness to study suspect, but ever since we left the snooty private school, his grades had been steadily improving. I guess without the distraction of being a working-class Adept kid in a school full of rich Mundanes, he had more time to focus.

"Need any help?" I asked, trying to be a decent parental figure.

He shot me a suspicious look.

"What?"

"What do you know about chemistry?"

"Um, I spent the majority of my youth cooking potions, so I know a thing or two about how chemicals behave."

"Yeah, but that was dirty magic."

"It might have been dirty but it was still alchemy, which was the foundation of modern chemistry."

"All right," he said in a challenging tone. "Which law states that the pressure of a gas is inversely proportional to the value of a gas at a constant pressure?"

The hand on the wall clock ticked five times before I answered.

"Boyle's Law."

His eyes grew wide. "I seriously didn't think you'd get that."

I crossed my arms and tilted my head at him. "I'm just saying if you need help, I'm here for you."

His smile was genuine but surprised. "I think I got this one, but I'll let you know."

Quitting while I was ahead, I turned to resume my mail shuffling. "How's everything else at school?"

"Fine."

"You met any new friends in your classes?"

"Not really. There are a couple of guys that are all right, but people mainly leave me alone." Instead of sounding depressed by this, he seemed relieved.

I didn't comment on that, because the more I suggested he try harder to make friends, the more he'd withdraw from me. The trick, I'd learned, was to give him some space while also watching like a hawk. If I wanted to suggest something, I had to be tricky about it because teenagers could smell meddling from a mile away.

The fourth piece of mail in the stack looked different from the others. Instead of being another credit card offer or piece of junk mail, this one was a thick envelope made of high-quality cream paper. The return address was from something called the Conservatory for the Arcane Arts. It was addressed to the Parents of Danny Prospero.

"What's this?" I asked, holding it up.

He came and took it from me. When he read the return address, his face paled. "Um."

I raised a brow and let the silence speak for itself.

"So, uh, a few months ago, I heard something about a new school opening up—"

"What kind of school is it and where?"

"It's a magnet school for Adept kids. They're opening it in the Cauldron this fall." He shrugged. "Anyway, I sort of applied."

Tick, tick, tick went the clock. This time, the silence stretched until I could respond in a calm voice. It was a lot of ticks.

"You...applied? You would have needed a guardian's signature."

As if summoned, Baba came through the door in a cloud of white hair and patchouli stink. She was a seventyish-year-old witch who used to be our next-door neighbor, but she'd moved in with us several months earlier after the landlord raised her rent more than she could afford. The situation worked out well for me because she cooked and looked after Danny. Plus she was a hoot when she wasn't meddling or forcing her witch's brews on us.

She took one look at our stand-off and froze. "Uh-oh, what happened?"

I snatched the envelope from Danny and waved it. "He was just explaining how he applied to some school without telling me. You know anything about that?"

Two spots of pink appeared on her papery cheeks, but her expression remained neutral. "Why would I know about it?"

"Baba."

"Kate." Her bullish expression was the kind achieved only by women who'd lived long enough to know that patience won more arguments than shouting.

I turned to my brother. "Who signed the application?"

"I did," he said.

"You forged my signature?"

He pointed at the old woman. "But she knew!"

The betrayal morphed Baba's expression from innocence to a promise of retribution. "You're a devil, Danny Prospero."

"I'm not going down alone," he muttered.

His response was so classic Prospero that I almost laughed. Almost.

Baba sighed. "Then you better tell her about Volos."

No name on earth was guaranteed to ruin my mood more than that one. "What about Volos?" I enunciated each word careful so I wouldn't yell them.

Mayor John Volos and I had a somewhat complicated and shady shared history. We grew up together in the Votary coven, and we'd been teenaged sweethearts. After I left the coven, we didn't speak for about ten years. But ever since I got on the MEA task force, he'd been back in my life causing lots of trouble, including, apparently, encouraging my little brother to sneak behind my back.

Danny sighed. "He's involved in the school somehow, and he told me about it."

I threw up my hands. "Why didn't anyone tell *me* about it?"

"It was a while ago. Back before I was in the hospital."

The previous year, Danny had been targeted by a wizard I was chasing. He hexed my little brother with a potion that turned him into something like a werewolf. Then he unleashed my brother on me in the city's abandoned subway tunnels. Curing Danny had required me to team up with Volos to create an anti-potion. Afterward, he tried to use the fact I'd cooked illegally to blackmail me.

Yeah, he was a real peach, that guy.

"Remember that day I went to see John and you came to get me?" Danny said. "He mentioned it before you got there. Later, he got in touch to tell me applications were available."

I waved the envelope like a murder weapon. "Why didn't you tell me then?"

"Because you were so rigid about magic back then," Baba said.

The words hit me like a slap. My mouth opened and closed as I struggled to find words to deny her claim. None appeared, because there was no denying I had been completely irrational in my insistence that Danny stay far away from anything remotely related to magic back then.

Before I could come up with an appropriate response, Danny held up his hands. "Guys, can we hold off on the argument until we find out if I got in?" He nodded toward the envelope, urging me to open it.

Across the kitchen, Baba leaned back against the stove with her arms crossed and an annoyed expression on her face. But I could tell she was just as eager as the kid to find out if he got in.

I ripped open the envelope and pulled out the stack of folded sheets inside. The top page contained a letter. I cleared my throat and read aloud.

"Dear Parents of Danny Prospero, we are pleased to inform you that Danny has been accepted—"

The rest of the words were lost in a volley of squeals and shouts from my companions. Danny ran to Baba and high-fived her before she wrapped him in a big hug.

"You did it, kiddo!" she said.

I stood to the side with the letter, feeling a completely opposite set of emotions.

"We have to call Mez," Danny said.

"Why would you call him?" I said, my tone quiet as a tomb.

"Oh, crap," he said, face falling. "It's just— after I started taking lessons with him, I mentioned the school thing. Turns out he knew the principal because they went to school together. He called her and put a good word in for me, so I thought he'd want to know I got in."

Knowing that even Mez knew about this made me feel like I'd just swallowed a shit sandwich. "You might want to hold off on alerting anyone."

"Why?" Danny asked.

"Because I haven't said yes."

The mood in the room plummeted.

"Kate," Baba started, "don't be like that."

I slammed the papers on the counter. "Don't be like what? Don't be angry that you hid this from me?"

Danny's shoulders slumped. "Why can't you just be happy for me?"

"Why can't you stop hiding shit from me?" I shot back.

My little brother, who was not so little anymore, stood up straighter, looked me dead in the eyes, and said, "Because I knew you'd make it about you. But guess what, Kate, this is my life. You made your choices and now I'm making mine."

With that, Danny started to gather his things from the table. I watched him in stunned silence. I didn't trust myself to respond yet because his words had hit too close to home.

"I'm going to go study." He picked up the flashcards he'd been reviewing earlier and froze. He held up the top card and waved it at me accusingly. It said *Boyle's Law*. "You cheated."

I tipped my head and shot him an ironic look. "Ditto."

* * *

An hour later, I sat on the back patio, staring at an empty beer bottle. I stared at it in the hopes that it would spontaneously refill itself, since I didn't trust myself to go back in the house and risk running into Danny or Baba.

So I sat and I stared, and I tried like hell not to think about how I'd brought this school thing on myself.

"Pizza's here! The delivery guy pulled up at the same time I did."

Pen held a large pizza box in one hand and the remaining five-pack of beer in the other. When she saw the look on my face, she paused on the back step with her foot hovering in midair. She wore the same black yoga pants I'd seen her in the last three times we'd been together, but the yellow T-shirt made her brown skin glow. "Uh-oh. Should I leave?"

"I'll never speak to you again if you do. Bring that beer over here."

She continued to the patio table and set down her goodies. She opened a beer and passed it to me.

"I love you," I said.

"I love you, too, but you look like you're ready to commit a murder."

"Multiple murders. Many, many murders." I took a long swig.

"I assume that Baba is one of your intended victims."

"How did you know?"

"When she let me into the kitchen, she was waving a lit sage bundle around. When I asked her why, she muttered something about the house needing a spiritual cleansing to get rid of bad karma."

I pursed my lips. "I'll show her karma."

Pen dropped into the chair across from me and nudged my foot with her own. "Spill it."

I finally looked up and really saw my friend for the first time since she'd arrived. Guilt slammed into me hard as I realized I hadn't even said hello to her. It had been a few weeks since we'd spent any real time together, and she had walked in to another Prospero drama show.

"You know what?" I said. "Let's not. Tonight's about you. How's the job hunt?"

She winced. "Honestly, I was hoping to talk about something other than my problems tonight."

"Well, I'm not ready to talk about what they did to piss me off yet," I said. "Pick something else."

"All right," she said, "how's the hunk?"

I laughed. "Smooth transition."

She winked at me. "Tell me everything."

I flipped open the pizza box and handed her a piece before taking one of my own. I was totally putting off spilling the beans on Morales, but I also knew it was a futile gesture. Pen would sit there until I told her every juicy detail.

"There's not much to tell," I hedged.

"Girl, please. Do you really expect me to believe that boy isn't worth gossiping about?"

It was hard to argue with that. Morales was basically an action figure come to life. I literally had not had a boring moment with him since I met him—either in or out of the bedroom.

"I mean, it's fun, yeah. Really fun. But we're keeping it casual, you know?" I shrugged and took a bite of pizza.

"Does *he* know that?"

I plucked a pepperoni from the top of the pie and ate it before answering. "Of course."

She didn't look convinced. "Last time I saw you two together he didn't look at you like a man with casual things on his mind. That was weeks ago, Kate."

"You're imagining things."

She ate some pizza, but I could tell she wasn't done. Chewing was just an excuse to regroup her thoughts in order to launch another attack.

"Well, I'm glad you're finally getting some on the regular."

"Thanks, I think," I said. "Maybe you need a fuck buddy, too. Get your mind off your work situation."

"I've been wearing the same pants for five days. I'm not exactly prime fuck-buddy material."

"Ah, sweetie, don't sell yourself short. If I were a guy, I'd totally do you."

"Thanks." She snorted. "Anyway, I've never been into flings. I have this annoying habit of developing lasting attachments to men who give me orgasms."

"You can be fond without forming expectations," I said. "I mean, Morales is my partner. In my line of work, you end up forming this intimacy with the people you work with, like family. I would have taken a bullet for the guy before he started giving me orgasms, you know?"

She shot me an odd look. "Yes, I know."

"But that doesn't mean that I'm ready to commit myself to him."

She shook her head but swallowed whatever she'd been about to say with a mouthful of beer.

"What?" I didn't really want to hear it, but I was enough of a masochist to be curious.

"Oh, nothing. It's just funny that you're willing to die for the guy, but you're not willing to call yourself his girlfriend."

"It's not the same, Pen. You wouldn't understand."

I'd finished my second beer. I wanted a third. I really, really wanted a third, but I also needed to keep my wits about me. Pen had entered the phase of the night where she tried to fix me, and if I gave her enough of an opening, she'd make me face some things I didn't want to deal with yet.

She pointed her bottle at me. "I understand more than you think, but I also know that there's no talking to you about this stuff. When you're ready, you'll either get over yourself and accept that you care more for that boy than you want to admit, or you'll create a total shit show."

"Hey! That's not fair. I haven't created a shit show in months."

She nodded her head toward the house. "You got one brewing in there, right?"

"That one's not my fault. Danny applied to a new school without telling me. Volos told him about it, and Baba and Mez helped him apply."

Pen, who'd been the counselor at Danny's old school, perked up. "Which school?"

"Some new magnet for Adept kids."

"The Conservatory?" she said. "That place would be sort of awesome for him, Kate."

"You're missing the point. They all lied to me, and now I only have a couple of days to learn everything about this place before his acceptance letter needs a response."

"He got in?" She practically squealed it.

I paused. "Yeah, why?"

"That place is really hard to qualify for. From what I've heard, it's basically for the best of the best Adept kids."

"Apparently Mez spoke to the principal on Danny's behalf." I clenched my jaw as a new wave of anger washed through me.

"I know you're pissed about them lying, but this is a huge opportunity for him."

"Sure, if I want him to become a wiz for some huge clean magic company."

"Why wouldn't you want that for him?"

I stilled, thinking it over. The wizards who created potions for the legal clean magic market could make a very good living. If Danny landed a job at a place like Sortilege Inc., creating new laundry potions and age-defying magic for cosmetics for the average American household, he'd be set.

But that kind of security came at a cost.

"What if he decides he wants to do something else with his life? This is basically forcing him into that track. If he stayed in the Mundane high school, he'd be able to go into any field he wanted. But this Conservatory seems like it would lead him straight to the labs."

"That's what he wants, Kate."

"That's what he wants *now*." I held her gaze to let her know my concerns wouldn't be dismissed so easily. "I know everyone thinks I'm too strict about magic, but I've already compromised a lot, and look where it's gotten us." I waved toward the house to indicate tonight's current predicament. "I let him become Mez's apprentice, and now I find out they're sneaking behind my back. How am I not supposed to wonder if I made the wrong decision now? How can I trust that letting him go down this path won't lead him to the darker sides of magic?"

She leaned forward and put her hand on my knee. "No parent knows that about their kids. He's sixteen, not six. You have to let him make some decisions for himself. And then you have to let him learn how to pick himself up if he makes a mistake. But this controlling approach you have is just asking for him to rebel against you."

I leaned my head back to look up at the sky. Babylon's light pollution made it impossible to see more than a couple of weak stars. If I were a superstitious woman, I might have wished on one of those stars for some guidance. But I didn't see any stars, and besides, the only person I wanted guidance from was dead.

"I'm missing my mom tonight." The thought came from out of nowhere. It wasn't the kind of thing I'd admit to just anyone, but Pen was the closest thing I'd ever had to a sister.

"I know it's hard, honey. You want the best for him, but if you think about it, she didn't have much more mothering experience than you do. And, all due respect to the dead, but you've provided a lot more stability for Danny than she gave you."

I dragged my gaze from the sky. "Huh, I guess you're right."

I'd been seventeen when she died, and Danny was now already sixteen. The difference was she'd been raising a teen daughter who was following in the family business, which happened to be cooking and distributing illegal and addictive dirty magic potions. Danny, who I'd raised on my own since he was six, was a solid B student who rarely got in trouble. Mom had been a prostitute for a sex magic coven. I was a detective who busted people like my mom for a living.

"Be that as it may," I said, "sometimes I wish it were her dealing with these conundrums instead of me."

"This is going to sound terrible, but do you really think you and Danny would have been better off if she'd lived?"

After so many years thinking of my mother as some sort of saint or martyr, it was disorienting to think of her as the total opposite. It was only about six weeks earlier that I'd found out that it hadn't been a potion I'd cooked that caused her death. I'd carried unnecessary guilt around for a decade until John Volos finally admitted that my Uncle Abe had been the one to order the kill of his own sister. Obviously, finding that out hadn't done much to endear me to Volos, but getting that weight off my conscience had let new ideas in—like the fact that I was managing to be a better mother than she'd been, which made me feel both proud and terribly guilty at the same time.

"You want to talk about what you're feeling right now?" Pen said softly.

I blinked away the sting in my eyes and opened the third beer.

"Damn it," I said after I'd downed enough to wash away the sting in the back of my throat. "Tonight was supposed to be about cheering you up."

"No, it was about us being together," she corrected. "I've missed hanging out like this. It's done me more good than you can imagine."

"That's good. Me, too." I smiled. A new idea sprang up in my mind. "Hey! Have you thought about applying at the Conservatory? I bet they need counselors."

Her smile was pained. "Yeah. I checked. They only want Adept faculty and staff."

"Shit," I said. "That sucks."

She nodded. "Trust me, I've gone to every school in a fifty-mile radius. They're all either not hiring or they're friendly with the stiffs at Meadowlake and won't touch me."

"I'm sorry, Pen. What about going into private practice?"

"I don't have the capital to start my own, and most of the existing ones require clinical experience I don't have." She picked at the edge of the bottle's label. "I've been thinking maybe about trying something else. A nonprofit or something."

"That would be cool!" I enthused, trying to encourage.

"We'll see. In the meantime, Rufus called and said he needs some help organizing some Arcane Anonymous events. It's a volunteer gig, but it'll get me out of the house."

Rufus was the leader of the AA group Pen and I had belonged to for years. I quit AA the previous year because my work in the MEA required me to use magic, but Pen still went to meetings religiously. She'd been the one with the actual addiction to potions in college. I'd only gone to meetings to remind myself of the cost of making those potions on human lives.

"That's a fantastic idea," I said.

"Still, I need something to turn up soon. I'm almost out of my savings."

Because she'd quit her job at Meadowlake, she hadn't been eligible for unemployment benefits. "Listen, if you need help—"

"Nope."

"Pen, don't—"

"I said no," she said in her best and-that's-final voice. "If something doesn't turn up soon, I'll get a part-time gig or something, but I'm not about to take a handout."

"Don't be silly. It's not handout if it's from family."

"In my family, it was and they'd never let you forget it."

"Fuck them," I said. "They're not here now. I am. And what's mine is yours, no strings. Got it?"

She opened her mouth to say something, but my phone buzzed with an incoming text. I figured it was Morales checking in, so I didn't pick it up.

"Anyway," I said, but the phone rang. I glanced at the screen and realized it was Gardner. "Shit, hold on." Into the phone, I said, "Prospero."

"You need to get to the morgue."

"What's up?"

"Franklin's got a couple of bodies. Something about maybe they're tied to the Valentine case."

"Yes, sir."

"Morales with you?"

"No."

"Huh," she said. "I assume you know where to find him?"

My situation with Morales wasn't a secret, but Gardner had never actually spoken to us about it. At that moment, I wasn't real excited about discussing with my boss that he planned to come over for a booty call soon. "I can probably rustle him up."

"Uh-huh. I'll expect an update first thing in the morning."

"Yes, sir."

When I hung up, Pen was already gathering her things.

"Sorry, that was—"

"Work, I know," she said. "Why don't you head out. I'll clean this up."

"No, I can do it. You go on."

She shook her head. "I don't think I'm ready to go home yet. I'll probably just hang out with Baba and watch TV or something."

I hesitated. "Are you sure?"

"Of course!" Her smile was forced, but I didn't have time to do anything about it. I had to get in touch with Morales and arrange to either pick him up or meet him at the morgue.

I pulled her in for a quick, hard hug. "I love you. Everything's going to work out."

She sighed and relaxed into me a little. "Love you, too." She pulled back, her smile more genuine now. "Now git on with you. I got some episodes of the *Blue Devils* to catch up on with Baba."

CHAPTER FOUR

We arrived at the morgue an hour later. I'd picked Morales up from the sports bar in my Jeep, Sybil, since he'd gotten a ride there from his buddy and it was on my way.

"Well, well, well, look what the cat dragged in," Franklin called.

"You got any coffee?" I asked. It was almost one a.m. and any night that ended at the morgue was bound to be a long one.

He pointed to a yellowed carafe in a machine that looked like it had been chugging out coffee since the Eisenhower administration. "Tastes like shit, but it's strong. You're gonna need it for what I have to show you." He jerked a thumb toward the exam room behind him.

I grabbed a two paper cups from the counter and filled them with coffee that was roughly the color and consistency of hot tar. I held one up and looked over my shoulder at Morales. He nodded and came forward to take it.

I took an experimental sip of mine and winced. "What'd you brew it with—jet fuel?"

Franklin snorted. "That's right."

"All right, Franky," I said. "What you got for us?"

"Deceased's name was Sergei Kostorov."

Morales shrugged. "Doesn't ring a bell. What coven's he in?"

Franklin smiled. "Ain't in no coven, Special Agent."

"Then why are we here?"

Franklin shot him a withering look. "He isn't in a coven, but I'd bet good money he's visited one recently." He waved a hand. "Follow me, kids, but don't touch anything."

Morales and I shared look before following the M.E. into the exam room.

Inside, there were four tables spread out at even intervals. Two of the tables were empty. The last table on the left held a closed body bag. The table just to the right of the door held the other body, which was covered with a white sheet. About halfway down the length of the table, something tented the cloth. I prayed it was an instrument Franklin had left impaled in the body, but I had a bad feeling that was one prayer that would never be answered.

"Mr. Kostorov was brought in this afternoon after I got your boy back from the lab explosion," Franklin began. "Aged seventy-two, married. No history of pre-existing disease, non-smoker. He died at Babylon General. Heart attack."

"Okay," I said slowly, "what does this have to do with the Valentine case?"

"Who told you it did?" he said.

"Gardner," I said.

He shrugged. "I might have given her that impression, but we'll get to that in a second. But first, check this out."

He ripped the cloth off the body. Just as I feared, the protrusion had not been an instrument, but an erect penis.

It was as hard as Babe Ruth's bat.

"Holy shit," Morales said.

"Gives new meaning to *stiff*, right?" Franklin joked.

I couldn't stop staring at it. "How is it still..." I held my index finger straight up.

"That, my friends, is why you're here. After he died, the attending physician called for an autopsy."

"Why?" Morales said. "Heart attack isn't exactly surprising for a guy that age."

"Right, except that the widow Kostorov admitted that night before last was their anniversary. Seems the mister decided to surprise her with a little party favor to celebrate."

I dragged my gaze from the dead man's penis. "Huh?"

"He bought a virility potion."

"Let me guess—his old ticker couldn't handle all the excitement," I said.

"Wrong," Franklin said. "His ticker couldn't handle the eighteen-hour erection."

Morales's mouth fell open. "You're shitting me."

"According to the intake nurse, Mrs. Kostorov didn't bring him in until twelve hours in. Said she tried everything she could think of to get it to go down."

A hysterical giggle gathered in the base of my throat. "That's terrible," I choked out.

"Once they got him checked into the hospital, the doc tried everything to undo the potion's effect. Apparently, this sort of thing is more common than you think with virility potions." He turned to Morales. "Remember that, Slick."

Morales flipped him the bird. I covered my smirk with a cough.

"Anyway, the issue didn't resolve using the normal anti-magic interventions. After a few hours at the hospital, Kostorov's heart just gave out. Attending sent him to me to find out what was in that potion."

"What did your exam reveal?"

"Now, this is where things get interesting." Franklin pulled out his clipboard and flipped through a couple of pages. "Like I said, there weren't any traces of pre-existing issues. I tested the blood here for some of the common ingredients in virility potions—dragon's blood or vervain. Neither were present."

"Translation?" Morales asked.

"First, the two main ingredients in the majority of virility potions used in Babylon weren't there. Second, for me to find out which chemicals were in the potion, I need to send it to the regional lab."

"And?" Morales said.

"And," I answered for Franklin as realization dawned, "it'll be weeks if not months to see results."

Franklin winked at me. "Always knew you were smart, Detective."

"So you asked us here because you want to use MEA resources to test the blood." Morales sounded incredulous. "Mr. Kostorov ain't got nothing on your balls, Franklin."

"Shit," he said, dragging the word out to contain five syllables, "what you take me for? You really think I'd bring you out here just for my own selfish purposes?"

Morales raised his hands. "We're waiting."

Franklin waggled his fingers in invitation for us to follow him to the other occupied table. "This one came in two hours ago. Darrell Hill, aged twenty-seven."

Franklin unzipped the bulky body bag. When he reached the waist, an erection sprang out of the bag. "I had the doctor test the blood before he came down. No dragon's blood or vervain."

"So what?" Morales said. "You think there's a serial killer out there who lures men in to take virility potions that makes their hearts quit?"

I shot Morales a warning look.

"No, hotshot," Franklin snapped, "I think there's a sex magic practitioner that's selling an extremely dangerous virility potion. Before you got here, I called around to a couple other hospitals. Memorial had a case four nights ago with same cause of death, except it was a sixteen-year-old."

"Jesus," I whispered.

"No shit." Franklin used a gloved hand to tuck Mr. Hill's dick back into the bag.

Morales had paled when Franklin revealed that there was a third death. He reached into his pocket and pulled out his cell. "Mez, it's Morales. I need you down at the morgue. Dr. Franklin's going to give you some blood samples—"

Franklin interrupted. "Semen, too."

Morales shot him a long-suffering look. "And some semen. We need you to do a test to find out what alchemical components were used in a potion taken by three different men." He pulled the phone from his ear, and the tinny sound of Mez's shouts filled the room. "Trust me, I am well aware what time it is." He clicked off. "He'll be by within the hour for the samples."

"I'll have it all ready to go by then," Franklin said. "Thanks for this."

I blew out a breath. "Any new findings on Valentine's body?"

He moved over to a desk and pulled out a file. "Didn't find any fragments of a bullet in the head, and there's an exit wound." He pulled out an image of Basil's charred head and pointed to a spot that was supposed to be the exit wound. I couldn't see much besides a mess, so I took his word for it. "Last I heard, CSI wizes hadn't found the casing or any fragments on site, either."

"Which means someone wasn't looking hard enough," I said.

"Or whoever shot Basil did a cleanup before they torched the lab," Franklin offered.

"So, no tracing a gun," Morales concluded.

"Of course not," I said. "That'd be too easy." To Franklin, I said, "Go ahead and give your report to Mez when he comes. Looks like we're officially taking the case from the BPD."

Morales added, "And let us know if you turn up any other DOAs that match the Kostorov potion."

"I know you're taking the Valentine case, but should I loop Duffy in on this virility potion thing?" Franklin asked.

"At best, we'd be able to pin manslaughter on the wizard, but you know how hard it is to get that shit to stick," I said. "Besides, you heard Duffy at the scene yesterday. He's not real eager to pick up new cases at the moment."

"Understood," Franklin said. "You got any ideas of where to start tracking down the source of this shit?"

"We'll have to do some digging," Morales said. "You got the widow's information?"

Franklin shook his head. "I got the attending's phone number, though. He can give it to you."

I took down the doctor's name. "We'll do our best to track this down, but we're already working the Valentine investigation. Gardner's not gonna be real thrilled about using resources if this turns out to be some low-level wiz selling bad potions out of his van or whatever."

"Tell that to the widow," he said, his tone uncharacteristically grim. "Or that kid's mom. Your brother's about that age, right?"

It was a low blow and he knew it, but he didn't look the least bit apologetic.

"All right," I said, "I get it. We'll see what we can do. Just don't expect a miracle."

He laughed but the sound held little humor. "In this business, miracles are in short supply, Prospero."

CHAPTER FIVE

We got to the gym bright and early the next day. After our trip to the morgue, it was one of those mornings where it felt like even an IV drip of coffee wouldn't be enough to get me through the day. But now that we were potentially juggling a murder case and Franklin's virility potion case, the To Do list had grown exponentially, so there was no sleeping in.

The light in Gardner's office was on, indicating she was already at work, and judging from the noises coming from Mez's lab, he'd pulled an all-nighter following his visit to the morgue. But the doorway into his lab had a heavy curtain pulled across it, which meant he wouldn't welcome an interruption. We needed to talk to both of them, but first we had a couple of calls to make.

"You take the widow and I'll reach out to Val to see about getting evidence from the lab?" Morales said.

I nodded and dialed the phone number for Kostorov's attending physician. After navigating my way through the hospital phone tree for about five minutes and getting a generic voicemail box, I hung up. In my cell, I found the number for a nurse named Maggie Smith that I knew at the hospital who might be able to help. Luckily, I had her direct line.

"Kate? Is everything okay?"

She was right to worry, since I only seemed to call when there was an emergency. We'd met after Danny had been hexed by a dirty magic potion, and the last time we'd talked had been after Pen had had a terrible car accident.

"Yes, everyone's good," I said. "I was actually hoping you could help me on a case. I was supposed to talk to a Dr. Singh, but I can't seem to reach him."

She snorted. "Yeah, he worked a double shift. He's probably in a self-induced coma about now."

"Well, the thing is I'm trying to get ahold of the widow of one of his patients who passed away last night."

"I was working last night. Who's the deceased?"

I told her Kostorov's name.

She made an ain't-that-a-shame noise with her mouth. "Yeah, hard to forget that one. What do you need the widow's info for?"

"Medical examiner called us in for a consult. Need to talk to the wife to find out exactly what he took."

"Geez, Kate, I'd love to help, but I can't give out her address or phone number without her permission or a warrant."

I stifled a curse. Stupid laws protecting people's privacy. Made my job a real pain in the ass sometimes. "I get it. Any way you could call her and ask her to get in touch with me?"

"That should work."

"I'd owe you a big one, Maggie."

"Sure thing. One of my girlfriends who works over at Memorial said they had a guy come in with the same problem. Whatever they took is nasty. I hope you find whoever's putting it out."

"That's the plan. Listen, if you hear of any similar cases coming in, can you give me a heads-up? Since you're on the front line, so to speak."

"Sure thing. I'll text you once I've gotten in touch with Mrs. Kostorov."

After I hung up, I chewed on my lip for a moment. I needed to talk to Mez to discuss the work he'd done on the Valentine potions, but before I could grab Morales from his phone to go talk to the wizard, Gardner's door opened. "Morales, Prospero—I need an update."

Morales hung up from the call with Val. Together, we went to Gardner's office to fill her in.

"How'd it go at the morgue?" she asked without preamble.

"Franklin has three bodies he believes are tied to the same virility potion," Morales said.

She frowned. "When he called, I assumed he was bringing us information on the Valentine case."

This is where things were going to get tricky. Technically, the favor we were doing for Franklin wasn't exactly kosher, so we needed to sell it to Gardner.

"He's got three dead men who all appear to have taken the same virility potion that stopped their hearts," he continued. "Based on Franklin's initial findings, the potions probably didn't come from Aphrodite's crew."

She didn't look convinced. "Three men dying from hard-ons isn't exactly shocking in this town, Prospero."

"One of the vics was a sixteen-year-old," I said. "Whatever this potion is, it's extremely dangerous, and it's possible a new outfit is moving into town to sell it. If we ignore this and the press gets wind of it later, we'll be crucified."

She sighed. "You talk to Duffy about this?"

"So far, we don't have any reason to believe these are homicides," Morales said.

She pursed her lips, thinking it over. "All right. Once we have Mez's results, we'll assess the need for further involvement. But this is not your priority—the Valentine case gets top billing."

"Got it," he said.

She looked down and wrote something on a pad. "Speaking of, any progress there?"

"We spoke to Aphrodite yesterday. Something strange is going on with them."

"Them?"

"Long story," he said. "Anyway, the Hierophant is planning a wedding."

"Whose wedding?"

"It's an alchemical wedding," I said. "Aphrodite is marrying their masculine and feminine sides to each other."

"What's that got to do with Valentine?"

"We're not sure yet," Morales said. "But Aphrodite's acting strange and seemed to imply there might be some upheaval happening in the covens."

"There's always upheaval in the covens," Gardner observed in a dry tone.

"Yes, but now we've got multiple dead men who took virility potions that aren't connected to Aphrodite, and someone killed their nephew, to boot," I said. "Something's going on."

"I need more than speculation here. Bring me facts and evidence."

"Understood," Morales said. "Aphrodite also said that Basil might have been dating a Votary girl. We're going to track her down today."

She nodded. "Good. I talked to Eldritch first thing this morning and told him we were officially taking the case. He offered full cooperation, but you come to me first before you go to Duffy."

"Yep. I talked to Val Frederickson before we came in," Morales said. "She's sending over some evidence collected at the scene. They found Basil's cell phone in a trash can near the scene. If it's okay with you, I'd like to bring Dixon in on that to track down call history and texts."

"Sounds good," Gardner said. "Let me know if you need extra hands beyond that. Shadi's team can be available for surveillance or leg work. I want this case in the win column ASAP."

We both nodded.

"Well?" she said. "Why are you still sitting there? Get to work."

* * *

By the time Morales and I exited Gardner's office, the lab "door" was open.

"I'm going to go talk to Mez," I said.

He nodded. "I'll see if I can get bead on Little Man and Mary."

Walking into the lab, I called, "How's my favorite lab rat today?" My tone sounded forced to my own ears. As much as I tried to keep work and private life separate, lack of sleep made it hard not to bring my frustration over the Danny school situation into the lab with me.

He looked up from the worktable where he was labeling samples. "Tired. I was up all night, processing everything from the arson scene and the morgue."

"Sorry, man." I let my resentment melt away. It was hard to stay mad at a man who'd stayed up all night processing semen samples for you.

"I tell you," he said, "some days I wish I were a vampire."

"Nah," I shot back, "you'd look terrible with a widow's peak."

"I'd rock a cape, though."

"True enough." I wandered over to the lab setup, which had green and blue liquids simmering away in Erlenmeyer flasks while other liquids crawled through clear tubing. "All right, let's start with the arson labs."

He pulled out a file folder filled with handwritten notes and computer printouts. "We got about two hundred potion patches of Buffalo."

Buffalo was one of the main potions currently being peddled by the Votary coven. Its full name was White Buffalo, which was due to its main ingredient being peyote. It was a potion that promised to expand consciousness, but usually ended up making its addicts schizophrenic.

I whistled. "Damn."

He nodded. "It's a nice haul, but that's not all we got." He tapped his pen on the clipboard where he had all his data. "There was also a stash of Chains. A big one."

"Chains" was one of the most abused dirty potions sold in the Cauldron. They called it that because it was super addictive, but it also created a paralytic affect in the user, akin to being bound in chains. Recently we'd had reports that it had started leaking to other cities, which meant the regional office was going to be really happy once news of the eventual bust hit the front page.

"That's a great haul. Did you tell Gardner?"

"I will once we're done here." He motioned for me to join him at a microscope set up near the windows.

"There was a third potion in the freezer. The stash was small—only about fifteen vials."

"What is it?"

"I've never seen anything like it before."

A rack near the microscope held three vials containing a red liquid. On the rubber lid of each, there was an Asian symbol I didn't recognize. "What's that symbol?"

"It's Chinese," he said. "Cinnabar."

"That's odd."

"I've never seen anything like this in Babylon. Have you?"

"The cinnabar, yes. It was a trademark ingredient of my Uncle Abe's potions. But you don't normally see Chinese symbols on anything here."

"Okay, so in the same stash, I also found about fifty red pills." He poured a few pills out on a scale. They were red with the number 69 on them.

"I've never seen those before either, but someone's not into subtlety, are they?" I asked, referring to the sophomoric symbolism.

"So, here's the thing," Mez said. "Based on my lab work, I think that the stuff in the vials is pretty similar to the formula in the pills."

"How so?"

"Look in the microscope."

Closing my right eye, I looked with my left. Had I been looking at a Mundane chemical compound, I would have seen a bunch of squiggles. But since I had the ability to *read* magic and the compound was arcane in nature, there was a sort of hologram of a dragon hovering just above the squiggles. Problem was, I couldn't tell Mez that I saw the hologram, because he didn't know I could *read*. The reasons I'd hidden it from most of the team were complicated, but normally, it wasn't an issue because evidence collected via arcane means, such as *reading* potions to find out who made them, wasn't admissible in court.

"What am I looking for here?" I asked.

"That's the slide containing the liquid potion. See how there are wiggly bits and straight bits?"

I focused on looking past the roaring dragon to the potion itself. "Okay, I see them."

"Move aside for a moment."

I stepped over to let him put a new slide in the 'scope. "Okay, this slide has the powdered pill on it."

He moved out of the way and I looked again. This slide had the dragon, but the image was weaker. In addition, a cupid with a bow was superimposed. I pulled away, blinking to clear my eyes from the confusing imagery. I wondered if the cupid was Basil's signature. When I looked again, I looked past the holograms to the potion itself for more clues.

"I see straight and wiggly pieces and—" I blinked and looked again.

"You see them?" he asked.

I adjusted the focus on the microscope. "Little black Xs."

"Right, those are consistent with yohimbe bark."

I stood up and crossed my arms. The holograms had told me part of the story, but I couldn't tell Mez that. So, I played dumb and let him connect the dots. "Yohimbe is found in diet and impotence potions, right?"

"Right," he said. "The pill contains the potion from the vials. But whoever made the pills was an idiot, because the lines were cinnabar and the squiggles were yerba mate. They're commonly used in Asian lust potions, but the idiot who made the pills added the yohimbe, too." He shook his head at what he clearly felt was a rookie move.

"So, basically, they took a lust potion and turned it into a super-lust potion?"

"Pretty much. Anyone who took that pill would have to have the heart of an ox to survive it."

I froze. "Have you tested the samples from the morgue yet?"

"I conducted some preliminary tests. Why?"

"Didn't Franklin fill you in on the situation?"

"He was busy, so his assistant gave me the samples."

"The body he called us to view was a seventy-year-old who'd died from an eighteen-hour erection made his heart fail. He knew of at least two other cases that had died in the last few days, including a sixteen-year-old."

"Shit," Mez said. "That definitely sounds consistent with what that pill would do."

"If we can tie all those bodies to whoever killed Valentine, the case would go from big to massive. I need you to test Franklin's samples for yohimbe."

"I'll start on those right away, then."

I stared down at the vials and pills, thinking through all the angles. "What I can't figure out is why there were so few pills and vials."

He nodded. "Especially since there was so much of the other potions."

I paced for a minute before a theory formed. "When I worked for

Abe, he'd sometimes give free samples out to the hexheads. Said it accomplished two things. First, if all the junkies died, the batch clearly wasn't ready."

"Charming," Mez said.

"The man's a sweetheart, right? Anyway, the other reason was that if the potion was good, giving samples to the hexheads created the market."

Mez nodded. "Makes sense in a really fucked-up way. But something else has my instincts firing off."

"Agreed. Whoever made those vials isn't a Votary wizard."

"How do you know?"

I froze, realizing I'd revealed more about what I'd seen than I intended. "I mean, that Chinese symbol, right?"

"Right," he said. "The Votary coven uses European alchemical symbolism on their potions."

"And sometimes the Sangs use Egyptian hieroglyphs, but I've never seen Asian symbolism in Babylon." I tapped my chin, playing along. "It could mean the Votary wizards are using new suppliers."

"I'd say that's a strong possibility," he said, "and that the suppliers are probably Fangshi."

I kept myself from pumping my fist as he came to the proper conclusion.

"What about the Fangshi?" Morales said from the doorway.

I turned and filled him in quickly on what we knew. "Do you think the Fangshi could be making a play in Babylon?"

"Anything's possible," he said.

"Didn't you work undercover with the Fangshi in Los Angeles?" Mez asked.

Morales gave him a curt nod. "Yeah, but I'd be shocked if any of the big players in the Fangshi would waste their time with a low-level guy like Basil Valentine." He avoided looking at me, but I could feel the tension coming off of him. We'd have a lot to discuss once we were alone.

"All right," Mez said, "We'll know more once I get the morgue samples processed. I'll let you know as soon as I know something."

I nodded and started to go.

"Kate?" he said, his voice suddenly hesitant.

"What's up?" I said, looking toward the door. Morales hovered there, looking impatient for me to wrap it up.

"Baba called me last night."

I held up a hand. "Look, Mez, I really don't want to get into this here. So, if you're planning to lecture me about how I need to raise my little brother, you can save your breath."

He shuffled his boots a little. "It's not that. I just wanted to apologize for my role in everything. They swore they were going to tell you."

I sighed. "Look, I don't have time for this right now."

"I know," he said, "but for what it's worth, I understand why you might have reservations, but I know Dr. Hidalgo personally. We went to Thoth U together. She'll take good care of him."

"Prospero," Morales called. "Tick-tock."

I ignored him for a moment and focused on Mez. "Look, I get that everyone just wants what's best for Danny, but I'm playing catch-up here. I need some time and space to think about this before I make a decision."

"Okay," he said. "I just wanted to make sure we're good."

"Yeah, we're good." I actively released the tension in my shoulders. "Just promise me that next time, you'll come to me."

"You got it." He smiled to seal the pact.

I turned to go, passing Morales, who followed in my wake.

"What was all that about?" he asked when we reached the sidewalk outside.

"Nothing," I snapped and threw open the door to go out to the street.

He caught my arm and spun me around. "Will you talk to me?"

"Why? So you can lecture me about how I'm a shitty mom too?"

He pulled back. "What?"

I quickly told him about the school drama. When I mentioned Volos's involvement, his jaw tightened but he didn't interrupt.

When I was done, he sighed. "What are you going to do?"

"I'll do my homework on the school and then I'll make a decision."

"That feels like the right move. You can't let them gaslight you into believing their deceit is somehow your fault."

Hearing him put it that way went a long way toward easing my anger. He'd put his finger on precisely the issue I hadn't been able to articulate for myself. "Exactly, yes. Thank you."

I smiled at him across the car. Something sparked in his face, and I felt a corresponding ignition in my chest.

"You're doing good by that kid. You'll figure out the right thing when the time comes."

"Thanks."

"You're welcome. Now, can you do me a favor?"

I cross my arms. It was as close to agreement as I could give him right then.

"Next time there's personal stuff happening in your life, can you tell me about it so I don't have to find out secondhand at work?"

My first instinct was to deny that I'd hidden anything, but he was totally right. I'd had plenty of opportunities from the time I picked him up to go to the morgue up until we got to work this morning to fill him in on what happened. Pen's pointed words about me saying I'd take a bullet for him but not call him my boyfriend came back to haunt me. "I'm sorry. I should have looped you in. There was just a lot going on."

We were in full view of the office windows, so he settled for bumping my shoulder. "Understood." He dipped his head until I looked him in the eye. "You know I'm here for you, right?"

"Of course," I said automatically.

"I mean it, Kate."

"I know."

He hesitated with his key halfway to the ignition. I braced myself, praying he'd let it go so we didn't have to have some sort of messy emotional conversation. Luckily, he thought better of whatever he'd been about to say and started the car.

"All righty," he said, "let's go see the Wonder Twins."

CHAPTER SIX

Since it was springtime, the twins had resumed their daily visits to the city park near the old steel factories. Originally, the park had been built for the families of steel workers, but since the steel bust, it was little more than an empty lot with junked-out playground equipment and a few chipped benches.

We left the SUV parked at the curb and started over toward their bench. The back of Mary's head was swathed in sunlight, which illuminated the patches of pink scalp showing through her greasy brown hair. Not wanting to startle her, I cleared my throat as we approached. She turned her head sideways to look at us from the corner of her eye.

"It's Lady and Macho." She tilted her head down as she announced our arrival to her brother.

"No shit?" The voice that responded to her sounded like it belonged to a thirty-year-old man who'd grown up hard.

He might sound mature, but Little Man was no larger than a six-month-old baby. Mary toted him around in a carrier strapped to her chest, but he was no infant. Instead, Little Man was her conjoined twin. Technically he was a homunculus—the product of their mother's addiction to a nasty fertility potion. Mary had gotten all of the physical strength, but Little Man's mind ran the show.

"I was hoping we'd see you two assholes today," he said with characteristic charm.

I crossed my arms and smiled down at LM. "You miss us, LM?"

"Nah, just need some money for cigarettes and a sammich." His laugh sounded like the grinding of rusty gears. He raised his two chubby arms. "What can we do for you?"

"You hear about Basil Valentine?" I asked.

Little Man chuffed out an offended breath. "That's a rhetorical question, right?"

"What you hearing?"

He leaned an elbow back on his sister's flat chest. "Other than Basil got shot before he got blowed up, you mean?"

"Right."

He sucked on his front baby teeth. "There's some rumors."

"What kind of rumors?" Morales said.

"Expensive ones." Little Man rubbed his tiny hand over his belly. "Sure am hungry."

Morales pulled a twenty from his wallet and shoved it toward the homunculus. Mary's hand reached out to snatch and stash it.

Once the transaction was made, LM smiled. "Rumor is Basil got himself tied up in some shady shit at the urging of his lady."

"Who's his lady?"

"You ain't heard?" He crossed his chubby arms over his belly. "Sad day when the law don't have any idea what's going on in their own town."

"Cut the shit, LM. Give us her name."

"Y'all are no fun today." He turned his cupid's bow mouth down into a pout. "Her name's Krystal LeMay."

"Is she in porn?" Morales asked.

Little Man laughed. "You ain't too far off, Macho. She runs a rub 'n' tug joint over on Blackmoore Avenue."

"What's her story?" I asked.

"I'm disappointed in you, Prospero. You of all people should know who's running your uncle's outfit now."

My mouth fell open. "Bullshit."

"Scout's honor," Little Man said. He held up two fingers in salute. "She was dating that asshole Puck Simmons before he went away for killing Charm."

Morales and I exchanged a shocked look. "Hold on," I said. "You're saying Puck's ex, who sold him out to BPD, is also the new head of the Votaries who happened to be dating the victim of our murder investigation?"

"Pretty much."

I grabbed Morales's arm. "We saw her before, remember? At Charm's wake."

"Was that the time you broke Puck's finger?" he asked.

"Yep."

"I remember her. She kept glaring at you like the two of you had some old beef."

"Which was weird, seeing how I'd never met her in my life."

"What's this about Krystal selling out Puck?" Little Man asked. He tried to sound casual, but I realized our error too late. We were supposed to be getting gossip from Little Man, not providing it.

"Oh, no, I meant they were dating when Puck went away."

His eyes narrowed. "Uh-huh. Anyway, that's who you need to talk to."

"You mentioned something about Basil getting into shady shit because of her?"

Little Man wiggled his fingers again.

I crossed my arms and tilted my chin down at him. "We already paid you."

"A pittance," he said. "When I give you so much."

"Tell you what," Morales said. "You tell us and we'll decide whether it's worth an additional payment."

He pressed his lips together, clearly annoyed. "So, Basil used to work for the O's, right? Seeing how he's Aphrodite's nephew, he got special insight into the sex potion business. Apparently, Krystal decided to use that."

"But you said Krystal's Votary. Why would she want a cut of the sex magic trade?"

"Who knows? Bottom line is I heard she and Basil made some deal with some Chinese motherfuckers to distribute their shit."

"The Fangshi?" I said.

"Never thought I'd see the day the Chinese would be selling on Babylon's streets." Little Man shook his head sadly, but his tone betrayed anticipation instead of disappointment.

"I'm thinking Aphrodite won't be too happy with that development," Morales said, shooting me a look.

"They did mention something about young wizes," I said.

Little Man leaned forward, suddenly very interested. "Hold up, you went to Aphrodite before you came to see me? The shemale working for y'all or what?"

"Relax, LM," I said. "Aphrodite would no sooner work for the MEA than give you a blow job."

He leered. "Please, that he-bitch would pay me for a taste of my prime beef."

I threw up a little in my mouth, considering the beef in question was currently encased in a full diaper.

"Anyway, that actually is pretty helpful, LM." I pulled an extra ten from my wallet and handed it to him. "So, thanks."

He handed the bill to Mary and laid his hands across his bare belly. "So...you two fucking, huh?"

The change in topic was so fast, I got vertigo. "Whoa."

"Don't be ridiculous," Morales said.

"Please. You got the look of a lady who been getting it on the regular, and he's strutting around like he's dipping his wick in a special candle."

It was nice to hear that he thought of me as a "special candle," but there was no way in hell I was going to discuss my private life with a horny homunculus. As much as I'd relied on Little Man's intel to help solve cases, I was under no illusion that he was on our side. He was a businessman who sold information. If word got out on the street that Morales and I were romantically involved, it could eventually be used against us by any number of lowlifes.

"You need to cut back on whatever you've been smoking." I shot Morales a grossed-out look. "I know better than to shit where I eat."

Morales's brow shot up, but he played along. "Yeah, gross."

"Don't bullshit a bullshitter." LM tipped his chin to shoot me a frank look. "Hey, no judgments. I get it. Y'all working long hours together. Things are bound to get horizontal. Just sayin', though, shit's gonna get messy."

"We don't pay you for relationship advice, Little Man," Morales said.

He smirked at us. "Nah, I do that for free."

Mary, who until that point had been sort of staring off into the middle distance, perked up. "Macho and Lady sitting in a tree," she sing-songed.

Little Man cackled like a loon. "F-u-c-k-i-n-g."

I shook my head and waved away their perverted nursery rhyme. "You two ain't right in the head." I plucked at Morales's shirt. "Let's go."

As we walked away, the sound of Little Man's laughter followed us. But then he yelled, "Don't arrest Krystal today."

I stopped and turned. "Why not?"

He made a jerk-off motion in the air. "I got an appointment tomorrow morning!"

* * *

Once we got to the car, I called my friend Joyce at the county clerk's office. According to the records on file, Krystal LeMay had gotten permits to open a massage parlor five weeks earlier.

After I hung up with Joyce and told Morales what I learned, he said, "Timing is interesting."

Krystal's ex-boyfriend Puck had been arrested a week before she got her permit. Sometime between choosing not to corroborate her boyfriend's alibi and opening the salon, she'd come into enough money to open a business.

"Something to ask about when we chat with her," I said.

"Do you really buy LM's claim she's running the Votaries now?"

"On one hand, he's rarely wrong. But on the other, she didn't strike me as the type."

He shot me a look.

"What?"

"You met her for what? Ten minutes in that bar that one time. And you two didn't even talk."

"Morales, I grew up in that coven, remember? You learn how to size people up quickly."

"Well, she had Puck fooled, so maybe she's a good actress."

"Maybe." I shrugged. "You want to talk about the fact that it's looking more and more likely that the Fangshi have infiltrated Babylon?"

A muscle in his jaw clenched. "Not especially."

Several years earlier, Morales had been undercover in the Fangshi. While he was there, the coven killed a dirty cop and Morales had helped them cover up the murder. It had been a secret he'd carried by himself for a long time, but the previous fall, a psycho wizard dosed us both with a truth serum and the truth had come out. Later, we discovered that Mayor Volos also knew his dirty secret and even had a written account of the crime signed by a member of the coven named Gan Ji, who'd been there when it happened.

"You know once Gardner finds out, she's going to start asking questions and your past in that coven is going to come up."

He shifted in his seat and veered the SUV into traffic. "Kate, there is no way that the wizards I dealt with in Los Angeles are in Babylon now. From the sound of it, it's a low-level guy wanting to earn some quick cash."

"But Gardner—"

He cut me off. "If L.A. comes up, I'll tell her everything I know about the inner workings of the Chinese coven so far as it pertains to closing the case. There's no reason for the incident to come up."

By that time, we'd pulled onto the street where the massage parlor sat. It was not the nicest area of the Cauldron, but it wasn't the worst, either. The block held a couple of dive bars, a check cashing joint, and had a bus stop on the corner. We parked across the street.

The massage place was in the center of the block with a pink neon sign in the window that read, HAPPY ENDING MASSAGE PARLOR.

"Well," Morales said, "that answers that question."

I shot him a look and reached for the door. "Behave," I warned him. "And don't touch anything."

The air inside smelled like coconut oil and stale semen. The combination was less pleasant than it sounds.

Behind the front desk, a woman with orange skin was talking on the phone. The hue was the result of a fake-tanning potion. The clean magic version of the potion was expensive and gave a convincing sun glow to the skin. The dirty version was cheap and left one looking like they'd rolled in cheese-puff dust. This chick clearly had gone for the discount version.

As she talked on the phone, she smacked her gum and filed her nails into daggerlike points. "So I tells him, you gotta warn a girl before you put it there—"

"Excuse me," I said.

She held up one of her fingers. "And he said, 'It slipped.' Can you believe it?"

"Hey, it happens," Morales said to me, straight-faced.

"It better not," I said to him, darkly. To the lady behind the desk, I said, "Ma'am." I held up my badge. "You need to hang up now."

She paused mid-smack and squinted at the badge. "I'm gonna have to call you back." She dropped the phone into the cradle. "We don't do couples massages."

"You have a lot of cops come in asking for massages?" I asked.

"You'd be surprised who we get in here." She shrugged. "What do you want?"

"We need to see the boss lady," Morales said.

"You got an appointment?" *Smack, smack, smack.*

I looked up at the video camera behind the desk and waved. "Come out now or I'll have my friends come raid your back rooms."

The phone on the desk rang. The Smacker answered. "Yeah…Uh-huh. Yep." She hung up. "You can go on back. Third door on the right. The right, you hear? You do not want to go left."

"Got it," I said.

With that, Morales and I walked through the lobby to the curtained doorway. The hallway was dark and each of the doors was closed. Suspicious moans filtered out into the cramped space.

"We should go left, right?" Morales joked at my back.

"Very funny." I opened the third on the right. Even though I shared my partner's amusement about the location of our errand, I was tense about the reason for our visit. If Krystal really was the new leader of the coven, she wasn't someone to underestimate.

The door opened into a storage room. Shelves lined with dingy white towels and industrial-sized bottles of massage oil lined the walls. I shuddered upon seeing boxes upon boxes of rubber gloves.

Just past all the shelves, a doorway was blocked by a bamboo-beaded curtain. Morales went through first, but he stopped short on the other side, which forced me to run into his back.

"Hey!"

He pulled me around him so I could see what he was looking at. Instead of entering an office, we'd entered a control room. A semicircle of TV monitors displayed the action inside all of the massage rooms. Nothing really prepares a person for seeing half a dozen illegal hand jobs projected on large screens, but it's not something I cared to repeat—ever.

"Jesus!" I looked at the floor so fast, I experienced vertigo. "Warn me next time."

"I didn't get any warning," he muttered.

"Why are so many of them weeping?" I asked.

"Nothing sadder than paying for an apathetic handie," Morales said in a philosophical tone.

"Excuse me," said a bitchy voice.

The woman sitting in the office chair monitoring all of the TVs spun around. She had blond hair and wore too much makeup. Last time I'd seen her, she'd been dressed like the girlfriend of an up-and-coming coven member—that is to say, showing lots of skin and attitude. However, that day, she wore a tailored skirt suit in a flattering light blue. The cut bordered on being just a tad too sexy for business, but considering the woman's business was discount hand jobs, it worked. She also wore a pair of nude heels with the tell-tale red on the sole that meant she'd paid way too much for them.

"I'm afraid we don't service ladies," she quipped. Then she looked at Morales. "But if you play your cards right, handsome, you can have one on the house."

He smirked. "That's so nice, but I prefer to live a hepatitis-free lifestyle."

She sniffed. "What do you want, then?"

"Would you mind turning those off?" I asked.

"Didn't know you were a prude, Kate."

"That's Detective Prospero to you, sweetheart, and I'm not a prude. That's just the saddest porn ever."

She pursed her lips and hit a button. All the screens went blessedly blank.

"There," she said. "Now, make it quick. I've got a business to run."

I wasn't sure how watching bored massage therapists dole out manual stimulation counted as busy, but what did I know?

"We've met before," I said. "At the Red Horse."

"Oh, really?" she said in a bored tone. She remembered, but she wanted me to believe she didn't. "I don't recall."

Considering she'd just called me by name, she knew exactly who the hell I was. "Yeah," I said, "I normally don't remember coven wizes' arm candy, but that day was special, seeing how it had been Charm's wake and all."

Her eyes had flared at my characterization of her as Puck's flavor of the week. "Oh, that's right," she said, "You're that girl who betrayed the entire coven."

I smiled. "That what Puck told you?"

"No, actually, your uncle did. He also said you were nothing special. That's why I didn't pay much attention."

"You talk to Abe often?" Morales cut in.

She shrugged.

"Because we've been hearing some things about you," he continued.

"Oh, yeah? What kind of things?" She crossed her legs in a way she probably thought was seductive. "I didn't catch your name, Detective—"

"Special Agent Morales," he said. "MEA."

Her eyes widened. "Impressive."

"Uh-huh," I said. "We heard that you sold out Puck."

"Who?"

"Your boyfriend. Puck Simmons. Some people called him 'Pain.'"

"Oh, him? What can I say? He broke the law. I couldn't continue to associate with him."

I smiled at her. "We also heard that you took over the Votaries once he was gone."

She had a donkey's laugh. "That's the funniest thing I've heard in ages," she brayed. "How hilarious!"

"According to the tax records, you opened this place up a couple of weeks after Puck was arrested."

"So?"

"Where'd you get the money?" I asked.

"Since when is it illegal to be an entrepreneur?"

"You didn't answer my question."

"I got the money the old-fashioned way—I worked for it."

"Hey, Morales?" I said, turning to him.

"Yeah?"

"What's the start-up cost for an outfit like this, do you figure?"

He rubbed his chin. "I'm no expert, mind you, but rents in this area have to run, what? Two grand a month? Any landlord worth their salt would demand first and last's deposit, too. Plus there's all the massage oil to buy."

"And the rubber gloves," I added.

"Sure, can't forget those. Let's call it ten grand minimum."

"That's an awful lot of hand jobs."

"Indeed," he said.

"I suppose someone could get a loan from the bank," I responded conversationally.

"Sure, but remember? The records on file listed the business was started in cash."

She jumped out of her chair. "Shut up, all right! If you want to come back here with a warrant, you can try it, but you have zero PC."

"All evidence to the contrary," I observed, tipping my head to the screens.

"You're MEA, right? There's no potions here. It ain't your jurisdiction."

"Honey, I don't know who told you that, but they don't know shit about how jurisdictions work."

"Maybe Puck taught her," Morales said. "Or Abe."

"Uncle Abe knows better than that, but he does like to take young ladies under his belt, so to speak," I said. "They still got those conjugal visit trailers at Crowley, Krystal?"

Her cheeks had flushed red with anger. "Get the hell out of here and don't come back without a warrant. But I'll warn you both, I have a very good lawyer."

"Let me guess, his name is Dicky Goldman," I said.

She looked shocked at my guess. "How did you know?"

"Because Dicky is Uncle Abe's lawyer. Makes sense that he'd want to protect his new puppet."

"I am nobody's puppet."

"Does Abe know that?"

Her voice shook with rage. "Get. Out!"

I held up my hands. "We're going, we're going. But one last thing. You might want to watch your ass with the Fangshi."

Despite her flushed cheeks, she managed to school her features when she responded. "The who?"

But it was too late. I'd seen the flash of knowledge in her eyes. "We'll be seeing you real soon, Krystal."

"Not if I see you first."

Morales pulled my sleeve. "Let's go."

We pushed through the beaded curtain, out of the storage area, and back into the hallway of sadness. Neither of us spoke, because it was a safe bet that Krystal had audio to go with the video surveillance. By the time we made it back outside, I inhaled and exhaled like my life depended on getting fresh air into my lungs.

"I need a shower and a drink."

"In that order?"

I shook my head. "Drink first. Definitely."

"I know just the place."

CHAPTER SEVEN

The place in question turned out to be the Irish Rover, a cop watering hole that served decent bar food. Since neither of us had had lunch, we ordered a couple of sandwiches with our beers.

We waited until we'd each gulped half our mugs before discussing what went down at Krystal's place.

"So," he said, "she's totally not in charge."

"I told you." I shoved two fries in my mouth.

"You were right. No way Abe would install someone that easy to rile up at the head of the coven."

"The weird part is, I get the impression she sort of thinks she's in charge."

"I got that feeling too." He nodded. "She did have an interesting reaction when you mentioned the Fangshi."

My phone rang. "It's Mez." Into the phone I said, "What's up?"

"I got the results on Franklin's samples. Mr. Kostorov's blood has traces of the two ingredients of the red pills plus the yohimbe."

"You're sure it's the same?"

"The results are consistent."

"I'll be damned," I said. "Two cases just became one."

Beside me, Morales shot me an interested look as finished off his sandwich.

"You tell Franklin yet?" I asked Mez.

"Yep. He said 'shiiiiiit,'" he said, doing his best impersonation of the M.E.

"Sounds about right. Did you fill in Gardner?"

"She seemed pleased, for Gardner. Something along the lines of 'They better not fuck it up now.'"

"Talk about a vote of confidence." After that, I quickly hung up with him and filled Morales in on the situation. By the time I was done, he'd finished his beer and mine was growing warm.

"So, Valentine was peddling a bad potion that caused killer erections. He got the ingredients for some of that potion from the Chinese coven. My guess is the Chinese found out he was screwing up their potion and decided to take him out of the equation."

"Right. We really need to talk to that widow."

"But we can't talk to her unless she gets in touch with us. So, we're basically at another dead end."

I took a long swallow of room-temperature beer. "What do you think about setting up surveillance at the massage parlor?"

"I'll call Shadi. Gardner already okayed the manpower."

My phone rang again. I didn't recognize the number, but with so many balls in the air, I never knew who would call. "Prospero."

"Leave me alone," a raspy female voice yelled.

I hesitated. "Um, you called me. Who is this?"

"Mona Kostorov."

"Oh, hi, ma'am. Thank you for calling."

She made a disgusted sound.

"Anyway," I said slowly, "it's really important that we have a chance to talk to you. Is there any way we could set up a place to meet? We'd be happy to come to you."

"I said, leave me alone!" She hung up.

I looked at the phone for a few moments, as if it might offer some sort of clue about what just happened.

"Who was that?" Morales asked.

"The widow Kostorov."

"How'd it go?"

"She yelled and hung up on me."

"So, she goes in the hostile witness column, then?"

I tossed my phone on the table. "What a pain in the ass."

"Kate, her husband just died."

"*She* called me."

"Well, you have her number now. We can try again tomorrow. But maybe next time, I should do the talking."

* * *

When I arrived home that evening, I opened the door into a kitchen filled with smoke.

Through the haze, I located a backside sticking out of my oven. "Damn it all to Hera!" the voice echoed from inside.

"Baba?" I called. "Are you okay?"

"My pierogis are burned, but otherwise I'm hunky dory." She pulled her body out of the oven and held out a tray bearing a dozen blackened lumps. She tossed it on top of the stove with a muttered Polish curse. "Now what am I going to take?"

I set my bag on the table and went to open the window over the sink. "Take where?"

She tossed her long gray braid over her shoulder. That evening, she was wearing a purple tie-dyed T-shirt that read, DON'T BE A BASIC WITCH. Beneath that, she wore a pair of denim shorts that hung down to her knees, and a pair of Birkenstocks with purple socks that came up to mid-calf. "One of my friends' husbands died last night."

"Oh, no," I said. "What happened?"

"I haven't gotten the whole story, but it's probably the usual—

ticker gave out." She delivered this news in the same tone someone might use to share the time.

Living with a septuagenarian meant I got a whole new perspective on mortality. It seemed like every few weeks, one of Baba's friends passed away. If my friends were dying that frequently, I'd be a wreck. But Baba and the rest of her buddies took it all in stride. I asked her about it one time and she said, "Well, I don't understand how you see all that violence every day, but you manage."

"Anyway," she continued, "me and some of the other ladies are organizing a food delivery." She glanced at the remains of her efforts. "Luckily, I made some cookies earlier and I can take over one of my special medicinal teas." She held up a large mason jar filled with a liquid the color of swamp water. "I call this one Widow Juice."

I stifled a groan. Baba wasn't an Adept, but she was a witch. It's sort of the difference between a professional chef and a home cook. She made all sorts of home remedies, including therapeutic teas and bath oils, as one might expect. But she also had this weird hobby of making strange teas that she claimed cured everything from psoriasis to being unattractive to the opposite sex. With a name like *Widow Juice*, I was too scared to ask what it did.

"That's nice," I said diplomatically.

She shook her head. "Poor Mona," she said, half to herself. "Sergei died on their anniversary."

I froze. "Mona?"

She nodded.

"Your friend's last name wouldn't be Kostorov, would it?"

"How did you know?"

"Unbelievable," I muttered. "I had a chat with Mona earlier."

She held up a hand. "Back up—how do you know them?"

I sighed and threw the bills on the table. "I can't get into particulars, but we have reason to believe Mr. Kostorov's death is tied to one of our cases."

She gasped and put a hand to her chest. "He was murdered?"

"No, nothing like that." I had to tread carefully since I was pretty sure Mona wouldn't appreciate me starting a rumor about the manner of her husband's death. Baba was great, but she was a terrible gossip. "I tried to connect with Mona about meeting with us, but she seemed…reluctant," I said diplomatically.

"I'm sure she's a wreck right now."

"Of course," I said quickly. "It's just, we think Mr. Kostorov saw something that could help up put a pretty bad guy away."

She nodded as if she understood. "I'm sure if you tried again in a few days…"

"The problem is, we don't have a few days. The guy in question did murder someone and he's putting some bad potions on the street, so more could die. I don't suppose—" I cut myself off.

She looked up, her eyes hawkish. "Don't play your cop tricks on me, Kate Prospero. I might be old, but I'm still wily."

I laughed. "I know, I know. Look, I know it's an imposition, but if you could maybe just mention that you know me? That might grease the wheels a little next time I try to call."

She crossed her arms and huffed out a breath. "What's in it for me?"

"Free rent," I said, pointedly.

She snorted. "I already get that. What else?"

"What do you want?"

She pursed her lips and thought it over. "I want you to go easy on the boy for this school thing."

I sighed and held up my fingers in a mockery of a scout salute. "I promise I'll be fair, but I won't promise he'll go totally unpunished."

She nodded resolutely. "Throw in a bottle of that cheap whiskey I like and we've got a deal."

I laughed. Staying mad at Baba was impossible. "Fine."

"All right, I'll ask her tonight." She held up a hand when I started to celebrate. "But don't expect a miracle. The woman's grieving hard."

"Understood."

She tossed down the dish towel she'd been toying with. "Okay, I need to go put on my nice clothes before I meet up with the ladies. You going out with that hunk tonight or what?"

"The hunk is on a stakeout. I'm reading up on high schools."

"Oh."

I nodded.

"Kate, listen," she said, "if you ever want me to make myself scarce, you just have to say the word."

I frowned at her. "I'm not mad enough to kick you out, Baba."

She waved a hand. "No, I mean if you and Macho want some time alone. I don't want to be in the way."

"Don't be silly," I said. "You're not in the way."

"Oh, good. Because I really look forward to seeing him in his boxers in the morning."

I waggled a finger at her as I fought the laughter bubbling in my throat. "You're a dirty old woman."

She cackled. "Damned straight!"

* * *

Once Baba was gone, I settled myself at the kitchen table with the information from the high school and Danny's laptop. He was at a friend's house that night working on a project, so I had the place to myself for once.

About an hour into it, I had to admit that the Conservatory seemed like a pretty awesome place for Danny to go to high school. All of the coursework revolved around teaching the students how to cook using clean magic methods. They studied the normal subjects, too, but even those involved magic instruction somehow. Like, in History they might read the *Malleus Maleficarum* and discuss the way misogyny and fear of magic were used to control the masses.

In fact, the more I read about the curriculum, the more jealous I was that I didn't have access to that kind of school as a kid myself. Of course, if they'd had schools like that back then, Uncle Abe would have just encouraged me to use my classes in clean magic to learn how to make dirtier potions.

As I read, there were only two concerns. First, it was a brand-new school. Danny would start as a junior, which meant he'd only be there for two years, and he'd have to start thinking about college a year in. That meant if he went and hated the Conservatory or, worse, failed out, it would really set him back on getting into college.

The second concern involved John Volos. Danny had mentioned that our esteemed mayor was involved in the school, but he hadn't said that Volos Real Estate Development was a major contributor to the school. That meant his money would go to help fund Danny's education and that his word would hold a lot of sway in the decisions of the administration. If I decided to let Danny attend, I'd need to make it clear with Volos that any meddling in my brother's life would result in major consequences.

I threw the papers on the table and grabbed a beer from the fridge. As I popped the top, I couldn't believe I was having to think about my little brother going to college. In less than two years, he could potentially be moving out of my house and going off to a bright future on his own. The thought both depressed and excited me. It was depressing because it meant I was getting older and so was he. Time had passed so freaking fast, I couldn't believe it. It seemed just yesterday that he was so tiny that my hand dwarfed his. Now he was taller than me, and his hands made mine look petite.

The exciting part was that in two years, I could potentially recover the life that had been interrupted a decade earlier. The life where I was just Danny's sister and I had a life of my own. The possibilities sort of blew my mind. I'd be able to work late nights without guilt chasing me around. Plus, even though Baba would still be around, I'd have more opportunities to have the house to myself.

I shook my head and took a very long pull of my beer. The future suddenly loomed like a big question mark on the horizon, and it would come whether I wanted it to or not. I shut the fridge and went to the laptop.

I pulled up the principal's email address and sent her a quick note requesting a meeting. I didn't mention the situation, just that I had some questions that would help me make a final decision.

That done, I went and grabbed my backpack. Before I'd left for the day, I stuck some old case files in there to review.

The top file contained all the information I could find about Krystal LeMay in the Arcane Crimes Database, a clearing house of information from all the Arcane crimes in the country. She didn't have much of a rap sheet. Just an adolescent misdemeanor charge for graffiti. However, she had come up on ACD in connection with a couple of Votary Coven nasties. She'd also filed a battery charge on a live-in boyfriend. According to the file, he'd been arrested a few years before that for distributing arcane substances. The name seemed vaguely familiar, so I assumed he was Votary. Another said she was in the car when another boyfriend was arrested for DUI and possession of a deadly weapon. She also showed up in all the files connected to the arrest of Puck Simmons.

As I reread the notes on that case, which Morales had typed into the database a few weeks earlier, a plan started forming in my mind. Even though Krystal claimed she didn't corroborate his alibi because she didn't want a criminal living with her, she clearly had a history of cavorting with lowlifes. Morales and I had been working with the theory that she'd turned on him because with him out of the way, there was a power vacuum for her to fill in the coven. But she obviously wasn't going to confirm that theory. Nor would she confirm the idea that the reason so much shit was happening in the coven was that she was a terrible leader.

I tapped the table with my fingers as I thought through all the angles. Once I felt confident in my plan, I picked up the phone and called Morales.

"How's the high school drama going?" he asked.

"Turns out they were probably right, but I'm going to let them all sweat it out a little longer."

"Remind me never to cross you, Cupcake."

I smiled at the rasp in his voice. I imagined him sitting in the dark and easing back in his seat to talk to me. I didn't love surveillance gigs, but part of me longed to go join him there just for the company.

"So, I've been thinking about Puck Simmons."

"That's…disappointing."

"Why?"

"I thought you were calling to flirt with me."

"I have never flirted with you."

"Uh-huh," he said. "So, what's this about Puck?"

"I think we need to go visit him at County."

The silence that greeted my great plan was not the reaction I'd been hoping to receive.

"Think about it," I continued, undaunted. "He's in County because Krystal screwed him over. Can you think of a better source of intel on her or the temperature of the coven right now?"

He let out a long breath. "Gonna be a tough sell to Grey."

"I'm hoping we won't need to involve him."

"How you figure?"

Assistant U.S. Attorney Aiden Grey was the prosecutor assigned to the task force. In order for him to offer a deal to Puck, we'd have to convince him that we could get enough juicy intel for our efforts to make it worth his time. But a deal would involve a lot of time and paperwork I didn't have the patience for at the moment.

"I'm hoping Puck will talk to us if we use the Krystal angle. Revenge is a potent motivator. It'll be a tough sell but it's worth a try. I think."

"Well, you did break his finger and we helped frame him for two murders."

"The finger thing is true, but he doesn't know about the framing."

Truth was, Puck wasn't innocent of all his charges. He had actually helped kill Charm Parsons. The problem was he didn't have anything to do with the murder of Pantera Souza, his accomplice in that crime. Pantera had been murdered by Mayor Volos. We just hadn't taken Volos down for that crime. Yet.

"I like the plan, though," Morales said. "Puck was in the line of succession for the coven, so he'd know what was in play before he went down for Charm's murder. Maybe he can tell us if there were plans to partner with the Chinese—or anyone else."

"Right."

"You have smart ideas when you take the night off."

"That wasn't my only smart idea."

"Oh, yeah?"

"How about you come over after you're done?" Earlier, he'd told me that Gardner had approved putting Shadi's team onto the surveillance rotation. McGinty was supposed to relieve him in an hour.

"Forget *smart*—you're a freaking genius."

"Damned straight."

"See you soon."

CHAPTER EIGHT

There's no easy way to storm into the mayor's office. Back when John was just a tycoon, it had been way easier. But now there was all sorts of security and layers of secretaries to get through. So, like anyone else, I had to make an appointment.

When I first called that morning, his assistant told me I'd have to wait a week to get into see Mr. Mayor. However, fifteen minutes later, she called back and said he had an opening at ten a.m. She tried to play it like his schedule had opened up miraculously, but I knew better. As much as I hated to admit it, I kind of enjoyed being a person Volos cleared the decks for at a moment's notice. Not that I'd ever tell him that.

I told Morales I'd meet him at the county jail for our noon meeting with Puck. He didn't try to talk me out of it, but I could feel the tension radiating off of him. To his credit, he advised me to take advantage of the meeting to do some digging while I was there to see if Volos was aware of the Fangshi's infiltration of the city. "Just do it before you read him the riot act, okay?" he'd said.

City Hall had been built in 1916 when Babylon was a jewel in the world's steel crown. It was a stately building with lots of columns and steps. But time hadn't been kind to the structure. Acid rain had left the stone face pockmarked and streaked with black. Regiments of pigeons strutted across the stairs, completely unfazed by any humans who dared tread on their turf.

The building was in the Mundane section of downtown, but that didn't keep the hexheads away. At the top of the steps, a man wearing a lady's turban and muumuu lazily attempted to feed the pigeons imaginary food. Every few seconds, a pigeon would come up to him, realize he didn't actually have any food, and peck his hand before stomping away. He cackled each time. He had no teeth to speak of and his skin was the color of key lime pie.

As I approached him, he pulled his attention from the pigeons. "Oh," he said. "It's you. Hey!"

"Hey," I snapped.

"She's coming," he said conversationally.

"That's nice," I tossed over my shoulder as I passed.

"And when He opened the third seal, I heard the third living creature saying, 'Come.' And I saw, and behold, a black horse, and he who sits on it had a balance in his hand."

I paused and turned. "What?"

He looked up at me. I'd expected his expression to reveal his obvious madness, but the brown eyes were clear and sane. "Revelation, sweetheart. You ain't read your bible?"

I frowned at him. "Why are you quoting scripture to me?"

He shrugged. "Peewee told me to." He nodded down to the white pigeon at his feet.

"The pigeon told you to quote the Book of Revelation to me?"

He nodded so vigorously that his turban went askew. "The end is nigh. Best start preparing."

"You need to lay off the potions, buddy."

He held up a hand for me to wait. Then he leaned down, offering his ear to the bird. The pigeon warbled something that had him nodding sagely. "Yes, that's right," he said to the bird. He looked up again. "Peewee says you need to make peace with the man in the tower and the man in the dungeon." He pointed out toward Lake Erie. "Or all will be lost."

I took a handful of change from my pocket and tossed it into the bucket at the guy's feet. "Thanks for the advice." Then I walked away.

Behind me, he called cheerfully, "Peewee says you're welcome!"

By the time I made it inside, I was in a much lighter mood. I might have some problems, but I didn't have man-wearing-a-muumuu-and-talking-to-pigeons problems, so I figured I was doing pretty okay.

A few moments later, I arrived at the top floor of the building where the office of the mayor was located. The waiting room was done in wood paneling and leather with touches of hunter green. It was quite a change from the offices Volos had had at his real estate company, which were decorated in a style I called "corporate samurai." But now he was all legit and favored a more Mundane traditionalist style. Volos was nothing if not adaptable, especially if doing so increased his power base.

The middle-aged woman behind the desk had the hard look of someone who'd been wading through a bureaucratic cesspool for most of her professional life. When I walked up to the desk, she didn't offer a greeting or a smile.

"Kate Prospero," I said.

Something about my name deepened her frown lines into troughs. "Oh. You." She turned and punched a code into the phone on her desk. A button lit up in response. "You can go in."

There was no rising to see me to the door or parting smile. I'm not sure what I'd done to offend the lady, but I wasn't about to let her ruin my mood. Once I got in that office, it would go downhill pretty fast on its own.

I walked to the door and opened it without knocking. "You son of a bitch," I said, marching inside.

Mayor Volos looked up from his desk.

As did the man sitting across from him—Captain Eldritch, my boss.

In the wake of my declaration, the office was dead silent. I stood frozen with my hand on the doorknob, looking between the two men who held my career in their hands.

Volos recovered first, rising smoothly from behind his massive desk. "Kate, it's good of you to come," he said, as if he'd invited me instead of me having requested the meeting, "Captain Eldritch and I were just talking about you."

Mention of his name seemed to snap Eldritch out of stasis. He leapt out of his seat, blustering. "Apologize to the mayor immediately, Prospero."

"I—"

Volos waved a hand. "It's not necessary." To Eldritch he said, "Since we go way back and I'm sure she meant it as a term of endearment. Right, Katie?"

My shock and embarrassment dissolved. "No, I meant it as an insult."

"Kate!" The captain gasped.

The mayor laughed out loud. "It's fine," he said. "Old friends, remember?" he said to Eldritch.

The captain looked from Volos to me, squinting as if he was weighing the most politically advantageous reaction.

On one hand, I resented the hell out of the familiarity, but on the other, he was also offering me protection from my own boss. Word on the street for a while was that Chief Adams might be promoted to commissioner by Volos. If that happened, Eldritch was in line for chief. But in order to snag those extra brass bars, he needed to stay in Volos's good graces. I cared less about Volos's approval, but I also didn't want to create any bad blood at the BPD, since my tenure on the MEA task force wasn't necessarily permanent.

"Sorry, sir. He's right. It's an old joke between us."

Eldritch chuckled like he was in on the joke. "Of course. I knew that."

Volos flashed me an amused look that he quickly covered with his politician's smile. "I understand that you're pitching in to help the BPD with a homicide case, Kate."

I hesitated. "Uh, yeah. We're happy to help Detective Duffy."

He nodded approvingly. "Excellent. I know Captain Eldritch is relieved to have such capable representation on the MEA task force."

"Absolutely," Eldritch said quickly. "Detective Prospero is one of our best."

"Excellent. Have a nice day, Captain."

The dismissal was sudden but absolute. Eldritch was left with no choice but to pick his hat up off the chair and make his goodbyes. After he shook the mayor's hand, he came to me. His handclasp was punishing and there was a glint in his eye that promised retribution down the road. I wasn't really sure what I'd specifically done this time to piss him off, but I was pretty used to being on Eldritch's shit list. "Good to see you, sir."

"Check in at the station house soon. I'd love a chance to discuss your progress with the task force."

"Sure."

With his thinly veiled threat delivered, he strolled out of the office.

Once the door closed behind him, Volos relaxed his politician's stiffness and smiled at me like a conspirator. "Jesus, he's an insufferable ass."

"Yeah, well, that ass is my boss, so I'd appreciate it if you didn't put me in weird situations like that."

"You're the one who walked in here hurling insults."

I crossed my arms. "Well-deserved insults."

He crossed his arms, too, and the move pulled back the cuffs of his expensive suit to show a flash of gold. The watch probably cost more than my rent and the Blue Book value of Sybil combined. "What did I do this time?"

The amusement in his tone made my molars itch. He'd lied, cheated, and murdered a man in front of me, but seemed to think my objections to him were nothing more than trifles.

"Danny got into the Conservatory," I said.

"That's great." He appeared genuinely happy. "He'll do well there."

"If he goes," I said. "I haven't decided."

"Don't be ridiculous. Why wouldn't you allow it?"

"You know why."

He sighed. "That's your pride talking. Think about the future this sets up for that kid."

I flashed him pointed look. "Trust me, I've glimpsed that kind of future and, frankly, I'm not real impressed."

He laughed, but there was a bitter note to the sound. "You'd prefer him to continue in that Mundane school training to be a middle manager at a widget company?"

"If it kept him safe, yes."

"Safe from what?"

"People like you."

The temperature in the office seemed to drop ten degrees. "That's a low blow, Kate. I care about that boy."

"Not as much as I do, John."

He nodded to concede that point. "Love can lead to irrational decisions. Overprotection. The need to control."

"I'm not here to debate the merits of the school. I promised Danny I'd consider it, but you're the last person I'd come to for advice on this matter."

He lowered his arms and leaned against his desk. "So, why are you here?"

"To threaten you."

A shocked laugh escaped his lips. "Oh? This should be good."

"You're the mayor, so I can't escape dealing with you professionally on occasion. But if you ever tamper with my private life again, mayor or no, I will come after you so hard, your head's going to spin."

He smirked. So cool and confident. The tiger playing with its food. "What are you going to do, Katie? Call me bad names?"

"You have a bad habit of underestimating me. It's been that way since we were kids. You always thought you had me under your thumb, but I turned the tables on you, didn't I?"

My reminder of how I'd walked away a decade earlier sat between us like a tossed gauntlet.

"I'm older now. Stronger. And if you think you're the only one with dirt on your enemies, you're not only naive but incredibly stupid."

I'd expected him to become angry, but a look bordering on lust crossed his face. "What damage you got on me?" He'd dropped the polished diction of the mayor and had reverted to the street slang we used to use as kids.

I lifted my chin. "Try me and see."

Very slowly, so I was sure to see it, the tip of his tongue wet his bottom lip. "You're wrong, you know."

"About what?" I tried to focus on his eyes and not the wet glint on that lip.

"I don't underestimate you. If anything, I've been waiting for you to stop underestimating yourself."

I laughed. "You patronizing ass."

"Maybe, but I'm not wrong. When I saw you again for the first time when you got on the MEA team, you looked like you wanted to run and hide from me. But now?" He tilted his head as if looking at me from a different angle would reveal the answers he was looking for. "Something's different. You're more…something."

"Maybe it was there all along," I said. "And you never wanted to see it."

He shook his head. "No, it's new. Something's changed."

I crossed my arms and smiled at him. Letting him wonder.

Finally, he spoke, his expression neutral, "So, the rumors are true."

"What rumors?"

"You and your partner..." He trailed off, as if saying the rest was beneath him. "I can't say I'm surprised, though it is disappointing."

"Believe it or not, your opinion has no bearing on who I take to my bed."

His jaw tightened. "You're going to hurt him, Kate."

I frowned, thrown off guard by the switch in direction. What was he playing at? I didn't have to wait long to hear his reasoning.

"He's going to try to domesticate you because he doesn't know better."

"I'm not a fucking housecat."

"No, sweetheart, you're a Prospero. Any man you're with has to understand that going in."

This man was the last person I wanted to discuss this topic with, so I changed the subject.

"Did you know the Fangshi are moving in on Aphrodite's territory?"

He blinked, and I allowed myself a brief moment to enjoy catching him off guard for a change.

"Why do you assume I keep up with what's happening in the covens?"

I shrugged. "Old habits die hard."

"As it happens, I'm aware of legitimate Chinese-American businesses coming into the city. In fact, I have a meeting with a representative in about ten minutes." He glanced at his watch. "But I'm unaware of the Fangshi making any moves in town."

I watched him for a moment but couldn't detect a lie on him. That didn't mean much. John Volos lied as easily as most people breathed.

"Is that the direction this Valentine case is taking you?" he asked.

I tilted my head. "I thought you didn't lower yourself to keep up with coven business."

His mouth twitched. "I bother myself with issues concerning the safety of this city. A potion lab exploding near downtown is a pretty big deal to my constituents."

I tipped my chin, accepting that explanation for now. "We don't have much hard evidence to go on yet, but we have reason to believe the Chinese are in town and may have been doing business with Basil."

"Interesting," he said in a noncommittal tone.

I glanced at the clock. "I need to head out." I paused until I was sure I had his full attention. "Do not contact Danny. If you need to speak to him, you go through me."

He looked distracted, as if his wheels were still turning. "I'm willing to give you some space, if that's what you'd prefer, but sooner or later, you're going to have to come to terms with the fact that we're connected in ways that can never be severed."

"Jesus, do you ever listen to yourself? You sound like a stalker."

His eyes narrowed. "I won't be mocked, Katherine."

I leaned forward until I was in his face. He smelled like money and ozone. "And I won't be managed, John."

"Trust me," he said in a sardonic tone. "I know."

He showed me to the door and opened it for me. As I brushed past him, he said, "See you soon."

I turned to tell him I hoped not, but a man in the waiting room caught my eye. Middle-aged and handsome, he exuded the confidence of a man used to being in charge. Volos had mentioned a meeting with a representative from a Chinese-American business, but this man had CEO written all over him.

Volos stepped around me and approached the man, offering his hand. Relieved to be forgotten, I slid toward the exit. But before I made it out the door, I heard Volos say, "Sorry to keep you waiting, Mr. Hung."

It was the first time I'd ever heard John Volos defer to anyone. It was surprising enough that when I got into the hall, I wrote the man's name down with the intention of researching him and his business when I got a chance.

* * *

On my way out of City Hall, I passed the pigeon man again. This time, he called out, "Beware the five."

I stopped. "The five what?"

He shrugged. "Peewee tells me what to say. Not what it means."

I crossed my arms and looked down at him. "You could ask him."

The man threw back his head and laughed. "Oh, there's no talking to Peewee."

He shot the pigeon at his feet the same look a mom might give to her naughty but beloved child.

"What's your name?"

He started, as if no one had ever asked him before. Given his profession was acting as a medium for a psychic pigeon, I couldn't say I was surprised. "Sweet Ray. What's yours?"

"I'm Kate." I held out my left hand to shake his.

He hesitated a moment before offering his right hand. "Pleased to meet you, Detective Kate."

I shook his green fingers. "How'd you know I'm a cop?"

He withdrew his hand and pointed at my waist. I looked down and saw the badge on my waistband was peeking out of my jacket.

"Ah," I said, "I thought maybe Peewee told you that, too."

"Don't be ridiculous."

Sweet Ray was as mad as a loon, but I found him charming. "What potion you use?"

He held up his hands. "I ain't looking for no beef with you, cop lady."

"I bust the dealers and suppliers, not the users."

"Regardless, Peewee isn't comfortable sharing that kind of information."

I looked to the pigeon, who was busy pecking at the concrete. "I didn't ask Peewee—I asked you."

Sweet Ray crossed his arms. "I ain't comfortable either."

"Naturally. Listen, you here every day?"

"Every damned day. Peewee doesn't like to move anyplace new."

"You ever see the mayor coming and going?"

He nodded. "Peewee doesn't like him."

I was beginning to like Peewee. "Why not?"

"Says the mayor man keeps some shady company."

"Listen, I have a favor to ask Peewee. Do you think you could ask him for me?"

Sweet Ray huffed. "Hello? He don't like it when you talk about him like he can't hear you."

"Of course." I looked at the fidgety pigeon and said, "Sorry, Peewee. Would you mind keeping an eye on the mayor for me? Like maybe if I came by in a few days, you can tell me who all has been by to see him."

Sweet Ray leaned down near the pigeon, who shied away from him. I noticed then that Sweet Ray wore flip-flops, and that his feet were swollen and covered in lesions. I was no doctor, but they looked a lot like the sort of sores diabetics got on their feet. Which might explain why he was called Sweet Ray.

"Peewee says we'll do it for one million dollars a week."

I raised a brow. "How about twenty bucks?"

He leaned down to the bird again. A moment later, he nodded. The turban made it all feel very formal. "All right, we'll accept those terms."

"Good," I said. "Just write down anyone who seems out of the ordinary." I handed him my card. "If anything especially weird happens, call me. Otherwise, I'll come by to check in with you."

He looked at the card for a moment before offering it for Peewee's inspection. The bird pecked at the card halfheartedly before wobbling off in the other direction. "It's a deal, Detective Kate."

I reached in to my pocket and removed a twenty. "Here's a down payment."

Sweet Ray snatched it out of my hand and had it stashed inside his turban before I could blink. "Much obliged."

"Tell me again what you're looking for?"

He looked put out, like he expected that after our brief acquaintance, I should already trust him. "Write down any unusual visitors. Call if something weird happens."

"Something weird concerning Mayor Volos directly," I corrected. The last thing I needed was for a man who had talked to flying rats calling me about every little thing he might deem odd. "All right, I'll be talking to you soon."

"Bye," he said, looking away as if he'd already dismissed me from his mind.

I was five steps down when he called out, "Wait! You forgot to say goodbye to Peewee!"

A woman in a business suit was walking up the steps and heard what he'd said. She shot me an odd look. I ignored her. "Bye, Peewee," I called.

I jogged down the rest of the steps to the parking spot where I'd left my Jeep. I didn't have a lot of faith that my new off-the-books CI and his feathered friend would actually net me much intel, but the worst I had to lose was twenty bucks. However, if Sweet Ray was actually saner than he let on, which I had a feeling he was, he could potentially see something that might be useful down the road when Volos finally went too far.

I left City Hall, feeling like I'd gotten a couple of new ticks in the win column that day. That feeling lasted only as long as it took me to reach County.

CHAPTER NINE

County Jail sat in the Mundane side of downtown, back across the Bessemer Bridge from the Cauldron. Most of our cases required us to go to Crowley Penitentiary for Arcane Criminals on an island in the middle of Lake Erie. But in this case, the felon we came to see had been brought up on a Mundane homicide rap, so he was at County awaiting trial.

Puck had been arrested a few weeks earlier for murdering Pantera Souza, a henchman for the Brazilian coven. Souza's associate had also died that night in a fight with the MEA team that no one else knew about, so Puck had gotten pinned for that one, too. In addition, he was also charged with being an accessory to murder in the death of Alexander Parsons aka Charm, whose body had been found decapitated in an abandoned church.

Problem was, the evidence the BPD had on Puck was mostly circumstantial because the murder weapon was sitting under the floorboards in a closet at my house. Obviously, the reasons Puck had been charged were complicated and highly illegal, which was one of the reasons I hadn't been in favor of Assistant U.S. Attorney Grey joining us.

The meeting rooms at County were smaller than the average

broom closet. The guard turned out to be a friend of Dixon's, so we used the connection to convince him to let us meet with Puck in the area where inmates met with family during visitation hours every Saturday. Since it was Wednesday, the room was cleared. There were about twenty tables and Puck sat alone at one in the very center.

Before we went inside, we watched Puck through the windows. "Been a few hard weeks for our boy," Morales said in a grave tone.

When we'd last seen Puck, he was full of piss and vinegar. He'd had a mohawk that stood straight up from his scalp like some sort of metaphor for his erection. Now it lay limp and to the side, like he'd been swimming in cold water. Yellowing bruises decorated the right side of his face, and the left held some newer, purple souvenirs. He looked up and saw us standing at the windows watching him and smiled. The move made the split in his lip start bleeding down his chin.

I held up my middle finger. I felt bad he'd been framed, but that didn't mean I liked him.

"Kate, we want him in a good mood."

I lowered my hand but didn't apologize. "If we're too nice, he'll shut down even more."

Morales said something under his breath that sounded a lot like "I hate it when you're right." Then he pushed open the door. "Let's get this over with."

As we approached, Puck crossed his arms. "I ain't got nothing to say to you."

"Play nice and we'll put a good word in for you with Grey," Morales said.

"I don't need you doing me any favors. I'm innocent."

I snorted. "Sure, you are."

"Bitch, you know I didn't cap Panther."

"Yeah, yeah," I said. "We're not here about that."

He pursed his lips and looked at me, daring me with his eyes to beg him to talk. I met his stare and held it. Morales stood quietly, waiting for the test of wills to play out.

After about a full minute, Puck finally looked away. "You're a real bitch, you know that? Damn!"

"You listen to me," I began in my lowest, meanest tone, "my partner might want to help you with Grey, but I got different priorities. If I get to him first, he's gonna send you to maximum security in whatever cell block is the heart of *A Morte* territory. Whoever put those marks on your face? They're nothing compared to the Brazilians."

Some of the wind leaked out of his sails. "Why you gotta play me, Prospero?"

"Why you gotta waste my time posturing? I were you, I'd drop the act and get down to answering my questions before you find yourself the recipient of *O olho de Deus*, my friend."

O olho de Deus meant "eye of God." It was one of the Brazilian coven's calling cards to stab their enemies in the eye socket with a knife called a *facón*. Puck had clearly heard about it, because he didn't ask me to explain. He just swallowed hard and slid a little further into his seat.

"I didn't kill him," he repeated lamely.

"We know."

His head jerked up. "You know who did?"

I shrugged.

"Oh, I see. You know, Prospero, I thought you left the game behind a long time ago. Turns out the cop game's just as dirty, right?"

"Spare us the street morality routine," Morales said. "We're here because your ex-girlfriend is tied up in the case we're working. We want you to tell us everything you know about it."

"Krystal." He said the name with about as much warmth as one might say *Nazis*.

Morales shook his head. "Must have been tough. Your own girl." He clucked his tongue. "Had to sting, man."

Puck perked up and his cheeks got some color. "She's a suspect?"

"Her new boyfriend got murdered."

"Her new boyfriend?" His voice rose. "Who?"

"Basil Valentine."

His eyes widened and his hand clenched into a fist. "That pussy-ass pimp? Goddamn!"

"It's only been what, Prospero?" Morales said.

"Six weeks," I said in a dismayed tone. "That's awfully quick to find herself a new man."

Puck drew in a deep breath, like he was trying to get his temper under control.

"You know what I heard?" Morales said to him. "Krystal sold you out because she wanted to take over the Votaries. Did you know she had ambitions to take over the coven?"

Puck sucked on his teeth. "She said she wanted to open a nail salon. Was taking business classes."

"Oh, she opened a business, all right." I smiled. "A massage parlor that specializes in happy endings."

"That scheming bitch," he growled. "Watch and see—she'll be dead before the month is out."

"Why?"

"She ain't street. Not as smart as she thinks, either. They'll eat her alive."

"Who will?" Morales said. "The Chinese?"

Puck rubbed his bottom lip, smearing the blood from his wound. He looked down at the smear of red on his left hand and huffed out a humorless laugh. He lifted it up to show us. "I got this tattoo the day I turned sixteen."

He nodded at the snake-eating-its-own-tail tattoo on his left wrist. I had a similar one on my left wrist. It marked us as made members of the Votary coven. I remembered the day I got mine, too. How proud I'd been.

"The thing they told us over and over was never to snitch on your family. Right?" He looked right at me as he said it. I nodded because there was no use pretending I didn't get that same lecture. "Where's the family now? Who's got my back? Fuck 'em. I'll tell you what I know."

I was surprised to feel a twinge in my gut. Maybe it was just that I knew what snitching cost a company man. You don't rat out your coven—or anyone, for that matter. It's the first and last commandment of the streets. But since I'd been a cop, I'd seen the screws get turned on enough street toughs to know that it took a pair of steel balls to sacrifice your own life for the good of the coven. However, I also knew that the first people to snitch to save their own asses when they got nabbed were the bosses themselves, the very ones who'd beaten the "no snitch" law into their troops.

"The Chinese," Morales prompted softly.

"Right. So, before the shit went down with the Brazilians, there was some new marching orders came down from the top."

"From Abe?" Morales asked.

"Yeah. Through Charm."

"How did Abe communicate with Charm?" I asked.

"Couple of ways," he said. "Abe's got a private phone in his cell at Crowley so he can call whenever he wanted. But he knew that was monitored, so he also has a guard on payroll who acts as a mule."

The fact Abe had his own phone or a guard under his thumb wasn't exactly a surprise. If power brokers like Abe were denied anything, the warden might find his favorite son floating in the family pool when he got home.

"So, what were the orders?" I asked.

"We were supposed to start moving a new package on our corners. Something we ain't seen before."

"What kind of potion?"

"Charm didn't say. Just that it was some new formula and we were supposed to hand out samples to get the hexheads hooked."

"It was a Votary potion?" Morales asked.

"Nah. It was from outside the state. The vials I saw had some weird markings I ain't seen before."

"Could you recognize it if you saw it again?" I asked. "Or draw it?"

"I think so."

I slid a piece of paper and a pen across the table. After a moment, he handed over the rough drawing.

Morales studied it for a moment before handing it to me for a look. It was the same symbol that had been on the vials from Basil's house—the Chinese symbol for cinnabar.

"Why would Abe make a deal with the Chinese?"

Puck shook his head. "Don't know. Charm wasn't so open to answering questions, you feel me? But knowing Abe, he wouldn't do it unless there was some big win in it for him."

"When did all of this happen in relation to you helping Pantera Souza kill Charm?" Morales asked.

Puck paused, staring hard at Morales.

"You already pled guilty to that crime," Morales pointed out.

"A couple of weeks before. See, Charm said we had to keep the new package on the down low."

"From who?" I asked.

He leaned back, his demeanor changed from that of a man offering confession to one about to launch a grenade.

"Aphrodite. Charm said if the Hierophant found out, it could cause problems."

Instead of pursuing that path like he wanted me to, I detoured back. "Why did you kill Charm?"

He sneered. "Because I saw where it was all headed. It was only a matter of time until Aphrodite found out what we were doing. Figured I'd get poisoned or we'd find ourselves in the middle of a turf war."

"So, you figured you off Charm and take over the coven?"

"Something like."

"Guess that didn't work out so well, did it?"

"We ain't at war, are we?"

I tilted my head. "Why all the love for Aphrodite?"

"I don't give a shit about the hermaphrodite. I just don't want to see the Votaries get destroyed because Abe's gone crazy in the clink, you know?"

"What makes you think he's crazy?" I asked.

He looked down at his prison-issued canvas shoes. "The Chinese aren't the only alliance he's made."

"Well?" Morales prompted.

"Look, you want to know about the Chinese, I told you. But there's some shit I won't talk about."

"Why?" Morales asked.

He laughed. "There's people running trade in this town that I don't want gunning for me, is all. Getting stabbed in the eye by the Brazilians or poisoned by Aphrodite would be a relief compared to what they'd do to me."

"Who the hell is left?" I counted people off on my fingers. "Abe's in prison, Harry Bane's mean but dumb—every other major player is dead or in jail."

Puck looked at me with an expression bordering on pity. "Ain't my job to cure your blindness."

I let that bait float by, since he obviously had no intention of doing more than taunting us. Better to focus on the case at hand. "If Krystal is the leader of the Votaries now, do you know why she'd choose to carry out the original plan to work with the Chinese?"

He shrugged. "She probably thinks carrying out Abe's marching orders will protect her."

"Do you know who Charm's connect was in the Fangshi?" Morales asked.

"Never met anyone specific, but I saw him talking to this Chinese-looking dude one time."

"Can you describe him?"

"Didn't see him too good. He was driving a black Mercedes."

"When was that?"

"The day before we killed him." There was no emotion in his tone. Simply stating a basic fact. Murder was a means to an end. Not anything worth being emotional about.

"You ever see that man again?" I asked.

"Nah. After Charm died, things got a little crazy, you feel me?"

Considering Morales and I had been in charge of investigating that crime, we were pretty familiar with exactly how crazy it had gotten.

"You got anything else for us?"

He held up his hands, as if to signal he was empty. "I been locked up in here with these Mundane motherfuckers for weeks. It's not exactly a hotbed of Cauldron gossip."

"All right," I said, standing. "If you think of anything else, call us."

He crossed his arms. "If I think of anything else, I'm calling Grey. You want my help going forward, I'm gonna want a deal."

"We don't control that shit," I said. "If you want Grey to help you, you got to deliver the goods on a big fish."

"One of these days, you're gonna need what I know and you'll come running with a real sweetheart of a deal." He flashed a smug expression. "I can't wait."

"Judging by the look of you, you're going to be lucky to survive here long enough for your hearing, asshole. So, I suggest that if you have something big, you call Grey before they fit you with your toe tag."

* * *

As we walked out of the jail, my cell rang. It was Baba.

"I talked to Mona," she said. "I had to give her my spot at the bingo table and promise her a gallon of Widow Juice, but she finally agreed."

"Your bingo spot?"

"It was a prime spot, Kate. Right next to Ernie Lipshitz."

"Who's that?" My phone chimed to indicate another call coming in. I ignored it for the moment.

She made a pitying noise. "Only the hottest widower at the senior center."

"Her husband just died. Isn't that sort of fast?"

"At our age, you got to lock it down quick."

I shuddered, not really wanting to know what exactly was getting locked down. "Okay," I said, "when does she want to meet?"

"Tomorrow around eleven."

I pumped a fist in the air. "That's amazing, Baba. I owe you one."

"Don't mention it, kiddo. Just remember your promise."

The reminder that I told her I'd go easy on Danny reminded me that he and I had barely spoken since our argument in the kitchen. I made a mental note to make an effort with him once I had a minute to breathe on the case. "Roger that."

I hung up with her and filled Morales in on the plan. By that time, we had reached the car and busied ourselves climbing in and buckling up. He was pulling the SUV out of the jail's lot when he finally brought up the meeting with Puck.

"Was that a waste of time?" he asked.

I thought about it for minute. "I don't think so. I mean, he didn't exactly tell us anything we didn't already suspect, but I did find the news that the Chinese deal came down from Abe interesting."

"You think he was telling the truth?"

"Seems like," I said. "I just wish we knew what angle Abe was playing. He never partnered with outside covens in the past. Why start now?"

"You think we need to pay him a visit?"

"Not until we know more. If we go in with half-cocked ideas, he'll eat our lunch."

"So, what now?" he said.

"Tonight, I'm running surveillance on Krystal's house of hand jobs. How about you?"

"I'm going to get in touch with some of my contacts in L.A. See if someone's heard anything about the Fangshi partnering with the Votaries."

My phone dinged to let me know I had a new voicemail. I'd forgotten about the call that came in while I was talking to Baba. "Hold on. I need to see what this is." I clicked the button and lifted the phone to my ear.

"Detective Prospero, this is Dr. Lynn Hidalgo, principal of the Conservatory for the Arcane Arts. I received your email and wanted to reach out to see if you'd like to meet to discuss the prospect of Danny joining us this fall. I'd really love to answer any of your questions and give you a chance to see the school itself. Please let me know when it would be convenient for you to come by for a chat."

I hung up and cursed.

"What's wrong?" Morales asked.

"That was the principal at that school."

"And?"

"I think Volos called her."

"Why?"

"Well, I emailed her last night, but I didn't give her my phone number. And this morning, I talked to John about Danny and the school. I think he put a bug in her ear and gave her my cell number."

"I guess that means your meeting with him didn't go well."

"I thought it went fine. I told him not to contact Danny except through me. He urged me to let Danny go to the school. I told him he didn't get a say."

"Obviously, he's trying to keep you in his sphere of influence." He shot me a side-eye. "Face it, Kate, the guy's got a long game planned where you're concerned."

I looked out the side window. This was not a conversation I wanted to have again. It's not that I believed Morales was wrong, but believing Volos did what he did out of some emotional place made it harder for me to keep my own emotions in the safe red zone. Anger was way easier to live with than any of the more complex feelings that sometimes raised their ugly heads when it came to my ex.

"Whatever," I said finally, "he's exceptionally good at backing me into corners."

"So, tell Danny he can't go to the school and have that be that."

I shook my head. "It's not that easy."

"Isn't it?"

"No, it's not. I can't ignore Danny's wishes just because I have personal shit with Volos. It's not fair to the kid."

"What about what's fair to you? You ask me, you let him guilt you into whatever he wants too much. Maybe try saying no for a change."

It was the first time since we started seeing each other that Morales had tried to express his opinion about my parenting. Unfortunately, he said the perfectly wrong thing.

"When I need your parenting advice, I'll ask for it, okay?"

"Whoa," he said, "chill. I'm just saying don't let your guilt—"

I slashed a hand through the air. "Drop it."

A chilly silence settled inside the car. Morales punched the accelerator to beat a yellow light. I crossed my arms and settled in for an indignant pout.

Only, once we made it through the intersection, he let out a long breath. "I'm sorry."

I looked up hesitantly, not trusting the olive branch he appeared to be offering. "All right," I said slowly.

"We've been pretty good at keeping work and personal separate, but sometimes it's gonna rear up. Volos has been tangled up in our work since the beginning, and now he's weaseling himself into your personal life more and more. On a professional level, it's concerning because I don't trust him for a lot of good reasons. On a personal one?" He paused and shook his head. "I'm not proud to say this, but I'm jealous as hell of the guy."

My mouth fell open. "What?"

"He was your first love. That's potent stuff. Not to mention he's now a powerful millionaire and political mogul."

"You forgot to mention that he's an asshole."

Morales pulled the car over to the side of the road and put the car in PARK. He turned to me. "That's the thing, Kate. Distrust, I'd believe. Anger, for sure. But you hate him."

"Right," I said slowly. "What's your point?"

"Hate is a passionate emotion. We don't hate something unless it gets under our skin. Unless we actually care a whole hell of a lot."

I blinked at him, letting the implications sink in. I opened my mouth to respond, but I was so dumbfounded that the words dried up on my tongue.

"I'm not saying you're secretly in love with him or whatever. Jesus, I hope not," he said almost to himself. "But there are unresolved issues there. I have to wonder if there's a part of you that enjoys the cat-and-mouse game you two have going on."

I threw up my hands. "That's the most ridiculous thing I've ever heard."

He arched a brow.

"Seriously, Drew. You're mental."

"Regardless, you can't blame me for being a little jealous, can you?"

"Yes, actually, I can." I crossed my arms and refused to look at him.

"All right," he said, "then answer me this. Did you tell him about us?"

"He already knew," I said.

That stopped him. "Really? What did he say?"

You're going to hurt him, Kate.

I huffed out a breath. "Nothing worth repeating." Time to change the subject. "I forgot to tell you that I asked him about the Chinese."

"And?"

"He had a meeting with some high-powered Chinese guy right after I left. I saw him but didn't recognize him."

"Did Volos say anything about the Fangshi?"

I shrugged. "He claims he hasn't heard anything about them. Just said there's some legit Chinese businesses moving into town."

"Yeah, because that timing's not suspicious."

"Right. Might be worth checking out the business section of the newspaper today to see if there's word of some Chinese outfit moving in."

"I'll handle that tonight while you're on stakeout duty."

"Sounds good," I said.

The car was quiet for a few seconds. Then he said, "Are we cool?" He kept his eyes on the road.

"Yeah."

He nodded.

And that was that. But as much as I wanted to believe our minor tension over Volos was just a blip, the ghost of it lingered between us. And the problem with ghosts is it's only a matter of time until they get restless and start causing trouble.

CHAPTER TEN

B eing on a stakeout is sort of like taking a really boring road trip. The scenery never changes and you don't really get anywhere, but at least there are lots of snacks.

That evening, I sat in the beater car with Shadi, surrounded by bags of M&Ms and beef jerky. A good pig-out required a balance of sweet and salty. "It's a good thing I don't do this more often or I'd have an ass like a weather balloon," I said, shoving a handful of pretzels into my face.

Shadi shot me a judgey glance. She did stakeouts all the time, but she managed to have a tight caboose and a midsection you could wash clothes on. While my side of the car looked like I was cramming for finals, her side had a bottle of water and a pack of chewing gum. That's it.

"I could have handled this alone," she said.

This was her subtle way of telling me she would have preferred I not be there. Guess my jerky wasn't the only thing salty in that car. "And miss all this bonding time?" I said. "No way."

She pressed her lips together and turned to look out the window again.

I'd fully expected to do the stakeout alone that night, but when I showed up, Shadi was already there. She told me she could take the shift and tried to send me home. But I was the only member of the team who hadn't taken a turn yet, so I refused.

"Hey, Shadi," I said.

"What?"

"Why'd you stay tonight?"

She shifted in her seat. "Nothin' better to do."

I frowned at the back of her head. "Seriously? Literally anything would have been better."

She sighed and turned to look at me. "My kid's at my ex's for the week."

"So?"

She narrowed her eyes as she weighed her options. Eventually, she realized that I wouldn't let up and spilled it. "I had to put my mom in a senior center a couple of months ago. House is too damned quiet with them gone."

I put down my pretzels. "Are you crazy? You've got the house to yourself and no responsibility for a week? You should be out living it up."

"I don't know. I mean, don't misunderstand—I can still catch a cat, you know?"

I nodded. Morales had told me all about how Shadi was quite the ladies' lady.

"But one-night stands lose their appeal after a while. It's just easier to throw myself into the job. That way, I don't have to think about going to that lonely house or dealing with some chick blowing up my phone because I didn't text her the next day."

I blew out a breath. "Well, hell—I don't know what to say." This literally was the longest and most personal conversation I'd ever had with her.

"Don't say anything at all would be my vote."

I huffed out a breath and shoved more snacks into my mouth instead of commenting. But after a while, I didn't like the fact Shadi's story had made me think about how lonely my house would be in a couple of years. So, I decided to bug her again rather than swim in my own maudlin thoughts.

"How are things working out with Dixon and McGinty?"

She sighed, giving me a chance to redact my question and let her sit in silence. I just waited. The truth was Shadi scared the heck out of me, but she was also fun to mess with.

"They're fine," she said, finally. "Dixon's got lots of potential and he's good with tech shit. McGinty's...well, he's McGinty." Her tone hinted that she might be having some issues with the veteran cop, but I was torn about whether to push my luck by asking more questions.

After another couple of moments, she said, "The thing is, you can tell he used to be real police, you know? A natural?"

Not wanting to chance saying the wrong thing, I just murmured something vaguely affirmative and nodded.

"But now he's tired. Like he's just putting in his time until retirement. Spends most of his days arguing with Dixon and reading the sports page."

"Does he have enough to do? I mean, he can't exactly go to the buys like Dixon."

Dixon's black skin and youth meant he could go undercover pretty easily. Same went for Shadi. But if McGinty tried to stroll through the Cauldron trying to buy potions, they'd smell the bacon on him in a heartbeat.

"Maybe not. I mean he's good at planning and shit, but with the cases we're working, there's not a lot he can do." She sighed and looked over. "You and Morales want him?"

"We could probably use some help with tracking stuff down."

"Really?"

"Sure," I said. "I'm sure Gardner wouldn't mind us sharing him as a floater when we need desk work."

"The thing is," she said, "I don't know that that would be a good use for him either. Did you know he used to be homicide?"

"Why did he stop?"

"Some shit went down. That's my guess, anyway. He doesn't talk about it. But I figure he must have pissed off the brass. That's the only way Eldritch would give us anyone, right?"

It was hard to argue with her theory. Since the beginning, Gardner had been fighting with Eldritch for more manpower from the BPD to round out the task force, but he'd resisted and had lots of excuses. Then, a few weeks earlier, he suddenly handed us McGinty, all magnanimous like we were lucky to have him.

"How old is he?" I asked.

"Forty-nine," she said.

He looked like he was at least a decade older than that. "Past his twenty," I said.

After twenty years of service, most cops could retire and earn fifty percent of their pension. Lots of unis took that deal and started new careers. Others, who had the option, stayed on because they were able to move up the ranks into brass positions. But McGinty had stayed on despite the lack of promotions.

"His wife left him six years ago and they didn't have any kids," Shadi went on. "I think he stayed on because he didn't have anything else to do."

"It's sad. Especially if he's as talented as you say. Maybe you should talk to Gardner about giving him more challenging assignments."

"Yeah, you're probably right."

We fell silent as we each pondered the possibilities for McGinty. I wasn't sure about Shadi, but talking about retirement got me thinking about my own future again. I was still a couple of years shy of thirty, so I still had plenty of time before I was eligible to retire. But once Danny went off to start his own life, would I end up alone with nothing outside the work to give me purpose?

"Hey," Shadi said, cutting into my thoughts, "you seeing the bogey at six o'clock?"

I picked up my binoculars and took a gander. A man was walking around the corner and headed toward the massage parlor. "Asian male, mid-forties?"

"That's the one. Pretty expensive suit for a man going to a five-dollar hand-job joint."

"Hold on," I said, refocusing. "I'll be damned."

"What?"

"I swear I saw that same man in the mayor's office this morning. Last name's Hung. Didn't get the first. Volos said he's looking to move his company headquarters to Babylon."

Shadi nudged my arm and I handed over the binoculars. While she looked, I pulled out the book where Morales had left his notes from the night before. I didn't see any mention of a man matching the description on the list of people seen coming in or out of the place.

"You sure it's the same guy?" she asked.

"He was wearing that same suit," I said. "What do you want to do?"

"Let's see what he does first."

Hung went to the front door of the parlor and walked inside. Using the binoculars, I looked through the front window and saw him speaking to the lady behind the front desk. She handed him a package wrapped in brown paper. He bowed to her and left, coming back out the front door.

This time, he looked around for potential threats as he hurried down the street, with the package tucked under his jacket.

"Want to guess what's in that package?" Shadi said.

"Let's follow and find out."

We slowly pulled out of our parking space. Meanwhile, Hung got into a black Mercedes parked on the street about half a block up from the massage parlor. Once he'd made it to the light down the street, Shadi followed half a block behind him.

Something was niggling at me, but I couldn't put my finger on it.

It was more than just the fact I'd seen Hung at the mayor's office that morning.

"California plates," Shadi said.

I jotted down the number to call it in later. "Got it."

"Surely they're not dumb enough to make an exchange that much in the open."

"Maybe not of potions, but cash? Absolutely." I pointed. "He's turning right on Exposition."

She smoothly followed, still far enough back not to be obvious. "Do you think this Krystal chick has really taken over the coven?"

I shook my head. "I think Abe's calling the shots and she's just his eyes and ears."

"Why would your uncle make a partnership with the Chinese?"

"Who knows? Maybe they made him an offer he couldn't refuse."

"Like what?"

"I'm actually too scared to contemplate the possibilities."

Half to herself she said. "Is he going to that restaurant?"

Sure enough, the Mercedes pulled up on a side street next to a Chinese restaurant that was designed with a green pagoda roof. The sign out front identified it as Jade Moon.

"Maybe he's hungry?" I said, tongue in cheek.

"He's going around the back."

We watched as he pulled around the building and into the alley behind. Shadi slowly drove by the mouth of the alley, not too slow but slow enough for me to get a look at Hung going in the back door of the place.

"You want to go inside?" Shadi asked.

I shook my head. "Don't want to tip them off yet. Let's knock off."

I pulled out the notebook again and copied down the address. In the morning, I'd call in the plate and track down the owner of the restaurant.

"Well, that's something," she said. "You want me to drop you at your car?"

"Yeah."

She nodded and turned in the direction of the gym, where I'd left Sybil. "You meeting up with Morales after this?"

I stopped writing and looked up. "No, why?"

She shrugged. "Just wondering."

Her tone was too casual to just be a casual comment. "All right," I said, and went back to writing. When she was ready to say her piece, she'd do it.

Five minutes later, she stopped the car at a red light and turned to me. "Drew's one of my best friends," she said.

I didn't look up. "Mine, too."

"For real, though, he's my people. You understand?"

I sighed and set down my pen. Coming from Volos, the talk had been invasive and inappropriate. But coming from Shadi, it was actually pretty sweet. She wasn't exactly the emotive type, but she and Morales were pretty tight. "Is this the part where you tell me that if I break his heart, you'll break my legs?"

She looked me in the eyes. "Something like that."

"I'll save you the breath, then. I'm well aware of the stakes here, and I have no intention of not playing fair."

She nodded. "Just so we understand each other."

"Loud and clear."

She turned back to the road just as the light turned green. "Good." She hit the gas and zoomed through the intersection. I went back to making notes with a smile on my face.

CHAPTER ELEVEN

Mona Kostorov lived in a small bungalow on the Mundane side of town. The area had been settled by Russian and Polish immigrants, and, while lots of upwardly mobile young professionals were moving in now, there were still enough old-timers that the streets still smelled like cooked cabbage on Sundays.

An American flag swayed in the breeze from a bracket on the porch. Two hanging baskets overflowing with purple petunias hung from under the eaves, and on the bottom step, a statue of St. Francis stood guard.

"How do you want to play this?" Morales asked as we approached the house. He sounded more nervous about interviewing an old woman than he ever sounded going into an interrogation of a hexed-out criminal.

"Relax. Old ladies love me."

"Mmm-hmm," he said.

"You seem to forget that I live with a senior citizen."

"I'm not forgetting anyone. I just don't think you can judge the entire old lady population's opinion of you based on Baba. She's not exactly average."

"She's...spirited."

"Last time I spent the night, I got up to pee and saw her dancing naked in the backyard."

I snorted. "It was a full moon."

"Yes, and I got an eyeful of it."

"Okay so Baba's not normal, but I still have a way with older ladies. Just let me do the talking."

He muttered something under his breath that I didn't catch.

The front door was painted green and had a straw welcome mat in front. I rang the bell and stood back with a friendly smile on my face. The door cracked open a fraction of an inch.

"What do you want?"

"Mrs. Kostorov? Hi, I'm Detective Prospero. My friend Baba—"

A loud snort cut me off. "I told that old bat I didn't want nothin' to do with no cops."

"She said you were expecting us," I said. "I promise it'll just take a moment of your time."

She didn't answer, and I chose to believe the lack of angry response was a good sign. So, I forged ahead.

"Ma'am? We're trying to track down the wizard who sold your husband the potion he took."

"He bought that potion legally. You can't arrest me!"

I held up my hands. "No one wants to arrest you, ma'am. It's the person who sold the potion we're after. You said your husband bought it legally? Do you know where?"

"Store in the Cauldron."

"Do you know the name of the store? Or a street?"

"No, now, I told you—I don't want to talk to you. I'm in mourning."

"We appreciate that this is a difficult time, but anything you can tell us would be really help—"

The door slammed in my face.

A male snicker sounded behind me. I rounded on my traitorous partner. "You think you can do better? Be my guest."

His brow rose at my challenge. "All right." He cleared his throat. "Step aside."

I held out my hands and stepped out of the way.

He knocked on the door lightly. "Mrs. Kostorov, I just have one more question."

"What?" The reply was muffled by the door.

"Do you have any more of the potion inside the house?"

No answer.

"As my partner said," he continued, "we're not here to arrest anyone, but if you have any of the sample left, it would really help us track down the guy who's responsible for your husband's death."

Silence.

"Or if you can remember what the pills looked like, that could help too. We'll put the bad guy away for a long time."

When no response came again, I tugged on his sleeve. "Let's try later," I whispered.

But he held up a finger. "I know what it's like to lose a loved one to magic, Mrs. Kostorov. People shouldn't be allowed to harm others with potions."

His admission shocked me. Morales didn't talk a lot about how his father and little sister, Blanca, had died in a terrible accident when his father tried to make a potion. Drew was eight years old at the time and tried to go into the burning house to save them, but it had been too late. All he had to show for his effort was a scarred left hand and a lot of guilt.

The locks on the doors clicked. A moment later, the panel opened to reveal a birdlike woman with a nest of blue hair perched on her tiny head. She wore a black dress and sandals with pantyhose. Her eyes were red-rimmed and swollen.

I instantly felt guilty for my annoyance at her lack of cooperation.

"He got them at an apothecary called the Golden Thread. Friend of his told him to ask a guy there for it. The code word is *Priapus*."

Her hand shot out and put something in Morales's scarred left palm. "You find that bastard."

Morales looked solemnly down at the woman. "You have my word."

He held his hand behind his back to show me a tiny plastic zip-top bag with some powdery residue inside. The outside of the bag had a red cupid with a bow and arrow printed on the front. We'd deliver it to Mez, but it was pretty clear Mr. Kostorov had purchased Basil's bad potion.

She turned to me. "And you tell that Baba that I need some more of her Widow Juice."

I nodded. "Yes, ma'am."

The tiny woman pulled herself up, as if having done her duty she felt a weight lifted from her shoulders. "Now, if you'll excuse me, I need to go lay down."

"Of course," Morales said, "thank you." He handed her his business card. "If you think of any more information or need anything, please call."

She looked at the card for a moment, and when she looked up, tears flowed freely from her eyes. "My Sergei was big like you. I miss him."

He put his hand on hers and squeezed. "He was a lucky man, Mrs. Kostorov."

"We were both lucky," she corrected. "You married?"

"No, ma'am."

She patted his hand. "Big man like you won't stay on the market for long. Just be sure you don't marry one like that one." She pointed at me.

"Hey!" I protested.

"Why's that?" Morales asked, ignoring my indignation. I couldn't see his face, but his tone sounded strangled, as if he was fighting laughter.

"Man like you needs a soft woman. Woman who'll give him children and bake bread." She shot me a look that was so full of scorn, I gasped. "That one over there don't appreciate a good man. She's probably a feminist." She spat out the word like a curse. "They're all trying so hard to be like men that they forget to be women."

"Listen here—" I began, but she cut me off.

"Hush, man-hater."

I sucked in a breath to respond, but Morales began pushing me toward the steps. "That's really good advice," he said to Mrs. Kostorov. "I'll be sure to look for a woman who likes men."

She nodded, as if they'd made a deal. "All right, you go now. I'll call if I think of anything else." She patted him again before withdrawing back inside. As she closed the door, she looked at me with a scornful sniff.

Once it was closed, Morales turned and put an arm around my stiff shoulders. I tried to keep glaring at the closed door, but he steered me away. "Come on, man-hater. We got work to do."

He wrangled me into the SUV and ran around to get in and take off before I exploded.

"Can you believe— Who the hell did she think—" I sputtered before we'd made it twenty feet.

"She's just old-fashioned."

"Old-fashioned is when someone prefers penny candy, print books, and Norman Rockwell paintings. That woman sounded like she resented getting the right to vote!"

He shrugged. "Who cares?"

I shook my head. "I can't believe how mean she was."

"She did just lose the love of her life, Kate."

"She seemed nice enough to you."

He smirked down at me. "Guess that makes *me* the granny whisperer."

We rode along in silence for a few minutes. Finally, I couldn't stand it any longer. "Do you agree with what she said?"

"Which part?"

I rolled my eyes. "About how you need a woman who'll give you lots of babies and bake bread."

He shot me a side-eye. "She really got under your skin, huh?"

"I don't know." I sighed. "I mean, this isn't the first time someone's acted like me being a cop is a betrayal of my gender."

"Do you think you're betraying your gender?" he asked carefully.

"Hell, no."

"Good. Because honestly? I'm terrified of the idea of you cooking."

"Excuse me, I can cook. I made a bad-ass potion back in the day."

"You cooked dirty magic potions. That's not exactly the same as making bread."

"Right, it takes way more skill. Just because I don't cook doesn't mean I can't. I'm usually just too tired from chasing down bad guys to make something."

"I'll believe it when I see it."

I turned and shot him a suspicious look. "You're trying to get me to cook for you like that old lady wanted!"

"What can I say? I'm a product of the patriarchy."

"You're full of shit. The truth is, you'd be bored as hell with some mousey woman who never challenged you."

He looked at me. "There's challenging and then there's pain in the ass." He left little doubt about which category I fell into.

CHAPTER TWELVE

A fter we left Mrs. Kostorov's, we decided to check out the apothecary she'd told us about. On the way there, I got a call from Dixon.

"Finally got something useful on Basil Valentine's phone."

I blinked. I'd totally forgotten I'd asked Dixon to take a look at it. "What'd you find?"

"Tracked a number back to Seattle. Looked like a dead end at first —a dry cleaner. But just in case, I plugged it into ACD," he said. "That number was tied to an FBI investigation. I guess when I looked it up, it notified an agent who'd worked on it, and he called me just now. Agent Rick Logan. He said they had a case going into a money-laundering operation tied to that dry cleaner a couple of years back."

"What happened with that case?"

"According to Logan, they had to drop the case when their lead witness showed up dead next to the Fremont troll."

"Figures." Witnesses in federal cases had a nasty habit of coming down with a bad case of death. "Who were they going after, though?"

"Logan said they were trying to tie the laundering operation to the Fangshi."

"Of course."

"Yep. Said they even had the Seattle field office of the MEA in on the investigation, but they couldn't turn up shit either. After one of their agents was executed, the trail went cold."

"Fuck me."

Morales stopped the car at a light and turned to watch me. I held up a finger.

"I wish I could say that made me happy," I said to Dixon, "but, you know."

He snorted. "Yeah, I get it. Also, I ran those plates from the Mercedes. According to my buddy at the DMV, the car is registered to a man named Alexander Hung."

"Yep, that's the guy."

"I checked him out in ACD, too."

"Well? Don't keep me in suspense."

"He's been sued a bunch of times, but no criminal convictions. His name pops up in connection to several criminal cases—no charges, though. Last agent who made notes said they thought he was a hit man for the Fangshi. Officially, though, he's a legit businessman."

"What kind of business?"

"Dry cleaners."

I huffed out an ironic laugh. "Naturally."

"He came up with some new alchemical cleaning process," Dixon continued. "He's got at least a dozen stores on the West Coast."

"Christ. And last night, we saw him getting a payoff from a Votary outfit. What the hell is going on?"

"That's starting to feel like something we may be better off not knowing."

"No shit." I sighed. "Thanks, Dixon. This is really helpful."

"You got it."

I hung up. "Fuck."

"Tell me," Morales said.

I gave him the rundown.

"Hold up," he said. "Didn't Puck say something about Charm meeting with a Chinese guy in a black Mercedes?"

"Crap, you're right. When I saw the car last night, it niggled at me, but I didn't make the connection. Has to be the same guy."

"Signs are definitely pointing to yes. While you were on stakeout last night, I did some research. You'd mentioned yesterday that Volos was working a deal with a Chinese company, so I looked at recent news in the business section."

"And?"

"And turns out Alexander Hung owns several businesses."

"Dry cleaning," I said, repeating what Dixon had said.

He nodded. "Yeah, but he also owns a company called Waidan Imports."

"What kind of company is that?"

"They distribute imported alchemical supplies—beakers, herbs, and shit. That's the company he's relocating here. I guess they're refurbishing one of the old steel factories. It's supposed to bring a lot of jobs to Babylon."

I shook my head. "Good luck convincing people of that."

"What do you mean?"

"I forget you're not from around here. It goes back to the steel bust. The alchemist who came up with the new way of processing steel was a Chinese alchemist. Once all the jobs moved overseas, it left a lot of raw feelings in the hearts of all the steel workers who lost their livelihoods."

"I guess that makes sense, sort of."

"It's one of the reasons people are so pro buying 'made in America' crap," I said. "There was this period back in the '80s where people would publicly burn any products marked MADE IN CHINA."

"Well, that explains why I can't find any decent dim sum here."

"Yeah. But I guess maybe it's been long enough and people are desperate enough for jobs that they'd be willing to overlook it."

"You're forgetting that Waidan is an American company. Alexander Hung is Chinese-American."

I laughed. "To lots of people around here, anyone who ain't white ain't American. You know that."

"Sadly true."

I looked out the window at the broken-down buildings that made up the Cauldron. The city needed an infusion if it was going to survive. John Volos thought more magic would fix things, but I wasn't so convinced.

Letting that depressing train of thought slip away, something else occurred to me. "I don't suppose you ran into this Alexander Hung when you were undercover," I said.

"Never heard of him before, but if he's high enough up the food chain, he'd keep himself clear of the street-level shit."

"I guess this sort of ruins your theory that the Fangshi players in town are probably small potatoes."

He pulled the SUV into a spot down the block from our destination. "The Fangshi is a huge syndicate. There's no reason to believe Hung or any of the other potential players here are in any way tied to my past."

"I hope you're right."

He tossed me a careless wink. "'Course I am, Cupcake."

The Golden Thread was one of several apothecaries in the Cauldron that sold clean magic potions. They were basically like drug stores in that they also sold convenience items, but the potions were dispensed by a registered wizard instead of a pharmacist. The other difference was that with the right word, a lot of those wizards might also sell you dirty magic potions they cooked on the side or distributed for the covens.

The business was located about three blocks from the massage parlor. There was nothing special about the decor to differentiate it from any other apothecary. The area nearest the door held a long counter from which the wizard dispensed his potions from glass jars stored on the shelves that lined the back wall. The center of the wall held a pass-through window where another wizard worked to cook more complex potions. At the back of the store, there were stand-alone cases that held sundries.

"Welcome to the Golden Thread," he said. "How can I help you?"

The man behind the counter had long blond hair pulled back into a neat ponytail. His apothecary uniform consisted of a starched white apron and dark jeans. A name tag on the apron read, JAKE. It was common for wizards who worked with the public to wear aprons instead of wizard's robes because the general Mundane population didn't like the reminder that they were buying magical products. Much easier to digest the idea that wizards were like chefs who cooked rather than sorcerers who cast spells to create potions.

"Hi," Morales said, "my friend told me I could get a special potion here."

Jake's smile remained polite. "Well, potions are our business."

I hung back behind Morales, which gave me a chance to watch the wizard. He had an ouroboros tattoo on his left wrist that match the one on mine. That meant he was both a made member of the Votary coven as well as a certified apothecary owner, which was odd since he'd have had to go through rigorous testing to be certified to make and sell clean magic. Not to mention there were government oversight and pesky taxes involved in running a legit potion business. Of course, like me, he could have left the coven and gone legit, but seeing how he was running an apothecary in the middle of Votary territory, it was sort of a stretch. Especially since we knew he sold at least one person an illegal and dangerous virility potion.

Playing it cool, Morales leaned in to whisper to the guy. "I was supposed to say *Priapus*?"

Jake's expression morphed from professional to feral. "Get the fuck out of here.

Morales reared back and held his hand up. "Whoa, calm down, guy."

"Are you a fucking cop?" he growled.

I put my hand on my sidearm, which had been hidden under my jacket. "Everyone relax."

"Hey, Lenny, we got a couple of pigs out here asking about that shit Basil sold us."

A pale face surrounded by long shaggy hair appeared in the pass-through window. "Fucking Basil."

"Look, man," Jake said, "we didn't know that shit was dirty."

Morales crossed his arms. "Oh, yeah? Then why was there a secret password to get it?"

Jake looked around quickly, as if he knew he was caught. "All right, we knew it was dirty-ish. But we tossed the rest of the pills, I swear. I don't want no beef with them dragon ladies."

I perked up. "What do you mean?"

"The day after Basil got his ass exploded, Krystal LeMay came in with a little old Chinese lady and four chicks dressed like ninjas and shit. Said if we had any more of Basil's shit, we had to give it to them. We said we sold out, but once they were gone, we flushed that shit."

"What did they look like?" Morales asked.

Jake rolled his eyes. "I told you, man—they looked Asian and shit. The ninja chicks were hot, though."

"Damn straight," said Lenny sing-songed like a chorus.

And they were all women, which ruled out Alexander Hung, I thought.

"Oh" Jake continued, "and the old broad had a horn."

"A horn?" I asked.

"Fuck," Morales whispered.

He lifted his index finger to his forehead and pointed to a spot just to the right of center. "One tiny horn, just here. It was green. Like a fucked-up unicorn or some shit."

"We heard the Votaries were partnering with the Chinese," I said because Morales had gone uncharacteristically quiet. "Why would they be hassling you?"

He made a disgusted sound with his mouth. "I plead the Fifth."

I shook my head. "You're not under arrest, idiot. We're looking for the person who killed Basil. But if you keep giving us a hassle, we'll make an exception."

"I don't know what to tell you." He sighed and raised his hands, all innocence. "I'm legit, but occasionally I'll connect an interested customer with a special product." He shrugged. "Times are tough, you know?"

"Uh-huh," I said. "The Chinese," I prompted.

"So, Basil came to me a few weeks back and said he had this new connect. Chinese wiz who's running a special potion. Said it's super hush-hush because it's a sex potion."

"He didn't want Aphrodite to find out," I said, nodding.

"Right. The Hierophant ain't exactly forgiving, if you get my drift."

"We're acquainted," I said.

"Anyway, Basil had this plan. He was going to get the pure product from the Chinese and pad it with some cheap shit and put it in pill form to double the supply."

My eyes widened. "Which would double his profit and screw the suppliers out of some of the take."

"Right. But I guess they figured out what he was doing, because we only sold a few doses before Basil went boom. Couple days later, the Chinese showed up and we closed up shop on that potion."

"Who's calling the shots? The Votaries or the Chinese?"

Jake shrugged. "That's above my pay grade."

"Have you seen the horned lady or her handmaidens again since they came in?" Morales said. I frowned at the word *handmaidens*. The way he'd said it sounded an awful lot like he'd heard of them before.

He shook his head. "Message received, you know?"

"You heard of anyone else around here having problems with them?"

"Tell them about the massage parlor," Lenny said.

"Hush, asshole," Jake hissed.

"Hey!"

I raised my brows. "The Happy Ending? What about it?"

Jake paused his lips and crossed his arms.

I sighed. "All right, you have the right to remain silent—"

"Hold up!" Jake interrupted. "No need for all that. I'll tell you."

"Go on," Morales said.

"This is just rumor, mind you," he said.

I circled my hand in the air to hurry him up.

"I heard Krystal is paying protection money to the Chinese."

I played dumb even though I'd seen it with my own eyes the night before. "Why?"

"On account of the fact that no one recognizes her as the legit leader. Lots of people haven't forgotten she sold out Puck."

"Bitch," Lenny said from the window.

"Yeah, that's right," Jake said. "At first, everyone was falling in line because word was the big guy himself had tapped her to take over."

Morales shifted his weight. "You mean Abe?"

Jake nodded. "But it didn't take long for word to spread about what she did to Puck. Then no one wanted to follow her. So, I guess she made a deal with the Chinese."

"Hold up, let me get this straight," I said. "Abe tapped Krystal to take over. Krystal betrayed Puck to make sure it happened. Then once she was in charge, she had to pay the Chinese to protect her from her own coven?"

Morales frowned. "Why wouldn't Abe's bona fide be enough to protect her?"

We looked at Jake. "Don't look at me," he said.

We turned our attention to Lenny. He waved his hands in a not-my-business gesture and disappeared back into his lab.

"That doesn't make any sense," I said as Morales ducked into the lab's doorway.

Jake looked relieved. "Maybe you should go talk to Krystal. Like right now."

I tapped the glass counter. "We will. Right after we book you and Lenny."

Ruckus sounds came from inside the lab, but before I could verify Morales had Lenny cuffed, Jake leapt over the counter and took off toward the door.

I cursed under my breath. "Morales, we've got a runner."

The sky had been threatening to open up all morning, and by the time I followed Jake outside, it was pouring. I spotted his apron flapping in the wind as he turned the corner down an alley. My feet pounded the slick pavement. I pulled my phone from my pocket and hit the speed dial button for Shadi.

"What's up?"

I talked into the phone as I turned into the alley. "You down near Blackmoore and Liberty?"

"Why are you breathing heavy?"

"I'm chasing an asshole down an alley."

"I'm two blocks away."

"I'm headed west in an alley. We'll be coming out on Elm."

Through the phone, I heard her car's engine rev up. "I'm on my way. Stay on the line, though."

"10-4."

Up ahead, Jake had almost reached the end of the alley. I dug in to speed up so I wouldn't lose him once he hit the street. He reached the end and turned left. "He's headed north on Elm now," I said. "Blond, ponytail. Wearing an apron."

"Almost there," she said. "Turning on Elm now."

I finally reached the end of the alley in time to see Jake running and a crappy blue sedan barreling toward him in the background.

I said into the phone, "That's him headed toward you."

"I got him." A banging noise came through the phone as she

dropped it to focus on snatching her prize. Suddenly, the car veered to the left and jumped the curb. She slammed it into PARK and flew out of the door. She was on Jake so fast, he barely saw her coming. She tackled him like a cowboy wrangling a wayward calf.

I sped up to go help, but by the time I reached her, she already had a zip tie around his wrist. She rose and put a foot on his bound wrists. I was gasping for breath, but she was barely winded.

"You want to take him in?" she asked. "Or do you want me to do it?"

I held up my hand and tried to catch my breath. Finally, I said, "Morales has another one a couple blocks back."

She nodded resolutely. "Let's go see."

She pulled Jake off the ground. Once he was upright, the height disparity between them was comical. Shadi might be small, but she stored a lot of power in a small package. She maneuvered Jake into the back seat of the car and waited for me to join him in the other side of the back seat before she shut the door.

"What the hell just happened?" he said, sounding dazed.

"Jake, meet Special Agent Pruitt."

"Damn, girl," he said, wincing. "I think you broke my collarbone."

"Quitcherbitchin," she said. "Where am I going, Prospero?"

I gave her the address and she backed off of the curb and took off toward the apothecary. I pulled out my cell and called Morales.

"Where are you?" he asked, sounding worried.

"With Shadi. She was nearby, so she helped me scoop up Jake. How are things there?"

He let out a relieved breath. "Lenny and I were trying to find you."

"There he is," she said.

I leaned to the side to be able to see through the windshield. Sure enough, there was Morales all but dragging cuffed Lenny up the road.

"Stay where you are," I said. "We'll pick you up."

CHAPTER THIRTEEN

I hadn't been to the Cauldron precinct in several weeks. I didn't want to be there that day, either, but we couldn't have asked Shadi to handle Tweedles Dee and Dum by herself.

We led them inside and straight to booking. This had been my old turf back when I was a street cop. The cop on duty in booking was an old warhorse named Butch. He'd seen pretty much everything, so he wore an expression that could only be described as "perpetual lack of surprise."

We deposited Lenny and Jake at the benches along the wall and went to go start the procedure.

"Hey, Butch," I said.

He looked up from his computer monitor. "Prospero. Long time no see." His tone was so even, you could lay a level across the words and the bubble would stay dead center. "What you got for me today?"

"Two warm bodies. Charged with resisting arrest—"

He shook his head. "Fill out the form. I'll get it entered once they're processed."

"That's new," I said. We used to have to walk each perp through the process and then fill out all the paperwork. It meant booking could take all day sometimes.

"You been gone awhile," he said.

"True enough." I took two clipboards and pens. "Thanks, Butch."

He didn't acknowledge the words. Just looked back down at his monitor and started typing again.

Morales and I took the clipboards into the break room to fill out. Cops in uniform milled around, getting snacks or energy-potion drinks from the vending machines. I only recognized a couple, who gave me the briefest of nods.

I leaned in to begin filling out the forms. "Well, it's official."

"What is?" Morales said, squinting at his own forms.

"I'm not one of them anymore. Not that I ever really was, I guess."

Back when I'd been a beat cop, I'd worked on my own and liked it that way. It was easier than dealing with partners who thought my last name and my dominant left hand meant I was still a criminal.

"Fuck 'em," he said.

He'd been monosyllabic since we left the apothecary. I wanted to question him about it, but it would have to wait until we left the precinct.

I took a sip from my paper cup and immediately regretted it. "At least the MEA has better coffee."

He huffed out a forced laugh but didn't look up from his paperwork.

We worked for several minutes, occasionally asking each other questions about what went down at the apothecary so our reports would be accurate and identical. I was almost done when a voice called from the doorway.

"That paperwork better be for the Valentine murder."

I glanced up to see Duffy glaring at us from the doorway. "It's related, yeah."

"My office," he snapped.

Morales and I exchanged an unimpressed look and then put our heads back down to continue working.

Two minutes later, Duffy reappeared. "Hello?"

I signed my report with a flourish. "What's up?"

"I just asked you to meet with me in my office."

"Actually, you just said, 'My office.'" I looked at Morales. "You want to go grab some food once we drop these with Butch?"

He stretched and yawned. "Sure. Chasing people works up an appetite."

"Jesus H.," Duffy said. "Will you come to my office? Now. Please."

"Oh, fine," I said, "but only because you asked so nicely."

He hovered by the door this time to make sure we got up to follow him. Once we left the breakroom, we followed him until I detoured toward booking to give Butch the paperwork. Morales stayed with him so he wouldn't blow a gasket.

When I ducked in to give everything to Butch, I saw that Lenny and Jake were gone from the bench. Butch saw me looking and said, "They're getting mug shots now."

I turned in the report and slid my business card across the desk. "You run into any trouble, call me."

He lifted the card and read it. "Aren't you fancy?"

"Yeah, it's all designer coffee and white-collar crime up in the MEA." There could be no missing the sarcasm in my tone. "Thanks, Butch."

When I entered Duffy's office a few moments later, the two men weren't talking. I'd kind of been hoping Morales could handle whatever bullshit Duffy was pulling, but I guess it just wasn't my day.

"What's up?" I asked, taking my seat.

"What's up is it's been four days and I ain't had a single update on the Valentine case." A vein in Duffy's neck bulged and his eyes were red, like he hadn't slept in a while.

"Maybe it's time to switch to decaf, Duffy."

"Fuck you, Prospero. I'm serious. Gardner told Eldritch we'd be kept in the loop on this."

"Hey, you're the one who begged us to take the case because you were too overworked. We figured you'd appreciate not being bothered."

He tilted his head. "How generous of you. But since you're here…" He leaned back in his chair and raised his arms, as if to offer us the floor.

"The two scumbags we just brought in were selling a potion for Valentine. Virility pills," I said. "According to them, a couple of days after the lab exploded, Valentine's girlfriend showed up with some Chinese wizards who demanded they stop selling the pills."

He frowned. "Chinese wizards?"

I nodded. "Fangshi. Mostly a West Coast gang. We think they're trying to move into the Cauldron and Valentine was helping. The girl-friend's involved too."

"What's her name?"

"Krystal LeMay. She's a Votary girl."

Duffy frowned as if he was having trouble keeping up. He was an Adept but had spent most of his career working homicides on the Mundane side of town. He'd been promoted to head of the Cauldron precinct murder squad several months earlier after he'd helped on a big case. Personally, I thought he was a good cop, but he didn't know enough about Cauldron politics to be in charge of solving all the murders there.

"So, you figure the Chinese killed Valentine. What's the motive?"

I glanced at Morales in case he wanted to jump in, but he looked about as ready to talk as a perp in an interrogation room. Realizing I was on my own, I continued to explain to Duffy. "Valentine—probably with the help of his girlfriend—screwed over the Chinese."

"How?"

"The Fangshi wizes supplied Valentine with a virility potion that he was supposed to put out to test the market. Only, Valentine got greedy. He cut the Fangshi potion with a dangerous ingredient and put it out in pill form. That doubled the supply so he could double his profits."

"Which cut the Fangshi out of more profit," Duffy supplied.

"Exactly. Only, the thing he added? It made the potion unstable and we've connected it to at least three recent deaths."

"Which begs the question—why haven't you arrested the girl-friend or any of these Fangshi people?"

I laughed. "Because we literally got confirmation of the connection less than an hour ago."

He didn't look convinced. "If it were me—"

"Yeah, well, it's not you," I cut in. "Remember? You couldn't handle it so you asked us to take over?"

He lifted his coffee mug to his lips. Finding it empty, he muttered a curse and slapped it down again. "Look, I'm not trying to bust your balls, Prospero."

"Yeah, you are, and you seem to forget that we don't report to you. You work your cases and let us work ours."

"I'm just saying it's only a matter of time before Eldritch comes in here and puts my balls in the vise. When I tell him you haven't made an arrest, he's gonna be knocking on Gardner's door. Then guess whose balls will be in a vise?"

"Enough with the 'balls' already, man," I deadpanned. "It aggra-vates my penis envy."

He cleared his throat. "Sorry, but you know what I mean."

"Look, Gardner wants this case closed too, but not by cutting corners and making arrests based on hearsay. If the Fangshi are involved, there's no evidence thus far connecting them to the crime scene except some potions."

His expression cleared. "Huh."

"What?" I snapped.

"Nothing, it's just—well, it's refreshing to hear someone worried more about making a strong case than getting a closure on the score card."

"Thanks, I think," I said. "Look, we'll loop you in once we have something concrete. If you have questions, you can certainly call. But until then, I figure you got enough on your plate without us checking in every day."

He scrubbed a hand over his face. "You're right. Sorry. About earlier…and the ball thing."

"Don't lose any sleep over it. I worked this precinct for five years, remember? I know how it gets."

"Yeah, well, according to what I'm hearing, it's worse now. Ever since Volos became the mayor and made it his mission to reduce violent crime in the Cauldron, the heat's been on." He shook his head. "Makes me wish I was still across the river. Mundane murder cases can get plenty fucked up, but they ain't got nothing on the crazy shit the covens pull on each other."

I almost felt bad for the guy, but I also knew he was more of a political animal than he'd ever admit. He wouldn't have taken this post if he didn't think it would pay off in promotions down the road.

I glanced at the clock on his desk. "All right, we good?"

He nodded. "Believe it or not, I do appreciate you taking this off my plate."

With that, I stood. Morales was looking at his phone, so I had to nudge him. He glanced up sharply and then realized the meeting was over. "We good?"

Dragging him after me, I called over my shoulder, "See ya, Duffy."

I held my tongue until we were outside the precinct and on our way to the car. "All right, what's eating you?"

"Nothing."

"Bullshit. You've been weird ever since we arrested those two jackasses."

He stopped walking and ran a hand over his scruff. "We're in trouble."

Thinking he'd gotten some message from Gardner while we were in the precinct, I frowned. "Shit, what did we do now?"

He let out a frustrated breath. "No, I mean, back at the apothecary? That horned lady they mentioned who came in with Krystal—she's bad news." The pained expression on his face revealed how much the admission cost him.

"What kind of bad news are we talking here?" I was afraid of his answer. Morales was the kind of guy who downplayed trouble, which meant bad news was really terrible news.

"The kind of bad that hates my guts and wants me dead." He took off toward his car again.

I tried to keep up. "Who is she?"

"They call her Yü Nü. It means 'Jade Maiden.' Rumor has it she's immortal."

I laughed. "What? That's crazy."

"Kate, she's the real deal. A master of Taoist alchemy from the old country. Some believe she's the head of the Fangshi worldwide. The four women with her were the Handmaidens. They're her private army of martial alchemists."

"But you said the Fangshi wouldn't bother sending big players to Babylon."

He threw up his hands. "I was wrong."

"Shit. What does she have on you?"

He stopped walking because we'd reached the car. He pulled the keys out of his pocket and toyed with them nervously. "She was involved in the murder of the dirty cop. After I got pulled out from undercover, I offered testimony that resulted in the arrest of several members of her family. I didn't implicate her or anyone else at the cop killing, because they'd come after me. That didn't stop her from putting a price on my head, though. That's why I haven't been back to Los Angeles."

I put a hand on his arm. "You have to go to Gardner with this."

He jerked away. "And have her fire me? I can't."

"She won't fire you. There were extenuating circumstances. People have to do all sorts of crazy shit undercover."

"You don't understand. I can't take the risk of the MEA firing me over this. I won't have anything left. Promise me you won't tell her."

I pulled back, stung that he thought I'd rat him out. "Of course not."

"Good, let's go. I need to go home and think this through. If Yü Nü is calling the shots, we're going to have to change up our approach in this case."

I nodded. "All right, we can order in and—"

He cut me off. "No, I need to be alone."

"All right. No problem." I kept my tone light to cover the fact I was feeling rejected. "I need to spend some time with Danny, anyway."

"I'm sorry," he said. "I just need to get my head on right."

"Don't worry about it. Just drop me off at the gym and we can regroup tomorrow."

I just hoped that was enough time for him to figure out how to tie the Fangshi to the murder beyond the shadow of a doubt, because the longer we spent investigating this case, the higher the chance of Morales's past biting us all in the ass.

CHAPTER FOURTEEN

B y the time I got home, I felt like death warmed over. Between being verbally abused by an old woman, chasing a punk through downtown Babylon, and hanging at the Cauldron precinct, I wanted to bathe in beer—or at least drink a beer in the bathtub.

My family had other plans.

I dragged myself into the kitchen and found Pen and Danny sitting at the table, waiting for me. I stopped just inside the doorway and dropped my backpack in its usual spot.

"What's up, guys?"

"Kate, if you could sit down," Pen said in her best therapist's tone. "Danny has something he'd like to discuss with you."

I tilted my head, every sense screaming caution. "Where's Baba?"

"She went to take something to a friend," Pen said. "Please sit."

"What's this about?" I hedged.

Danny tapped a finger on the edge of the table nervously. Whatever they had to talk to me about must be a big deal. I resisted the urge to grab a beer from the fridge before I sat down. As I took my seat, I realized I just need to be quiet and stay as calm until they told me what was going on.

"Thank you," Pen said. "Kate, Danny asked me to help facilitate a conversation he'd like to have with you concerning the Conservatory. I'm not here as your friend or Danny's. I'm here as an impartial mediator to help you to both discuss a very important issue.

I held up my hands in what I hoped was an encouraging and calm gesture. "You guys, this really isn't necessary."

Pen shot me a warning look. "Go ahead, Danny," she prompted.

He looked at her nervously but she encouraged him with a nod. I tapped my heel against the floor and tried to remain calm. "Kate." He paused to take a deep breath and looked down at a sheet on the table covered in his handwriting. "A few days ago, you discovered that I had not been honest with you. I am really, um, sorry and stuff for lying to you." He glanced up at me from under his hair. "But I really want to go to the Conservatory."

"I know you do."

"Please only listen now," Pen said in a prim tone.

I gritted my teeth but managed a nod.

Danny continued. "I have been studying magic with Mez for a few months now and he thinks I have a real talent. Plus, I love it. I really want to go to a school with other people like me. I'm tired of being treated like some sort of freak because I'm a Leftie."

A pang hit my midsection. I'd gotten Danny out of the Cauldron and stuck him in a Mundane school as soon as I could when he was younger. When I'd made the decision, I thought I'd been saving him lots of trouble, but I actually sort of doomed him to being around people who would always treat him as an outsider.

"Also, I'm excited about the idea of getting to study magic in school. They have really cool classes in stuff like metallurgy, spagyrics, and the physics of magic."

My brows rose because those did sound pretty cool.

"I know you are afraid that if I follow the path of magic, I will end up like Uncle Abe or whatever, but I promise you that I will only study clean magic and that I will use it for good."

145

I didn't have the heart to tell him that clean magic wasn't automatically good any more than dirty magic was always evil. He was too young to grasp that all magic was chaos, and that the minute you thought you controlled it, it would turn on you.

"In conclusion," he said, "I know you are angry and I don't blame you, but I hope you can see past that to allow me to pursue the future I really want."

From beneath the table, Pen pulled out a file folder. She opened it and removed a sheet of paper. She slid it across the table with dramatic flair.

Frowning, I picked it up and realized it was the acceptance letter the school had sent in the packet.

"Here's a pen." She slid that across, as well.

I stared down at the paper because I didn't trust myself to speak. I felt totally ambushed. The thing was, I knew it wasn't Danny's doing at all. Despite her claim to the contrary, she wasn't there as an impartial mediator. She'd coached the kid on what to say and orchestrated the offering of the form like a puppet master.

"Kate?" she prompted.

I looked up. Whatever was on my face must have warned her, because her benevolent smile fell. "Danny," I said, "can you give Pen and me a couple of moments alone?"

"Is everything okay?" he asked, sounding worried.

"Everything's fine," I said in a bright tone. "I just need to talk to her for a second."

He rose hesitantly and headed to the doorway into the living room. Before he went through, he cast a worried look back at both of us. We both smiled, all reassurance.

Once he was gone and I'd heard his footfalls on the stairs down to his room, I turned to my best friend, crossed my hands in front of me on the table, and laid into her. "What the hell is wrong with you?"

She pulled back, looking like I'd slapped her. "What? I'm trying to help."

I laughed, a low, bitter sound. "You're trying to meddle. There's a big fucking difference, Pen."

She huffed out an offended breath. "Danny called me last night and said he wanted help figuring out how to convince you to let him go to the school."

"And instead of encouraging him to have an adult conversation with me, you orchestrated this manipulative farce. Nice touch sliding the form across, by the way. You almost had me before that bullshit."

She rose from her chair. "Screw you, Kate. Maybe if you were around for him, he wouldn't have to come to me for help."

The punch didn't land like she wanted it to. I knew I hadn't been around the last couple of days, but I knew she was being unfair just to knock me down. "Look, I know you're lost right now, but that doesn't give you the right to pull this kind of shit."

She paled. "I'm not lost."

"Yes, you are. You're wearing the same damned yoga pants you had on four nights ago, for Chrissakes."

Her face morphed into an indignant mask. "This is a different pair!"

I leaned back in my chair. "Regardless, I can't have you coming in here trying to fix things because you can't fix your own life."

She crossed her arms. "That's unfair, Kate."

"No, unfair is putting me in a position where I'm ambushed and backed into a corner. You didn't even check with me first to take my temperature. You just tried to steamroll me, and you dragged Danny along for the ride."

She bent down and grabbed her purse. "I don't have to listen to this."

"Fine," I said. "Don't."

With that, she stormed out the door and slammed it behind her. A few moments later, the sound of her car's engine turning over reached me. Even that sounded righteously indignant.

"Kate?" Danny's voice came from the living room. "Is everything okay?"

I took a deep breath before answering. "Yeah. Come on in."

He looked around as he entered. "Where's Pen?"

"She had to go home."

"Did you yell at her?"

I nodded. "Kind of, yeah."

"Crap, I didn't mean to—"

"It's not your fault." I waved him over. "Why don't you sit down."

He moved carefully, as if he were afraid that one wrong move set me off. I kept my posture relaxed and tried to look unintimidating.

"All right, here's the deal," I began. "I won't be signing that paper right now."

He opened his mouth to argue, but I held up a hand. "You said your piece—now it's my turn." He nodded reluctantly and I continued. "The reason I can't sign it yet is that I haven't even seen this school. It wouldn't be responsible of me as your guardian to send you to a place until I've checked it out first."

"I guess that makes sense."

"As it happens, I talked to the principal yesterday."

His head jerked up. "You did?"

"Yeah, we're trying to find a time to set up a meeting to discuss all of this and so I can see the school itself."

"I—I didn't know."

"How about I plan it for a time when you can come with me?"

His face transformed, and for the first time in a long time, I got to see that dimple that used to charm me out of grounding him when he was younger. "That would be awesome."

"I can't promise that I'll like it, but I can promise that I'll give it a chance."

He exhaled a deep, accepting sigh. "That's fair, I guess."

"In return, you have to promise me that you'll stop recruiting

Baba, Pen, Mez, or anyone else to help you when you want to work around me. We've been through a lot, you and me. I know things have been tough the last couple of years and there's been a lot of changes, but we're family, Danny."

"I know," he said in his best defensive-teenager tone.

"And I know I've been a pain in the ass about a lot of stuff. Right?"

His lip twitched. "Sort of, yeah."

"I promise I'll try to listen to you more. But you've got to meet me halfway and be honest. Okay?"

He thought about it a second before nodding. "Yeah, all right."

I pushed my chair back and went around. "Stand up."

He glared up at me. "No hugging."

I held my arms open. "You're not getting out of it. Might as well give in."

He sighed the sigh of the put-upon. "Gawd, Katie."

"Hug or no deal."

He rolled his eyes like a pro before pushing out of his seat. The hug was probably the fastest ever recorded, but beggars couldn't be choosers.

"Now, you want to help me send the email to Dr. Hidalgo?"

The corner of his mouth lifted. "Yeah."

I threw my arm around his neck and pulled him toward the living room so we could use the laptop. "I have to give you credit, though. That speech was pretty good."

He ducked his head. "Pen helped me."

I pulled my arm away and felt some of my victorious feeling fade. "Yeah, I figured."

"She was kind of intense about it, honestly."

"That doesn't surprise me." I knew the topic wasn't done with Pen, but I'd give her a couple of days before I called to hash it out. Pushing that aside, I prepared to take the next step in helping my brother move toward his future—whatever that held.

CHAPTER FIFTEEN

The next morning on my way into work, I swung by City Hall to check on Sweet Ray and Peewee. Like before, I found them on the top step. Well, I found Sweet Ray. There was a pigeon at his feet, but it was gray, not white like the one had been a few days earlier.

"Morning," I said. "Do you remember me?"

He looked offended. "Of course. You're Joan of Arc, right?"

"Very funny."

He shrugged, which made the gold braid on the shoulders of his crushed velvet housecoat sway. "I gotta get my kicks where I can, because Peewee isn't speaking to me." He tipped the stained turban toward the gray pigeon.

"Um, I thought Peewee was white."

"You racist?" he said sharply. "Because I won't work for an intolerant person."

"No," I said, dragging out the syllable. "I just thought Peewee had white feathers."

Sweet Ray spread his arms wide. "All of them are Peewee."

I looked out over the dozens of pigeons strutting around on the shit-spackled steps. "All of those are Peewee?"

"Don't be ridiculous." He shook his head. "Every pigeon on earth is Peewee. They share a consciousness. Pigeons are very enlightened, you know."

As far as conversations went, that one really felt like a dead end, so I let it go. "All right, so it's been a few days. You got anything good for me?"

He shrugged and tossed a couple of imaginary crumbs toward the confused gray bird. "People come, people go."

"Any particular people?"

"Mostly cheap assholes."

"Fair enough. Did you see anyone from any of the covens come through?"

He tilted his head at the sky, thinking it over. The move was so birdlike, I had to smile. "Peewee says he saw one lady."

"Adept or Mundane?"

He shrugged. "Peewee didn't like her."

Thinking of the lady that had Morales worried, I said, "Did she by chance have a horn?"

Sweet Ray looked at me as if I were the birdbrain. "You sure you're not using, girl?"

"No horn, then?"

He leaned down to confer with the pigeon. "Peewee says no. She had brown skin."

"Asian? Latina? Black?" I paused. "Wait, can pigeons even see color?"

"Duh. Of course they can. Their eyesight is excellent." He flicked a feather off his hem. "And Peewee just said 'brown.' If he'd want you to know more, he would have told you."

I crossed my arms. "You know, if Peewee is just fucking with me, I'm not going to be happy."

He shrugged. "I'm just the medium here."

"You're also the guy who won't get paid."

He sighed. "Look, I don't know what you want from me. A lady came by two days ago to see the mayor. She didn't look like nothing special to me, but Peewee got all excited and told me to tell you about her."

"All right, all right," I said, "I got it. Anything else?"

"Yeah, actually, last night the mayor left about six o'clock like normal. But then he came back at like ten."

"Sweet Ray, do you really sit here that long every day? Where do you sleep?"

He nodded and rocked a little bit, as if my question made him uncomfortable. "I got a place nearby," he said defensively. "But I like to be here in case Peewee has to tell me something."

"Okay," I said. Judging from the deeper green hue of his skin, he managed to slip away to use, too. "What happened when the mayor came back at ten?"

"He had a man with him. Asian." He peeked from under his lashes at me. "And a pretty lady with red hair."

The lady was Volos's lawyer and girlfriend, Jade. But I was obviously curious to learn who the mysterious Asian dude might be. "Did you manage to hear them talking about anything when they went by?"

"The redhead was saying that she wanted them to meet somewhere else, but the non-mayor man said there was no time."

"Hmm," I said. "Did they mention his name or anything?"

He shook his head. "Peewee says he's tired now."

I pulled a twenty from my pocket and handed it to it. He slipped it under the turban.

"Listen, next time the mayor comes back late at night like that, you give me a call, okay?" Clearly, the reports after the fact weren't going to help me much. I'd need to see what was happening with my own eyes despite Sweet Ray's claims about the superiority of Peewee's vision.

"You said only call if something is strange," he said.

"Well, now I'm asking you to call if you see the mayor with anyone who looks Chinese or who you know works for the covens."

He sighed. "I don't know. This sounds a lot like of work."

"How do you figure?"

"If I want to call, I gotta go find a phone. They won't let me inside the building, so that means I gotta go three blocks to the bodega. Plus, I gotta find change."

"You don't have a phone?"

He shot me a very lucid bitch-please look. "You think I'd spend my days on this step talking to pigeons if I could afford a cell-a-phone?"

Thus far, my new CI was turning out to be a huge pain in the ass, but he was the perfect person to keep an eye on Volos for me without the mayor knowing he was being watched. "Tell you what. If you actually ever manage to bring me something useful, I'll buy you a burner phone."

His brows disappeared behind the turban. "No shit?"

"No shit."

He sat up straighter. "Girl, I'm gonna bring you the best shit. Just you wait."

"I can't wait," I said, trying to sound optimistic. "Take care of yourself, Sweet Ray. I'll look forward to that call."

With that, I left the man to brag to the pigeons that he'd have his very own "cell-a-phone" soon.

CHAPTER SIXTEEN

I rolled into the gym around ten a.m. I expected the workday to be in full swing, but when I walked in, I only found Shadi, Dixon and McGinty sitting in the boxing ring.

"Where is everyone?" I asked.

"Mez is in the john," Shadi said, "and Gardner's in her office. She wants a team meeting once she's off her call."

I frowned because no one told me we were having a meeting. "Morales checked in?"

"Just called him about the meeting. Why aren't y'all together?"

"I had an errand to run first thing. He on his way?"

She shrugged. "Left a message."

"Now that you're here," McGinty called, "maybe you can settle something for us."

"Settle what?"

"Dixon here has a theory. He says cops fall into two categories."

"Oh, yeah? Which ones?"

Dixon leaned forward in his chair. "Supermen and Batmen."

I just stared at him.

He shifted in his seat, warming up to having a bigger audience as Shadi climbed into the ring to listen as well. "On one hand, you got the Superman. He's a real hero, right? Plays by the rules. Got into the game because he wants to help people. Really good guy."

Shadi pressed her lips together and shook her head. I caught her eye and smirked. "And the other?" I said, egging him on.

"The Batman cop is a hero, too, but a reluctant one. He went into the business because he wants to make bad guys pay. He isn't afraid to dirty his hands to get the work done."

I rolled my eyes. "Let me guess—you're a Superman."

His face fell. "No, I'm a Batman."

Shadi laughed out loud. "Please. You're a Boy Scout, Dixon."

"I got darkness in me," he protested.

I met McGinty's eyes. He was grinning like he was enjoying fucking with the new guy. "Dixon was just educating me on which category each of us fell into based on his astute observations."

I climbed into the ring. "And?"

"Morales is a straight-up Batman."

He clearly loved the idea of being in the same column as Morales.

"Mez, too, although technically he's more like Alfred," he said. "Seeing how he makes all the cool toys for the team."

"I'm sure Mez would love to know you think of him as a stuffy old white guy," Shadi said.

"What about McGinty?" I tipped my chin toward the veteran cop.

"He used to be a Superman before the job made him all jaded."

McGinty just shook his head and took a pull from his coffee mug, which I'd bet cash money was ninety-proof.

"What do you think, Shadi?" I asked. "What are we?"

She shook her head. "I think that patriarchal bullshit don't apply to us."

"Huh?" This from Dixon.

"Listen, white boy, it might get you off to imagine that you're Batman, but girls like us? We didn't have superheroes to look up to when we was girls. We were given Barbies and told to pretend to be someone's mama."

I laughed out loud. "Speak for yourself. We couldn't afford Barbies, so I played Wiz and the Fuzz with the rest of the Cauldron boys."

"Are you saying you looked up to superheroes?"

"Nah," I said. "You're partly right. I knew even back then those weren't supposed to be role models for me."

"Who'd you look up to, then?" Dixon asked with breathtaking cluelessness.

I didn't bother to admit I looked up to my Uncle Abe. Instead, I searched my memory banks for some version of a female role model I could remember. Finally, I said, "Xena."

"The motherfucking Warrior Princess?" Shadi said, laughing. "Hell, yeah."

"Right? She kicked all sorts of ass."

"Got her some ass, too," Shadi said, waggling her eyebrows, "from that cute little blonde."

"Shut up," I said, "Xena and Gabrielle didn't have sex."

"Bitch, please." Shadi gave me a pitying look. "They totally scissored by the campfire at night."

"I don't remember any indication they were a couple."

"That's your hetero bias showing, girl. If you had been a little lesbian girl, you would have seen it all over that show."

"Well, either way," I said, "we can agree she was a badass."

Shadi high-fived me. "Amen, sister."

I looked over to see Dixon and McGinty furiously typing into their phones.

"What are you doing?" I asked.

"Checking to see where I can find this Xena show."

"When you do, let me know," McGinty said.

"Perverts," Shadi said without heat.

"Who's a pervert?" Mez asked, coming out of the locker room.

"These two," Shadi said, hooking her thumb at them.

"I knew I liked them," he said. "What's shaking, Prospero? Where's your partner?"

I opened my mouth to say I didn't know, but the sound of the door downstairs opening interrupted. I listened for a second. Once I heard the telltale strike of boots on wood, I said, "Speak of the devil."

A moment later, he appeared at the top of the steps. We hadn't spoken since the previous afternoon when he dropped me off at my car. I studied his face for signs of trouble or hope, but his poker face wasn't giving anything away. But he did search me out of the group with his eyes and nod. That was something I guess.

"Am I late for the party?" he said.

Gardner's door opened and she rushed out. "Good, you're all here. I want an update on the Valentine case. Morales, go."

She climbed into the ring like a fighter preparing for a bout. Morales followed more slowly, like a man who didn't expect to win this round.

"Evidence is pointing to a deal gone bad between the Votaries and the Fangshi," he said.

Gardner's expression brightened. "That's interesting."

Morales propped a boot on the lower rope of the ring. "A few separate sources fingered Krystal LeMay as Valentine's girlfriend. She's also reported to be the new head of the Votary coven."

"Two nights ago," I added, "Shadi and I witnessed a woman who works for Krystal handing a payoff to a suspected Fangshi operative."

"What's the motive for offing Valentine?" Gardner said.

"Mez?" I said.

The wizard came forward. He wore a lab coat over his embroidered vest and slacks. The gentleman-wizard look was rounded out by the pair of goggles perched on his dreadlocks. "We believe that the Chinese supplied the potion and Valentine was supposed to distribute it. But he got greedy and cut the potion with yohimbe, which doubled his supply and, thus, his take, but also made the batch extremely unstable and dangerous."

"That's where the Kostorov case comes in," I said. "We talked to the widow, who pointed us to an apothecary that was distributing the potion for Valentine. According to them, two days after Valentine died, Krystal showed up with some Chinese people and warned him to stop selling the bad potion."

"Fangshi Chinese?" she asked.

Morales said, "We believe so, yes."

"Anyone you know?" she said.

My stomach tightened in sympathy.

"No, sir." He kept his expression schooled and refused to look my direction. "Dixon tracked down a connection to a suspected Fangshi hitman named Alexander Hung, who works out of Seattle and California. We believe that, in addition to being in contact with Krystal, he might also have met with Charm Parsons prior to his death."

Gravity suddenly doubled. He made no mention of Yü Nü, who he knew very well. I knew he wanted to keep his past from catching up with him, but I didn't expect him to lie to Gardner's face.

Gardner jumped on the mention of Charm. "Explain the Charm connection."

"We met with Puck Simmons. He said that before Charm died, word came down from Abe that he wanted corner boys to start running Fangshi product. He said that he witnessed Charm meeting with a man who matched Hung's description as much as six weeks ago."

"You got anyone watching Hung now?" she looked around the room.

"Not yet, sir," Morales said. "That was our next step."

"Why don't you give a rundown on the Fangshi for the team?" she said.

He cleared his throat and appeared to be gathering his thoughts. I leaned back against the ropes and prayed he didn't dig us into a hole we'd not be able to climb out of.

"First thing to know is that the Fangshi aren't like the covens here."

"How so?" She folded her arms across her chest, putting her faith in his knowledge and experience.

"The covens here are basically street gangs, but the Fangshi are more organized. Almost corporate." He rose and went to the board where we'd pasted pictures of the suspects in the case. "My guess is Alexander Hung is probably like a middle manager. Someone else is pulling the strings from L.A. It's probably someone high up in one of the Tongs."

Shadi piped up. "What the fuck is a Tong?"

"Benevolent societies," he said. "Many are legit and offer protection and support for Chinese communities. But some are associated with the Fangshi. Those Tongs are wrapped up in murder for hire, prostitution, potion trafficking, gambling, you name it. Many infiltrate legit businesses to give them deep cover and money-laundering capabilities."

"Like dry cleaners?" Dixon asked.

"Yeah," Morales said, "a lot of the business owners who belong to the Tongs are law-abiding, but they don't have a choice in helping the Fangshi if they want the Tongs' protection.

"So, what the hell are they doing in Babylon?" Shadi asked. "There ain't many Chinese here."

Morales shrugged. "Potions are the most lucrative part of the Fangshi's interests, and if there's one thing Babylon has plenty of, it's hexheads."

Gardner walked up to the board. "All right, Shadi, your team is on Hung. I want to know where he's staying and who he's meeting." She turned to look at Morales and me. "You two I want on the girlfriend. Even if she didn't pull the trigger, if she's running the Votaries now, she's our main target. Bring her in. Today if possible."

Morales started to argue, but I interrupted him. "We're on it, sir."

That earned me a glare from my partner. We'd be having a

conversation once we left the gym, but I didn't care. The truth was, we did need to bring in Krystal. If she was the head of the Votaries, she was a prime catch, and her testimony might also bring us the Fangshi—especially if she was paying them off because they had something on her. Shadi and her team weren't going to find out about Morales's past by checking in on Alexander Hung, anyway.

Gardner turned toward Shadi to ask something, but a loud slam sounded from the door downstairs. It was quickly followed by sound of feet stomping up the risers. We all turned to see the new arrival. A few moments later, a pile of blond hair emerged over the top step followed by about two hundred and fifty pounds of curves encased in spandex and patent leather. She didn't walk so much as undulate, like she was screwing the air.

"Hey, y'all," she called as she stopped and stared at us expectantly, "is this the MEA office?" Sweet tea dripped from her words.

"Who's asking?" Gardner said.

The woman placed her hot-pink manicure against her bosom. "I'm Fontina Douglas, darlin'—who the hell are you?"

Morales and I exchanged a look as we both realized she was Aphrodite's cousin from Atlanta. The Hierophant had obviously been telling the truth about her cousin taking over the coven. The question was what was she doing at our office?

"I'm looking for Morales and Prospero," she said when no one answered her initial question.

"That's us," Morales said with about as much enthusiasm as a man facing an executioner.

"Lawd," she exclaimed, "my cousin didn't tell me what a tall drink of water you are, Mr. Morales." She batted her eyes at him. She clearly used one of those new potions that made a woman's lashes resemble tarantula legs.

"Special Agent," he corrected.

"Whatever you say, doll," she said. "I'm here to make a delivery."

"This should be good," Gardner said under her breath.

We climbed out of the ring to approach Fontina. She waved an envelope in the air. The heavy cardstock had a pearlescent finish, and spring-green ribbons trailed from the edge.

"It's an invite to Aphrodite's wedding," Fontina said. "I have one for every member of the team, but Aphrodite said I should personally hand this one to both of you. They also told me to say that they would take it as a personal insult if you decline."

Considering that the last time we'd seen Aphrodite, they'd kicked us out of their temple, this was quite a surprise. However, any reaction on our part would be reported right back to the Hierophant, so I downplayed my shock. "Thanks," I said. "It's an honor to have them hand-delivered by a Hierophant of the Atlanta O coven."

"Well, I'll be the Hierophant of the Babylon O's soon enough."

"Oh?" Morales said. "Aphrodite made it sound like they would still be active in the running of the coven once the wedding was done."

"Sure, that's what I mean." She smiled big, showing lots of pearly whites. "Anyway, I don't want to interrupt your important work." She glanced toward the boxing ring and the board we had on display. Gardner deliberately turned the panel so the case information was facing the other direction.

Fontina tittered. "Y'all have a nice day, now, y'hear?"

With that, she turned on her skyscraper heels and sashayed to the stairs. We all listened as she clip-clopped her way down the steps. Once the door downstairs opened and closed, I let out an audible breath.

"She's a peach," I said.

"I almost wish Aphrodite was staying in charge," Morales said.

"You two want to fill us in on who the hell that was?" Gardner demanded.

"Her name's Fontina Douglas. Up until recently, she ran a sex magic temple in Atlanta. She's Aphrodite's cousin and I guess she's taking over the day-to-day operation of the Temple of Cosmic Love once Aphrodite marries themself."

"Hold up—who's marrying who, now?" McGinty said.

We quickly gave the rundown. When we were done, Mez chimed in. "Ooh, that's going to be interesting. Any of you been to an alchemical wedding before?"

"Can't say I've had the pleasure," Morales said.

I shook my head. Shadi and the others didn't bother responding, since they didn't move much in magical circles.

"They're pretty rare," he said. "On account of you have to have a sacred hermaphrodite to pull one off."

"Wait," Morales said, "I thought this would be like a typical wedding with Aphrodite wearing half a tux and half a dress like Victor Victoria."

Mez shook his head, warming up to having the crowd's attention. "It's an alchemical wedding, not a Christian one. There's a period of ritualistic preparation to achieve spiritual mastery."

I nodded. "When we saw Aphrodite last, they were meditating and spouting a bunch of stuff about cleansing their karma and shit."

"Right," he said. "The wedding itself usually happens during a total solar eclipse." He took my invitation and looked at the date. "Which there happens to be on the date of Aphrodite's shindig. The ceremony itself will involve a lot of alchemical imagery and some ingesting of potions and stuff. Some people believe the hermaphrodite becomes immortal during the ceremony, but I think that's mainly symbolic. More likely they just attain some new level of enlighten-ment. Anyway, it'll be a gas."

"And knowing Aphrodite, there will be a lot of dramatic flair to boot," I added.

"Well, I don't know about you guys," Mez said, "but I'm totally going."

I exchanged a look with Morales. "I guess it's safe to say we'll be there too, considering Aphrodite basically had Fontina threaten us."

Gardner cleared her throat and shot a pointed look at her watch. "If you're all done with your wedding plans, we have a murder to solve and possibly two covens to take down for it."

Mez ducked his head. "Sorry, sir."

"Prospero, Morales. Head over and see if you can get a bead on Krystal. I want her in custody by end of the day."

From the corner of my eye, I saw Morales's jaw clench, but I put on a smile. "Yes, sir." To Shadi, I said, "Let us know if you find anything on Hung."

"10-4," she said.

"All right, team," Gardner said. "Let's roll. I want potions and money on the table and bad guys and gals behind bars ASA-fucking-P."

CHAPTER SEVENTEEN

T he ride to the massage parlor was tense, to say the least. It took a good six blocks before Morales even acknowledged me.

"'We're on it, sir,'" he said in a mocking tone. Clearly, he was still hot under the collar over me talking over him when he was about to ask Gardner if we could have Hung duty instead of Shadi.

I pursed my lips and turned my best Prospero glare on him. "Don't give me that shit. If it were up to you, we'd be on our way to antagonizing a man who has the power to destroy your career. At least this way, we're able to keep an eye on his movements without him knowing."

His jaw tightened dangerously—the way it always did when I was right and he didn't want to admit it. "It wasn't your call."

I laughed out loud at his offended tone. "You don't get to pull rank when it suits you, Macho. Unless you're willing to come clean with Gardner, then this has the potential of blowing back on both of us—that means I get a say in how this plays out."

He blew out a breath. "For the record, I really hate this case."

"I hate to be the one to say this, but"—I reached out and patted his arm—"I told you so."

He laughed out loud and shook his head at me. Once that subsided, he shot me an apologetic look. "Sorry."

"Don't sweat it," I said. "Lord knows we've had cases that haven't brought out my best, either."

He snorted. "No shit."

By that time, we'd turned onto the street near Krystal's place. We parked down the street and walked toward the entrance.

"Is it just me," Morales said, "or does business seem unusually slow for this time of day?"

The massage parlor's neon sign winked suggestively from the front window. But when I tried to open the door, it was locked tight. I knocked on the glass and put my cupped palms to the pane to look inside.

"Don't see any lights on," I said.

Morales rapped on the pane to see if he could summon someone from the back. We waited a few moments, but no one ducked out from the back hall.

I checked my watch. It wasn't even noon yet. "They should be open."

Morales pulled his cell phone out and dialed the parlor's phone number after reading it off the sign. After a few moments, he sighed and ended the call. "Voicemail. Let's go around back."

An alley behind the building gave us access to a gray metal door with the massage parlor's name painted across it.

"Should I knock?" I asked.

He shook his head and reached around me. A quick tug and the door was open.

I frowned up at him. "That's odd."

"Look alive." His expression took on deadly focus.

I pulled my salt flare from its holster. Morales pulled out his Glock and nodded. I opened the door wide enough for him to look inside. We paused to listen. When no sounds emerged, he ducked inside and I had his back.

The door closed behind me, blocking out the sunlight and leaving the space unnaturally dark even though it was just after lunchtime. It took a moment for my eyes to adjust to the darkened hallway to look for signs of a threat.

Even though I couldn't see well, I could certainly smell. The acidic stench of vomit hit my nose like a punch.

All of the treatment-room doors were closed and no light came from below. We made quick work of clearing those just in case before we headed toward the storeroom and office. That doorway was open and light spilled from it into the hall.

Signaling to each other, we took position to execute a safe entry into the room. If someone was in there, and armed, they could easily set up facing the doorway and take us out. He nodded to me to begin the process.

"Babylon Police," I called out. Since I was still a detective, I usually led with that because the MEA tended to make for itchy trigger fingers.

Morales grabbed a towel from a nearby table. He waved it across the doorway. When no shots rang out, he spun and fell into a crouch with his gun pointed into the room. "Clear," he said, moving out of the death funnel.

We walked around the shelving and froze.

Krystal's body lay in a puddle of yellow vomit. Blue light from the screens above her cast the body in a ghostly light.

"That explains the smell," I said.

Morales tiptoed over the mess to squat next to her to check the pulse. After a moment, he shook his head and rose.

I didn't see any signs of a struggle. But she had no wounds that we could see, and the broken teapot near the body had probably been knocked over when she fell.

We stepped out of the room so we wouldn't contaminate the crime scene.

"I'll call Gardner," he said. "You call Duffy."

I cursed under my breath. "We're never going to hear the end of this."

* * *

Two hours later, Duffy was still not talking to us. As he watched Franklin and the CSI crew work, he would occasionally look over and shake his head. Meanwhile, Gardner and Eldritch were across the room, having a heated discussion that we'd probably be hearing about soon.

I couldn't blame Duffy for being pissed, but I wasn't feeling so chipper myself.

Morales took a sip of weak coffee and winced. "Think they'd notice if we snuck off to a bar?"

"Don't tempt me."

Before he could deliver the retort on his smiling lips, a uniformed officer ducked into the hallway from the front room. The entrance to the massage joint had been opened up and the people milled around the waiting room as they processed the scene or worked some other angle of the case. I didn't recognize the uni, but he looked like he'd worked enough scenes to not be a problem. "Prospero?" he called, looking around.

I walked over. "Yeah?"

"The receptionist is here."

"Thanks." I waved Morales over. We'd sent a couple of patrolmen to the receptionist's house to bring her in for questioning. Even though it was technically a murder scene and fell under Duffy's purview, we were proceeding as if we were in charge until a victor was declared following Eldritch and Gardner's argument.

Out in the waiting room, the receptionist we'd seen the first time we'd come to the parlor waited by the front desk. She wore a pair of yoga pants and a hot pink T-shirt with the word SASSY airbrushed across her fake boobs.

"Ms. Harper?" I said, approaching her. "If you'll follow us?"

According to the records we found in the filing cabinet, Felicia Harper had worked for Krystal since the massage parlor opened. Her address was in a Mundane neighborhood where the ratio of liquor stores to schools was five to one. She had no priors, but based on the way she was working the wad of chewing gum in her mouth, I was prepared to arrest her for disturbing my peace.

The uni had set up a makeshift interview space in the first treatment room. It held a massage table covered in white paper and two straight-backed chairs. I motioned for her to take a seat up on the table. The paper crinkled as she climbed on.

"What is this all about?" she said. "I do not appreciate being pulled away from my stories without an explanation."

"Weren't you supposed to be working today?" I asked.

She nodded. "I came this morning, but the door was locked. I tried to call Krystal like five times, but she didn't answer." She smacked her gum like most people used punctuation.

"You didn't have a key?"

"Only Krystal has a key. The girl's got trust issues."

Considering she was dead in a puddle of vomit, I had trouble judging Krystal for that personality deficit. Besides, she had plenty of other ones to resent.

I also noted she used the present tense. She didn't strike me as smart enough to be a good-enough actress to pull off that sort of misdirection if she had been the killer.

"What'd you do when Krystal didn't answer?" Morales asked.

She shrugged. "I went home."

"It didn't occur to you that something might be wrong?"

"Not really." *Smack, smack, smack.* "This wasn't the first time she didn't show up to open the place. I left because I didn't want to have to deal with bitching from a bunch of horny guys who couldn't get their wieners yanked, you know?"

I looked down at my paper to cover my smile. Morales, much

better at maintaining his poker face than I, soldiered on. "Can anyone verify what time you got home?"

"My neighbor saw me come home. She was unloading some groceries from her car and I waved."

"And her name?"

She offered it.

"When was the last time you saw Krystal?" Morales asked.

She looked up as if thinking back and methodically chewed like a cow enjoying some cud. "Last night. She was in her office. She asked me to stay and clean the treatment rooms, but I told her I was off the clock."

"Did she argue with you?"

She shook her head. "Nah, she seemed distracted. Told me to go ahead and go. Said she'd lock up."

"What was distracting her?" I asked.

"She was opening a package."

"Any idea what was in it?"

"Like a teapot thingy."

My brows shot up. It had to have been the one I'd seen broken next to the body. "Did she say who it was from?"

"I asked her." Smack, smack. "She didn't answer. There was a card, though. I saw her tuck it in her bra."

Morales and I nodded, as if she'd said something of little consequence, but my blood pressure had just shot up. I pulled out my phone and texted to Franklin. *Someone sent the teapot last night. Check the vic's bra for a gift note.*

"You still haven't told me what happened. Were we robbed or something?" She looked around the room as if it might hold clues.

My phone dinged. *Bra, got it.*

I loved that Franklin didn't demand an explanation. He just got to work. Total pro, that guy.

I nodded at Morales to let him know Franklin was on it. He acknowledged it with a quick nod and turned to speak to Felicia.

"Krystal was found dead in her office. I'm sorry."

She stopped her smacking for one blessed moment. "Oh." And then it resumed.

"Oh?" I frowned at her. "That's all?"

"Well, whadaya want from me?" She snorted. "She didn't pay me enough for tears."

Morales glanced at me and shrugged.

"Do you know of anyone who might have held a grudge against Krystal?"

"Oh, shit, lady." She cackled. "How much time you got?"

"Detective," I muttered.

Morales placed a hand on my shoulder. "Does anyone in particular come to mind? Have you witnessed any recent altercations with anyone?"

She studied her fingernails for a moment. "I dunno. I mean, a couple of days ago, that Chinaman came in and was hollering about his payment."

"What was his name?" I asked even though I knew who it was.

"Fuck if I know. He didn't exactly make small talk, ya know?" She waved her hand and smacked her gum. "All's I know is he comes by once a week to pick up money. He's a real asshole. Acting all high and mighty when I don't have the package ready the second he comes in the door."

She smacked the gum philosophically for a moment before continuing. "Anyway, he came in a couple of days ago. I ran out to grab some food, so Krystal was working the desk. When I got back, she and this guy were facing off in the lobby. He was shouting or whatever."

"What did he say?" I asked.

She shrugged.

"What did Krystal do?"

"She said that she'd bring him the package the next day. Something about her boss being behind or something."

"Her boss?"

"That's what she said."

"Did she mention a name?"

"Nope. Just 'my boss'—Krystal was a bitch but she wasn't dumb, you know?" She paused. "Except I guess she wasn't so smart if she got herself offed, right?"

I withheld my opinion on the matter. "Did you see the man after that?"

"Nah. I assumed she delivered the package as promised. And she never said anything to me about it after that. Like nothing happened."

After that, we wrapped up the interview after asking her to stay available in case we had any more questions. We were rising to show her out when a knock sounded on the door and Mez stuck his head in. "Got a sec?"

We handed Felicia off to a uni in the hallway, who led her back to the lobby. "What's up?" I asked Mez.

"Gardner wants to see you guys outside."

I frowned. "Does that mean Duffy's taking over?"

He shook his head. "Eldritch wants us to continue to take point, but we have to keep Duffy updated on the regular. Shadi and McGinty are doing door-to-doors, and Dixon's reviewing the CCTV footage." He laughed. "Poor bastard."

Remembering what Krystal had filmed on those cameras, I winced on Dixon's behalf. "We'll definitely owe him lots of beers for that."

"Franklin's about to wrap up. He found the note in Krystal's bra like you suggested." He held up a baggie with the card inside. It was rectangular and blue, and someone had typed,

To Good Fortune and a Long Life

-A

"I'm taking that with me to run prints," Mez said. "Also found the gift box and a tea tin. I'll let you know what I find once I run all the labs."

"Who you think this A is? And why did they kill her?" Morales asked.

"Asshole in the massage parlor with the poisoned tea?" he deadpanned. "Once I run the tests, I'll be able to track down what kind of poison was used. The why is your job."

After that, Mez ran off, leaving us to go look for Gardner outside. I didn't have to ask why she preferred not to talk inside the parlor. Who knew where else Krystal's cameras were broadcasting?

We found Gardner out in the alley on her cell phone. As we approached, she ended the call. "That was the commissioner. Apparently, Mayor Volos is threatening to pull the plug on the whole coven investigation and give the murder cases back to Duffy."

"Mez said Eldritch agreed to letting us continue," Morales said.

"He did. Last thing he wants is another murder added to his stats. But apparently, Volos isn't too keen on letting the MEA get the win on this one now that it's looking like a bigger case. Luckily, the commissioner held him off, but we don't have long to get this wrapped up."

I blew out a breath and looked up at the sky. The sun was going down, and the moon was starting to rise over the Steel River. Only a couple days until the full moon. Since there'd be an eclipse to go with it, the power would be amplified, and that always causes problems in a town filled with beings capable of wielding magic. "Did Shadi and those guys find anything on Hung?"

"They didn't have a chance to get too far before I pulled them off to come help out here," she said. "But McGinty traced his name to a deed for a Chinese restaurant."

"The Jade Moon?" I asked. "That's where he went when Shadi and I followed him the other night."

"He's one of the investors," she said. "Otherwise, Shadi got a tip that Hung's staying in one of Volos's properties while he's getting Waidan up and running in town."

"Probably the Phoenix," I said.

"Start with the restaurant. The longer we can put off being on Volos's radar with this, the better."

Morales cocked a brow at me. "You hungry?"

"I could go for some cashew chicken, yeah."

"All right," Gardner said in her enough-of-the-funny-business voice, "you two watch your asses. Corpses are piling up, and if Hung is responsible, he's also got the mayor's ear."

We sobered up. "Yes, sir," we said in unison.

"Don't hesitate to call in the cavalry if shit starts going pear-shaped."

"Got it."

"And, Prospero?" she said.

"Yeah?"

"You might also be interested to know that your uncle is part owner of Jade Moon too."

"I'll be damned," I said.

"Looks like we need to make a trip out to Crowley soon," Morales said.

"Oh, joy. Something else to look forward to. Come on, let's go."

CHAPTER EIGHTEEN

The Jade Moon was only a couple of blocks away. That meant it sat squarely in Votary territory, which was interesting, all things considered.

"I wonder when this place opened," I mused aloud.

We drove over and parked a few doors down. Morales checked his cell while I watched the front entrance. "According to the notes Dixon just emailed me, February."

"Interesting. Two months ago. That means Abe was setting up a Fangshi partnership a lot earlier than we thought."

"How you want to play this?" he said, nodding toward the restaurant.

"Well, we don't know if he's there, so busting in with guns probably isn't a great idea."

"How about we play it casual? Couple on a date or whatever?"

I cocked a brow at him. "I love how you wait until we're on the trail of a murderer to ask me on a date."

"You want poetry?" he said. "Fine. Roses are red, corpses are blue…"

I held up a hand to prevent another horrifying stanza. "You're not right, son. But since this a work date, you're paying."

He grinned. "If it's a work date, then Gardner's paying."

"It's a date, then."

We exited the car and walked arm-in-arm down the road. Since we were only pretending to be on a date, we'd automatically relaxed some of our no-affection-on-the-job rules. Even though I'd given him hell about it, the date idea was pretty solid. Flashing badges in a place like this would mean an automatic circling of wagons in the Fangshi. Us pretending to be grabbing a romantic dinner would buy us some leeway to case the joint before we decided on the best move.

He steered me toward the entrance. The door was tucked under a pagoda-shaped overhang. Wind chimes hung on either side of the doorway, and when we walked in, an invisible gong sounded.

"Nice," I said.

The interior of the restaurant seemed awfully nice for the Cauldron. Considering we were only a couple of blocks from the massage parlor, it felt weird to see a sit-down place instead of a drive-thru.

"Only the best." He winked as he showed me toward the host. I noticed that his demeanor had softened from his normal workaday gruffness. Of course, once upon a time, Morales had worked undercover in Los Angeles, which meant he could be a good actor when he wanted to be. Now, apparently, was one of those times, as he pretended to be a man trying to woo a lady.

It was a disorienting feeling. Since we'd never actually been on a date, it was fascinating to get a glimpse at his date behavior without actually being on one with him.

"Welcome to Jade Moon," said the host. He was Chinese and wore a white coat with a Mandarin collar and black pants. "Table for two? Right this way."

As we made our way through the restaurant, I noted a few important details. First, it was almost six o'clock, well into the dinner rush, but only two other tables were occupied. One booth in the far corner had another couple in it, and a table near the kitchen held four men in business suits, having what looked like a meeting. None of them were Alexander Hung, though.

The other thing I noticed was that even though the entrance was pretty nice, the dining room itself had vinyl tablecloths and the general air of a place pretending to be nicer than it actually was. Once we were seated, a waitress rushed up and instructed us that we were there for happy hour, and that when we were ready, we could just help ourselves to the buffet in the other room. Morales ordered us a couple of Tsingtaos.

Once she went to go get the beers, he leaned on the edge of the table. "So, now what, Nancy Drew?"

I smiled at him from under my lashes. "The businessmen are all packing." I'd seen the outline of their shoulder holsters through their suit coats.

He reached across the table and took my hand. "There are four cameras set up around the dining room."

"I noticed another two on the way in." I winked at him.

The waitress dropped off the beers. Once she was gone again, he continued.

"What do you say we go hit the buffet and see what we see?"

"Not yet. I want to go powder my nose first and see if there are any secret rooms in the back."

"Take your phone."

"Be sure to watch my ass as I walk away to make it convincing."

"I was planning on it." He lifted his beer to his lips. Before he took a swig, he said, "Hit the panic button if something goes south."

The button he was referring to could be found on the protective amulet we all wore when we were on the job. Mez had made them, and they'd saved my ass more than once. The circular amulet had a bubble of glass filled with a green liquid. All I had to do was break the glass and it would alert the rest of the team of my GPS coordinates.

"You got it," I said. "Grab me an eggroll."

As I walked to the back, I was very aware of my rear end, which I might have swayed bit more than usual. I also made sure to take note of all the exits and that the couple in the booth were having a humdinger of a whispered argument.

Past the kitchen doors, there was a hallway that held extra high chairs, two restroom doors, and a set of swinging double doors. Since I had the hallway to myself and I didn't see any camera there to witness my snooping, I went for the double doors. I pushed one in a couple of inches and peeked inside.

Rows of metal shelves hinted that the space was used as a storeroom. But remembering that Hung had come in through a rear entrance to the restaurant, I wondered if there was more back there. Naturally, instead of wasting the opportunity by doing something smart like going to get my partner, I went through the doors on my own.

The room had the musty-sweet smell of uncooked rice, which made sense, given the dozens of large bags lined up on some of the shelves. There were also thick metal doors leading to what I assumed were walk-in freezers.

I passed the shelves, careful to listen for voices and look for cameras. I walked down a row formed by two shelving units. As I neared the end, voices reached me. They were speaking in Chinese, so I had no idea what the words were, but based on the volume and velocity of the words, the man and woman were arguing. I peeked between the shelves to see them each wearing the uniforms of waitstaff.

I stopped to listen in case they suddenly decided to switch to English. Unfortunately, they selfishly continued to argue in their mother tongue. Plus, I'd been gone too long for a normal potty break. I backed down the aisle again and went to the other end of the storage room. There, I found a metal door that had some high-tech security keeping it on lockdown.

It was only when I turned around to go that I saw the camera pointing at that door, and the damning red light that blinked to indicate I was being filmed.

With my heart thumping, I scurried out the double doors and back down the hall. I ducked into the bathroom, smeared on some lip balm —the closest thing I had to makeup—and went back out. It wasn't easy to act natural when you'd just been caught snooping, but I gave it the old college try. I slowed my steps to a normal pace and tried to look like a woman who was headed back from the john.

However, the instant I sat back down, Morales said, "What did you do?"

I made a show of pulling a pair of chopsticks from their paper. "Nothing, why?"

"You're a terrible liar."

I sighed. "A camera caught me snooping in the storeroom."

"We should go." He started to rise, but I grabbed his arm.

"Not yet. For all they know, I wandered back there by mistake. We need to find Hung, and my gut's telling me he's here. There's a door back there with enough security on it, it practically screamed 'villain's lair.'"

He looked about as thrilled by that plan as he would have if I'd suggested we get his-and-hers colonics. "Did you know I never had high blood pressure before I met you?"

I smiled. "It'll be fine. Come on—I'm starving."

As we passed through he archway to the buffet room, I whispered, "By the way, there's a back exit to this place, so if something happens, run like hell."

He nodded. "Also, the bartender's armed."

"Good to know."

"And while you were gone, the couple in the booth broke up and the woman is now getting loaded at the bar."

I looked back across the restaurant to where the bar was located, and sure enough, the blonde was slumped on a stool while she attacked a cosmo and told her sad tale to a thin, stoic Chinese man behind the bar. He looked like he was trying to figure out whether he should shoot her or himself just to end it.

I piled some cashew chicken on my plate. "This is fun, right?"

Morales focused on scooping some rice on his plate, but his brows rose in a contrary manner. "Your idea of fun worries me."

"I mean the date part. Maybe we should try it for real some time."

He set down the rice spoon and turned to me. "Yeah? You'd be into that?"

I frowned at him. "Why wouldn't I be?"

He shrugged and busied himself piling more food on his plate. "You just seemed like you wanted to keep everything casual."

"I said a date, not a wedding."

He snorted. "Understood."

Behind us, a door opened and a kitchen worker came out to refill one of the food trays.

"Does it seem odd to you that they have so much food coming out when there are so few customers?" I asked.

"Maybe they have a late dinner rush." I piled some beef and broccoli on my plate and tried to move down the line, but I ran into Morales's back. I went up on my tiptoes to see what the problem was and spotted a man in a black suit barring our way.

The man dipped his chin in a mockery of a bow. "Detective Prospero. Special Agent. Please come with me." There was no question in his words, no request. He was clearly sent to deliver a command. "She's waiting for you in the kitchen."

Morales and I exchanged a look. There was no time to debate. The smart side of my brain—the one that kept me alive all those years—wanted to cut our losses and run. But the other side of me—the cop side that wanted to solve the case by any means necessary—was in charge. She told my smart side to pipe down and pay attention.

"Lead the way," I said.

As I expected, he made his way toward the ornate door on the side of the restaurant farthest from the buffet. I tried not to imagine a gang of martial arts experts waiting to ambush us on the other side.

"Guess this answers the question of whether anyone was watching the camera's feed," Morales observed.

The man walked in front of us, seeming unconcerned that we might run. I glanced behind me and finally understood the reason— the four businessmen from the other table with suspicious bulges under their jackets had situated themselves in front of each of the restaurant's exits.

I got Morales's attention and jerked my head toward the closest guard. His expression grew even grimmer.

I should have felt comforted that they hadn't requested that we surrender our weapons, but we were so outgunned, it didn't matter. I reached up to break my amulet, but Morales grabbed my arm.

"Bad idea," he whispered.

"Why?"

"It'll only anger her."

I wanted to ask who *her* was, but I had a bad feeling I already knew.

"Whatever you do," he continued in a low tone, "don't stare directly at the horn."

I'd expected our host to lead us into a private dining room. Instead, he took us back down that dark hallway and through a pair of swinging doors that led into the massive kitchen. After the empty dining room's calm, this place was a riot of noise and movement. Even the air was chaotic with the warring scents of hot oil, sizzling meat, and the delicious aroma of sautéed ginger and garlic. But instead of making my mouth water, the scene we walked into made my tongue go dry.

Four women in matching embroidered tunics made of green silk and black pants stood in a line. Their hands were folded in front of them, and no weapons I could see. However, I got the definite sense that they'd be able to kick both our asses easily if we made a wrong move.

They parted like a green tide to reveal the petite figure of a woman who looked like someone's grandmother. She stood behind a butcher block that was shiny from age and stained from use. She wore a simple black tunic and wide-legged pants. She wore no makeup and her hair was pulled back into a bun. No frills, no fuss.

Of course, she didn't really need to accessorize with the horn jutting from her forehead like a crooked jade finger.

Remembering Morales's warning, I tried really hard not to stare at it, but even for the Cauldron, a woman with a horn was pretty bizarre.

"Do you have a warrant, Special Agent Morales?" Her voice was deeper and more resonant than I expected. She also clearly had not forgotten Morales. That didn't seem like a good development.

"I don't know what you mean," he said. "We're just on a date."

"A date. Of course." She smiled but the emotion didn't reach her eyes. "In that case, you have to try our house specialty." She nodded to one of her handmaidens, who removed a roasted duck carcass from the row of hooks over the counter.

"You ever have Peking duck, Detective Prospero?"

"You have me at a loss," I said. "You know who I am, but I haven't had the pleasure."

She bowed over the duck. "They call me Yü Nü."

I tipped my chin. Not a bow, but not a rejection of respect, either. I had a feeling she took that sort of thing pretty seriously. "You know what? Thanks for the offer." I placed a hand over my belly. "But I'm really not hungry. We were just about to leave, in fact."

"First you lie to me, and now you reject my hospitality." She shook her head, making the light spark off the tip of her jade horn. "A less generous person might be insulted."

Since Morales was the one with experience with this crew, I decided to keep quiet. He held up his hands. "We meant no disrespect. By all means, we would love to try your duck."

She nodded briefly and ran a small hand over the crisp skin of the duck's carcass. "Peking duck is a delicacy where I come from."

"Hell?" I guessed.

She ignored my joke. "Beijing. Luckily, my people brought the recipe with us when we moved to Los Angeles. You ever try it when you were there, Special Agent Morales?"

His jaw twitched. "You made it for me on several occasions and you know it."

Yü Nü pulled a cleaver out from under the butcher block. My hand automatically went to my sidearm. She paused and gave me a disappointed look.

"Relax, Detective. It's for the duck."

To punctuate her point, she brought the blade down in the center of the duck's back. The butcher knife chopped through the crispy skin easily. I wasn't sure whether I should feel worried or hungry, but I was both.

"I knew a man looked like you," she said in a conversational tone, "but he called himself by another name. What was it?"

"Tommy Swan." Morales bit off the name like a curse, only it sounded like he was damning himself instead of her.

She looked at me. "Did you know your partner used to go by an alias?"

I didn't move or answer.

She lifted the cleaver again. "Tommy Swan disappeared right after my cousin got arrested."

Morales crossed his arms. "He sold dangerous potions to minors." He looked at me. "Sold at illegal raves. Last count, about twenty kids OD'd on his shit before we tracked him down at the supplier."

"Ouch," I said.

"Did Tommy ever tell you about the night that cop died? Sure didn't seem like the law then."

Morales had never mentioned that he'd actually been there the night that cop had been murdered. He'd only told me he helped cover up the murder in an effort to continue his part of the investigation. I shot him a sideways glance. He refused to look at me.

"I'll take that as a no," Yü Nü said with a smirk. "Anyway, I know why you are here." With a single, decisive whack of her left hand, she lopped the duck's neck clean from its body. "You harassing us because we're immigrants."

Morales tilted his chin to a don't-bullshit-a-bullshitter angle. "Give me a break, lady. We're Arcane agents, not INS."

"Arcane, huh?" The cleaver came down on the torso again, cleanly cutting it in two. The carcass split open to reveal the glistening meat. "We simple restaurant folk."

When we'd come in, she'd barely had an accent, but now she was talking like a caricature of a Chinese immigrant.

"Simple, sure," I said. "Why would simple folk be in business with Abe Prospero?"

"Who he?"

"He's the head of the Votary coven," Morales said. "Just like you're the head of the Fangshi."

She tilted her head back and cackled. "You crazy. Yü Nü is simple cook. No Fangshi here."

"Most cooks don't have a private security team." Morales tilted his head at the women standing in a semicircle behind Yü Nü.

She hacked off a wing. "Babylon is dangerous. Never know who gonna stab you in the back." She sliced a chunk of meat from the duck's breast. Juice and fat oozed from the roasted meat.

My shoulder blades tingled. I glanced over my shoulder. To my relief, no one was sneaking up behind me.

Morales took a step forward. The Handmaidens tensed, their hands going to their voluminous sleeves, where Lord only knew what kind of weapons were waiting to be employed.

Morales held up his hands. "Easy, ladies." To Yü Nü he said, "Look, we all know how this is going to go down from here. Once you let us go, the first thing we're going to do is call a judge to get a warrant. I figure we already got you on threatening federal officers, unregistered firearms, and a few hygiene violations, not to mention I haven't eaten since breakfast and I tend to get pretty angry if I don't eat."

"It's true," I said. "He's a bear when he's hungry." I shuddered theatrically. "Which means I'll have to spend some time trying to get him to calm down and not try to get your restaurant shut down altogether."

The cleaver came down on the duck's other breast, lopping the entire thing off. "No one has threatened you and you're free to go whenever you'd like. You came to me, remember?"

I noticed she'd dropped the fake immigrant accent now that we were getting down to the real business.

"As for the firearms," she continued, "my Handmaidens are merely mentees of mine, and the armed guards outside work for the Benevolent Society of the Thousand Suns."

Beside me, I heard Morales curse under his breath. I shot him a look but only received a quick headshake in return.

"As for closing down this restaurant, you are more than welcome to try." She slammed the cleaver down on a wing, severing it from the torso, to punctuate her words. "I should warn you, though, that Mayor Volos loves our duck."

I started laughing before she finished talking. Beside me, Morales cracked a smile. I slapped my knee and wiped my eyes. "Woo, thanks for that!"

Yü Nü's scowl scored deep grooves on either side of her down-turned mouth. "What's so funny?" she demanded.

I cleared my throat and got ahold of myself. "'I'm close personal friends with Mayor Volos,'" I mimicked. "Lady, you have no idea how little that scares me. In fact, it sorts of makes me want to try that much harder to bring you down."

"Kate," Morales said in a warning tone.

She clearly wasn't keeping up, which was fine with me. Instead of continuing the back-and-forth over our errant mayor, she changed tacks. "You can stomp around in your boots and issue threats all you want, but you're just a little girl playing a dangerous game." Her hands glistening with fat, she began scooping the bits of skin and meat into a takeout container. She moved with an economy that hinted at years of experience butchering roasted meat in busy kitchens. "He said you'd be trouble."

The bait she'd tossed was hard to resist, but I managed not to ask for a name. "Damn straight."

She took my cockiness in stride. "Little girl, I been around too long to trust the word of any wizard. Especially ones that carry a badge."

"You don't look so tough," I said.

Morales cursed under his breath.

Yü Nü held my gaze and lifted the cleaver into the air with her left hand. She placed her right hand flat on the chopping block, fingers spread. "You daring me, girlie?"

"Um, no?"

Her eyes glowed with disturbing zeal. Without looking down, she swung the blade. The unforgiving edge hacked right through her thumb.

Bile rushed up the back of my throat, but I forced myself not to close my eyes.

Yü Nü didn't cringe or cry. She smiled.

The chopping block was splattered with blood. She didn't move her hand. Watching her, I wondered what she was trying to accomplish by cutting off her damned thumb.

It didn't take long to get my answer. The green horn began to glow, as if lit from inside. Yü Nü finally closed her eyes and the light spread until she was bathed in it.

The thumb on the chopping block began to vibrate. I blinked, wondering if it was a trick of the light. But when I reopened my eyes, sure enough, the thumb was moving toward the hand.

The light intensified once the thumb touched the wound. I stepped forward for a closer look. The skin where the thumb had been severed bubbled and hissed. It was almost as if the horn's light was cooking the thumb back in place.

Once the smoke cleared and the light receded, Yü Nü lifted her hand. One of her maidens came forward with a basin. She dipped the hand in, carefully washing off the gore. When Yü Nü lifted it out of the water, the skin was unblemished.

Yü Nü clenched her hand into a fist and then wiggled the thumb to demonstrated that it was uninjured.

I swallowed hard. Morales had said she was rumored to be immortal, but I hadn't believed him. Wizards, especially ones who worked in alchemy, were always claiming to have found the elixir. But I'd never actually met one.

Despite the kitchen's heat, I suddenly felt chilled to the bone.

"You want to try?" Yü Nü said tauntingly.

I put my hands behind my back. "I'll pass."

She cackled.

"All right," Morales said. "Where's Alexander Hung?"

She scraped the edge of her blade over the cutting board's bloody surface. "Who?"

"Part owner of this restaurant."

She licked the fingers of her left hand. "Don't know investors. Just cook."

"Bullshit," I said.

She raised her greasy hands and looked around, wide-eyed. "Do you see him?"

"I saw him come here the other night," I said.

"Maybe he picked up some egg rolls," she said without missing a beat.

"All right," Morales said to me. "It's time to go."

I nodded and started to turn away.

"Take this with you," Yü Nü's voice rang out. "The least I can do for interrupting your dinner." She held out a white plastic bag with a large yellow smiley face on the front. "I threw in some fortune cookies, too."

When we hesitated, she sighed and came from around the back of the counter. She shoved the bag into Morales's hand but held on, forcing him to look at her. "You listen," she said in an undertone, "Coming after Yü Nü is a waste of your time. I didn't kill anyone."

He pulled back. "Oddly, I don't feel inclined to take your word for it." He handed the bag back to her. "And I've lost my appetite. Let's go, Kate."

He turned to walk out. Instead of following immediately, I snatched the bag out of Yü Nü's hands. "I haven't lost my appetite." And then I turned on my heel and marched past the armed men.

"Detective Prospero?" she called.

I turned and raise a brow.

"He's going down soon. You want to sink with him?"

I laughed. "For what?" I held up the duck. "All I did was pick up dinner. You're the one putting on the display here."

"The Fangshi have resources you can't begin to imagine. We'll find something that will stick."

"Not if we do first."

She raised her chin and the light caught the jade horn, making it spark milky green. "You don't want to start a war with Yü Nü, little girl."

I snorted. "No, lady, you don't want to start a war with a Prospero."

CHAPTER NINETEEN

T he last thing we wanted to do after leaving Jade Moon was go back to Gardner and let her know we didn't have Alexander Hung. I was pretty sure telling her we managed to get ourselves on the shitlist of a Chinese sorceress was also not news that would excite her.

Also? Morales hadn't spoken to me since we left the restaurant.

"Do you think Yü Nü put the hit out on Krystal?" I said, as he pulled the SUV from the curb.

He stared out the windshield as if I hadn't spoken.

"Hello?"

"What?"

"Earth to Morales, it's me—your partner." I leaned forward and waved my arms. "Don't shut down on me now, okay?"

He finally looked over. "We just kicked a hornet's nest in there."

"All the more reason to find Hung and bring him in for questioning."

He shook himself, getting back in the game. "Let's head over to the apartment building. See if we can rustle him up."

Ten minutes later, we pulled up in front of the Phoenix, a luxury apartment building on the Steel River. The project had been built by

Volos's real estate development company as part of their larger project to revitalize the Cauldron. Volos lived on the fourth floor, which, according to Shadi's notes that Gardner texted me, was the same floor where Hung was staying.

"Hold on," I said. "Hung is staying in the apartment where Mayor Owens used to live."

Mayor Skip Owens had run Babylon until a psycho who thought he was the second coming of Dionysus killed him and tried to frame Aphrodite for the crime. He had lived in one of the penthouses in the building and Volos had the other, but now I guessed Volos owned both. Typical.

"Looks like," Morales said. "I hope they at least put a new bed in there."

Owens had been poisoned and his body had been found wearing a gimp mask and arranged like the Hanged Man from the tarot.

"Odd that Volos is keeping Hung so close," I said.

"Is it really?" he said, getting out of the car. I jumped out to, and when we met up again on the sidewalk, he said, "It's looking more and more like the Chinese are making lots of interesting alliances in town."

We headed toward the art deco doors. "What I'm curious about is whether Volos and Abe know about each other. Seems like the Chinese would want to keep each of their side pieces unaware of each other."

Inside the lobby, there was a security guard dressed in a slick navy suit. He had jet black hair and a scowl as imposing as the Great Wall. Oh, yeah, and he was of Asian descent.

Surprise, surprise.

"Who are you here to see?" he demanded. Guess they didn't teach public relations at scary security guard school.

I was pretty sure that the second we told him we were looking for Alexander Hung, he'd push a button on a console to alert our quarry to scurry out the building's back exit. "Mayor Volos," I said.

Morales didn't turn to look at me, but he did nudge my ankle with his toe—a subtle *What the fuck?* signal.

"He expecting you?"

I shook my head. "No, but he'll see us. Tell him Kate's in the lobby. We're old friends."

The guard didn't look convinced but he did pick up the black phone from the console. He turned away as he spoke quietly. After a couple of moments, he looked back at us over his shoulder and said into the mouthpiece, "I understand, sir."

My stomach dropped. Had my visit to the mayor's office ruined any pull I had over Volos?

The guard hung up the phone. "He says he wasn't expecting you."

I licked my lips nervously and opened my mouth to try to BS my way out of this, but the guard wasn't done.

His face cleared. "But he said you can head on up."

Shock held me motionless for a second, but then Morales tugged on my sleeve. Next thing I knew, we were alone in the elevator, on our way up to the fourth floor.

I could practically feel Morales holding back on a lecture he didn't dare deliver. Volos had every inch of the public spaces in that building under surveillance. There was no doubt he was watching and listening to us.

"Nice night," I said.

"Uh-huh." Morales crossed his arms.

Fine, so he wasn't happy. I could handle that. If we could have talked, I would have told him that I made the play because I knew the guard wouldn't let us up there if we mentioned Hung's name. This way, we could get to the fourth floor, no problem. We just had to figure out how to shake Volos and get over to Hung's place.

The elevator dinged and the doors opened. I'd sort of been hoping we could just sidle out and head to Hung's place. However, Volos waited for us in the open doorway of his apartment.

"Kate, Morales—what a nice surprise!"

"Shit," I said.

"Lucy, you've got some 'splainin' to do when this is all done," Morales said under his breath.

"Just follow my lead," I said under my breath.

Before he could point out we were in that situation because I'd taken the lead, I raised a hand to wave. "Hey, Mr. Mayor."

Volos's posture changed from a *gotcha* stance to that of an animal who smells an ambush. "What brings you here?"

We exited the elevator. "Actually, the guard misunderstood," I said. "We were on our way to meet your new neighbor."

He crossed his arms and leaned against the door jamb. "Is that right?"

"You didn't mention Alexander Hung was living in your building when I saw him at your office the other day."

"Did think it was any of your business, Detective."

The switch in address was meaningful. When he thought he had the upper hand, he called me "Kate" or "Katie." When he thought I had something on him, it was always "Detective."

"Anyway, we'll just show ourselves over." I turned toward the door on the opposite end. Halfway there, I realized two things. First, Morales wasn't behind me. Second, Volos wasn't trying to stop me.

I turned to see them both watching me with their arms crossed and near-identical expressions of masculine annoyance on their faces.

"What?" I demanded, feeling pretty annoyed myself.

"He left this morning." Volos pushed off from the jamb. "Anyone else need a drink?"

"I thought you'd never ask," Morales said, and followed him inside.

I stood alone in the hall for a second, wondering what just happened. Volos and Morales never agreed on anything. Why in the hell did they have to pick being pissed off at me as their first time?

I heaved a martyred sigh and marched into the apartment. Inside,

Volos was at the bar, pouring three drinks, and Morales stood at the windows, looking out over the darkened water.

"What do you mean, *he left this morning*?" I demanded.

"What isn't clear about that statement?" Volos shrugged and offered me a glass with two fingers of something amber-colored.

"He's a suspect in a murder investigation, John. Don't fuck with us here."

He lifted his glass in a toast. "Hung didn't kill Krystal LeMay."

I slammed the glass on the coffee table in his sunken living room. "How do you know?"

He swirled his drink and took a lingering sip before answering. "No motive."

I pursed my lips and pinned him with my best cop glare. "You stick to running the city and let us worry about motives, all right? Where is he?"

"I'm not his keeper, Kate. He was in town to meet about moving his company here. I offered him a place to stay while he was in town. I assume he left because he had business to tend to on the West Coast."

"He left town?" My raised voice echoed in the cavernous penthouse.

"He vacated the apartment. I don't know if he left town or not."

"What's his guard still doing here, then?" I demanded.

He quirked a brow. "Mike works for me. And I believe his family came over from the Philippines."

"Sure."

He tilted his head. "Do you think every Asian in Babylon is Chinese or just that all Asians are Fangshi?"

I shifted uncomfortably. Obviously, I didn't like the idea of being called on biases, but it was also likely Volos was using this to throw me off. "I just assume anyone who associates with you is crooked. How about that?"

Before he could retort, I pulled out my phone and called Dixon.

"Hey, I need you to contact the airport and see if Alexander Hung was on a flight headed somewhere on the West Coast today."

"Gee, Kate, I'm sort of up to my eyeballs in hand-job videos here."

"Then ask McGinty to do it." I punched the button to end the call. When I looked up, I realized Morales still hadn't moved from his spot by the windows. His untouched drink rested in his right hand. "Hey!"

He turned slowly. "What?"

I threw up my hands. "Murder investigation? Remember?"

He shrugged. "The guy's not here." He drained his drink in two long gulps. He walked across the room and handed the glass back to Volos. "Thanks, man." Then he turned and walked to the door. "I'll be in the car."

I watched him go with my mouth hanging open. I suddenly felt like I'd entered the Twilight Zone, only instead of a gremlin on the airplane wings, I was witnessing my partner losing his damned mind. "Well, that's just great," I muttered.

"Trouble in paradise?" Volos said, smirking over the rim of his glass.

"Will you shut up?"

He looked pleased with himself but was smart enough not to say anything else on the matter.

"I was telling the truth, you know. Hung's innocent."

I shot him an ironic glare.

"Of this crime," he amended.

"Why do you know so much about it?"

He watched me for a moment, as if weighing his options. My patience was thin, so I raised my brows and shot him an any-day-now look. Finally, he sighed. "When did Krystal die?"

"We don't have the final report yet, but I'm guessing it happened last night."

He ran a finger along the glass's rim. "I was with Hung and one of his associates until one a.m."

"Which associate?"

"A woman."

"Cut the shit, John. Was it the chick with the horn?"

He paused. "You know her?"

"I just watched her butcher a duck," I said, "and cut off her own thumb."

He scowled. "Stay away from her."

"You know, you have a really bad habit of believing you have a say in my decisions. We interviewed her as part of an official murder investigation."

"And I'm telling you, she and Hung both have alibis for last night."

I didn't mention to him that whoever killed Krystal wasn't there last night when she died. They could have sent that package over at any time. But he didn't have the right to know every detail of my cases. "You willing to testify to that effect in court?"

He laughed softly and emptied his glass. "Don't be ridiculous."

"I thought so," I said. "I don't know what you have going with the Chinese, but you saying you were with them doesn't exactly exonerate anyone. For all I know, all three of you killed her."

He scoffed. "Why in the hell would I want to kill the girl?"

"Because she was running the Votaries."

The look he slanted at me could have frozen water. "Don't insult me. You don't believe that."

"What I believe is that you have gotten yourself in yet another dirty deal and it's blowing up in your face."

"The only deal I'm involved in is trying to stimulate this city's economy by bringing in new businesses—legit ones."

"Hung is a rumored hitman and Yü Nü is believed to be the head of the Fangshi worldwide. Plus, she's scary as hell."

"Luckily, rumors aren't admissible in court, Detective. And neither are your personal feelings about Yü Nü—or me."

"Whatever. I'm going now."

I was almost at the door before he spoke again, softly this time. "I can pull the plug on this."

Turning to face him, I said, "You wouldn't dare."

"Want to try me, Katie?"

"You're the one talking about too much to lose." I crossed my arms. "You interfere in my case and I'll be forced to do some digging into business dealings, Mr. Mayor—among other things."

"You're not the only one who has dirt. Only a matter of time until Morales goes down now that the Fangshi are in town."

I walked up to him and took his drink. After I drained it, I let out an *ahh*. I licked my lips slowly, and his eyes flared. "If I were you, I'd be more worried about the BPD getting wind of a murder weapon in the Pantera Souza case." I shoved the glass into his chest, forcing him to reach up to grab it. "Never ask your enemy to get rid of evidence that implicates you in murder, asshole."

As I walked away, he breathed, "I'll be damned."

I smiled but didn't look back. Inside I was experiencing the dual emotions of elation and panic. The excitement was due to having the upper hand for once. The panic was the result of showing my cards. Now that he knew I had the gun that killed Pantera Souza with his prints all over it, I'd have a target on my back. I just had to make sure he never found out where I'd hidden it. As long as he had to worry about who I'd shown it to, I'd be safe.

Morales was downstairs in the lobby, where he and the guard were trying real hard to pretend they were ignoring each other. I walked past him and went out into the night air. The cool breeze off the river lifted my hair off my neck.

"Took you long enough," he snapped behind me.

I stopped and turned. Instead of responding, I watched him. Gave him the opportunity to take it back or apologize. He declined by not meeting my eyes. "All right," I said, "What's your problem?"

He tried to stonewall me. His jaw went hard and a hand shoved into his jeans pocket, like he was thinking about starting a fight.

I held up a hand. "Whatever story you're telling yourself right now? It's bullshit. I stayed behind because I knew if I pressed a little more, Volos would give up something useful. And I was right."

His brow quirked. He didn't ask the question, though.

"He said he was with Yü Nü and Hung last night."

"So? They could have sent the tea at any point."

"Yes, but I didn't tell Volos how Krystal died. He seemed to assume she was shot or something. That tells me he wasn't privy to the plans, but it does place him in cahoots with both Yü Nü and Hung."

"Christ." He ran a hand through his hair. "But Hung's MIA, so we can't pull him in."

I placed a hand on his shoulder, forcing him to look at me. "You need to get your shit together."

He pulled back. "I'm fine."

"No," I said, "you're not fucking fine. Yü Nü rattled you. I get it. But you need to keep your head in the game if we don't want everything to blow up in our faces."

He sucked a deep breath in through his nose, held it for a couple of beats, and blew it out like he was exorcising some demons. "Sorry. You're right."

I winked at him and threw his own words back at him. "'Course I am, Cupcake."

He nudged me with his shoulder. "So, what's our next move?"

"There's someone we haven't talked to who's up to his knees in this bullshit."

"Don't say it." The words were gruff, but the sparkle returned to his eyes.

"I think it's time we paid a visit to Uncle Abe."

CHAPTER TWENTY

etting to Crowley Penitentiary for Arcane Criminals wasn't supposed to be easy. The only way to get to Crook's Point Island was via ferry. The prison itself sat atop a cliff like a gothic fortress overlooking the iron sand beaches and dark waters below.

The day we went, the lake churned in advance of a massive spring storm. The gunmetal gray sky pressed down on top of us, and waves knocked the boat around like a kid's toy in a washing machine. We were about halfway across the lake when the sky opened up, forcing us into the pilothouse. Rain fell in sheets that obscured the view.

With nothing left to do, Morales and I sat on the benches and tried not to knock each other over as waves crashed into the boat.

"Nice day for sailing, huh?" he said.

Nausea made me woozy, and I imagined my skin had to be about as green as Sweet Ray's after a bender. But Morales looked like he was enjoying himself. After the tension from the night before, it was nice to see him more relaxed. However, I wasn't fool enough to think it would last. Not only did we still not have any idea where Hung was, we were also about to be in a room with my uncle, who was really good at destroying a person's chill.

"Why don't you make yourself useful and distract me?" I said, hoping to keep the good mood going as long as possible.

He raised an eyebrow.

I swatted his arm. "Talk, I mean."

"Oh," he said, "all right. How about we talk about the fact Aphrodite's wedding is tomorrow."

"All right, I approve of that topic." I sat up straighter. "What are the chances it's going to be a clusterfuck?"

"Pretty high, I'd say."

"When I mentioned it to Baba, she said that on one of her daytime talk shows, a woman married herself because she thought all guys were jerks."

"Why didn't she just marry another woman?"

"I asked the same thing," I said. "According to Baba, the lady didn't want to, and I quote, 'chomp bush.'"

He snorted. "Were those the lady's words or Baba's?"

"Baba's."

"Naturally. Although, honestly, don't knock it until you've tried it."

I couldn't take a stance on that one, so I let it sail by. "In alchemy, the sacred marriage is the holy union of the sun and the moon. It's a symbolic deal that represents the communion of female and masculine aspect to create the Lesser Stone."

"Well, that certainly applies literally in this case, since Aphrodite is marrying her male and female sides to each other."

"Yes, it'll be a big deal for the covens. Aphrodite is already pretty revered for being a sacred hermaphrodite. Once they're married, though, they'll ascend to a higher state of respect. Like a guru or whatever."

"Can you imagine how insufferable they'll be then?"

"No shit. Although, I have to question how enlightened a glorified pimp can actually become."

"Especially one that still has a thriving poison garden," he added. "Any idea what the ceremony will be like?"

I shook my head. "The invitation said it'll be at the old Orpheum Theater, so it's bound to be quite a to do."

"I don't know the Orpheum."

"Used to be a big deal when the town was booming. Real ornate and all that. But after the steel mills closed, no one wanted to go see the opera. It sat abandoned for years, but you-know-who arranged for some company to buy it last year. They've been renovating it to use for concerts and events."

"You-know-who?" he prompted.

"The mayor."

"Ah." He plucked at the edge of his sleeve. "So, you never told me what else he said last night besides trying to give an alibi to Hung and Yü Nü."

I looked out the window to the stormy lake. "He made some vague threats about pulling us off the case if we hassled them."

"Good."

Shocked, I pulled my gaze from the window. "How do you figure?"

"Let him try to explain obstructing our case in court. We really should sit down and write up all these instances for use down the road. It's only a matter of time until he's going down."

"Good idea." I swallowed and looked down at my hands. I'd had a few months to tell Morales about the gun. On the night I'd taken it, things had been really crazy and Morales didn't see me make the decision not to toss it in the lake. I'd had plenty of opportunity to tell him about it since, but I held back. I told myself it was because I knew once he found out, he'd be angling to make a case against Volos ASAP. I felt it was too soon, since Volos had dirt on us, too. We had to wait until we had something huge to use, and then the gun could be just another nail in the coffin.

But now I realized there was another reason I hadn't told my partner. Hell, I'd barely admitted it to myself. As much as I hated John Volos, I knew he was better than whatever would replace him. As shady as he could be, he'd done a lot for Adepts in Babylon. If we took him down now, it would confirm for a lot of old-school Mundanes what they'd already suspected—all Adepts are criminals.

Morales bumped my shoulder. "I wonder if he'll be at the wedding," he said, unaware of my woolgathering. "Can you imagine? The mayor attending the self-wedding of a hermaphrodite who runs a brothel."

"Actually," I said, "it's not that farfetched. The Adept community will see this as a big deal. Dirty magic or no, a sacred hermaphrodite is revered by all Adepts, regardless of whether they're trained in the alchemical traditions or not. If he didn't go, it would be noticed."

"But the Mundane community will notice if he does go, and not in a good way." Morales shrugged. "Regardless, I hope we're at different tables at the reception. That guy seriously ruins my appetite."

The boat's motor downshifted, saving me from responding. I looked up to see the cliffs that held the prison looming. The driving rain softened the edges but intensified the feeling of gloom that hung over the place.

The boat bumped into the dock, shifting my weight into him. His hands came up to steady me. For a minute, I allowed my weight to settle against him.

"You okay?" he asked into my hair.

I nodded. "Yeah," I lied. Visiting my uncle always felt like entering psychological warfare.

"Good." He gently eased away and rose, holding out a hand to help me up. "Because it's showtime."

* * *

Half an hour later, we cleared the security gauntlet and were shown to the interview room. Since Abe had a restraining order against me, I was required to stay a certain number of feet away from him. This meant Morales would be taking lead on the conversation, and I'd be stuck behind a two-way mirror, watching. There was an intercom in the room I was in, so I could ask questions, but it put me at a disadvantage, which was exactly what my uncle wanted.

Even though I hated the necessity of being stuck behind glass, I was kind of relieved Morales had to take the lead on this. Facing down Uncle Able always took every one of my wits. Abraxas Prospero hadn't stayed on top of the dirty-magic food chain in Babylon as long as he had by being an idiot.

The interview room door opened, and two guards led in the prisoner. He wore an orange jumpsuit and a pair of white canvas sneakers with manacles clamped around his ankles. His hands were cuffed too, and attached to a length of chain looped around his waist. His white hair had thinned out a little more since the last time I'd seen him, and his bald spot had grown a little larger. But his eyes were still as bright and dangerously cunning as they'd ever been.

"Special Agent Morales," he said, "this is a pleasant surprise."

"I wish I could say the same, Abe."

My uncle didn't react to the barb. "And shall I assume that my prodigal niece is ensconced behind the mirror." He faced the mirror, almost exactly where I was standing. "Hello, Katie Girl. It's a shame you can't join us." The words dripped with cheerful scorn.

I pressed the intercom button. "Remove the restraining order and I can."

"And risk you losing your temper again and attacking me?" He laughed. "We're all safer this way."

Morales held out a hand. "Please sit."

"Actually, we have another party joining us."

Morales glanced at the mirror. I shrugged even though he couldn't see me. "Who is it?" I asked over the intercom.

"An old friend," he said. "But while we wait, why don't you tell me how Danny's doing? He's what—a sophomore now?"

"Yeah, we're not having that conversation."

As if I hadn't spoken, he continued, "I do hope you're seeing to his magical education."

It was one thing for Baba or Pen to butt in and tell me what to do about Danny's schooling. But Uncle Abe was a whole other level of nope.

So, I decided to fuck with him. "Actually, Danny's decided to live life as a Mundane. He's even been training himself to write with his right hand."

A thunderstorm crossed Abe's face. "Over my dead body. That boy has too much inherent talent to squander on a Mundane existence."

"He said he couldn't stomach doing magic because it reminds him too much of our family's shameful past."

Morales's grin was all teeth as leaned back in his chair, enjoying the sparring match.

"That's your brainwashing talking, Katherine," Abe said through clenched teeth.

"He wants to be an accountant," I added, twisting the knife a little deeper.

"You—" Whatever he'd been about to yell cut off when the door opened again.

The white man who entered wore wire-rimmed glasses, a slick navy suit, and brown hair so thick it had to be plugs. His pink tie was decorated with embroidered green dollar signs. "You didn't say anything, did you?" he said to Uncle Abe.

"Let me guess," Morales said in an ironic tone, "you're the lawyer."

"Dicky Goldman," I growled.

Luckily, I'd already released the intercom button. I glared through the mirror as Abe did the introductions in the other room. I'd never officially met Dicky Goldman, but I'd seen him at work. He'd represented my uncle during his trial, which had been televised. The guy was as slick as shit through a goose and twice as dirty.

"She in there?" Dicky said to Morales once the introductions were done.

"If you mean Detective Prospero, yes."

The lawyer nodded dismissively. "My client wishes you both to know that moving forward, all interviews should be arranged through me. Further, you will no longer be speaking to my client without my presence, so you can't frame him for any additional crimes."

"He's already in prison for the rest of his life, Dicky," I said into the intercom.

He smiled tightly. "We'll see."

Both the meaning of his words and the utter confidence with which they were spoken sent a chill through me. I knew he wouldn't answer if I asked what the hell that meant, so I took another tactic. "Uncle Abe didn't know we were coming out here today. How'd you get here so fast?"

He waved a hand, which revealed a huge gold watch that glinted so bright, it nearly blinded me through the glass. "You have ten minutes today, so I suggest you get down to business."

"Morales? A minute?" I said calmly.

Uncle Abe smiled. Dicky checked his watch. Morales ducked out of the room and met me in the hallway.

"You know, if he wasn't such a pain in my ass, I'd almost admire your uncle's moxie."

"We don't have much time," I said. "I'm not sure what he's playing at, but we need to be extra careful. Dicky's a real shark."

"I wonder if we should just leave it. He probably won't allow Abe even to share his birth date now."

"If we back down now, they'll think they won."

"Kate, they kind of have."

I shook my head. "Nope. Get back in there and ask him about the Fangshi. If nothing else, it tells him we're on his scent."

He sighed. "All right, but I'd like to go on the record that I think this is a waste of time."

"Noted. Now get in there, Tiger." I smacked him on the ass and marched back into the room.

Once I was back behind the mirror, I watched Morales return to his seat. Abe rocked back on two chair legs, a smug smile on his face, as if he fully expected Morales to cancel the interview.

"Thanks for waiting. I'll try to make this quick." He made a show of opening the case file filled with all the paperwork Dixon had dug up on the Fangshi's business interests in Babylon.

Abe froze and shot his lawyer a look. Dicky shook his head and made an easy-now gesture with his right hand. Dicky took a box of cigarettes, lit one, and handed did over to Abe without being asked.

My uncle took a long drag of the purple Viceroyal and exhaled slowly. "Let me guess, you've stalled on a case and need my help."

"No, actually, we have a couple of questions about your business interests in the Cauldron." Morales clasped his hands on the table top.

"You have us at a disadvantage, Special Agent," Dicky said. "My client obviously doesn't have access to any of his records in here."

"Which is why it's so convenient you're here, Mr. Goldman." Morales smiled. "Seeing how as his attorney, you'd be involved in setting up any business for Mr. Prospero."

Dicky laughed. "I'm a criminal attorney."

"I couldn't have said it any better myself."

While Dicky stiffened with offense, Morales turned to Abe. "We have questions about some properties we believe you own."

Dicky jumped in. "As you're well aware, anything owned by Mr. Prospero that wasn't seized by the state was placed in a trust to be managed by an executor on behalf of my client and his heirs."

"Who is the executor?" Morales asked in a reasonable tone.

Dicky smiled a shark's smile. "Where's your warrant?"

"We were hoping this might be a friendly chat." Morales shifted in his seat and tried a different tactic. "The property in question is a Chinese restaurant called the Jade Moon. It's owned in a joint venture between Waidan Imports and Cockatrice Holdings."

"Who told you that?" Abe snapped, but Dicky put a hand on his arm.

"Again, I would advise my client not to answer that question—"

"I didn't ask a question yet," Morales pointed out.

The muscle in Dicky's jaw spasmed. "By all means."

"There was another business recently opened in a building under the Cockatrice Holdings umbrella." He pretended to refer to the notes in his notebook. "It's called the Happy Ending Massage Parlor."

"And?" Dicky said. "We're still waiting for a question."

Morales's eyebrow snapped up. "That's an interesting reaction from you, Mr. Goldman. Wasn't the proprietress one of your clients?"

Dicky sucked on his teeth. "I have a lot of clients."

Morales slid across a picture of Krystal's body from the crime scene. "Her name was Krystal LeMay. She was found murdered yesterday. In a building owned by Abe."

Abe sat up straighter to stare at the picture. "Did you know this?" he asked Dicky.

Dicky leaned in to whisper something to Abe. I leaned forward fruitlessly, unable to hear from the distance.

Once Dicky finished saying his piece to Abe, the two men turned back to face Morales, who kept his expression neutral. "My client had not heard of Miss LeMay's passing yet, Special Agent. Obviously, he's willing to work with the homicide detective in any way he can."

Morales smiled. "BPD's not handling this one. We are."

Abe's face went stony.

"And," Morales continued, "my question from before was—why

wouldn't Mr. Prospero try harder to hide his alliance with the Fangshi?"

"The who?" Dicky said, without missing a damned beat.

Abe, on the other hand, had gone very still.

I didn't believe for a moment that Dicky didn't know who the Fangshi were any more than I believed that Abe wasn't wondering how in the hell his attorney managed to be so careless.

"We have Krystal to thank for helping us make the connection, actually." Morales shook his head sadly. "In fact, the timing of her death is just awfully interesting. First her boyfriend dies in a horrible potion lab explosion, and now she's killed right after we start investigating the Fangshi for Valentine's death? Like I said, interesting."

The cigarette between Abe's fingers trembled. "You're fishing."

Morales laughed and leaned back. "Trust me, this hook is well baited."

Dicky opened his hands in a magnanimous gesture. "If you have evidence, show it."

"We're not ready to formally charge anyone. Yet." Morales paused, let it sink in. "Consider this a courtesy call."

Abe's head tilted. "How do you figure?"

"Well, first of all, you've got to get yourself a better lawyer."

Dicky sputtered. "How dare—"

Morales talked over him. "And second, someone just murdered the head of your coven. You ask me, it's time to reconsider your new friendship with the Chinese."

At that, the mood shifted again. Abe's posture relaxed and a wide smile spread across his face. "Krystal was the head, sure."

He leaned back in his chair and swiveled until he faced the mirror. His shit-eating smirk made my skin crawl. "Excellent detective work, as usual, Katherine."

"Shit," I said to the empty viewing room.

I'd suspected that Krystal was a misdirection, but Abe's smugness was worrisome. Someone else was calling the shots on the streets. But who?

In the other room, Dicky tapped his Rolex. "Time's up, Special Agent." He rose and encourage Abe to rise as well. "Next time, be sure you're not wasting my client's time. He may be incarcerated, but he's a busy man."

"Oh, yeah?" Morales shot back. "You got yourself a hobby on the inside, Abe?"

Abe glared daggers at him.

"For your information, my client is working to better himself. He's enrolled in college courses."

"What are you studying?" I asked over the intercom.

"Criminal justice." Abe turned fully to face the mirror. "Figured if they let you be a cop, anyone can do it. Besides, the way you're handling this case? There'll be an opening soon."

Dicky grabbed Abe's elbow and helped him rise. The pair went to the door and knocked for the guard.

"Just one more question," Morales said in a casual tone. "Why'd you bother getting into the virility potion game? Weren't you worried about creating a beef with Aphrodite?"

"You're making quite a leap if you think I would bother with sex magic, Special Agent." Abe scoffed. "But if I did lower myself to meddling with that sort of potion, Aphrodite wouldn't dare come after me. The Hierophant knows their place."

I didn't comment on the fact that Abe seemed to be up-to-date on the change in Aphrodite's preferred pronoun, but it was interesting. "But you've been stuck in here for years and Aphrodite's out there," I said into the intercom. "Besides, they're ascending. That will make them even more powerful."

"Ascending," he scoffed. "Nothing more than a publicity stunt."

"To what end?" I asked.

"You're the detective. Figure it out." Abe shot me a pitying smile. "Despite what Aphrodite wants everyone to believe, I'm still Abraxas

Prospero. These walls?" He jerked his head toward the metal-barred window set in the wall. "They might as well be ether."

There was a note to his voice that I hadn't heard in the previous meetings. It sounded like the confidence a man got when he held a secret over you. And it scared the hell out of me.

"You two take care, now." With that, he allowed the guards to open the door and accompany him back to his cell.

CHAPTER TWENTY-ONE

T wo hours later, I pulled Sybil into the parking lot in front of a two-story brick building that had once housed a factory. After the meeting with Uncle Abe, I felt like I'd spent my morning swimming in a sewer, but I hadn't had time to grab a shower before I had to pick Danny up for the meeting at the Conservatory.

I felt sort of bad abandoning Morales, but I also hadn't been super excited about going back to the gym and telling Gardner we were no closer to making an arrest in the Valentine and LeMay murders.

"We need to hurry." Danny had the door open before I put the car in PARK.

"Relax. The meeting doesn't start for five more minutes."

I'd never seen Danny worried about punctuality, but he was clearly eager to make a good impression on the principal of the Conservatory for Arcane Arts.

"Just relax."

He rolled his eyes at me in that teenaged way that made me feel like I was short on gray matter. "I am relaxed. I just want to get inside before you get called away."

Guilt flared like heartburn in my chest. The case had been keeping me away from home a lot, and it had been a bit of an ordeal to schedule the meeting with Hidalgo, who was pretty busy herself trying to launch a brand-new school.

"I already told the team I was unavailable," I said. "They can survive without me for an hour."

The Conservatory sat on the edge of an area of the Cauldron that had undergone an impressive revitalization effort. Sitting along the Steel River, the tall red brick building had huge metal-framed windows and tall smokestacks with blackened tips. A construction crew swarmed over the lot as they completed the transformation from failed factory to high school of the future.

Danny was five steps ahead of me the entire way to the front door, and he kept looking back to make sure I was coming. I stifled a grin at his enthusiasm. I had to admit it was nice to see him excited about school for change. However, I couldn't overlook my qualms about fitting into such a new school, and my old habits died hard when it came to Danny doing magic.

The building looked like an old factory from the outside, but inside it looked like a hip dot-com office. Several levels of open loft-like spaces looked down on the atrium. A Latina woman wearing a trendy pantsuit met us at the white lacquered desk.

"Ms. Prospero?" she said, holding out her left hand.

"Kate," I said, shaking it. "Dr. Hidalgo?"

"Lynn." She smiled warmly. "And you must be Danny. Welcome to the Conservatory."

She offered her left hand to Danny, too. He paused and took a second to realize he'd automatically held up his right. I realized with a start that by raising him in Mundane circles, I'd failed to school him in proper Adept etiquette. Luckily, he recovered quickly and gave her a confident Leftie handshake.

"I'm excited to be here, ma'am."

I blinked at my brother's first use of the word *ma'am* ever.

"You'll have to forgive our dust," she said. "Most of the major interior construction is complete, but we've got a lot of work left to get ready for our launch in August."

"This sure doesn't look like any high school I've ever seen," I said.

"That's because we're not going to be like any other high school." Her smile was friendly, but I had the feeling this speech was rehearsed. "The Conservatory for the Arcane Arts will be the first charter high school in the nation focused on incorporating magic into the curriculum."

"So, all of the students will be Adepts?" Danny asked.

She shook her head. "Since we're a public school, we're legally required to accept any student who wishes to attend, if there is room. If we have more applicants than space, we use a lottery system." She waved us toward a set of elevators and pushed the button.

"How can a Mundane student thrive in a school where the curriculum is for Adepts?" I asked as we entered the car.

"First, we don't use the term *Mundane* here. We call those students *traditional learners*." She pushed the button for the second floor. "Second, the core classes are just like in other schools. What separates us is the types of electives we offer. For example, our Adept learners might take a spagyrics class, but our traditional learners might opt for a class in herbalism. All students also take the history of magic classes. The fact is that there are careers for TLs in the magic industry, so there's much for them to learn and use for the future."

"Where did most of your students attend middle school?" I asked

"A quarter of the incoming first years attended the Sir Isaac Newton Academy school. I used to be the principal there."

"Never heard of it," I said.

"It's a private school that serves K through eight. It's located in Highland Hills."

That explained why I hadn't heard of it. Highland Hills was where Adepts who worked for Big Magic lived. No one from the Cauldron could afford to send their kids there for a proper education in clean magic.

"Why would those families come all the way into the Cauldron?" I asked.

"Because of me." She delivered this information as if I should have already known the answer.

"How many students do you have who haven't gone to Newton?" Danny asked. He sounded worried, and I couldn't blame him. After the shit show of privilege we'd dealt with at Meadowlake, we were both wary about him mixing with a bunch of snobs again.

"The first-year class is made up of a mix of students from all the middle schools in Babylon. However, for the upper classes, we got special permission to be more deliberate about who we admitted."

"What does that mean?" I asked.

"We recruited students from local high schools who showed promise in the arcane arts. Most of them are Adepts, but there are several traditional learners who showed promise in witchcraft or practical magic."

Danny and I exchanged a look. He'd been studying with Mez informally for the last couple of months, but he was still pretty new. I worried that he might struggle to catch up to the students who'd been trained for years.

The elevator dinged and we all exited. The floor was wide open, with glass-enclosed labs. "Thanks to our corporate sponsors, we offer our students state-of-the-art labs. We also have our own greenhouse, so students have access to the freshest herbs and plants for their experiments."

"Wow," Danny said. "Right, Katie?" He elbowed me in the ribs, as if reminding me to play it up to Hidalgo.

"Cool," I said, lamely. It's not that I wasn't impressed. I was. It was just a wave of jealousy caught me off guard. The kids at this school would have no idea how lucky they were. There were still parts of the world where Adept kids might be beaten because their parents thought being a Leftie was a sign of a demon's curse.

"You grew up in the Cauldron, didn't you, Kate?" Hidalgo asked.

She showed us into a lobby outside a suite of offices, which I assumed belonged to the administration.

"I did," I said. "Not far from here, actually."

"Working for Abe Prospero?"

I paused, trying to decide whether I was imagining the judgment in her tone. "He's my uncle. I'm sure our mutual friend mentioned that."

"Yes, Mayor Volos hinted you were childhood friends. Not hard to put it all together with the last name."

Danny groaned.

She turned to him with a warm smile. "Looks like you come by your powers naturally, young man."

He sat up straighter. "You're not worried that I'm a Prospero?"

She shook her head. "Should I be?"

"Danny wasn't old enough to learn to cook dirty when we left," I snapped. "His training has all been clean."

"That was never in question," she said. "Although it would have been fine if he had. Magic is magic. What makes it clean, dirty, good, or bad is mostly based on the intentions of the Adept."

The fact her philosophy so closely resembled my own brought me up short. She was slowly chiseling away at the chip on my shoulder, but I wasn't sure yet it that was a good thing or if she'd been briefed by Volos on how to handle me.

She opened the door to her office. I'd been expecting something bordering on corporate neutrality. Beige everything and a polite picture of her family on her desk.

Instead, the room had a huge window looking out on the river. But the excellent view competed with the loud décor inside. She'd painted the walls brilliant lime green. Along one wall, shelving held a display of arcane texts and magical implements and totems. Her desk was a large wooden slab varnished to a blond shine with a natural edge. And the pictures on display were mostly her in exotic locations with various shaman, priestesses, and other magic practitioners.

Lisa Hidalgo wasn't just a school principal. She was a well-traveled and clearly well-educated magic instructor.

"Please sit." She indicated two brightly painted wooden chairs and took her own seat. Instead of a proper desk chair, she had one of those yoga balls.

"So, as I understand it, Danny was somewhat...creative about his application process."

I frowned at her, but to Danny I said, "Can you give us a second?"

He shot me a suspicious look. Considering the last time I'd said it, I'd been about to chew Pen a new one, I couldn't blame him for being worried. Still, I wasn't about to let him sit there while I had some real talk with the good doctor.

Hidalgo watched him go with a neutral expression, and once he was gone, she simply looked at me with her brows raised.

"Who told you that?" I said.

"Detective Prospero, may I be frank?"

"I'd prefer that."

She opened her hands. "Mayor Volos is a donor, and he did advocate for Danny. But I'll tell you what I told him—I'll take his donations, but I'm no one's bitch."

A slow smile spread across my face. "Oh, I bet he liked that."

"Let's say that the call ended rather quickly after that." She grinned. "Anyway, my point is that I assure you that I'm confident Danny is a good fit here. Kichiri's recommendation holds a lot more weight for me than the mayor's."

It took me a second to remember that Kichiri was Mez's real name. "That's good to hear. Thank you for your candor." I sat forward. "Everything I've read about and seen here today looks good."

"But?"

"It's almost too good," I admitted. "You mentioned my background before. I'm sure you can understand I might have reservations about encouraging Danny to follow the path of magic."

She nodded and thought this over. "I can see that, I suppose. But if I may—I've been in education for a long time. Denying an eager student access to knowledge can make them more determined to learn it, not less.

"And let's face it—the economy is evolving. Our society has become so addicted to the convenience of magic that the balance of power is shifting. It won't be long until Adepts have a large portion of the economic and political clout in this country. Refusing to accept that fact out of pride or fear could leave Danny in the dust down the road."

I sighed. She wasn't wrong, but I didn't like it.

"I have an idea that I think might make everyone happy."

I crossed my arms. "All right."

"After school's over in a couple of weeks, we're offering a summer camp for Adepts. It's our way of orienting the new students to the Conservatory style of learning and allowing them to bond with each other so they have friends when school starts in the fall. Why not let Danny come? If he enjoys himself and does well on the exercises and classes at camp, then he can join us in the fall. If not?" She shrugged. "You can keep him in his current school."

I thought it over for a moment. "Where's the camp?"

"At Ohio University for the Arcane Arts. Only a couple of hours away. The students will live in the dorms. They'll have workshops and team-building things during the day and time for socializing and some outings at night. It's two weeks long."

It sounded like something Danny would love. "How much does it cost?"

She smiled. "Free—everything's included, too. He'll just need some spending money."

It all sounded too good to be true. Free magic camp, free top-notch training in clean magic, a kid excited about school. It was getting harder and harder to ignore the fact that the only cost here was to my own pride.

But the truth was, there wasn't a price I wouldn't pay for him to be happy. I just had to pray that a good start would ensure he had an easier time on the arcane path than I had.

"All right," I said finally, "we can try the camp."

"If you want, I'd be happy to meet with you again afterward to discuss how he did on the projects."

"That would be great." For some reason, there was a lump in my throat. Part of me wanted to believe it was just that Danny was growing up too fast making me emotional. But deep down, I knew it was something more fundamental. Somehow, I had managed to give Danny advantages I couldn't have dreamed of as a kid. Advantages that my mother wouldn't have been able to give him.

"You okay?" she asked. The empathy in her tone almost undid me, but I managed to keep it together.

"I really appreciate your understanding about all of this."

"I can only imagine how angry you must have been when you discovered his deception, but between you and me, it shows an incredible amount of drive on his part. We'll just have to make sure we give him an opportunity to focus that energy in a positive direction moving forward."

Something about her use of *we* made me feel enormously better. It also shifted something in my perspective.

For so long, all of the decisions for Danny's welfare had been on me. Now I had a whole crew of friends and coworkers to rely on. It had taken me a while to realize that I didn't have to do everything on my own, and to drop my defensiveness about needing help. Based on what I'd seen so far of Hidalgo, I was impressed by her ability to stand up to Volos and her obvious commitment to educating Adept kids.

She excused herself to go get the forms for the summer camp, and a moment later, Danny slinked through the door slowly. His head bowed in submission, as if preparing to hear the worst sort of news.

"You can relax," I said. "How do you feel about going to a summer camp hosted by the school?"

His face crumpled into a scowl. "Summer camp? Like for little kids?"

I shook my head. "It won't be like that. You'll stay in college dorms and take magic courses, and you'll also get to hang out with other students going here."

His face cleared. "That sounds pretty cool, I guess."

"Assuming that goes well"—I took a deep breath and dove off the cliff—"you'll be starting the Conservatory in the fall."

He let out a loud *whoop* and pumped a fist in the air. "This is going to be so lit."

"Yeah, well, you ever lie like that to me again, and I'm sending you to military school, so watch yourself."

His chest puffed out and his chin went up. "You won't regret this. I swear."

I wanted to hug him. To reassure myself that I could believe his oath. Instead, I smiled and nodded and tried to ignore the realization that when my two greatest adversaries—Uncle Abe and John Volos—each found out, they'd be ecstatic.

CHAPTER TWENTY-TWO

I was on my way back to the gym after dropping an elated Danny off at home when my cell rang. I didn't recognize the number.

"Prospero," I said.

"Peewee told me I had to call."

"Hey, Sweet Ray, what's up?"

"Chinese guy just showed up."

I hesitated. "And?"

An annoyed sigh came through the receiver. "And he went to the mayor's office."

I chose my words carefully. "Did Peewee tell you that?"

"No, dummy, the mayor was with him."

"Hold on, the mayor showed up with a Chinese guy? Did you see the car they got out of?"

"Mercedes, black."

"How long they been inside?"

"Five minutes. I can see the car from the pay phone down the street. It's still there."

"That's good, Sweet Ray. Real good. You keep an eye on it and call me back immediately if the Chinese guy comes back out."

"Did I earn it?"

I tucked the phone under my chin and took a turn to head toward City Hall. "Huh?"

"You said if I did good, you'd get me a cell-a-phone."

"Oh, uh, yeah, I think so. I'm gonna hang up now, but I should be there in about five minutes." I hit the button to end the call and punch another to ring Morales directly.

"Yo."

"Meet me at City Hall."

A beat of silence. "Why?"

"Hung is there, meeting with Volos right now."

The sound of his chair squeaking came through the phone, indicating he was on the move. "Be there in a sec. Be careful."

* * *

On my way to City Hall, I ran two red lights and almost hit a hexhead who was jaywalking across Reunion Boulevard. Luckily, I managed not to commit vehicular manslaughter and slid into a spot across the street from the municipal complex four minutes after I'd hung up with Morales.

Two minutes after I parked, Morales's SUV pulled up behind me. I jumped out and ran around to get in with him. The surge of excitement had my heart thundering.

He turned his back to the street to watch me. "What's going on?"

Before I could open my mouth to explain, Morales went for his weapon. "What the f—"

Something banged into the window behind me. I spun, reaching for my gun, too.

I wasn't sure what I'd been expecting to see, but it wasn't Sweet Ray's green face pressed into the tinted window. His turban was askew and his eyes were wild.

"Jesus Christ." I rolled down the window. "You scared the shit out me, Sweet Ray."

He threw up his hands. "Sorry," he hissed. "I tried to call to you before you got in the car, but you didn't hear me."

"Um, Prospero?" Morales said from behind me. "Who is that?"

I'd forgotten that I'd never told Morales about my new informant. "Shit, sorry. Sweet Ray, this is my partner, Morales." To Morales, I said, "Sweet Ray has been keeping an eye on the mayor's office for me."

Morales eyes went wide but he managed to say, "Hey, man."

"Charmed, I'm sure." Sweet Ray tipped his chin at my partner. To me, he said, "Where's my cell-a-phone?"

I tamped down my impatience. "You'll get it once I have confirmation Hung's really in there."

"Who's Hung?" he said.

"Great hire there, Cupcake."

"Hush," I hissed at him. "Where's the Mercedes?" I asked Sweet Ray.

He pointed farther up the road. Once the traffic cleared enough, I spotted the black Mercedes gleaming in the afternoon sunlight. I nodded and turned to Morales. "Sweet Ray said they've been in there about"—I paused to check the clock—"fifteen minutes now."

"Who's *they*?" Morales asked.

"Mr. Mayor and the Chinaman," Sweet Ray said. "Peewee said they're trying to call Liberace."

I closed my eyes and waited.

"Liberace?" Morales shot me a level look as he spoke.

Sweet Ray made a disgusted noise. "Hello? Liberace had the voice of an angel."

"Got it—thanks," he said, his tone strangled. "And who exactly is Peewee?"

I opened my eyes. Sweet Ray stared at my partner like he'd just insulted his mama. Morales was watching me like I'd lost every damned one of my marbles. "Peewee is Sweet Ray's friend," I answered evasively.

Sweet Ray snorted. "That's an understatement."

Morales nodded as if he understood, even though he was nowhere close to comprehending what the hexhead actually meant. "Okey-doke," he said, "so we wait until Hung comes out and take him in for questioning."

"All right, Sweet Ray," I said, "you can go back to your step."

"When do I get my cell-a-phone?" His tone bordered on petulant.

"I promise I'll bring it by tomorrow, okay?"

He shook his head. "But Peewee said the eclipse is bringing death for you."

All of the air got sucked out of the car.

"Step the fuck away from the vehicle." Morales had his weapon in hand and pointed at Sweet Ray before I could blink.

"No!" I yelled. "That's not—"

Before I could explain that Sweet Ray hadn't been threatening me, the hexhead took off. His turban flew off his head as he ran right into traffic.

"Shit!" I started to open the door, but Morales grabbed me.

"Kate, don't—"

Blaring horns interrupted him. We both looked up in time to see a car squeal to a stop mere inches from Sweet Ray. He executed a spin and jumped out of the way of another car before safely making it to the curb.

"Damn, he's got more moves than Frogger," Morales breathed.

I slapped him on the arm. "Why did you pull a gun on him?" My fear was making me surly.

He shoved his gun back into his shoulder rig. "He threatened you —or his buddy did, anyway."

I blew out a breath to get my temper under control. "You misunderstood. Peewee isn't his friend."

"But he said—"

"Shit, listen." I slashed a hand through the air. "Peewee is a pigeon, okay?"

Morales went so still, I worried he'd seen another threat outside the car. I looked around but didn't see any immediate danger. When I looked at him again, I said, "What?"

"Kate, have you been drinking?" He ran a hand through his hair. "It's fine if you have. I just need to know."

"No, jackass, although I will need one pretty fucking soon." He didn't speak, just waited for me to explain. "All right. Sweet Ray sits on the front steps of City Hall every day. He thinks he's a medium for a pigeon named Peewee." I didn't mention that Peewee wasn't just a single pigeon but the collective pigeon consciousness. There was only so much ammunition I was willing to provide for the eventual mental health review his look was promising.

"Let me get this straight. You hired a cross-dressing hexhead who believes he can communicate with a bird to be your informant?"

"When you put it like that, it sounds crazy." I crossed my arms and sank down in my seat. "It made sense at the time, though."

He scrubbed a hand across his face. "I'm not sure how to respond to any of this."

While he thought it over, I looked past him to make sure Sweet Ray made it back to his spot. Sure enough, he sat on his normal step with the flock. He looked vulnerable without his turban.

"Maybe we need to knock off for the day," Morales said. "It's been a crazy couple of— Son of a bitch!"

I jerked out of my contemplation of Sweet Ray's existence. "What?"

"Hung and Volos just got into the car." He pointed at the Mercedes zooming away from the curb. We both watched, open-mouthed, as the car rolled past on the opposite side of the road. Sure enough, Hung was driving and Volos was in the seat.

"Crap, what should we do?" I asked, looking over my shoulder to track the car's progress.

"It's going to be a clusterfuck if we pull that car over without an arrest warrant."

"Let's just follow them, then. See what they're up to."

He nodded resolutely. "All right. Call Gardner and tell her what's going on. That way, if shit gets messy, she's already in the loop."

While I pulled out my phone, he executed an illegal U-turn. I quickly filled Gardner in on the situation.

"Stay out of sight. Do not pull that car over with the mayor inside. You understand?"

"Got it."

"If they stop somewhere and you witness illegal activity, you call in backup. I can't have it being their word against yours."

"Got it," I said. "I'll be in touch soon."

"And, Prospero?"

"Yep."

"No fuckups."

"10-4." I hung up and filled Morales in on the plan. His only response was a tightening of his jaw and the engine of the SUV revving as he sped up.

Four blocks ahead, the Mercedes turned toward the river.

"Are they headed toward the docks?" Morales said, almost to himself.

I didn't answer because the car was already making another turn, away from the lake and toward the Bessemer Bridge. It smoothly merged into the late-afternoon traffic as downtown's Mundane worker bees fled to their safe suburban hives.

I leaned back in my seat and watched the sun ooze into Lake Erie through the side mirror. "Did you ever think of quitting?" I asked.

From the corner of my eye, I saw his head turn as if I'd shocked him. "What do you mean?"

"The MEA."

"Why in the hell would I quit?"

I turned to look at him. "Well, Los Angeles, for example—based on what you've said, it was pretty fucked up."

"Like Babylon isn't?"

He was trying to deflect with sarcasm. Since I'd practically invented that maneuver, I wasn't about to let him get away with it. "I'm serious. After the Fangshi killed that dirty cop, it didn't occur to you that maybe it was time to cut and run?"

His chest heaved with a massive sigh. "Why are you asking me about this?"

I toyed with a loose string on the hem of my jeans. "Just making conversation."

He laughed but it didn't sound amused. "Cut the shit, Prospero."

I finally looked up. "I'm just giving you a chance to tell me the whole truth."

"You calling me a liar?" The acid in those words threatened to eat away at the connection between us.

"I'm saying maybe you downplayed some details, is all," I said carefully. Truth was, ever since the meeting with Yü Nü, I'd been fighting a bad feeling about Morales's original version of the tale.

"Details are just decoration. What really matters is at the end of the day, I helped put away a lot of bad guys because of that case. "

It was such a perfect Morales answer that I laughed out loud instead of getting angry. "Ends justified the means? That's what you're going with here?"

"How's the weather up on that high horse, Cupcake?"

I cleared my throat and looked back out the window. He wanted a fight, but I wasn't playing that game. "What do you think Gardner will do if she finds out?"

He waited a beat too long before answering. "If I'm lucky, she'll just fire me."

"And if you're unlucky?"

"She'll have me arrested."

"Shit."

"Right."

An image of Morales being led in chains into a prison filled with people he put there made me shudder.

"Surely there were extenuating—"

"I said I didn't want to talk about it, okay?"

I bit my tongue to hold in my automatic retort. Morales and I often sparred verbally, but he rarely ever spoke to me in actual anger. Normally, he was the cool customer while I ranted and raved. What's more—and I didn't want to really admit this to myself—it stung me in a soft spot that I rarely acknowledged. As much as I kept him at arm's length in some ways, I'd taken his commitment to me for granted. The fact he'd keep me at arm's length over something this big and impactful on both his career and our relationship from me made me feel insecure—and that made me angry.

But Morales and me? We didn't do heart-to-hearts. So, I didn't call him on it. I just let it lie there between us like a pile of dog shit we'd both tiptoe around for the next couple of days instead of cleaning it up.

"He's turning," he said.

Several car lengths ahead of us, Hung had exited the bridge and turned right.

"They're going toward the cafe district," I said. "It's really going to suck if all of this trouble was just to catch them grabbing some chow."

"Even if that's the case, why risk it?" Morales said. "Volos knows we'd cry obstruction if we caught him with Hung. Why bring him out in public like this?"

From long experience, I'd learned that my guesses about Volos's motives were usually not nearly as fucked-up as the truth, so I didn't bother responding.

Morales followed the Mercedes through traffic into the trendy area where the wealthy members of Babylon society ate appetizers and overpriced, tiny entrees in converted warehouse lofts that overlooked the river. The area used to be the Mundane version of slums, but ambitious developers, including Mayor Volos, had invested in the area and transformed it into a place where the hip and beautiful went to see and be seen.

The Mercedes pulled up to a valet stand in front of a two-story red brick restaurant called Nirvana. After we watched the pair walk inside, we drove up the block to find a space that wouldn't require us waiting on a valet guy to bring the car if we needed to get out of there quickly.

"Okay," I said, "What's the plan?"

"I think we should go inside, ask for a table, and see if they're meeting someone."

"We're not going to be able to get a table in a place like that."

"So, we'll go to the bar or I'll distract the hostess while you see what you can see," he said. "Actually, reverse that. The last time you went to do recon, we ended up being threatened with a duck."

I couldn't really argue with that, so I just nodded. "Let's do this."

As it turned out, Nirvana was a Buddhist-themed restaurant, which meant there were about a million Buddha statues inside and no meat or alcohol.

Without a bar to hide in, we had no choice but to ask for a table. Just beyond the massive smiling Buddha that sat behind the reception area, diners sat on grass mats on the floor with low tables between them. The lady at the reception wore a simple gray smock and her head was bald as a baby's.

"We just had a cancellation, so we do have a table available," she said in a serene voice. "If you'll follow me."

Morales and I exchanged a shocked glance, but we didn't exactly relax. The entire way to our table, we both clocked the open space for signs of Hung and Volos. But they weren't in the main dining room. Before I knew it, we were sitting in haphazard half-lotuses on grass mats.

I leaned forward, both to ease the pain in my hips and to whisper to my partner. "You see them?"

A server appeared to pour fragrant tea into our cups. He didn't speak or make eye contact, which was fine, since we weren't there to chat.

"I'm betting they're upstairs," Morales said.

On the far side of the restaurant, a set of bamboo stairs led to the second floor. I hadn't noticed the hostess showing anyone else up there, but I did see some anxious-looking servers scurrying up there with trays laden with covered dishes.

"Welcome to Nirvana." The man wore the saffron robes of a monk. He had no hair, and a smile as serene as a spring meadow. "I am Bodhi, your guide on this enlightened culinary journey."

"Hey, Bodhi," I said. "What's upstairs?"

He blinked at my abruptness. "A couple of private dining rooms and the meditation chamber."

I nodded and looked at Morales. "Bingo."

"I'm afraid the private rooms are booked several weeks in advance."

"Tell me about the meditation chamber," Morales said.

"Any guest may use it for a few moments of quiet contemplation."

"Awesome," I said. "Thanks."

He lowered his chin and briefly closed his eyes to acknowledge his acceptance of my gratitude. "Your journey will begin with a salad made of pickled lotus roots. We will then move on to the main course of sweet zucchini dumplings and—"

I held up a hand. "Just bring us whatever."

Bodhi bowed and walked away, but I could have sworn I saw a muscle in his jaw clench at my behavior. As a rule, I tried not to be rude to people who handled my food, but this was an extenuating circumstance. We weren't really there to eat, and Bodhi talked so slowly and calmly that I was at risk of falling asleep in my jasmine tea.

"All right," I said, "get up there. If you run into trouble, hit the panic button."

He rose slowly. "Don't eat my lotus crap before I get back."

I toasted him with my tea. "No worries there."

Over the rim of my cup, I watched his progress across the room. He looked like a dark shadow against the enlightened background. I spotted three women and a couple of men tracking his progress, too. Guess they hadn't mastered the practice of not desiring things yet.

Morales was halfway up the bamboo steps when Bodhi reappeared with a tray. Two tiny plates on top each held what appeared to be a single black bean, a white cube and a dot of green sauce. "Oh, man," I said, "I don't know if I can eat all of that."

Bodhi didn't respond, because he was too busy looking around.

I waved my tea cup around. "Can I get a refill?"

He lifted the tea pot. "Where's your companion?"

"To the brim, please. I can't get enough of this stuff," I said, trying desperately to distract him by being obnoxious. I glanced over and realized Morales had made it up the stairs. "Anyway, he went to the little monk's room."

He seemed to accept this. "Please enjoy."

I wanted to ask him if more food was coming, but decided I'd pushed his buttons enough for now. "Thanks!" I beamed and made a show of picking up the single bean with my chopsticks. I popped it in my mouth. "Mmm." Truth was, the bean had about as much flavor as a mouthful of air.

Bodhi scurried back to the kitchen.

I was washing the nothingness off my tongue with tea when my phone buzzed.

A text from Morales: *They're in a private room. Third voice inside I don't recognize. There's two guards outside. White, look like L.E.*

L.E. as in *law enforcement*. I frowned. Volos and Hung had shown up without any security, which meant they had a dining companion in that room who needed lots of muscle. Interesting.

My phone beeped again. *In the meditation room. Walls thin so I can hear Volos meeting. Something about favors owed. Shit, hold on, someone just came in to meditate.*

I wrote back: *Do I need to come up?*

I still hadn't received an answer by the time Bodhi returned. To console myself during the wait, I'd eaten the rest of my "salad" as well as Morales's.

Bodhi took in the two empty plates and the empty chair across from me. "Is your companion ill?"

I shook my head. "He enjoyed that so much, he needed to go meditate on it."

He seemed to accept this and made quick work of clearing the plates.

"Actually," I said, "now that I think about it, I could probably use a little reflection, myself." I patted my lips and threw my napkin on the table. "I'll be back in a second."

At the top of the steps, I found a small altar with a statue of a laughing Buddha and lit candles. To my right, I clocked the door with the two guards. When I appeared, they looked up, hands going automatically to their hips.

I waved at them lamely and turned to the left toward a door with a discreet sign that read MEDITATION. I'd only taken two steps in that direction when the door behind the guards flew open. A round of male laughter escaped the room. I froze and turned to watch.

Hung emerged first, followed by a man I didn't recognize, but his power suit and bearing marked him as a power broker. He looked vaguely familiar, but I didn't get a good-enough look at him before the guards stepped between us.

Before I knew it, John Volos came into the hall. When he saw me, he froze. "Kate?"

"Morales!" I hissed over my shoulder.

The guards, sensing trouble, stepped in front of the man I didn't recognize.

Volos pushed one of them aside and came toward me. "What the hell are you doing here?"

"Hey, John," I said, my tone overly bright. "Morales!"

The door to the meditation room opened and my partner emerged.

"Volos, what the hell is the meaning of this?" the man behind the guard said.

"Take him out the back way," Volos tossed over his shoulder. "Now."

Before I realized what was happening, the guards took off like two ninjas, spiriting the man away down the back hall.

I started to go after them, but Morales grabbed me. "Focus on Hung," he said, his voice low but uncompromising.

"Step aside, Mr. Mayor," he said. "We have some questions for Mr. Hung."

Gardner's warning not to engage unless we saw some actual illegal activity came back to haunt me. "Hold on," I began, but Morales shot me a look that promised retribution if I didn't have his back. I sighed and backed down.

Volos took advantage of my uncharacteristic silence. "Special Agent Morales, I already told your partner that Mr. Hung has an alibi for the night of Krystal LeMay's murder."

"Yes, and you also told her that you weren't willing to put that in the official record. Unless you've changed your mind, we have no choice but to question him about the case."

Hung still hadn't said a word. He just stood there, looking unflappable and aloof. I watched him just in case he decided to run. His gaze met mine, and something in his eyes—a glint like the edge of a blade—sent a shiver of warning down my back.

"I warned you that if you didn't back off, I'd have you pulled from this case," Volos said.

"Yeah, you say lots of things," Morales shot back, "like when you said Hung left town."

"What do you have to say for yourself?" Volos said, ignoring Morales's zinger.

Realizing he'd been addressing me, I pulled my gaze from Hung to look at Volos. "Who was that guy?"

He pulled himself up straighter. He almost looked relieved. "Our business here has no bearing on your case, Detective. Unless you're willing to make a charge, I suggest you back down."

"Better yet," Hung cut in. Hearing his voice for the first time was a shock. I'd expected an accent, but he had the cultured diction of an Ivy Leaguer, smooth but with enough scorn to make you feel judged. "How about I call my lawyer and you can explain to him why you are harassing me."

He reached for his pocket.

"Watch yourself," I barked, pointing my gun at him.

His eyebrow quirked, as if I'd amused him. "Relax, Detective." He pulled out a state-of-the art smartphone—at least five generations better than the one I had in my pocket. He touched a couple of buttons and put it to his ear. Then he turned his back on us, like we were of no consequence to him anymore.

Meanwhile, Volos had pulled his cell out, too. I figured he was lawyering up, as well, until I heard him speak into the mouthpiece. "Gardner, it's Mayor Volos."

"Fuck," Morales whispered behind me.

"You want to explain to me why your top two agents are harassing me and my dinner guests?"

He winked at me as I seethed. Behind me, Morales radiated frustration bordering on rage.

"Yes, I'll send them on home. I'm sure you understand that I must insist that a real murder detective be put on the case from now on?"

That dig had me clenching my fists until my nails scored half-moons into my palms.

"Yes, that's fine." Volos held up his phone. "She'd like to speak to you."

Morales moved forward like a man walking to the gas chamber. He held the phone to his ear. He didn't say anything, but I could hear the high, tinny tones of Gardner's shrieks in the otherwise silent hallway.

Finally, he said, "I understand, sir."

He clicked a button and handed the phone back to Volos with exaggerated care.

"Now," John said, "Mr. Hung will make an official statement but only at the Cauldron Precinct and only to Detective Duffy. If either of you interfere in this investigation from this moment on, you will find yourselves unemployed. Am I clear?"

Morales's jaw twitched. I stared so hard at Volos, I was surprised lasers didn't shoot out of my eyes.

"That's all," he said in a cheerful tone.

Summarily dismissed, we both trudged down the steps. At the bottom of the stairs, Bodhi was waiting for us. I was closest, so he handed the check to me. "Please never come back."

I opened the bill to see that the going price for enlightenment was three hundred bucks.

"Oh, and namaste." Somehow, he managed to make the word sound a lot like *fuck you.*

CHAPTER TWENTY-THREE

W hen we got back to the gym, Gardner loomed at the top of the steps with her arms crossed. She looked like a parent who'd stayed up waiting past curfew. Except we weren't teenagers and our punishment would likely be a lot more painful than losing the car for a week.

"Office." She spat the word and turned on her heel before we even reached the top step.

Morales and I climbed the remaining steps in silence, ignored the pitying looks the rest of the team was shooting us, and made a beeline for Gardner's office.

She slammed the door behind us, but as she came around the desk, her movements had that slow, deliberate quality of a person trying to rein in their temper. She didn't sit down to address us. She just paced back and forth behind the desk.

"I just got off the phone with Eldritch. Apparently, Mayor Volos and Mr. Hung showed up to his precinct looking to file an official complaint against the two of you. In addition, Mr. Hung asked to make a statement to Duffy about his whereabouts on the night of Krystal LeMay's murder."

"Sir, LeMay was poisoned by tea delivered via a courier," I said. "Hung didn't have to be there—"

She slashed a hand through the air and kept pacing. I hunkered down in my seat and ignored the warning side-eye Morales shot me.

"Now, I was fairly certain when we talked earlier that I gave you a direct order not to approach the mayor or Mr. Hung unless you witnessed anything illegal. Is that correct?"

Neither of us dared speak, so we just nodded.

"I thought so," she said, "and based on the report I got from Mr. Volos, you interrupted a business meeting."

I raised my hand.

"Not now, Prospero."

"But sir, that's not what—"

"It doesn't matter what actually happened. Don't you get it? When it comes down to our word versus the mayor's, who do you think Eldritch is going to believe? Who do you think my bosses are going to believe if those official statements are sent to them?" She stopped herself and sucked in a deep breath. "How did you even know they were meeting?"

I hesitated because everything I'd said so far ended up pissing her off. Instead, Morales fielded the question. "Detective Prospero has a CI at City Hall who informed us of the meeting."

Her eyes widened. "What CI at City Hall? I never approved paperwork for that."

"He's sort of an unofficial informant, sir," I said. "I've been paying him out of my own pocket."

"Who is he?"

I shrugged. "Just a guy."

"What is his connection to Volos?"

"There isn't one, exactly. He's just always there and sees who's coming and going."

She tilted her head. "Prospero, please tell me you're not relying on a homeless person to spy on the Goddamned mayor."

"Forgive me, sir, but what does him being homeless have to do with it? He gave us good intel."

"I want official paperwork on this man."

I shook my head. "Absolutely not. I won't compromise him like that."

"You don't trust me to keep your information protected?"

"With all due respect, sir, I think you're too worried about not pissing off the mayor."

"Watch yourself."

I backed down and changed direction. "Look, I'm sorry, but there's some dirty shit happening between the Chinese and Volos."

"Your job was the find who killed Valentine and LeMay, not try to build some sort of conspiracy case around the mayor."

"Our job is follow the clues and intel to find evidence of crimes being committed. The clue led us to Hung. Hung is involved with both the Votaries and Volos. Don't you find that weird and troubling?"

"What I find troubling is your obsession with John Volos."

The air escaped me, as if she'd thrown a fastball at my chest. "Excuse me?"

"Face it, Prospero, you've been chasing after him since you joined this team."

My mouth fell open.

"That's a gross mischaracterization of the facts, sir," Morales said. "She's not responsible for Volos being tied into all of the dirty shit happening in this town."

"And you used to be my top agent," she spat. "Now you're letting her lead you around like a dog in heat."

I jumped out of my chair. "Whoa—where do you get off?"

She crossed her arms and stared at me. "Stand down, Detective."

"Fuck that." I raised my chin. "I don't know what angle you're playing politically, but I told you this case smelled bad from the beginning. If we have to give the murder cases over to Duffy, that's fine by me. But there is something rotten brewing in this town. It starts with the mayor and goes all the way down to the street corners."

"You think I don't know that?" she shot back. "I've been in this job longer than you've been able to drive, sweetheart. Everyone's always dirty. That's the world we live in. You don't throw your first punches at the highest guy on pyramid. You gotta kick out the foundations first. You get the corner boys to turn on their captains and on up until you got enough evidence to bring down the power brokers. You can't let them see you coming, either, because the minute they smell the ambition on you, they'll put a bullet between your eyes."

I clenched my jaw. I didn't want to admit she was right. It was easier to pin the blame on her. Harder to accept that we were fighting a war where our enemy wasn't bound by inconvenient ethics.

"Furthermore," she said, "you seem to be forgetting that Volos has all of us in a sling. We kidnapped Volos to get to Souza, and then we sat by and watched him murder a man. You think he's not already angling to bring each of us down one by one before we can get him?"

Guilt crept up the back of my throat like bile. Now was the chance for me to come clean about the gun I had hidden in the floorboards of my house. But I didn't, because something in my gut told me it wasn't good to be the only person in the room without secrets. Everything had gotten so complicated and political. Being the good girl who told her bosses everything she knew seemed like the sort of thing that would get me dead one day. And if there was one Prospero trait I needed to embody, it was the marrow-deep need to survive no matter what.

When I didn't respond, Gardner turned to Morales. "What do you have to say for yourself?"

He scrubbed a hand over his stubble. "Not much to say. We tried but couldn't get the solve."

She huffed out an ironic snort of laughter. "That's it?"

He raised his hands in a futile gesture. "What do you want from me? LeMay died twenty-four hours ago. We didn't even have the fucking labs back from Mez yet."

Her eyes flared. Normally, Morales was a real cool customer when he was dealing with the boss. I'd never heard him take that tone with her.

"Prospero, give us a moment."

I froze. "Uh."

Morales's face gave nothing away.

"Now," she said.

I shot Morales an apologetic look and slinked out the door. Once I closed it behind me, I walked calmly over to Shadi's desk, which sat along the side of the boxing ring.

She tossed down her pen. "Damn, girl, what did you two do this time?"

I kept my back to the door. "Tell me what's happening in there?"

She craned her neck to look around me. "Gardner just sat in the chair you vacated. She's talking calmly. Morales is shaking his head."

I blew out a long but not-so-calming breath. "Fuck."

"Now he's talking and she's shaking her head." Shadi looked up at me. "What the hell is going on?"

"This case," I said, "this fucking case. I knew it was bad news from the start."

I turned to lean against her desk and chanced at peek at the office door. I couldn't tell if it was a good or bad sign that they weren't yelling. Sometimes, quiet conversations had the loudest repercussions.

"Where are Dixon and McGinty?" I asked, trying to distract myself.

"Cut them loose once the boss lady started hollering."

About that time, Mez came out from his lab. He glanced around until he noticed the closed door to Gardner's office. "Hey, Prospero." He waved me toward his lab. "Come here."

I pushed away from Shadi's desk and went to see what he was up to. Once I stepped inside the lab, he pulled the curtain closed behind me. "What's up?"

He pulled me over to the counter, where a thick file folder sat. "Gardner told me to bundle all my lab reports to send over to Val since BPD's taking over the case." He tapped the stack. "But I thought you might be interested in seeing it before I do."

Part of me wanted to tell him there was no point, but something in the way his eyes were sparkling told me that'd be a mistake. "Tell me."

His mouth widened into a grin. He flipped open to the top page on the report. The sheet was covered in all sorts of columns with numbers and chemical symbols. "We were right—it was the tea. They sent Autumn Tieguanyin, which is a premium variety of oolong. Also called the 'Iron Goddess of Mercy.' The aroma is quite strong, which is probably what masked the presence of the poison."

"What kind of poison?"

He did a little dance, indicating he was excited about the answer to my question. "At first, I didn't believe it, because I'd never seen it before—just read about in obscure arcane books. Even then, it was only theoretical."

"What?"

He sighed as if disappointed I wasn't keeping up. "The poison in the tea is called *gu*. It's an ancient Chinese form of poison created when, on the fifth day of the fifth month, five venomous creatures were sealed inside a container. They fought and devoured one another until all of the toxins were concentrated into the single super toxin."

"Holy shit," I said. "That's hardcore."

"Right?"

I shuddered. "Good thing I'm a coffee drinker or that would put me off tea entirely."

"Anyway, that's what killed her. Looks like the Fangshi weren't going for subtlety on this."

I tapped a finger on the report and thought it through. "That doesn't make a lot of sense, though. I mean, our theory was that whoever killed Basil blew up the lab to try and cover up the murder, right?"

He nodded.

"So, why be so blatant with Krystal? Especially when they had to know we were sniffing around their operation."

"Who knows?" he said. "I mean, maybe it was a warning to the other covens not to fuck with them. After all, just because we found the link to Chinese magic in the poison, it doesn't help us identify the wizard who made the poison, right?"

I paused. "You got that sample?"

He went to grab a slide. "This is the tea sample. Why?"

Before I could figure out a way to convince him to let me look at it under a microscope without letting on I wanted to *read* the poisonous potion, Morales threw open the curtain.

"Prospero," he said, "time to roll."

"Where?" Part of me was hoping he was about to tell me we were going to go find Hung. I also was watching him to see if there were any clues about how his conversation with Gardner went. But he wasn't giving anything away.

"Home."

My shoulders fell. "Oh."

"We have to get ready for the wedding tomorrow."

I perked up again. "Oh?"

The corner of his mouth lifted. "You said it yourself—the who's who of the Cauldron will be there, right?"

"Yeah," I said. "But there's no way Gardner will let us go now."

A new voice came from the doorway. "Yes, she will." Gardner stepped inside. Shadi followed behind her, as if she'd been summoned as the boss passed by on her way to the lab.

"Morales convinced me we've been approaching this all wrong," Gardner continued.

Her words didn't make a lot of sense to me, but they sounded positive, so I just nodded and shot Morales a questioning look. He wouldn't meet my eyes. I'd left Gardner's office both hoping and worrying that he was about to come clean. Judging from her lack of shouting and his lack of eye contact, it had gone another direction.

"We have?" I asked.

"I'd been so focused on the murder angle that I missed an opportunity here with the Fangshi." She turned to Mez. "What you got there?"

I tried to read Morales, but he was busy not looking at me. Impatience made me itchy. I wanted to demand an explanation, but given the tension still echoing in the gym from the confrontation earlier, I thought it best not to test Gardner's suddenly improved mood.

Gardner reached for Mez's slide, but he pulled his gloved hand out of reach. "Watch yourself—this shit's nasty as they come." He quickly filled them in on the potion's components.

"Hold up," Shadi said, "they sent ancient Chinese poison hidden inside Chinese tea and a Chinese teapot?"

Gardner frowned at the report. "I thought you said the Fangshi were good," she said to Morales.

"They are. None of this makes any sense."

"Well, it's Duffy's problem now," she said. "I'll drop these off at the precinct on my way home tonight. I'll put a bug in his ear about this."

I watched her hand the poisoned tea slide back to Mez so he could bundle up the evidence for her to take to Duffy. There was no way I could get a chance to *read* the poison's signature now.

Morales caught my eye, as if to ask what was wrong. I looked away. He wasn't the only one who got to have secrets.

"I'm confused," Shadi said. "I thought we were going to the wedding to continue working on the case."

"No," Gardner said, "we're going to work an investigation I just opened into the Fangshi's conspiracy to distribute dirty magic in Babylon."

"We're still trying to get potions and money on the table?" I asked.

She shrugged. "We're the MEA, that's our job—not solving murders."

We all exchanged knowing looks to confirm that we understood what she was telling us.

Gardner clapped her hands. "All right, everyone be here early tomorrow to prepare. I want that entire theater cleared before the wedding begins. And, guys, try to look like guests, not cops, okay?"

"What's that supposed to mean?" Shadi said.

Gardner shot her a look. "It means dress up."

"Wait, you mean like an actual dress and shit?" she said. "God damn."

"I got one you can borrow," Mez said. "You need one, too, Kate?"

I shook my head, a plan forming in my mind. "I got someone I can borrow one from."

"All right," Gardner snapped, "now that we've all discussed what we're going to wear, I'll remind you all to watch your asses at this event. Judging on past experience in this town, this wedding is going to be a real shit show. Be ready for anything."

CHAPTER TWENTY-FOUR

An hour later, I parked Sybil on the street outside an old peach stucco apartment building. Morales and I had gone our separate ways after the meeting. Actually, what had really happened was he ran off once we left the gym as fast as he could after muttering something about needing to go buy some new socks for the wedding.

It was a bullshit excuse. He was avoiding telling me what really went down in Gardner's office. It was apparent from her good mood that he hadn't used to the opportunity to come clean. The good news was, he convinced her to let us keep working the Fangshi angle. The bad news was, he seemed determined to avoid talking to me about his reasons.

But instead of forcing another argument, I drove over to Pen's apartment with two goals in mind. The first being to apologize for being such an asshole to her about the Danny intervention episode. The second was seeing if she had any dresses that would accommodate a thigh holster.

When she opened the door, I held up the snack cakes and bottle of wine I'd picked up on the way over. "Don't slam the door in my face. I come bearing peace offerings."

She crossed her arms and pursed her lips, considering my meager gifts. "Is that the buttery chardonnay I like?"

"Yes, ma'am. It's even chilled." I offered the bottle for her inspection. She played it cool, raising a finger to poke at the condensation on the bottle's surface.

Finally, her frown broke and a bark of laughter escaped. "Get in here." She hauled me inside and slammed the door behind her.

I handed over the treats, which she took and set down on her coffee table. "You know, you can't just buy back my affection with alcohol and sugar, Katie."

I sighed. "That was just to get me in the door," I said. "I'm hoping my sincere apology will earn me the right to stay awhile."

She chewed on her bottom lip. "I'll accept it on one condition."

"Name it. Anything."

"That you accept my apology, too. You were right. I shouldn't have encouraged him to ambush you like that."

"Pen, no—"

She held up a hand. "Unfortunately, you were sort of right. I'd been so sick of myself and my problems that I was butting in where I shouldn't have as a way to distract myself."

"That's okay. I mean, don't do it again, but I understand."

She shot me an amused but contrite look. "Anyway, Baba said you met with the principal?"

"I'll tell you all about it while you open the wine."

"Deal." She took the bottle and spun on her bare feet to go grab an opener from the kitchen.

As she opened, I told her all about the meeting at the school and the compromise we'd come up with. She poured us each a glass and handed mine over when I was done. "That sounds like a good plan," she said. "Plus? Bonus two weeks without the kid this summer."

I paused to savor both the wine and the thought. "I hadn't considered that part yet."

"You and Morales can run around the house naked if you want."

I almost spit out my wine. "Oh, Baba would love that."

"How many times have you seen her naked since she moved in?"

"No, I mean, she literally will love it. I'm afraid Morales is going to charge her with sexual harassment."

"That woman ain't right." She snickered. "Where is Macho tonight, anyway?"

I sighed and set down my glass. "We have this wedding to go to tomorrow, so he's off making sure he's got the attire he needs."

She pointed her glass at me. "Why does it sound like there's trouble in paradise?"

"It's nothing. This case we're on is just stressing us out."

"You sure that's all?"

I nodded and took another swallow of cold wine to scrub the half-truths from my tongue. I was afraid if I spoke to Pen about my half-formed concerns, they'd become real.

Luckily, she seemed to have another topic she wanted to discuss. "So," she said, taking a coy sip of her wine. "I have some news."

I looked up, relieved to have a distraction. "What?"

"I got a job." She danced a little jig.

"Shut up! Where?"

"There's this new clinic opening in the Cauldron. It's a new approach to helping with addiction by treating the body and the mind. They'll have physicians and nurses on staff along with counselors."

"Wow, Pen, that sounds amazing."

"It's really exciting. They haven't even broken ground since they'll be opening in the fall. But the woman who's starting it was in town to interview prospective employees this week. I went in yesterday to interview, and she called me an hour ago to tell me I got the job."

"That's so great. You like this woman?"

She smiled over the rim of her glass. "We really hit it off. She's run clinics in New York for years and is expanding her practice to other areas that have high dirty magic epidemics. She said my own struggles with addiction in the past would help me be a more empathetic counselor."

I nodded. "Makes sense."

"The best part is, I'll be making more at this community clinic than I made at Meadowlake and the benefits are amazing."

"If they don't open until the fall, when will you start?"

"Nicola—that's my boss—is flying the new staff out to New York in a couple of weeks to tour her other clinics. We'll be there for a week, shadowing their staff and helping out. But after that, I'll be helping get everything ready here from writing procedure manuals to interviewing support staff."

I held up my wine for a toast. "Cheers to new beginnings."

She clinked her glass against mine. "And to old friends."

After we each took a celebratory sip, I looked at her over the rim. "Speaking of new beginnings, you know this wedding I need to go to tomorrow?"

She tilted her head and shot me a knowing look. "Is it black tie or cocktail attire?"

I made a pained face. "There's a difference?"

She grabbed my hand and pulled me toward the bedroom she'd converted into a closet. "Come on, Cinderella. Let's find something for you to wear to the magic ball."

CHAPTER TWENTY-FIVE

The next afternoon, Morales and I arrived early for the six o'clock wedding. By the time we got there, people were still rushing around, getting things ready, which lent a frantic energy to the Orpheum Theater. Of course, the solar eclipse might have had something to do with it too. Adepts were always more sensitive and magic more unstable when big celestial events occurred, like eclipses or blue moons.

"You look good in a suit," I said to Morales as we climbed the steps to the Orpheum's balcony. "You look like one of those sexy tycoons from Baba's romance novels."

He shot me a side-eye. "You clean up pretty nice, yourself, Cupcake."

It had taken two hours of trying on dresses for Pen to find something that fit both of our requirements. I demanded that it conceal weaponry and Pen wanted to be sure it flattered my assets. We'd finally found a sleeveless red dress with a deep neckline and something Pen called an "umpire waist." The skirt was long and flowy with a knee-high slit.

Judging from the looks Morales kept shooting my cleavage, Pen had accomplished her goal. And considering the amount of firepower I had hidden in my underpants, I'd succeeded in mine, as well.

"But why are you walking like that?" he added.

I looked down at the black high heels. "Pen wouldn't let me wear my boots. She made me wear these." They were only two inches tall, but I felt like I had two skyscrapers attached to my feet. "Also, I have a lot of metal strapped to my thighs."

"What?"

I waved my tiny purse. "I don't know why women bother with these. It only has enough space for lipstick and one lousy knife. I had to get creative and use a garter belt as a holster."

He missed a step. "Garter belt?"

"Sure." I walked ahead of him onto the balcony area. "It chafes something fierce, but it's good for holding my Glock and an extra magazine."

"That's not all it's good for," he whispered to himself.

"Are you coming?" I said over my shoulder.

He stopped and speared me a glare. "You're doing this on purpose, aren't you?"

I shot him a saucy smile. "Maybe."

"Devil woman."

A loud crash on the floor below us destroyed the moment. We both ran to the balcony railing. The sound of a high-pitched voice yelling echoed through the cavernous space.

"Goddamn it, Leon, be *careful*."

A slim man wearing a white tuxedo with a sparkly lavender cummerbund stood onstage with his hands on his hips. He was yelling at his assistant, who was rearranging some chairs on the floor. He also wore a white tux but his cummerbund and tie were black. He also looked to be on the verge of tears. "I'm sorry, Stefan!"

"Must be the wedding planners," Morales said.

"Charming." I dismissed the arguing pair and focused on surveying the room as a whole. "This place is pretty cool."

The people who renovated the Orpheum had decided not to polish all the surfaces or paint over all of the signs of decay. They'd cleaned it up and shored up the structure, but they hadn't replaced all the seating on the floor or restore the chipped mural on the ceiling. The entire effect was a sort of post-apocalyptic chic.

"I just wish Aphrodite had chosen an easier space for us to surveil."

Behind Stefan, a brand-new purple velvet curtain hung across the stage. In the center was the logo of the theater, a large golden lyre. Every now and then, a banging sound would sneak out from behind the curtain and Stefan would yell something. Apparently, he had other people working back there to prepare the backdrop for Aphrodite's nuptials.

"I used to sneak into this place in high school. The backstage area is basically a maze."

He cocked a brow at me. "Breaking and entering? I'm shocked."

"Hardly. There used to be huge holes in the walls. You could just walk right in. It was pretty cool if you didn't mind stumbling over homeless people having sex."

"Weirdly, that is something I mind."

I shrugged. "Potayto-potahto."

He nudged my arm. "Let's go check out the backstage, then. Make sure there aren't any horned women hiding in a supply closet."

He was joking, but the longer I was in that theater, the more my instincts warned me to be careful. Word was, Aphrodite had invited more than two hundred people to the wedding. That list included everyone from coven leaders to business associates and cops all the way up to the mayor. The potential dramas of mixing all those different strata of society was bad enough, but add the increased magical energy of a large-scale arcane ritual happening during an eclipse, and you had yourself a recipe for fireworks. Not to mention, neither of us trusted that the Fangshi were done making statements. If they wanted to send a message, this would be the place to do it.

"You look like you're thinking," he said. "I thought I warned you about that."

"Just thinking through the variables," I said. "When's the boss getting here?"

Dixon and McGinty were already in their sedan across the street from the theater to have an extra set of eyes on the entrance. Shadi was on the roof of the building behind the theater. She had the back exit covered. Mez was an invited guest, and he was bringing Gardner as his "date."

"Gardner said they'd be here thirty minutes before the ceremony."

We'd originally all planned to arrive together, but at the last minute, Gardner decided it would look too suspicious to have the entire MEA task force arrive *en masse*.

I looked at the exits around the building as we walked through the lobby. Security guards in tuxedos were already manning the door. They were Aphrodite's army, not law enforcement, so we couldn't count on them pitching in if we had an emergency situation.

"Relax," Morales said.

"I'll relax once this is over and I can take off these shoes."

We reached a door that led to the dressing rooms. Two of Aphrodite's guards stood in front of it like well-dressed statues. I didn't recognize either of them, because I usually dealt with Gregor. When we reached them, one raised a hand. "No one goes backstage."

I pulled my badge from the tiny purse. Morales opened his suit jacket, where his ID was hanging from the inside pocket. "Is Gregor around?" I asked "He knows us."

He shook his head. "We're on strict orders not to let anyone back there. Period."

"Call him—or Aphrodite," Morales said.

The guy shook his head. "No can do. The Hierophant is meditating."

"What the hell are you doing here?" a voice called from behind us.

We turned to see Duffy barreling our way.

"Here we go," Morales said under his breath.

"Hey, Duffy!" I called, all friendly. "You clean up nice."

He wore a gray suit that looked like it had been in a heap on his floor until about fifteen minutes earlier. The bags under his eyes told me he'd probably been up all night, too. I almost felt bad for the bastard, but his expression told me he was about to ruin that, too.

"I thought you were told to stay away from my case."

I raised my hands. "This is a wedding, not a crime scene. And last I checked, we were invited." I nudged Morales, who produced our invitations from his jacket pocket with a flourish of cream paper and green ribbons.

Duffy squinted at them. "Pains in my ass," he muttered. "You know, when this is all over, we need to have us a little chat about your friend Alexander Hung."

"You're mistaken," Morales said. "He's the mayor's friend, not ours."

Duffy crossed his arms and got that look he wore when he knew something we didn't. I braced myself out of habit. "Had some real interesting things to say about you," he said to Morales. "Real interesting."

"Oh, yeah?" Morales played it cool.

"Mmm hmm. Said you used to be part of the Fangshi. Under-cover, like."

"That's true, Duffy," he said. "I was undercover in Los Angeles for many years. I helped put away a lot of the Fangshi, too, so you'd best take anything one of their soldiers says about me with a massive grain of salt."

Duffy sucked his teeth. "He said you were obsessed with bringing down the Fangshi. Said this whole case was a witch hunt."

I snorted. "If this is just a witch hunt, why are so many bodies popping up?"

"According to Hung, another coven's responsible for the murders."

"You know, Duffy," I said, "criminals tend to lie. It's not generally a good idea to take their word for things."

He shrugged. "I don't know. I spent most of last night poring over the evidence—or lack thereof, I should say—that Gardner dropped off. Thanks for nothing, by the way."

"A lot of that was gathered by your own CSI team, so talk to them," Morales shot back.

"Anyway," Duffy continued, "I can't believe you two were working the Chinese angle so hard."

"Why's that?" I demanded.

"Seems to me someone was trying too hard to make it look like the Fangshi did Krystal."

I glanced at Morales uncertainly. Just last night, we'd discussed that possibility too. "Did Hung make any guesses about who's responsible when you spoke to him?"

"Said he didn't know. He had an alibi for both murders. As did his associate, Yü Nü, who came by to make a statement last night as well." He shuddered. "She's something else."

I grinned at him. "If she ever offers you some duck, say no."

"Huh?" He shook himself. "Anyway, I checked out the image Dixon sent over of the man who delivered the teapot to Krystal. You were wrong on that, too."

"How so?" Despite Duffy's obvious enjoyment of pointing out our alleged errors on the case, I was interested to hear his take on it.

"Turns out he's most likely Korean."

My brows popped up. "How can you tell?"

"You got the picture on your phone?" he asked.

I nodded and removed the images Dixon texted me. It was a frozen frame from the video capture at the massage parlor. In the first one, the Asian man was bending down to place the gift box by the door with his left hand. In the next frame, he was standing up. He wore a sleeveless black T-shirt, skinny jeans, and a courier bag strapped across his chest.

Duffy tapped on the second one. "Here, enlarge it." The three of us bent over my phone to look at the zoomed in picture. "See?" Duffy said. "That's a South Korean flag on his bag."

I squinted at the picture. "I'll be damned." I zoomed out again until we could see the whole image. Sure enough, there was a patch on the bag that looked like a Korean flag. "But it's hardly conclusive evidence. Who says the Fangshi don't have a couple of Koreans working for them?"

"Actually, the Korean and Chinese wizards hate each other," Morales said, almost to himself.

"Wait." I stared at the image again, holding it up to the light. "Where have we seen him?" I handed it to Morales.

He shrugged. "Could be anyone."

"Regardless," Duffy said, "I'm convinced you two were barking up the wrong tree here. And I think I know why."

"Cut the shit and say your piece," I snapped.

"I had a feeling in my gut from the beginning that the MEA task force was playing dirty. I knew something shady went down on that ship a couple months back, and now I got wizards telling me things about Morales's activities in Los Angeles. You ask me, it's only a matter of time until your entire team goes down."

"Actually, no one asked you," I said. "In fact, if you'll recall, both the Charm Parsons case and this one were originally yours, but you couldn't handle them. Maybe if you spent more time solving murders and less time lobbing accusations at your fellow law enforcement officers, you wouldn't be drowning in the Cauldron."

"And maybe if you spent more time following the law and less time pursuing your personal vendettas, you wouldn't be on the verge of an IA investigation."

My stomach dropped. "What the fuck?"

He grinned. "Tomorrow morning, I'm delivering the statements from both Mr. Hung and Yü Nü as well as evidence I gathered about the Parsons case to Internal Affairs. I can't work this up the chain at MEA, but I can bring you down from inside the BPD. It won't be long until they bring in the MEA brass, and then it'll be bye-bye time for the whole team."

"You son of a bitch," I seethed. "What is your problem?"

He stepped up, getting in my space.

"Watch yourself," Morales growled.

I waved him off and stepped closer to Duffy. "You best not come at me unless you're prepared to follow through."

"That's your problem, Prospero," Duffy said. "You think you're still on the street corner, jockeying for little slices of real estate with other two-bit wizes. But you're in law enforcement now, sweetheart. There's rules and they're the only thing that separates us from the junkies and hustlers."

"You're wrong," I said, "because if I was still on the street?" I placed my hands on the lapels of his jacket, enjoying it when he flinched. "And you told me you were about to snitch on me?" I looked him in the eye and shook my head sadly. "You'd be praying for a saline enema by the time I was done."

He knocked my hands away and stepped back. "You'll never be anything more than a criminal just like your uncle." He rounded on Morales. "And what's your excuse? Fucking murderer."

The word hung in the air like a curse.

"Duffy?" a voice called from down the hall. We turned to see Gardner striding toward us. Her high heels clicked purposefully against the concrete floor. She wore a black dress that flowed around her body, making her look like some sort of avenging spirit. Behind her, Mez, dressed in a black suit with a green silk waistcoat, rushed to keep up with her.

"What the hell is going on?" she demanded when they reached us.

"Duffy here was just telling us his theories about the case," Morales said, cool as can be.

Her gaze moved from Morales to Duffy and to me, as if trying to see the lies on us. Finally, she turned on Duffy. "I promised your captain we wouldn't interfere in the investigation. If you need help, you'll need to find it elsewhere."

I bit my lips to hide my smile at the way Gardner maneuvered the conversation to leave Duffy no wiggle room.

"Understood," he said, his voice tight. "If you'll excuse me, I need to go take my seat for the ceremony." With a final nod to Gardner, he turned on his heel and walked away without so much as a glace toward the rest of us.

Once he was out of earshot, Gardner said, "What was that really about?"

There was no point in lying to her. "He's planning on launching an IA investigation for the Parsons case, and he's using statements from the Chinese to indicate we mishandled this one, as well."

"Why's he going after Kate?" Mez demanded.

"Because she's still BPD," Gardner said. "This way, he gets around me because the IA investigators will go straight to my brass." She put her hands on her hips and looked down at the floor for a moment, thinking over her options. "Why now?" she said.

It was the perfect time for Morales to come clean. Once Duffy's report happened, it would only be a matter of time until the L.A. incident came to light. I looked at him, pleading with him silently to tell her. But he wouldn't meet my eyes. "He said he thinks I have a vendetta against the Fangshi so we were pushing the investigation in that direction so I could harass them."

It was only part of the truth.

A string quartet started playing in the theater's lobby. It was almost show time.

"All right," Gardner said, "we'll deal with this later. Prospero?"

I nodded.

"Don't worry about this. We've got your back." Behind her, Mez nodded emphatically.

"Thanks, sir."

I chanced a glance at Morales. He looked like he wanted to be somewhere else. Duffy's voice echoed in my head: *Murderer.*

A new version of the story he'd told me had started to take shape in my head. He'd claimed he'd covered up the murder, but had he actually killed that cop?

"Kate?"

I pulled myself out of my thoughts and looked up to find that Gardner and Mez were already gone.

"You okay?" His hot palm branded the bare skin of my shoulder. I resisted the urge to pull away, to get away from him long enough to get my head straight. "I need your head in the game right now." He leaned down and forced me to look him in the eye. "You trust me, right?"

I froze. Did I? If he'd asked me thirty minutes earlier, I wouldn't have hesitated. But now? I felt like maybe I'd fallen for the Morales he'd wanted everyone to see. The handsome hero, the good guy. But I'd just watched the good guy lie so easily to someone who trusted him.

He shook me a little. "We'll get through this, okay?"

"Did you do it?" The words were barely above a whisper.

"What?"

"Did you kill that cop?"

His expression hardened, like a door slamming shut between us. "How can you ask me that?"

"Because now my ass is on the line too, and you just lied to Gardner."

He ran a hand through his hair. Finally, he sighed, surrendering. "He was about to out me to Yü Nü. Said if I didn't pay him off, he'd blow my cover."

I swallowed that and let it sink to the pit of my stomach like an anchor.

"He was dirty, Kate. Fangshi were paying him off to protect them. So, I killed him and told Yü Nü that he was stealing from her."

"Was he?"

He nodded. "Of course."

I shook my head. "How could you do that?"

"How could I not?" His voice rose. The music coming from the theater was loud enough to drown it out. "Do you have any idea what people like that would do to an undercover cop?"

My Uncle Abe had had his own sister—my mother—murdered because he thought she was defecting to another coven. It wasn't hard to imagine the torture he would have put a cop through if he'd been exposed as a mole.

"Look," Morales said, "I know I didn't tell you the whole truth. I'm sorry. But I never thought it would go this far. I thought once we arrested Hung and Yü Nü, we could put it all behind us."

"Only, now they're still free and I'm about to be the one thrown to the wolves at IA," I said. "And here you are, still lying to Gardner to save your own ass."

He didn't say anything. He just stared at me as if I'd betrayed him. I resisted the urge to back down because I knew I'd be betraying myself.

"When you're ready to tell her, I'll be there. Until then, I'm going to need some space."

With that, I walked away with as much dignity as the high heels allowed. He didn't try to stop me.

CHAPTER TWENTY-SIX

As I stormed away from Morales, I realized I didn't have many choices when it came to escape routes. I could either go to the lobby, where guests were waiting for the doors to open into the theater, or I could find access the backstage area.

Since I didn't really feel like mingling with the who's who of Babylon Adept society at that moment, I went with the latter option. Luckily, I found an unguarded door tucked inside an alcove.

Inside the dark hallway, I stopped and leaned against the wall. My indignation was burning off fast, and taking its place was a cold, creeping dread.

Duffy was going to report me to Internal Affairs.

The irony would have been rich if it hadn't been my ass on the line. Ever since I joined the MEA, I'd been the one warning my teammates to follow protocol. I'd been pretty self-righteous at times, if I were being honest. But in the end, trying to do the right thing hadn't protected me. The political currents of law enforcement in Babylon had a strong undertow that could suck anyone down without warning. And there I was, without my water wings.

I took off my heels to give my feet some relief. I realized that I could just leave. Walk out of that theater, go home, and put on some sweats.

But, try as I might to convince myself otherwise, I wasn't the kind of person who hid when things got tough. I had a stubborn streak that saw trouble and dove in headfirst. Prosperos were like sharks that way—we never quit swimming.

With a sigh, I pushed myself off the wall and put the shoes back on my feet. But just before I turned to go back out into the reception area, someone down the hall began shouting. I followed the dark corridor toward the noise.

Up ahead, the hall opened onto a room to the left of the stage. When I walked in, I found the wedding planner smacking his assistant over the head with a handful of tulle. "I told you to use a square knot!" he shrieked.

"Yo!" I called.

The planner stopped and turned, the tulle raised high. "What?" he snapped.

"What the hell's your problem, buddy?"

"What business is it of yours, bitch?" He tossed the final word out like a dare.

I smiled. If he'd known me better, he might have recognized it as my oh-you're-fucked-now smile.

"Well, for starters, you're assaulting that man, and since I'm a cop, it is my business." I pulled my badge out of my purse. "What's your name?"

The guy under the tulle made a whimpering sound.

"I'm Stefan" the wedding planner said. "And I'm pretty sure this tulle isn't hurting anyone."

He lowered the fabric to reveal his assistant's face. I'd seen the pair earlier from far away, but now that I could see them up close, I realized that the assistant was Asian and he looked awfully familiar.

"Your name's Leon, right?" I asked.

He nodded.

"Can I see your IDs?"

Stefan huffed and put his hands on his hips. "This is ridiculous. We don't have time for this."

"Then I guess you better hurry," I said sweetly.

As they each complied, I pulled out my cell and pulled up the picture from earlier just in case. But I shouldn't have bothered. Stefan thrust his wallet at me. I spared it a quick glance.

Leon stood frozen, watching me with a wariness that seemed excessive given my simple request. "Sir? Your license?"

He whimpered. "It's in my bag." He pointed vaguely across the room at a chair that held a messenger bag.

One with a Korean flag patch.

"I'll be damned," I said. Leon, the put-upon assistant, was the guy from the massage parlor.

"Leon, hurry up and show it to her," Stefan said. "We have to get the crucifix set up!"

I frowned at the mention of a crucifix, but I kept my eyes on Leon. He looked from the bag to me to Stefan, then back to me.

I waved. "Hi, there. You been moonlighting as a tea courier lately?"

"What are you talking about?" Stefan said. "I told you we don't have time. Aphrodite will kill us if the ceremony starts even a minute late."

Meanwhile, Leon had gone pale at my mention of tea.

"Damn it, Leon!" Stefan said.

It happened fast. One second, Leon looked like a trapped mouse, and the next, his fist shot out and clipped Stefan in his porcelain veneers.

The resulting howl bounced around the room. Before I could recover from the shock, Leon took off, hurdling boxes of tulle and silk flowers like Jesse Owens. He vaulted the stairs to the stage and disappeared.

I kicked off my shoes and pulled my phone out of my purse as I took off after him. While the phone rang, I dodged workers who were doing last-minute setup of one of the most bizarre wedding sets I'd ever seen. Three little people dressed as cupids milled around a low altar in the center of the stage. Fontina Douglas stood behind it, straightening an archway draped with green and white ribbons. When she saw me, she froze and scrambled for a phone from her pocket.

I ran past her without a second glance as Gardner answered on her end.

"Where are you?" she snapped.

"Backstage. I found Duffy's Korean."

"What?"

"The guy who left the tea for Krystal. I'm chasing him backstage." I dodged a woman wearing a moon headdress. Stars dripped from the sleeves of her silvery gown. Next to her was a man in a sun headdress who wore a yellow leotard with painted orange and red flames licking up the side. "There are too many people back here and I need backup."

"Where's Morales?"

"I don't know." Not the time to explain that my partner and I were currently not speaking.

"I'll find him or Duffy. Stay on the line and keep me updated on your location."

"Copy." I lowered the phone but kept it connected. Up ahead, Leon shot a wild look back in my direction before ducking into the backstage area on the other side.

As I gave chase, my mind spun with the potential ramifications of Leon being at Aphrodite's wedding. Had the Chinese sent him to infiltrate the crew and sabotage things? Morales claimed the Koreans and the Chinese didn't play well together, but that was hardly conclusive proof Leon didn't work for the Fangshi.

I leapt down the steps on the other side of the stage and followed Leon down a ramp into the bowels of building. "Leon, I just want to talk to you!" I yelled.

He sped up.

I lifted the phone. "Sir, I'm going down a ramp on the west end of the building into the production areas."

"Morales and Duffy are both on their way. Mez and I are dealing with a situation in the lobby."

"What kind of situation?" I panted.

"Alexander Hung just arrived with four distraught Chinese women and Mayor Volos. They're claiming Yü Nü is missing."

"What the fuck?"

"Just focus on catching your guy. We've got this."

"Hanging up now. I'll call back once I have him."

I punched the button, shoved the phone in my cleavage, and bore down. Leon was fast, but I was determined to find out what the hell was going on. He turned down a new hallway, looked back over his shoulder to clock me, and tripped over a pile of black clothes.

He slid headlong into a closed door. I grabbed him by the coat and pushed him against the panel. It took me a second to catch my breath to speak. "Just wanted to talk to you," I said between gulps of air.

A low groan sounded behind me. I looked over my shoulder. Leon hadn't tripped over a pile of clothes, after all. He'd tripped over a beaten wizard.

"Harry?"

The leader of the Sanguinarian coven looked like ten pounds of shit in a five-pound sack. Whoever had beaten the wizard had been thorough. In fact, if not for the white hair and the vague outline of the black ankh behind the bruising, I might not have recognized him at all.

Leon wiggled in my grasp. "Let me go, lady," he said.

"Shut the fuck up, Leon. I need a minute."

"Harry?" I called again.

No response. Whoever had beaten him had left him for dead.

"Shit."

"I swear I didn't do anything." Leon whimpered.

I swiveled my face back at him. "Then why did you run, dumbass?"

His gaze skittered away.

"Prospero!" Morales's voice carried down the cavernous back-stage area.

"Down here!" I shouted back, relieved. Once he reached us, he could help me handle both Leon and the fact that someone had kicked the shit out of Harry Bane.

I turned my attention back to Leon. "Who are you working for?"

The sound of running footsteps told me that Morales and Duffy were almost on us. Once they arrived, Duffy would want to take over with Leon, and we'd have no choice but to let him. But I wanted to know the answer for my own sake.

"Did Alexander Hung hire you?"

Leon frowned. "Who?"

"Someone hired you to deliver that package to the massage parlor. Who was it?"

The door behind Leon flew open. He fell backward and I fell forward, landing in a heap at the feet of the person who opened the door. I saw two black shoes and black pants legs. Rolling over, I realized it was Gregor looming over me.

Then I saw the fist.

Then I didn't see much because a lightning bolt of pain flashed through my skull.

Shouts seemed to come at me from all angles.

And then everything went black.

CHAPTER TWENTY-SEVEN

Something poked my arm. It felt like a stick. My mind was so muddled that for a moment, I wondered how I ended up in a forest.

I opened the eye that wasn't swollen shut. My vision blurred and I instantly regretted my curiosity as pain slammed into the backs of my eyeballs. I blinked to clear away the static in my head.

Finally, my one-eyed vision cleared enough to see that I was lying on the floor, my hands bound behind my back, and that it had not been a stick that poked my arm, but Yü Nü's freaking horn.

She saw I was about to speak and shook her head. I squinted at her, and she jutted her chin to the side. I cut my eye toward the direction she'd pointed and caught my breath.

Aphrodite was dressed in white robes with a copper wreath on their bald head. At least, I thought it was Aphrodite. It was hard to tell because they wore a sun mask over their face and a moon mask over the back of their head. The effect was unsettling because no matter where you were, it seemed like one of those masks was watching.

The Hierophant paced in front of a pair of chairs that had been set up in the massive area. In those chairs sat Morales and Duffy. They were bound and bloodied, too. On either side of them stood massive guards with big guns.

"What's going on?" I whispered.

"The hermaphrodite lost her damned mind," Yü Nü hissed. "Wants to use me to become immortal."

"How?"

She looked up and crossed her eyes to look at the horn. "I told her she has to be pure and do the rites, but she said she don't have time. She gonna cut off my horn." The scorn in her voice indicated her opinion of that plan.

I nodded to show I understood enough of the gist to know we were in deep shit.

I rolled over a little to take stock of the situation.

A little wiggling revealed that while I was passed out, someone had divested me of all of my weapons. So, not only was I unarmed, I'd also been groped by some asshole to boot. I looked down where the amulet should have been rested between my cleavage, and noticed it was gone too. The only good news was someone had also taken my shoes, so my feet didn't hurt any more.

Yü Nü watched me wiggle with a passive stare. For someone being held captive, she sure seemed unworried. Easy for her, seeing how she was immortal.

Giving up on the possibility of calling in the cavalry or overpowering a guard with a weapon, I turned my attention to my surroundings.

The ceiling was high overhead, but it didn't look like a normal ceiling. The sound of clomping footsteps echoing from above told me that we were in a space under the main stage. A pulley system near the center of the ceiling indicated where the stage would open up so large set pieces could be raised from the basement level.

Directly below, on the floor, was a large platform holding a crucifix. I realized it must be the one Stefan mentioned earlier.

"What is going on?" I whispered.

"We got to get the fuck out of here," Yü Nü said.

"Oh, you're not going anywhere."

My heart stopped for a beat and then galloped ahead like a spooked horse. That voice, though muffled by the mask, had been Aphrodite's, and it told me two things. First, they knew I was awake. And second, they weren't too worried about the ramifications of kidnapping three cops, which meant they thought they had nothing left to lose.

Where the hell was our team, though?

Knowing I wouldn't have any answers until I jumped through the hermaphrodite's hoops, I schooled my features and prepared to play ball.

"This is the weirdest bachelorette party I've ever been to," I said. "When does the stripper get here?"

Aphrodite ripped off the mask. "Yes, laugh it up while you can." The voice had been calm with a hint of scorn, but those eyes were alight with a level of crazy I hadn't seen there before.

"How about you untie me so I can apologize?"

They snorted. "You'll be untied when the time comes. Until then, you will stay there and keep your mouth shut. Or I will make your boyfriend bleed."

Boyfriend. Somehow, Aphrodite had found out about my relationship with my partner and intended to use it against us.

My gaze jerked toward Morales. He looked relatively unharmed, but I didn't have a lot of hope that would remain the case. His eyes met mine across the room. He looked up toward the pulley system. I nodded to let him know I'd seen it too. At that point, it was probably our only chance for getting the hell out of there, since Aphrodite had armed guards posted at the locked door.

The Hierophant wandered behind Morales and ran a hand through his hair. He clenched his jaw and stayed totally still. "Every bride needs something old." They jerked their head toward Yü Nü. "Something new." They looked toward the crucifix. "Something borrowed—

that's you. And something black and blue." They patted Morales's face and laughed.

"And why, exactly, did you borrow me?" I asked, trying to stay calm.

Aphrodite walked over to the corner of the room where Harry's unconscious body had been dumped unceremoniously—at least I hoped he was just unconscious. "This asshole here fucked me over. Said he could help me cook the potion for immortality. But at the last minute, he chickened out." They nudged Harry with a golden sandal. "Pussy."

"Why would you ask Harry to make an immortality potion?" As the head of the Sanguinarian coven, his specialty was blood magic. While there probably were blood potions that could make someone live forever, I was pretty sure it would also turn them into something pretty close to a vampire. Not that Aphrodite couldn't rock a pair of fangs, but it didn't seem like their style.

"Because I couldn't trust any of the Votaries to help me," Aphrodite said. Then they laughed, bitterly. "Guess I should have known not to trust anyone in this godforsaken town. Used to be there was honor among the covens. We had each other's backs. But now you can't trust anyone not to fuck you over."

It struck me as odd that the person railing against the dearth of honor in Babylon was currently holding three law enforcement officers hostage, but I figured they wouldn't enjoy the irony. I did need to keep them talking, though.

"If you couldn't make Harry cooperate, how do you figure Yü Nü will instead?"

"Not willingly, of course." They laughed. "I have to thank you for being such a shitty detective, by the way. I mean, Jesus, how many clues did I need to plant for you to arrest someone from the Fangshi?" They shook their head as if we disgusted them. "Anyway, I never would have been able to get to that horn once she was in prison. So, thanks!"

"Leon works for you," I said, finally putting it together. "Not the Chinese."

"Ding, ding, ding!"

"Which means you killed Basil, too," Morales said. "Your own nephew."

"I knew you were the smart one," they said, winking at him. "Yes, I killed Basil. It wasn't my original intention, of course. I simply wanted to remind him of his loyalties. But that Votary bitch seduced him too well." Aphrodite sighed and shrugged. "After Gregor put him down, we saw the Chinese potions in the fridge and knew what the police would think—you are *so* predictable, after all. We torched the place and got out of there."

"Why kill Krystal?" Duffy asked.

"Well, she was just fun to kill. Plus, I needed to send a little message to my old friend Abe to remind him what happens when you fuck over Aphrodite Johnson."

"You went out of your way to make it look like it was the Chinese who did it." Morales said. "How does that send a message?"

"Abe was the one who taught me how to make *gu*. It was years ago, but trust me, he knows who killed Krystal." They laughed. "I'm afraid you were the only ones in the dark." They made a mocking pouty face.

"All of this was because you were pissed at Abe for partnering with the Fangshi?" I demanded.

"Among other things," they said coyly. "Anyway, that's all water under the bridge. I'd hoped to do all of this with less of a mess, but if my meditation practice has taught me anything, it's that you have to learn to let go of your need for control."

I levered myself into a sitting position, which earned me the attention of a very big gun and an even bigger man holding that gun. "Easy, there," I said. "My arm was just going to sleep."

"Oh, by all means," Aphrodite said, "you'll be needing both of your arms in a minute."

I didn't like the sound of that at all, but I refused to let them see my fear. "You know that Volos and Hung are looking for Yü Nü and our team will find us. It's only a matter of time."

Overhead, the sounds of music filtered down from the stage. Apparently, Aphrodite had considered it might take time to make the potion and scheduled other entertainment to divert the guests' attention.

"I had your partner send them a message that you were busy interrogating Leon and everything was hunky-dory, didn't I?" She looked at Morales. He nodded solemnly.

My stomach churned. The cavalry wasn't coming. Yet. Eventually, they'd get suspicious. Until then, we had to stay alive.

"They're probably enjoying the show." Aphrodite smiled up at the music and put on the sun mask again. Judging by the smugness of her tone, she'd orchestrated something shocking up there. "Fontina will keep the show going until it's time for us to join."

They snapped their fingers. In a sudden rush of motion, the guard with the gun had my hands untied and I was led over to the Hierophant.

"Oh, Kate, Kate, Kate. I'd lost hope of making the potion after Harry disappointed me. Then you literally fell into our laps when you chased poor Leon. It was divine providence that you showed up when you did."

I didn't ask where Leon was, but I wasn't real optimistic he was among the living. "Forgive me if I don't feel lucky."

They smirked. "Anyway, now that you're here, you can cook the recipe."

I froze.

"Oh, don't look so surprised. Immortality potions are an alchemist's specialty." They looked around wide-eyed. "Do you see any other alchemists here?"

"Yü Nü is way more powerful than I am."

They threw back their head and laughed. "Dumb girl, I wouldn't trust Yü Nü to make me dinner, much less a potion. She'd poison me in a heartbeat."

"You think I won't?"

"Of course not. Because if you fuck me, your boyfriend dies."

Before I could register their intention, Gregor rounded on Morales, raised his gun, and pulled the trigger.

The gunshot screamed a split second before Morales doubled over. My skin went cold and my pulse pounded in my ears, drowning out the sound of my screams. Rough hands held me back as I struggled to break away and go help him.

His chair fell over and he curled up in a ball. Next to him, Duffy tipped his own chair over and tried to check him over despite both of their hands being bound behind them.

"Duffy!" I yelled.

"They got him in the shoulder. Can't tell if it went through."

"Ouch," Aphrodite said. "I bet that hurts."

"Let me help him!" Duffy demanded. Aphrodite nodded to let the guard untie the detective. Once he was loose, he ripped off his shirt, untied Morales, and got him sitting upright. I watched the process with my breath held. Morales was pale and sweating, and his torso had way more blood staining it than I wanted to see, but he managed to nod in my direction.

"Better get to work before he loses too much blood. Or I get bored and have Gregor put another bullet in him."

I jerked out of my captor's hold. "You will fucking die today," I promised.

"Unless you want him to die, I suggest you make sure I don't, bitch." Those eyes flashed bright again, underscoring the promise. "The book is over there with the cooking supplies."

I looked to where they were pointing. The "lab" they'd indicated was little more than a plastic folding table with a shitty Bunsen burner, a few test tubes, and a few bottles with labels I couldn't read. "You've got to be kidding. There is no way I can cook with that shit."

"Best try." They waved their hand like sending me off to go pick out a puppy from a store window rather than forcing me to cook an immortality potion.

I went to the table and picked up the book. It was an old volume with a cracked leather spine and yellowed pages. The writing inside was done by hand, and it appeared to be some sort of grimoire kept by an old wizard who called himself The Bard.

The recipe's ingredients were fairly straightforward. Most alchemical processes were. But the simplicity of the ingredients was misleading. The true complexity of any alchemical potion was found in the skill of the wizard to transmute intention into magic. It wasn't just a matter of mixing a bunch of chemicals—it was about the right wizard mixing them in the right way and infusing them with the right energy.

I wasn't the right wizard for this job. I had power, yeah, but I hadn't had enough practice in the last decade to use it with the discipline needed for a powerful potion like this one.

"I'm going to need help," I said.

"Who?" Aphrodite asked.

I looked around the room. Morales was out for obvious reasons, Duffy looked about as rattled as I'd ever seen him, and Yü Nü wanted Morales dead. That left Harry Bane, who was unconscious and a blood wizard.

Or I could call in a wild card.

I looked the Hierophant in the eye and said, "Volos."

I felt Morales's gaze shoot my direction, but I pretended to ignore it. Aphrodite didn't laugh like I'd expected. "Why?" Their eyes narrowed.

"Because he's a better cook than I am. I can *read* the potion to make sure it'll work, but he's always been the stronger cook."

"You expect me to bring the mayor in here?"

"You want your fucking potion to work?" I lifted my chin. "Besides, he'll be added insurance for you. No one's going to risk shooting the mayor."

They stepped away to go confer with Gregor. My heart slammed into my ribs like a Rottweiler trying to get out of a cage. Calling in Volos was a huge gamble. But I wasn't lying. I wasn't sure I had the chops to cook that potion. Plus, I didn't know anyone more conniving than Volos. If anyone could fuck over Aphrodite and make sure we walked out alive, it was him.

I kept my expression neutral as they debated, because Aphrodite kept shooting suspicious glances my way. Finally, the Hierophant smiled like a snake. "He wouldn't do anything to risk her. Actually, it should be fun to watch him help her while she's trying to save her other man."

I clenched my jaw. At some point soon, I'd be paying Aphrodite back for all of this. Until I had that opening, I needed to play it smart. "Are we doing this or what?"

Gregor brought my cell phone and made me give him my code. Before they hit SEND on Volos's number, Aphrodite warned, "If you say one thing wrong, I will murder Duffy and put another bullet in Morales. Am I clear?"

I nodded and swallowed the bile in my throat. Aphrodite hit the number. The phone barely rang before Volos answered. "Kate, where the hell are you?"

"Shut up and listen to me. I need you to get away from the others and come help me."

"Where are you?"

"I can't say. Just promise you'll come alone."

"Of course."

Aphrodite covered the mouthpiece and said, "Tell him what happens if he tries to be a hero."

"They're going to kill us."

Aphrodite smiled.

"Who?" His voice had the controlled tone of a man resigned to committing premeditated murder.

"Aphrodite."

"I understand. Where?"

A wave of emotion rose up. If he came, it could mean his death, but he hadn't hesitated. "Wait alone in the alcove to the left of the theater entrance."

"On my way. Kate?"

"Yeah?"

"We'll figure this out together." Those simple words held complicated promises. I didn't want to think too hard about what this would cost me, needing him. But I knew that I had no choice.

After the call, I went to the table to start prepping the cook. Keeping my hands busy kept me from looking toward Morales. I told myself this was for his own good. The more distracted I was by his injury, the longer it would take to make the potion.

But the real truth was, I avoided looking at him for my own good. Because I knew he'd have a couple of strong opinions about me calling in Volos to help me. It wouldn't do any good to tell Morales I was only doing this to save him. But that wasn't the whole truth, and we'd both know it.

My hands shook as I fired up the Bunsen burner. With nothing left to do until my sous-chef arrived, I lifted the book and began to read. According to The Bard, a shortcut to the Philosopher's Stone, also known as the Panacea—or universal cure and key to immortality— was to use someone else's stone and combine it with the "Hand of the Philosophers."

Even though I'd studied dirty magic on the streets, I had passing familiarity with the idea behind the Hand. The term referred to five mineral salts that could be used to unlock the mineral or metallic essences. If I was reading the instructions right, The Bard was claiming that if you could steal someone's stone or get part of it and mix the with the five salts, you could unlock immortality. In this case, the Philosopher's Stone would be Yü Nü's horn.

The music upstairs reached a crescendo. The next moment,

pounding came from the door. I turned in time to see the guards open it for Gregor and Volos.

The instant Volos stepped across the threshold, the air in the room instantly ignited with a new electrical charge. It wasn't just me, either. Aphrodite shivered and Morales moaned, as if Volos's arrival brought him new physical pain.

Volos quickly scanned the room, but I knew he hadn't missed a single detail. When his eyes found me, they flared, as if he'd zeroed in on his target. He looked me up and down. When the gaze reached my battered face, his eyes narrowed dangerously. I shook my head to let him know I was fine. He seemed to relax a fraction, but not much.

"Welcome to the party," Aphrodite said, coming forward. "Kate will fill you in on the particulars. I'd advise you not to try to be the hero, John. It won't go well for any of you."

He didn't deign to speak to them. He simply nodded and marched toward me, a man with total focus.

When he reached me, he simply said, "What are we cooking?"

"You ever make an immortality potion?"

The corner of his mouth lifted. "Would it surprise you if I said yes?"

"Not at all. Any of them work?"

"Not a damned one."

"This one needs to or we're all dead."

He took the book from my hands. "Then we better get busy."

CHAPTER TWENTY-EIGHT

T hirty minutes later, we weren't smiling anymore. The chemicals we were working with normally required a secure lab, plenty of protective gear, and lots of luck. Not only were they extremely flammable, they were also caustic. But instead of thick gloves and goggles, we had our bare hands and lots of cursing and praying.

The cocktail of chemicals was so pungent that all of the guards had retreated to the other end of the room to escape the noxious odors. Even Aphrodite gave us a wide berth. Though they still managed to shout intermittent threats to remind us that one wrong move and they'd shoot someone.

We'd already created the Aqua Regia by mixing the Philosopher's Hand. The recipe called for four parts vitriol, one part alum, and six parts niter. Once those were mixed, we added sal ammoniac to the distillate. The resulting "King's Water" was strong enough to dissolve gold—or, we hoped, an immortal sorceress's horn.

I wiped sweat from my forehead and glanced toward Morales. He was dangerously pale and growing more so by the minute.

"All right," Volos said, "we need to get the horn."

He looked at me expectantly, as if somehow, I'd been elected horn harvester without my knowledge or consent.

"I'm not doing it!" I whispered.

We both glanced over to where Yü Nü sat in a half-lotus watching us cook. The serene expression on her face bordered on amused, which did nothing to help my confidence. If we'd done something wrong, she sure as hell wouldn't tell us.

"I'm not doing it," Volos said. "She scares the shit out of me. Besides, I already did my big heroic act of the day by coming down here to save your ass."

"What's the holdup?" Aphrodite yelled. "The sex acts are almost complete."

I rolled my eyes and tried to ignore the grunting and moaning coming from upstairs. Apparently, Aphrodite had recruited some of her employees to put on a sex magic ritual in preparation for the wedding. The sounds didn't do much for my concentration. Especially when I could feel Morales glaring at my back as I had my head down working with Volos on the potion to the dulcet sounds of a woman having multiple orgasms overhead.

"We're working on it," I snapped.

"Tut-tut," Aphrodite called. "No need to get snippy."

I blew out a deep breath, shot John one last glare, and marched over to face Yü Nü. As I approached, she watched me, unmoving. Up top, the woman peaked for the seventh time in a row.

"Hey, Aphrodite?" I called.

"What?"

"I need a knife."

"I don't think so."

I rounded on her. "How in the hell am I supposed to put that horn"—I pointed at the green horn—"into that potion"—I pointed toward the table—"without a Goddamned knife?"

Aphrodite stormed over and pulled a ceremonial dagger from a garter on their right thigh. "I'll do it."

They leapt forward and brandished the knife, like they meant to sever the entire horn from Yü Nü's head. But the second she touched the sorceress, Aphrodite wailed like they'd been burned. The knife went skittering across the floor.

I walked over and calmly picked it up. By the time I got back, Aphrodite was lobbing threats at a serene Yü Nü. "I swear to Cybele, if you don't give me that horn, I'm going to disembowel you with a spoon."

"Big talk for a glorified pimp," Yü Nü taunted. "You don't deserve immortality."

"Shoot them!" Aphrodite shrieked. "All of them."

The room filled with the sound of several guns priming for the kill. I held up my hands. "Hold on," I said. "If you shoot us, you're done for. This room will be full of cops so fast, your head will spin. Aphrodite, please. Let me talk to her."

Aphrodite crossed their arms and said, "You have one minute."

I nodded and stepped around her to face the sorceress. "Hey, Yü Nü," I said. "Look, the recipe doesn't say I need the whole horn."

She didn't speak.

"Yeah, so anyway, I just need to, like, chip off a piece or scrape off some shavings or whatever."

Those unblinking eyes watched me.

"I know you're pissed, and honestly, I'm not so thrilled to be here, either. But all I need is some of that horn and all of us have a chance of walking away."

"I am immortal, girlie. They can shoot all their bullets at me and I will survive." Yü Nü crossed her arms. "I won't let you use my magic to save a man who put my family in prison."

"Well, not to split hairs here, but your family did do a lot of illegal shit. If they weren't smart enough to cover their tracks, it's not his fault."

The sounds of male rumbling came from across the room. Apparently, Morales had some opinions about my handling of the situation.

But at that point, I wasn't real receptive to his advice on matters concerning the Fangshi.

"Look, Yü Nü, I know you hate him. I'm not too thrilled with him right now either. But he doesn't deserve to die because Aphrodite's lost their damned mind." I turned and looked over my shoulder. "No offense."

Aphrodite's lips pursed so hard, they resembled a prolapsed anus.

"I promise I'll only take a little. And once we're all out of here, I promise you can go back to wanting Morales dead."

She let out a big sigh. "Okay, fine. But only a little. And don't tell anyone I gave it to you, or every wizard will be knocking down my door wanting to shave my horn."

I held my hand over my heart. "You have my word."

She placed her hands in her lap and lifted her chin to give me access. The jade horn jutted up at me like a tiny middle finger. "Volos, I need a clean dish."

Rustling sounded behind me. I smelled his cologne before I saw the clear dish appear. "Thanks," I said, refusing to look at him. "Hold it steady."

I leaned in and brought the knife up horizontally. The entire room was quiet. Even the sex performers upstairs seemed to have fallen silent. I gently placed the edge of the knife along the bottom of the horn. "Ready?"

"Just do it," Yü Nü snapped.

And just like that, I scraped the horn. A screeching sound cut through the air, like nails on a chalkboard. I winced but kept scraping until several green shavings rested on the dish.

"I think that's enough," Volos murmured behind me.

I let out the breath I'd been holding. "Thanks."

I was close enough that only I heard the words she whispered. When they hit my ears, I froze, but as their meaning registered, I forced myself to act casual and walk away.

When I reached the table, I watched Volos lift the shavings to the light. I leaned in and repeated the words Yü Nü had said. "Once they drink it, run like hell."

Volos and I exchanged a look. I wished I'd been able to question the sorceress. Ask her if she meant that Aphrodite would kill us or that the potion would never work.

We didn't have the luxury of wondering. Our only choice was to move forward. Carefully.

Volos placed the shavings into the container of Aqua Regia. The mixture immediately bubbled and hissed. It had been gold in color, but now it transformed to black, white, yellow, and, finally, red.

Volos blew out a breath. "I think that's it."

"Finally!" Aphrodite shouted. "Let's get this show on the road."

"Hold on," I said, "I need to be sure."

"Kate," Morales said, his voice strained from pain and fatigue, "hurry."

He looked like he'd aged ten years. I gave him a weak thumbs-up and turned back to the task.

Volos, knowing what was coming, stepped back. I turned my back to everyone and closed my eyes. I heard him say something to the others in a low tone, but I actively blocked everything out after that.

Inhaling a deep breath, I scanned down my body, focusing on relaxing each limb. I willed my cells to tune into the vibrations of magic running through my body. When everything was humming, I finally opened my eyes.

The potion looked different now. Instead of the simple red liquid from earlier, it now glowed iridescent and thrummed with power. Above the glow, I saw the red dragon of Yü Nü's magic. Next to that were two crowned serpents swallowing each other's tails in an infinity symbol. I realized with a start that this image was supposed to be my magic mixed with Volos's power.

Swallowing hard, I focused on the images again, looking beyond the surface markers that identified the wizards who'd created the magic and beyond to the heart of the potion. There, circling in the air over the potion, was a soaring red phoenix.

I released all of my energy at once, nearly collapsing from the rush of power. Volos caught me and steadied me. "It's good," I gasped. "We did it."

Suddenly, there was a rush of movement around us. Gregor and the other guards ushered all of us onto the platform.

"Wait," I yelled, "we did what you asked. Let us go." I pointed at the blood coating Morales's torso. "He needs medical attention."

Aphrodite had that mask back on, a leering sun burning in the dark. "The proof will be in the pudding. No one is free until the rites are complete."

A guard dropped Morales at my feet. I knelt down to support him. "Hang in there, okay?"

He was paler now and his skin was coated in a fine sheen of cold sweat. I grabbed his hand to help him rise and Volos looped his arm under to support Morales's weight on the other side.

On the other side of the platform, Duffy and Yü Nü huddled together. Aphrodite climbed onto their crucifix. They seemed to have dismissed the unconscious Harry Bane in the corner. I'd seen him twitch a time or two, so I didn't think he was dead. In fact, he was probably the safest of all of us at that point because he wasn't going up to the stage for whatever horror show Aphrodite had planned.

"All right, kiddies, smile. It's show time." Aphrodite threw their head back to look up at the trap door overhead. "Send up the guards."

Half of the armed men left the basement. Presumably, they were going up to the stage to ensure Aphrodite's safety if any of the law enforcement agents in the audience decided to try to play hero.

From somewhere in the theater, trumpets blared. A cheer rose from the crowd.

Gregor placed a headset on the Hierophant's head. A moment later, when they spoke, the sound echoed from above, as if they were being broadcast into the theater.

"Ladies, gentlemen, and everyone in between, thank you so much for attending this sacred occasion tonight. In a moment, we will begin the rites. You will notice that some of my personal security staff are posted on the stage. Don't be alarmed. They are there to ensure the safety of everyone involved. We have also taken the liberty of locking the doors to the theater."

Gasps filtered down. Aphrodite smiled. A murmur of alarm rose in the theater.

"Again, this is for your own protection. Assuming everything goes to plan, no one will be harmed. Now, let the show begin!"

The pulley system squeaked and groaned. The platform lurched and then we were rising steadily toward the hole in the ceiling.

I looked at Volos, whose expression was uncharacteristically anxious. Morales squeezed my hand. I looked at him.

"That potion going to work?"

I nodded. "Looks like."

"How do you know?"

I sighed. "Because it's what I do."

"Meaning?" He frowned.

Time to come clean. "I can *read* magic. Tell who made it and what it does."

His face tightened. I braced myself for the recriminations. Defensive retorts already began to form in my head. But then his expression cleared and he leaned into me. "Jesus, Kate. I'm sorry," he said. "I'm so damned sorry."

"Don't." I closed my eyes and enjoyed the solid weight of him against me. Close by, I could feel Volos watching us, but I didn't care. "It doesn't matter right now. Just save your energy. We're going to need to be strong and fast to get out of this."

"Actually," Volos said, "if bullets start flying, it's going to take a fucking miracle." He glanced at Morales and me. A tight smile appeared on his lips. "But strong and fast won't hurt, either."

When Morales didn't try to get the final word in, I realized he must be in worse shape than I realized.

Shouting from up above echoed down to us. Guess the crowd hadn't been as reassured by Aphrodite's words as they'd hoped.

"When we get up there, Kate will stay with me," Aphrodite commanded. "Everyone else don't move, or my guards will not hesitate to take you out. No one must interfere with the ascension rites. Am I clear?"

We all muttered our understanding of the terms. I didn't bother asking why I was the only one required to stay with them. I was their insurance. Morales and Volos wouldn't go after them with me at their side, and the MEA and BPD in the building wouldn't risk shooting a cop.

Next thing I knew, we were emerging from the darkness and into the intense stage lights. They blinded all of us temporarily. After blinking several times, my vision cleared enough to look out over the packed theater. I couldn't make out distinct faces, but I had the impression of hundreds of worried faces watching the drama unfold onstage.

It didn't take long for people to start noticing the wounded among us, or that the mayor was one of the hostages. Shouts and screams came from the crowd. The sounds of confrontation reached us as some people tried to get through the exits.

A gunshot ripped through the theater.

"Enough!" Aphrodite screamed into her headset. "You came here for a show, didn't you? How often in your life do you get the privilege of witnessing a Hierophant ascend to the higher plane of existence? Do you think this process is pretty? Do you think magic is neat and tidy?" They laughed. "Children, I assure you, it is not."

They spoke from their perch on the crucifix. Fontina appeared and pulled the robe from their body. Now, Aphrodite wore a simple loincloth. The breast on the left side of their chest was exposed along with the pectoral of the right side.

"Take a good look. This earthly body is about to transmute into a sacred vessel of immortality!" They threw off their masks and removed their loincloth. Fontina clapped and cheered.

Gasps rippled through the shocked crowd. A flaccid penis sat just above a hairless vulva. I didn't find the display grotesque or shocking. It was all…just flesh.

Aphrodite was revered as some sort of mysterious figure, but really, they were just a person. I realized with a start that maybe in some ways, they were more human than the rest of us, being one of the few humans who knew what it was like to live inside the skin of both a man and a woman. Unfortunately, that knowing hadn't translated into wisdom.

From the corner of my eye, I saw Morales leaning into Volos as two guards pointed the muzzles of machine guns at their midsections. Across the stage, Yü Nü and Duffy were receiving the same treatment.

I looked out into the glow of the lights that created a barrier between us and the audience. Somewhere out there, Gardner and Mez, and, by now, probably Shadi, McGinty, and Dixon, were watching this profane tableau play out. Their guns were probably in their hands too.

I clasped my hand around the potion vial. Such a thin layer of glass separating me from an elixir that could give whoever took it everlasting life.

I looked up at Aphrodite again as they lectured the theater on how lucky they were to be there, and I felt sick to my stomach. No matter what any of us claimed or how much territory someone controlled in this town, none of us were magic's master.

Movement from the corner of my eye grabbed my attention. Morales and Volos were inching toward their guards. The pair of security goons were too busy listening to Aphrodite to pay adequate attention to the two most dangerous men in the room.

Morales caught my eye and nodded. I scratched my cheek to indicate that when they made the move, I'd be ready.

"Now," Aphrodite proclaimed, "I will ingest the potion to finally merge my masculine and feminine energies, thereby perfecting my nature and becoming immortal." They looked at me. "This potion was created by Kate Prospero, niece of Abraxas Prospero, the betrayer. Once I ingest this elixir, I will ascend as the supreme coven leader of all of Babylon!"

They paused, as if waiting for applause, but none came.

The speech made me pity them. I used to sort of admire Aphrodite's gumption, but now they'd let my Uncle Abe's bullshit get to their head. How many other people had been destroyed because he'd betrayed them? How many more would fall before he was done?

"Katherine, the potion, please."

Aphrodite smiled down at me. The lights caught the stubble growing in on the right side of their face. It made the sweat on their upper lip shine. Aphrodite imagined themself a god, but they were just a person. Another victim of magic's seductive force. I wondered if they'd even had a choice when a wizard turned them into a hermaphrodite as a child.

"Kate," they snapped, "now!"

I raised the vial with my left hand. "I'm sorry you suffered," I whispered. "But this won't fix things."

They frowned at me. Those lunatic eyes cleared for a moment, and I swear, in that brief instant, I saw something wholesome in there. But just as soon as it appeared, the lucidity evaporated.

Aphrodite snatched the potion from my hand. They raised the red liquid high, like an offering to a fickle god. Then they popped the cork and tossed it back in one gulp.

For a moment, the red liquid clung to their lips like blood. Their tongue darted out to get every last drop.

Time slowed. I stared transfixed, waiting for the miracle.

From far away, I heard my name. Beyond Aphrodite, bodies spun into chaotic motion.

Aphrodite lay their head back against the crossbars and smiled beatifically. The bones of their face undulated beneath the skin, as if reknitting together into a more cohesive structure.

Out of the chaos, I recognized the faces of the team as they emerged from the crowd to rush the stage. Mez deployed some sort of magical explosive that stunned the guards nearest the stairs they'd come up. Then Gardner was behind him, grabbing Morales and pulling him to safety.

Someone grabbed me from behind and pulled me off the platform. I fell back onto the floor, landing on someone solid. "Katie, we have to go." It was Volos. "It's not safe."

I couldn't take my eyes of off Aphrodite. The light hit their face like a beacon.

"Kate," John said more forcefully this time. But then he turned to fight one of the guards who'd come forward.

I moved close to the cross. I had to watch. Had to see the ascension.

At first, it seemed like things were going according to plan. Aphrodite's face changed, losing both its softness and its hard edges. But then the blisters appeared.

And the screams began.

Smoke billowed from their ears. The body vibrated and shook. Charred patches appeared at intervals, shot through with pink and red tissue. The air filled with the scent of burning human flesh.

All around, people ran and shouted. Someone called my name. I spun and watched Duffy barreling toward me, as if in slow motion.

Just behind him, Fontina raised a gun and pointed it at the detective's back.

Several thoughts occurred to me in a rush even as time slowed. Duffy threatening to report me to Internal Affairs. Me threatening him for snitching. Morales killing that dirty cop to save himself.

It would be so easy, I thought.

Even as my ego campaigned for an easy fix to my problems, my instincts had already made my decision.

I ran at Duffy and pushed him off to the side. He shouted and went down, falling off the stage.

Behind me, Volos screamed my name.

Deprived of her original target, Fontina aimed the gun at me.

She smiled and pulled the trigger.

A flash of color appeared. I thought it was my life passing before my eyes. However, at the exact moment I should have felt the pain of the bullet ripping through my flesh, a body tackled me.

My first thought was that somehow, Volos had managed a super-human feat and made it in time to save me. But when I rolled over, I realized that the body on top of me was too round and small to be his.

Yü Nü fell back into my arms. Her blood coated my hands.

Strong legs pressed into my back, supporting me as I held the sorceress. I looked up to see Volos standing over us with a gun. Without a second's hesitation, he pulled the trigger.

Fontina fell into a puddle of blood-stained chiffon and Southern-spiced curses. She wasn't dead, but she was done being a problem for the time being.

Up on the cross, the Hierophant threw back their head and screamed a column of flame.

Volos knelt next to me and the sorceress. "You two all right?"

I shook my head because I wasn't sure of anything. Yü Nü hadn't moved since we fell.

Volos took her chin and gingerly touched the horn. "Ow, shit!" he hissed, pulling his hand away.

Yü Nü's horn began to glow. Heat radiated through her body, seeping into my skin. "Don't touch the horn," she said with her eyes still closed.

My relief was short-lived. A keening wail came from center stage.

Gregor stood beneath the cross. Tears poured down his face. He removed his gun from his holster.

"We've got to move," Volos said. He lifted Yü Nü to carry her away. "Come on!"

I rose slowly, letting them go on without me because I was unable to tear my gaze from the drama unfolding at the cross. Gregor's lips moved in silent prayer. Then he pointed the gun at the column of flame, right above the heart. "I'm sorry, my love. I'm so sorry."

He pulled the trigger.

Someone grabbed me from behind and forced me to move. I turned to look over my shoulder. It was Volos. He'd come back to get me.

Just like he always will, I thought.

As he pulled me away, I watched five armed cops, including Shadi and McGinty, open fire on Aphrodite's bodyguard.

He fell dead at the foot of the person he'd loved. Above his too-still body, Aphrodite's corpse smoldered.

As I was carried away, people shouted and fussed. They seemed far away—or maybe that was me. I turned to look one more time at the tableau onstage.

Several men had found fire extinguishers and were dousing the last of the flames. I thought about that charred house where they'd found Basil's body—also shot and burned.

Some might call that justice.

But to me, it all seemed like such a fucking waste.

CHAPTER TWENTY-NINE

Three days later, reporters packed the hospital's conference room. Next to me, Morales sat in a wheelchair, looking handsome and wounded. His arm was in a sling and a bandage covered the large gash across his forehead. He'd been instructed not to speak during the press conference due to the cocktail of pain potions flowing through his system. I stood between him and Gardner, trying not to look as ambivalent as I felt.

On the table in front of us stood fat stacks of cash and piles of colorful potion ampoules, baggies filed with patches, and some additional alchemical props thrown in for effect. Most of the props had been gathered in a raid we'd done two days earlier at Aphrodite's temple. In the end, Gardner had gotten her potions and money on the table like she wanted.

She was wrapping up her spiel. "I have been in touch with AUSA Grey and his is already building a case against the remaining members of Aphrodite Johnson's coven, including the former madam of a sex magic temple in Atlanta, Fontina Douglas, for crimes including two counts of murder in the first degree, conspiracy to commit murder, racketeering, and a host of other crimes that should put several of them away in Crowley Penitentiary for a very long time." She waited for the applause to die down before continuing. "I speak on behalf of myself, the entire MEA, as well as Detective Prospero and Special Agent Morales, in thanking the Babylon Police Department, including Commissioner Adams, newly appointed Chief Eldritch, Fire Inspector Perry, and Detective Duffy for the help in this case. We could not do our work without their cooperation."

The men she'd name-checked stood and did their best to look humble.

Not one of us in that room had suspected Aphrodite Johnson as being behind those murders. Yet here we were, taking credit for their death.

A butterfly touch brushed my left hand. I glanced down and saw Morales shoot me a look. He was supposed to be hexed out of his gourd, but his eyes looked plenty clear to me. We'd worked together long enough that he could probably recite my thoughts to me verbatim. It helped that he usually shared my impatience for the spectacle. The difference between us was that he saw it as a necessary evil, whereas I just saw bullshit.

"We'll take a few questions," Gardner said.

Journalists leapt out of their chairs and waved hands to be called on. Gardner selected a Hispanic reporter I recognized from the local evening news. "Carmen Fuentes, Channel 10, Action News," she said. "My question is for Detective Prospero."

I stepped up and nodded, trying not to look like I wanted to run away. "Will you be under any sort of disciplinary action for cooking dirty magic for Aphrodite?"

A pocket of flame erupted in my gut at the gall of the question. Luckily, Gardner stepped in to field it. "Absolutely not. It is only thanks to the quick thinking of Detective Prospero and Mayor Volos that everyone walked away with their lives. In fact, I believe the mayor is working on a special commendation for the detective."

That was the first I'd heard of that possibility. With cameras on me and Morales at my side, I kept my expression blank. But inside, I was conflicted between embarrassment and dread. I hadn't spoken to Volos since he'd hauled me out of the theater. I probably owed him an apology for dragging him into that scene, and a thank-you for pulling me out of the shootout. But I hadn't allowed myself to wallow too much in the fact that I owed him. Again.

"Is it true that Detective Duffy is retiring from the force?" another reporter asked.

I perked up at that one. Duffy looked about as excited to address the press as he'd have been about getting his prostate exam. But he couldn't avoid the expectant looks.

"Yes, that's true," he said. "My last day will be in a few weeks. I've already started working with Chief Eldritch on identifying my replacement."

"What about Detective Prospero?" a reporter shouted.

All eyes turned to me. Duffy looked like he wanted to cry. Eldritch looked like someone had offered him a shit sandwich.

"What do you say, Detective?" someone shouted.

Morales nudged me. My feet felt like they weighed fifty pounds as I stepped up to the mic. "I wouldn't dream of trying to fill Detective Duffy's shoes," I said. "Besides, I'd love to keep working with the MEA as long as they'll have me."

Apparently, I said the right thing, because Eldritch visibly relaxed.

"That's all the questions we have time for today," Gardner said. "Thank you."

* * *

After the press conference, I accompanied Morales back to his room. Once the nurses got him settled, I let out a huge sigh of relief at the blessed silence.

He'd been pretty quiet through the conference and the ride up to his room.

"You all right?" I asked.

He'd been looking out the window while I chatted with the nurses, and now he turned his head on the pillow to look at me. The light slanting in highlighted the bruises under his eyes and the paleness of his skin. The doctor said he had at least another week to go in the hospital before he could go home, but he was looking at months of rehab for the arm.

After that? Well, we didn't talk about that yet.

"Drew?" I prompted when he didn't immediately answer.

"I was just thinking about Yü Nü," he said.

I frowned. "What about her?"

"How she jumped in front of you."

In all the craziness since he got shot, I hadn't had a lot of time to process everything that had gone down at the theater. But every night, I'd had a dream where I was dying and Yü Nü offered me an elixir. Each time, she whispered that a friend had sent her.

"Maybe it was a reflex," I said, brushing it off. I rose and busied myself pruning the flowers that lined the windowsill.

The corner of his mouth lifted. "Jumping in front of a bullet for someone is a pretty big deal."

"Not when you know you're immortal."

He lay his head back on the pillow and looked up at the ceiling philosophically. "Duffy's retiring."

"Yep." I threw a handful of dead red and white rose petals in the garbage. As I did, I spotted a discarded newspaper on top. A face in a picture on the front page grabbed my attention.

I removed it and held the image up to the light. The man in the picture looked a lot like the one who'd been meeting with Hung and Volos at the Buddhist restaurant. I scanned the photo's caption. *Senator Thomas Graves (R-NY) visits Babylon for a GOP fundraiser*

"I'll be damned," I breathed.

"Huh?"

The doctor had urged all of us to keep stress away from Morales to aid in healing. I was pretty sure if I told him Volos had a United

States Senator in his pocket, his blood pressure would skyrocket just like mine was.

"They're expecting rain tomorrow." I stashed the paper with my jacket before I went back to the bed. Later, I'd have to figure out why Volos, who was a Democrat, had business with a Republican senator from New York, but for now, Morales needed my attention.

I straightened the tray table across the bed, discarding bits of trash to distract myself from the theories popping up about Volos and the senator.

"I saw you," Morales said quietly.

I looked up, feeling guilty even though there was no way he'd know what I was thinking about. "When?"

"That night. I saw you save Duffy."

I looked around the room for something else to tidy. "Let's talk about something else, okay?"

He patted the edge of his bed. "C'm'ere." His lids looked heavy and his tone slurred a little. The nurses had given him a dose of pain potion before she left, and they were already kicking in.

I perched on the edge of his bed and took his left hand. His grip was surprisingly strong. I turned our joined hands over so I could look closer at the scars webbing across the surface. It hit me then that he'd probably have to relearn how to be a Leftie for a while.

"I told Gardner."

My stomach felt like it dropped ten stories. "When?"

"Apparently, it all came out when I was coming out of anesthesia." His tone was rueful.

"And?"

"And we're going to have a discussion once I get out of here. But it didn't sound like she was ready to send me to the clink."

"That's good." I smoothed a hand across his forehead. "That's real good."

He took my hand and held it in his left. "I can't change the past," he said, his words slurring.

"Shh. Let's talk about it later."

"Kate?" he murmured. His eyes were barely open now. I placed my right hand on his cheek, enjoying the rasp of whiskers against my palm. I'd been so afraid at the theater. There'd been so much blood and he'd lost consciousness before they loaded him in the ambulance. And for the first time, I had to imagine a life without him as my partner.

"Yeah?" I said, leaning down to kiss his forehead.

"You love me?"

I froze. His eyes cracked open a slit, and he looked at me with dilated pupils.

He was hexed-out and vulnerable, but he was asking me to love him.

"Of course," I said. "Of course I do."

"Good," he slurred. A smiled lifted the corners of his mouth. "I love me, too."

I huffed out a laugh and kissed him again, this time on the cheek. "Night, Prince Charming."

His hand went limp as he entered the underworld of magic-induced dreams. I rose from the bed and tried to ignore the ghost of guilt that clung to me as I walked toward the door.

I hadn't been lying. I did love him.

He was my partner and my best friend.

I loved him. I did.

I reached for the handle but paused to look back. Even in his sleep, he looked intimidating, with his dark whiskers and hard jaw. Losing him would have fucked me up for a really long time.

Yeah, I loved him.

But that wasn't really what he'd been asking. He didn't just want me to love him. He wanted me to be *in* love with him.

But how could I be in love with someone who lied to me?

And how could I claim to be in love with someone when I lied to them, too?

Before those thoughts could sink their claws too far into me, I threw open the door and marched out.

My body slammed into an immovable obstacle.

"Oh!" I gasped. Hands gripped my arms to steady me. I looked up.

"Kate? Are you okay?"

My traitorous heart whispered: *This one.*

I gasped and pulled away. "Damn it, John."

He loosened his hold but not enough to allow escape. "What's wrong?"

I pushed his hands away and retreated into myself. "You just surprised me," I snapped.

The warm, chypre scent of his cologne clung to me as tried to put space between us.

He nodded toward the door. "Is he okay?"

"He will be."

He nodded and put his hands in his pockets. "Good, that's good."

"Don't act like you care."

"I've made no secret about not liking the guy, but I don't want him dead."

"Why not? Your life would be a lot easier."

He was quiet for so long that I looked up at him to see what was taking so long. The fury on his face made me lose my breath. "I am not a monster, Kate. The last thing I want in this world is for anything to hurt you."

And that's when I knew. "Do you know why Yü Nü protected me?"

He blinked at the rapid change in topic and shifted uneasily in his expensive loafers. "Of course not."

I raised a brow. "Liar."

"I said I wasn't a monster. I never claimed to be honest." With that, he reached out and tucked a strand of hair behind my ear. "Take care of yourself, Kate."

The tenderness in his tone stunned me. He turned to go, but before he reached the door, I said his name.

He stopped and turned. "Yes?"

"Thanks," I said, "for, uh, helping Danny get into the Conservatory. And stuff."

He waited a couple of beats too long to answer. "Of course." A little unguarded smile lifted the corners of his mouth. He turned again.

"John?"

He stopped again with his brows raised.

"I'm sorry I pulled you into that mess. At the theater, I mean. I just didn't know what else to do."

"Don't sweat it," he said. "Turns out all those years cooking dirty pays off sometimes."

"I guess so." I'd never thought of it that way. "Anyway, I— Thanks."

He held my gaze and smiled a smile that I felt all the way to my toes. "It's always my pleasure, Detective."

With that, he left, leaving me behind trying to sort through the cocktail of conflicting emotions his deeply spoken *pleasure* created in my midsection.

It was only once I was in the elevator and out of his sphere of influence that I realized I hadn't asked him about the senator.

CHAPTER THIRTY

A few weeks later, I parked on the street in front of City Hall and left the engine running. "I'll just be a sec, okay?"

"Make it fast," Danny said. "I don't want to be late."

I waved to acknowledge the request and jumped out of the Jeep. The sun was still rising over the river, and the scent of green algae rode the wind off the water. I sucked a deep breath in through my nose to try to enjoy the experience of Babylon before all the people woke up and ruined it.

The front steps of City Hall were pretty empty except for the usual winged loiterers. Luckily, the person I'd come to see was an early riser.

Sweet Ray sat about halfway up the stairs. He wore a purple fez that morning with a Sergeant Pepper jacket. When he saw me jogging up the steps toward him, he turned to say something to the pigeons at his feet. I couldn't quite make it out except for the tone, which sounded pretty bitchy for six in the morning.

"What's happening, Sweet Ray?" I said.

"Peewee doesn't want to talk to you," he said, keeping his eyes averted.

"I'm not here to talk to Peewee. I'm here to talk to you."

His shoulders twitched in a halfhearted shrug. "What do I care?"

"Look," I said, perching a foot on a higher step, "I know I left you hanging, but things have been pretty fucked-up the last few weeks."

The last two weeks alone had been a blur. Morales had gotten out of the hospital and was home, but he had PT appointments several times a week. With him on medical leave, I'd been stuck with all the paperwork on our cases as well as pitching in with Shadi's. On top of all that, there'd been a scramble to get Danny ready for camp. Without Baba pitching in, I don't know how I would have juggled all of it.

Sweet Ray half-turned his head my direction. "We saw your picture in the paper. You looked like shit."

I laughed out loud. "I bet." I really owed Pen a new dress. I'd practically had to burn the other one.

"Did you really cook dirty for the Hierophant?"

I sobered. "Yeah."

"Where'd you learn to do that?"

I waved my left hand. "I grew up in the Cauldron."

He finally looked at me. "No shit? And now you're a cop?"

"Decided life was better on the other side," I said. Little had I known when I made that decision how much more complicated *better* would be. "Anyway, I got something for you."

He perked up. "You hear that, Peewee? She brought *me* a present."

The pigeons at his feet clucked and shuffled, clearly unimpressed.

I pulled the box from my jacket pocket. He looked at it for a moment, clearly not trusting that I wasn't fucking with him.

"Are you for real with that?"

I shoved the Babylon Mobile box into his hand. "It's nothing fancy. Just a burner. I put forty dollars on it, though. That should last you a little."

His hand trembled and the corners of his eyes got suspiciously bright. "A cell-a-phone?" He said it with the reverence one might have for a sacred religious artifact. "For me?"

Suddenly fighting some moisture in my own eyes, I cleared my throat. "Well, you earned it, didn't you? You gave me some good information. You and Peewee."

He sat up straighter. "Mostly me, though."

"Mostly you." I watched him open the box and pulled out the simple flip phone. "I programmed my number in there. In case you ever see anything else I need to know about."

He looked up from the phone. "You mean about Mr. Mayor?"

I hesitated, thinking about that day at the hospital. Volos had been off my radar for a few weeks, but I was pretty sure it was only a matter of time until he popped up again. "Sure," I said finally, "or any coven stuff."

"What if I run out of minutes?"

"I'll refill it when you bring me something useful," I said.

"All right." He pursed his lips.

"Hey, Sweet Ray?"

"Yeah?"

"You know how you said the eclipse would be death?"

He nodded solemnly.

"I mean, I lived and all, but things were close there for a little bit." I cleared my throat. "I guess I was wondering how you knew there'd be in trouble."

He smiled wide, exposing white gums and a few gray teeth set against his green lips. "I told you, Peewee sees everything."

"All right." I laughed. "You take care of yourself, okay?"

He waved the cell phone. "Thanks."

When I got back to the car, Danny looked up toward the stairs. "Who's that guy?"

I paused before starting Sybil. "That, my friend, is what happens to people who get involved with dirty magic."

"Whatever." He rolled his eyes like a pro. "Can we go now?"

* * *

We pulled into the parking lot about ten minutes later. The Conservatory building looked half-baked but full of promise in the golden rays of first light. I chose to see that as a positive portent.

"You can just drop me off." Danny opened the door before I even pulled to a complete stop.

"Hold it." I threw the car in Park, grabbed my travel mug of coffee, and turned off the Jeep. "You're stuck with me until that bus leaves."

He muttered under his breath, but I knew it was all an act. He'd been checking his hair in the visor mirror ever since we left the house, and he kept looking in his backpack to see if he forgot anything. The kid was nervous as hell. He might be able to convince himself that he didn't need me, but I wasn't naive enough to believe it. Besides, even if he didn't want me there, I needed to be there to see him off.

It was the first time we'd be apart this long. He'd spent the night with friends plenty of times, and had a couple of school trips over long weekends. But my little brother had never been out of my sight for two whole weeks before. Even Baba, who'd known him since he was about six years old, couldn't handle it. She'd refused to come to see him off because she was afraid she'd make too much of a scene. Instead, she opted to stay home to start making cookies to send him in care packages.

"Kate?" His impatient tone dragged me out of my reverie.

"Right. Sorry." I climbed out with my coffee, holding it like a security blanket.

I surveyed the parking lot for any familiar faces. The only one I spied was Principal Hidalgo. She stood next to the bus, checking kids in against a roster on a clipboard. She spotted us and waved, but then a group approached and she got caught up with their questions.

Around the lot, some of the other parents gathered in clusters to chat, but they didn't look like people I'd like. The moms all wore full faces of makeup and wrinkle-free clothing. I, on the other hand, wore no makeup and I was packing heat, which I was pretty sure wouldn't be a great conversation piece in that crowd.

I turned to tell Danny we should go check in with Hidalgo, but realized he was already halfway there. I smiled at his enthusiasm and resisted the urge to call him back to help me carry the rest of his stuff. In addition to the backpack, he had a trunk filled with clothes and toiletries, plus all of the alchemical supplies we'd had to buy for the camp.

Some of the other kids were pretending to look at their cell phones but casting each other cagey side-eyes to size up whether new arrivals were potential friends or foes. While I handled loading Danny's stuff into the bowels of the bus, he assumed the position near a cluster of two boys and a girl who looked about his age.

I was trying to wedge his trunk into the bus when I heard one of the guys say, "Your mom made you get a trunk, too? Lame, right?"

"She's my sister, not my mom, but yeah."

"Your sister's old," the girl said.

"She's almost thirty," Danny said in the same tone others might have used to say, "The disease is terminal."

I smiled and finished putting his gear into the bus. Then I wiped my hands on my jeans and stood. "Hey, Danny?"

"What?" He had the slouchy posture of a teen in full impress-the-new-friends mode. I saw the fear in his eyes, though. He was terrified I would embarrass him. I suddenly was overcome with a sense of relief.

Danny was fine. Hell, he was better than fine. He might be headed off to a summer camp for Adept kids, but he wasn't so different from the average American teen. His grades were solid, he never got into any major trouble, and he had a good head on his shoulders. On the other hand, by the time I was his age, I already had a tattoo, a smoking habit, and experience selling dirty potions on street corners.

Now I was a decorated detective on an elite task force, and I'd helped bring down some of the nastiest coven characters this city had ever produced.

I was under no illusions that I would never have a problem with Danny again. But for some reason, standing there that morning, I realized that I'd earned the right to feel confident that I could handle anything he threw my way.

"Um, hello? Earth to Kate?"

His new buddies snickered.

I shook myself. "Just wanted to let you know I'm headed out. You got the money I gave you?"

"Yeah."

"All right. I'll get going. Have fun and don't forget to call every now and then."

"Whatever."

Turning to walk away, I felt a mixture of pride and sadness. It wasn't easy letting him grow up. Hell, sometimes it was way harder than the things I ran into in my job. But I knew I'd done right by that kid.

I was almost at the car when I heard my name. I stopped and turned. Only to find myself the recipient of a quick side-hug.

"Thanks, Katie."

I closed my eyes and squeezed him tight. "You're welcome. Just do me a favor?"

He pulled away, looking bashful for an instant before the too-cool teen returned. "I know, I know. Don't get in trouble."

I shook my head. "Just promise me you'll never forget who you are."

"Like my name?"

"Some people might hear you're a Prospero and think you're bad news."

He shrugged. "Fuck that. I don't care what people think."

I barked out a laugh. He was lucky the swear jar was at home, but he did sort of have a point. "Right, fuck them. Because you know what? We get to decide what it means to be a Prospero now."

The bus driver honked the horn to indicate it was time to embark for the trip.

Danny squeezed me again. "I promise I'll try to follow your example and show the world that being a Prospero means acting like a total badass." He ran off, turning to taunt me as he went. "Behave yourself," he mocked. "Don't do anything that I wouldn't do."

With that, he ran off to join his new friends to climb on the bus. I forced myself to get into the car to watch them go so I wouldn't be the dumb woman crying in the parking lot. Once the bus drove off, trailing exhaust behind it, I saw the man leaning against a truck on the other side of the lot.

Cursing under my breath, I climbed out of the Jeep and walked toward him. As I got closer, I noticed the truck's bed was filled with luggage and fishing gear.

"You following me now?" I said.

Duffy didn't crack a smile. "That your kid?"

I leaned against the fender beside him. "Brother."

"How's your partner?" He crossed his arms and looked up at the sky, as if we were just two pals shooting the breeze.

"Better. Should return to work soon."

He turned his head to shoot me a meaningful look.

"What do you want, Duffy?"

He heaved a sigh. Whatever he'd come to say would cost him. I allowed myself to enjoy that. "To thank you."

I raised a brow and shot him a side-eye. "Oh, really?"

"You saved my life."

I opened my mouth to brush it off, but he cut in.

"It's not often someone surprises me, but you managed."

I huffed out an ironic laugh. "I suppose you meant that as a compliment, but I'm a little offended that you thought I'd let you die."

He cocked a brow. "You know I know what happened with Morales in Los Angeles, right?"

I nodded. "Yeah, and you know I'm not my partner, right?"

He paused, thinking it over for a moment before nodding. "True enough." He scrubbed a hand over his chin. "Anyway, thanks."

"I guess I should thank you, too," I said.

"How you figure?"

"Nothing would have stopped you from opening that IA investigation before you left the force. Could have gotten the last word in in a big way."

"Eh, it was a lot of paperwork," he said, underplaying it. "You hear they tapped McGinty?"

I nodded. "Last I saw him, he looked like he'd gotten a shot of adrenaline. It'll be a good more for him."

"He seems like good police. Hope he has an easier time than I did."

"What do you mean?"

He shrugged. "You know, I seen a lot of shit in my day. Working homicide for so long, you see the worst of people, right?"

"If you say so."

"I always avoided getting involved in the Arcane shit until Eldritch hired me to take over the Cauldron homicide beat. My daddy was an Arcane cop—you know that?"

I shook my head.

"Worked in the Cauldron, in fact."

"No shit?"

He nodded. "He was killed by a Votary wiz when I was seventeen."

I closed my eyes and cursed under my breath. All the sudden it made sense. Gardner had tried to hire Duffy multiple times to the task force because he was both a Leftie and a highly respected homicide detective. He'd turned her down flat each time. Now I knew why.

"He was an Adept too," he added. "Before he died, I heard him complain to my mom almost every night how the Mundane cops distrusted the Lefties on the force. So, when I became a cop, I did my best to distance myself from being an Adept. Played it straight and stayed as far from the Arcane shit as I could."

"Why are you telling me all of this?" I asked.

He licked his lips and sighed. "Because I was wrong."

"About what?"

"About you. I never thought that police work was black-and-white. I seen lots of gray on the homicide beat. But I still managed to stay on the right side of things most of my career. It wasn't until I got put on the Cauldron beat that those beliefs were challenged. Policing magic is complicated."

I laughed. "No shit."

"I mean it," he said. "After Krystal got whacked, the murders slowed down for about twenty-four hours. Turns out, all the Votary peons were fighting over whether to listen to her or not. But once she was gone? They started killing each other to see who got to be the next leader. It's endless. And all over what? Who got to control a few lousy street corners?" He shook his head at the futility of it.

"And then that night at the theater," he said, "you did everything against the book. But I also realized that there wasn't another option. It's like the rules on the Mundane side of things don't translate in the chaos of magic."

"I've never thought of it that way, but yeah, that's a good way to put it."

"Truth is, since the day I started working the Cauldron, I've constantly felt under water. But you're from here. You know how to swim through the currents." He held up his hands. "Don't get me wrong. I still believe a lot of your choices have been shady as hell, but I guess what I'm saying is I don't condone it but I get it."

I didn't know how to respond to him, so I just nodded and waited for him to continue.

"I tried to hack it here. Sure, I got a few good solves, but mostly I ran into case after case of shit that I didn't begin to understand. Then the wedding from hell happened. I've had nightmares about it ever since that night." He shuddered. "The screams."

"It got to me, too," I admitted.

We were quite for a moment, silently bonding over the shared memories of the horror of seeing Aphrodite burn.

Finally, Duffy sighed. "I gave my resignation the next morning. Realized life is too short. I never married or had kids, because I was so dedicated to the job. And here I am, with gray hair and nothing to show for all that work but nightmares."

I looked over my shoulder and nodded. "What's with the fishing gear?"

He patted a hand on the truck's bed. "Got a cousin has a place out in Montana. Gonna fish and drink beer all day."

"That sounds"—*boring*, I thought—"nice."

"You're a terrible liar," he said. "But don't worry. Your day's coming."

"Which day is that?"

"Day when you're too old for this shit too."

I laughed. "I've been too old for this shit since I was a teenager, Duffy."

He tilted his head and shot me a pointed look. "So, why are you still here?"

I didn't love the way that question caused my gut to twist, so I didn't say anything.

"I'm gonna give you some unsolicited advice, Kate," he said. "You should take that boy"—he nodded after the direction the bus had gone—"and get out of town. Go far away. Don't come back."

I twisted my lips into a cocky smile despite the inner turmoil. "Why's that?"

He sucked his front teeth, thinking it over. "Because you swim a little too well in these waters. If you're not careful, you might forget you're not a shark."

I tilted my head and watched him for a moment. Finally, I decided to forgo my usual sarcastic response and go with honesty. "I got unfinished business here."

"That's your pride talking. Listen to an old man. It's better to walk away with your life than to die proud."

I crossed my arms. "I don't plan on dying anytime soon."

"Neither did that hermaphrodite, girl. You saw what happened to them." He shot me a look heavy with irony. "And, not for nothing, but if your partner doesn't get you killed, then your association with that crooked mayor will do you in."

An electrical charge flashed under my skin. It was anger, but the reality was, I was just angry because he was telling the truth.

"Well, thanks for your advice," I snapped. "I'll take it under advisement."

I started to push away from the car, but he put out a hand to stop me.

"Tell me something. What really happened with that potion?" he asked. "The one you and Volos made?"

Now that he'd dropped the advice, I relaxed against the truck again. "I don't know. The cook was good. It should have worked."

He nodded and looked down, thinking it over.

"But I have a theory," I continued. "Aphrodite tried to cut corners to enlightenment. Just like a hexhead, they were looking for an outside fix—a potion made by someone else to solve their problems. But what I'm starting to realize is that inside problems require inside fixes."

"Sounds like you're closer to enlightenment than Aphrodite ever was."

I smiled. "Good thing I'm not trying to become immortal."

"Aren't you?" He looked me in the eye, daring me to deny it.

I wasn't touching that one. I pushed away from the truck. "Anyway, I hope you find what you're looking for in Montana."

"And I hope you find what you're looking for here. I just hope the price you'll pay on the way won't be too high."

"Goodbye, Duffy," I said.

His smile told me he wasn't offended that I ignored his advice. He seemed content now that he'd said his piece. "Bye, Detective Prospero."

With that, he got in the truck and drove off toward his easier life. I watched him go and thought over what he'd said. Maybe he was right. I should have left Babylon ten years earlier when I left the covens. But there was too much on the line to leave now.

I turned to watch the sun come the rest of the way up over the river. Since I'd started with the MEA, we'd brought down the leaders of two major covens. The only major player still on the street was Harry Bane, but he seemed to have an unfortunate habit of getting his ass kicked often enough to not be a real threat.

Nah, I thought, I wasn't about to cut and run. I'd fought too many battles to give up on this city now. Duffy was probably right that shit would get a lot worse before it got better. But the thing I knew for sure was that if people like me didn't fight the hard battles, nothing would ever change.

Prosperos never ran from a fight. We stood our ground, protected our turf, and when push came to shove, we fought dirty. And if there's one thing my time on the task force had taught me, it was that we'd never win the war against dirty magic by fighting clean.

ALSO BY JAYE WELLS

The Prospero's War Series

Dirty Magic

Cursed Moon

Fire Water (novella)

Deadly Spells

The Sabina Kane Series

Red-Headed Stepchild

Mage in Black

Violet Tendencies (Short Story)

Green-Eyed Demon

Silver-Tongued Devil

Blue-Blooded Vamp

Rusted Veins (Novella)

Fool's Gold (Novella)

Meridian Six Series

Meridian Six

Children of Ash

Other Works

The Uncanny Collection

ABOUT THE AUTHOR

USA Today Bestseller Jaye Wells is a former magazine editor whose award-winning speculative fiction novels have hit several bestseller lists. She holds an MFA in Writing Popular Fiction from Seton Hill University, and is a sought-after speaker on the craft of writing. When she's not writing or teaching, she loves to travel to exotic locales, experiment in her kitchen like a mad scientist, and try things that scare her so she can write about them in her books. She lives in Texas.

Find out more about Jaye Wells

www.jayewells.com

jaye@jayewells.com

GET A FREE BOOK

Sign up for Jaye's newsletter to get a free book. You'll also receive exclusive access to giveaways, excerpts, and release and event news. Each monthly newsletter also includes a recipe from Jaye's kitchen and the Fur Fan of the Month.

SIGN UP NOW!
JAYEWELLS.COM/NEWSLETTER

ACKNOWLEDGMENTS

My name may be on the cover of this book, but a lot of people helped me bring this story to you.

Lyndsey Llewellen at Llewellen Designs created the beautiful cover. She did a great job keeping the look and themes of the original covers created by Lauren Panepinto and the team at Orbit, but also put her own mark on it.

Melissa Hayden provided content editing and Richard Shealy provided copyediting. Thanks to their eagle eyes for catching all my typos and continuity issues. Any errors that made it through are my own.

Thanks to my assistant, Chelsea Klepfer, for keeping me organized and for all your excellent ideas.

Special thanks to Chia Hwa Chang for answering my Chinese language questions. Also Pat Hughes, who, in addition to being my uncle, is also an expert on fire fighting. He answered all my questions about drug lab explosions and provided excellent insights into what happens at the scene. In addition, his No BULLSHIT BEFORE 5 P.M. sign inspired the one in Gardner's office. Again, any errors in the story are my own.

I couldn't do what I do without the support of my readers, family, and friends. For this book, especially, I had a lot of encouragement and advice from some very smart writers, including Kathleen Baldwin, Kay Thomas, and Yasmine Galenorn. Thanks also to Team Awesome for your continued support and excitement for this series.

Last but not least, Zach and Austin Wells deserve medals for keeping me grounded and laughing. ILYNTB.

If you enjoy the Prospero's War series by Jaye Wells, be sure to read her post-apocalyptic thriller,
Meridian Six:

In a world at war, freedom is a luxury paid for with blood.

The daughter of a rebel leader, Meridian Six was used as a propaganda tool and blood slave to her vampire captors for years after her mother died. When she finally escapes, she runs toward a red light signal that leads the way to the underground world of human rebels.

All she wants is freedom, but what she finds instead of a rebellion in search of a hero--and for some reason they think she fits the bill. The vampires used her famous name as a tool of oppression, but now the humans want to use it to inspire a revolution.

MERDIAN SIX

One

The frigid air scraped my lungs raw. I pumped my legs faster, praying for a second wind. Stopping wasn't an option. Their breath beat at my back, and if they caught me, I'd be dead.

I turned the corner, running down an alley. Footsteps echoed behind me. Faster. I wrenched two trashcans back into their path. A male cursed and grunted. Metal scraped against concrete. I focused on the mouth of the alley and prayed for a miracle.

A black sedan screeched to a stop in front of me. I didn't hesitate. My legs ached with the exertion, but I just managed to launch myself onto the hood. On the other side, the landing lurched every joint in my body.

Keep running. Find the light. Red means life.

Behind me, deep voices argued. I continued down the street, cursing the heels the Castor had forced me to wear for the Prime's birthday celebration. I couldn't spare the precious moments to rid myself of the torture devices.

Finally, a speck of red appeared in the distance. All thoughts of sore feet and desperation evaporated. The beckoning light glowed from the porch of a squat, run-down house that looked more like a prewar crack den than a haven for the lost.

I kicked up my pace and pushed through the pain. Salvation drew closer.

My pursuers' harsh breathing echoed off the burnt out shells of buildings and trash- strewn streets. A weathered poster bearing my own face mocked me from the brick walls of an old induction center. In red ink along the bottom, the Troika's slogan, the hated words I'd repeated so often on radio broadcasts and in speeches to grim-faced prisoners: "Blood will make you free."

Not a soul lurked in the shadows. Most humans now slaved in work camps or blood camps. Rebels sought refuge in the burnt-out cities, but if any were watching me from the darkened windows, their survival instincts precluded them from interfering in Troika business. After all, my pursuers wore the telltale black uniforms of the secret police. The lightning symbol on their breasts had become a graphic promise of pain.

Not far now. If I could just--

Pain exploded on my scalp. My head whipped back with the force of the fist jerking back on the ponytail. My feet snapped out from under me. He used my hair to keep me from hitting the ground. The agony made me wish I'd hit concrete instead.

It was Sergei, one of the Prime's personal guards, who'd caught me. The one who always watched me while caressing his precious riding crop. "Got you, bitch." His eyes burned like hot coals. Fangs flashed as he panted for breath. "Now we can add evading arrest to your list of crimes."

His partner doubled over, trying to catch his breath. I didn't know his name, but he had the wild eyes of a male who enjoyed his job too much. He glanced up at the glowing red light on the front of the house, now only twenty feet away. "She almost made it."

"Almost doesn't count," Sergei said, tugging my hair harder. He leaned in at my grimace. "You like that?" he whispered. "There's more coming." I gritted my teeth and waited for my opportunity. "Call headquarters and have them send a rover to retrieve her."

With the partner distracted, I slapped his fist to my scalp, holding it in place and easing the pressure. I scraped my heel down his shin and stabbed the tip into his foot. With a yelp, he released me. I grabbed the crop from his slack hold and jerked it against his windpipe.

It happened so fast his friend didn't see it. He spoke into his radio, his back to me, "Repeat: Meridian Six has been subdued--" I grabbed the blade from my garter and made his last words dissolve into a wet gurgle. As he fell, I grabbed his gun from his hand and turned it on Sergei.

"You won't be allowed to live." His words the confidence of a man determined to deliver the deathblow. "You'd already be dead if Director Castor didn't want the pleasure for himself."

I put the gun to his head. Pulled the trigger. His body jerked. Wetness splashed my face. I dropped his body and hauled ass toward the steps.

It happened as if in slow motion. I ran toward the door, my hand rose to pound. The roar and vibration of the Troika's arriving craft shook the building. The panel in front of me flew open. A female in red robes opened her mouth in shock, reaching for me. The blast ripped through the night. Fire exploded in my left shoulder. I fell in slow motion, the world a blur of pain--fell across the threshold and into the acolyte's arms. Blood filled my vision.

Red means life.

MERIDIAN SIX

Two

Whispers woke me. I peeled open one eye. Two females watched me from the doorway. I didn't move so as not to alert them to my newly conscious state. Not until I had a chance to take stock.

Drab-colored clothes were folded in a neat pile on the chair by the door. The stained and ripped green silk dress I'd been wearing hung from a hook and the high heels lay beneath them on the floor like two drunks. Across from the bed, a canvas hung depicting the beatified visage of some patron saint of the Sanguinarians, the religion to which the Order of the Sisters of Crimson belonged. On the table beneath the painting, lay the dagger I'd stolen off the guard when I'd made my escape. When I'd arrived it was bloody, but now it shone like pristine, polished silver.

A thin, coarse blanket abraded my naked skin. The realization that I was totally at the mercy of these bloodthirsty holy women shocked my synapses into firing again.

They call me Meridian Six

"She is awake." The voice was feminine with an undercurrent of steel.

I used to be a tool for the Troika. But now I am their prey.

Turning my head, I focused on the pair by the door. The acolyte who'd helped me inside earlier stood next to a statuesque woman in crimson and black robes. All Sisters of Crimson wore red robes, but only those who'd achieved exalted status wore the sacred black as well.

Chatelaine...smart not to leave an acolyte alone with me. Not after the way I arrived.

She dismissed the acolyte with a nod. The door closed, and she moved forward slowly, almost gliding. She wasn't afraid to be alone with me.

"Welcome. I am Sister Agrippa, Chatelaine of this rectory."

She shushed me and placed a hand on my arm when I tried to sit up. "You must rest. The bullet grazed your shoulder, but you lost blood from your other wounds."

I didn't meet her eyes and pulled the sheet higher. She'd seen the bite marks on my thighs and breasts.

"What happened to your lower back?"

I looked up quickly, thankful she hadn't mentioned the other wounds. "Had to dig out the chip so they couldn't zap me."

She nodded but showed no emotion on her face. "You wouldn't have made it far if you hadn't." Something lit in her eyes—respect? "It's a miracle you made it out of the Fortress as it is, Miss Six."

I fell back onto the flat pillow. Even my bones felt exhausted. I wasn't surprised Sister Agrippa knew the name the vamps had given me. Everyone knew about Meridian Six, model Troika citizen. The instant I escaped I swore I'd never be called that name again, but I didn't want to offend the holy woman when the situation was still so fragile. "Thanks," I said instead.

She eyed me with frank curiosity. "I assume you are aware I am only able to offer you sanctuary for twenty-four hours. You slept twenty of those away, I'm afraid."

I cringed. Four hours wasn't much time. I needed to regroup and come up with a plan. "I understand, Sister. I appreciate your hospitality."

"I took the liberty of having my assistant bring a change of clothes." She nodded at a stack of garments on a chair next to the door. "I guessed at your size, but they'll be better than the filthy ones you wore when you arrived." Her face didn't betray any judgment but I found her choice of adjective telling. Had my harlot's clothes and the blood kiss marks on my inner thighs and chest betrayed my status as the Troika's blood whore?

I wasn't sure how to reply. Thanking her again would have felt too much like a confession.

"I'll leave you to your ablutions. The first mass of the evening begins in five minutes. Perhaps you'll join us? Spiritual renewal may offer you a modicum of strength for your journey."

"I think I'll pass." I hesitated before adding, "No offense."

"None taken. I didn't think you'd agree anyway." She moved to the door again. "Go ahead and get dressed. I'll have my assistant retrieve you after mass, and we can discuss next steps."

"Sister?"

"Hmm?" She paused by the door. The brighter light from the hall-ways fell around her like a halo.

"Aren't you going to ask why the Troika are after me?"

She paused and smiled, her small, white fangs flashing in the dim light. "Would you tell me the truth if I did?"

My lips quirked. I liked this woman's straightforward, no-bullshit attitude. "Probably not."

She nodded and left, closing the door behind her. I sat in silence for a few more moments, trying to will myself out of the warm cocoon of the bed. My soul ached to stay in this quiet place. My body ached for stillness. But my mind wasn't having any of that. I needed a plan—and fast. I'd have a lot more than aches to worry about if the Troika's men caught me when I left the convent.

Twenty minutes later, I'd completed my fortieth lap of the small room in the foreign-feeling clothes. The coarse woolen sweater and baggy denim weren't exactly the quality I was used to. I normally opted for simple garments of the highest caliber fabrics that wouldn't hamper movement or snag. Castor insisted that my clothes should also show off my form to its best advantage, which was why I didn't mind the shapeless garments the sisters provided. And the shoes! The soft leather moccasins hugged my feet like a dream. They'd be a hell of a lot easier to run in than the heels the Director of Propaganda insisted I wear.

His face flashed in my mind's eye. The lascivious gleam when he'd presented me with the dress and shoes. "And don't forget the hairpiece," he'd said, waving the green silk ribbon. "All birthday gifts should be topped with a bow." He'd giggled and left muttering to himself about how clever he was for thinking of the perfect birthday gift for the Prime.

Me.

A soft knock on the door announced the acolyte's return. "The Chatelaine will see you now."

I nodded and followed her out into the corridor. I'd considered wandering around earlier while I waited, but I didn't want to be rude. The corridor's ceilings hung low over sconces lining the walls, giving off a warm glow. Funny, from the outside this building seemed condemned, but inside it was clean and peaceful.

"Are we below ground?" I asked, noting the lack of windows.

She nodded meekly over her shoulder.

I waited for more information, but she didn't offer any. The sisters, I guessed, probably built this sanctuary in abandoned tunnels dug during the Blood Wars. I'd heard how the humans and vampire rebels had dug warrens under the cities for quick escapes during skirmishes. Now, the dirt walls had been plastered over, but the echoes of old fear clung to the air like the musk of turned earth.

We reached a door, and the acolyte knocked. "The Chatelaine is waiting."

"Thank you, Sister—" I let the word hang there for her to fill in.

She avoided my eyes and scuttled off. Her red robes swirled

around her ankles as she rounded the corner. I wondered briefly how she ended up living in abandoned tunnels below the city, offering succor to fugitives like me.

"Six?" The Chatelaine's voice pulled me out of my musings. I took a deep breath, raised my chin and marched into her inner sanctum.

She sat behind a battered wooden desk. A single low-watt bulb hung from the ceiling. The threadbare tapestries stretched across sections of the walls did nothing to dispel the chill. One depicted a unicorn bleeding in a cage and another a knight fighting a dragon.

"Nice," I said, more to get the conversation going than out of any real appreciation for the artistry.

"Functional," she countered. "They help insulate against the dankness."

I took the seat she offered. The ancient metal chair creaked in protest. I cringed as the sound echoed through the cave-like room.

The Chatelaine stared into a vid-screen, an alien bit of technology for such an ascetic setting, but, then, she was a vampire. And vampires loved their tech.

I couldn't see what she was looking at, but whatever it was, she found it damned interesting. Warning bells went off in my head. Noticing my sudden stiffness, she turned the screen toward me.

My own face stared back at me. My stomach fell as I read the ticker beneath the old photo. "Fugitive still at large. The Troika is offering a reward of ten thousand charns for her capture—dead or alive."

"Meridian Six, age twenty-three, daughter of rebel sympathizer, Alexis Sargosa," she read, her brows rising. "Wanted for violation of Troika code 439."

My stomach churned, and my hands grew damp. Given the conditions of the rectory, it was possible the Chatelaine was mentally tabulating the repairs she could make with that kind of reward.

I lifted my chin, waiting for her to make the next move.

"Code 439?" she said. "That's assault, correct?"

I gave a jerky nod to confirm that was, indeed, the crime assigned to Code 439, but I didn't feel the need to confess my innocence. After all, if things had gone as planned the charge would have been murder instead.

The nun's eyes took on a speculative gleam. My fingers slid down my leg toward the shard of metal I'd strapped to my ankle using a bit of bandage the nuns had left in my room. They'd been smart not to leave me with any glass or cutlery, but the metal bracket had torn away from the bed frame easily and its sharp corners could inflict some pain.

"Keep your weapon where it is, child. The Sisters of Crimson are no friends of the Troika, no matter how well they pay."

I paused and looked at her. "Ten thousand Cs would buy a lot of food for your acolytes, sister."

"True, but then I would have a debt on my soul I'm not prepared to repay."

"If you knew all of this I'm surprised you let me in here to begin with. Some consider me quite dangerous."

Her lips lifted in a slight smile. "Especially the Troika."

"What makes you say that?"

"Ten thousand charns seems a bit steep for assault," she said, leaning back in her chair. "No, I think they want you for another reason."

I looked down. How much should I tell her? Even if I knew I could trust her, I'd be risking her life by sharing information she shouldn't know.

"Let's just say I have intimate knowledge of a few skeletons in the Troika's closet," I said.

"Oh, I bet you do." Her lips twitched. "So they made up the code violation then?"

"Not necessarily." I didn't elaborate. I crossed my arms to let her know that was all I had to say about the matter.

"Fair enough," she said. "I suppose you've already guessed that a crowd of Troika guards have gathered outside?"

"I figured as much."

"You got a plan?"

"Run like hell."

"In other words, you've got no plan at all." She leaned forward with her elbows on the desk. If she hadn't been wearing the robes of a holy order, her expression would have reminded me of a conspirator. "Lucky for you, I do."

* * *

To learn more about Jaye Wells and her books, please visit www.jayewells.com.

CPSIA information can be obtained
at www.ICGtesting.com
Printed in the USA
LVOW12s2325081017
551717LV00001B/92/P